also by gabrielle zevin

Memoirs of a Teenage Amnesiac

Elsewhere

ALL
THESE
THINGS
I'VE DONE

ALL
THESE
THINGS
I'VE DONE

GABRIELLE ZEVIN

**SQUARE
FISH**

FARRAR STRAUS GIROUX
NEW YORK

SQUARE
FISH

An Imprint of Macmillan

Square Fish and the Square Fish logo are trademarks of Macmillan and
are used by Farrar Straus Giroux under license from Macmillan.

Library of Congress Cataloging-in-Publication Data
Zevin, Gabrielle.
    All these things I've done / Gabrielle Zevin.
        p.   cm. — (Birthright)
    Summary: In a future where chocolate and caffeine are contraband, teenage cellphone
use is illegal, and water and paper are carefully rationed, sixteen-year-old Anya Balanchine
finds herself thrust unwillingly into the spotlight as heir apparent to an important New
York City crime family.
    ISBN 978-1-250-01028-5
    [1. Organized crime—Fiction.   2. Celebrities—Fiction.   3. High schools—Fiction.
4. Schools—Fiction.   5. Family life—New York (State)—New York—Fiction.   6. New York
(N.Y.) —Fiction.   7. Science fiction.]   I. Title.   II. Title: All these things I've done.

PZ7.Z452All 2011
[Fic]—dc22

                                                                            2010035873

Originally published in the United States by Farrar Straus Giroux
First Square Fish Edition: May 2012
Square Fish logo designed by Filomena Tuosto
macteenbooks.com

10   9   8   7   6   5   4   3   2   1

AR: 4.4 / LEXILE: HL630L

To my dad, Richard Zevin, who knows everything

Whether I shall turn out to be the hero of my own life, or whether that station will be held by anybody else, these pages must show.

—Charles Dickens, *David Copperfield*

contents

I. i defend my own honor 3

II. i am punished; define *recidivism*; tend to family matters 31

III. i confess; contemplate mortality & teeth; lure a boy under
false pretenses; disappoint my brother 51

IV. i go to little egypt 66

V. i regret having gone to little egypt 77

VI. i entertain two unwelcome guests; am mistaken for someone else 90

VII. i am accused; make matters worse 95

VIII. i am sent to liberty; am also tattooed! 117

IX. i discover an influential friend & then, a foe 134

X. i convalesce; receive visitors; hear news of gable arsley 148

XI. i define *tragedy* for scarlet 162

XII. i relent; make an adequate witch 181

XIII. i tend to an obligation (ignore others); pose for a picture 195

XIV. i am forced to turn the other cheek 210

XV. we mourn again; i learn the definition of *internecine* 240

XVI. i apologize (repeatedly); am apologized to (once) 285

XVII. i make plans for the summer 295

XVIII. i am betrayed 305

XIX. i enact a fair trade 330

XX. i set my house in order; am returned to liberty 345

ALL
THESE
THINGS
I'VE DONE

I. i defend my own honor

THE NIGHT BEFORE JUNIOR YEAR—I was sixteen, *barely*—
Gable Arsley said he wanted to sleep with me. Not in the distant
or semidistant future either. Right then.

Admittedly, my taste in boys wasn't so great. I was attracted
to the sort who weren't in the habit of asking permission to do
anything. Boys like my father, I guess.

We'd just gotten back from the coffee speakeasy that used to
be off University Place, in the basement of a church. This was
back when caffeine, along with about a million other things, was
against the law. So much was illegal (paper without a permit,
phones with cameras, chocolate, etc.) and the laws changed so
quickly, you could be committing a crime and not even know it.
Not that it mattered. The boys in blue were totally overwhelmed. The city was bankrupt, and I'd say maybe 75 percent
of the force had been fired. The police that were left didn't have
time to worry about teens getting high on coffee.

I should have known something was up when Gable offered to escort me back to the apartment. At night at least, it was a pretty dangerous trek from the speakeasy to where I lived on East Ninetieth, and Gable usually left me to fend for myself. He lived downtown, and I guess he figured that I hadn't been killed making the trip yet.

We went into my apartment, which had been in the family practically forever—since 1995, the year my grandma Galina was born. Galina, who we called Nana and who I loved like nobody's business, was busy dying in her bedroom. She had the distinction of being both the oldest and the sickest person I had ever known. As soon as I opened the door, I could hear the machines that were keeping her heart and everything else pumping. The only reason they hadn't turned the machines off, like they would have for anyone else, was because she was responsible for my older brother, my little sister, and me. Her mind was still sharp, by the way. Even confined to the bed, not much got past her.

Gable had had, maybe, six espressos that night, two of them with shots of Prozac (also illegal)—and he was mad up. I'm not making excuses for him, only trying to explain a few things.

"Annie," he said, loosening his necktie and sitting down on the couch, "you gots to have some chocolate in here. I know you do. I'm gagging for it. Come on, baby, hook Daddy up." It was the caffeine talking. Gable sounded like a different person when he was on the stuff. I especially hated when he referred to himself as Daddy. I think he'd heard it in an old movie. I wanted to say, *You aren't my daddy. You're seventeen years old, for God's sake.*

Sometimes I did say this but mostly I let it go. My actual daddy used to say that if you didn't let some things go, you'd spend your whole life fighting. Chocolate was why Gable'd said he wanted to come up to the apartment in the first place. I told him he could have one piece and then he had to leave. The first day of school was tomorrow (my junior year as I mentioned; his senior), and I needed to get some sleep.

We kept our chocolate in Nana's room in a secret safe in the back of her closet. I tried to be real quiet as I walked past her bed. Not that there was much of a need for that. Her machines were as loud as the subway.

Nana's room smelled like death, a combination of day-old egg salad (poultry was rationed) and overripe honeydew melons (fruit was pretty scarce) and old shoes and cleaning products (purchase permitted with voucher). I went into her walk-in closet, pushed her coats out of the way, and entered the combination. Behind the guns was the chocolate, which was superdark, with hazelnuts, and came from Russia. I put a bar in my pocket and closed the safe. On my way out, I stopped to kiss my grandmother on the cheek, and she woke up.

"Anya," she croaked, "what time did you get home?"

I told her that I'd been home for a while. She'd never know the difference anyway and she'd only worry if she knew where I'd been. Then I told her to go back to sleep, that I hadn't meant to wake her. "You need your rest, Nana."

"What for? I'll be resting forever soon enough."

"Don't talk like that. You'll be alive a really long time," I lied.

"There's a difference between being alive and living," she

muttered before changing the subject. "First day of school to-morrow."

I was surprised she remembered.

"Go get yourself a nice chocolate bar from the closet, okay, Anyaschka?"

I did what she said. I put the bar from my pocket back in the safe and replaced it with a different, identical one.

"Don't show anybody," she said. "And don't share it unless it's with someone you really love."

Easier said than done, I thought, but I promised I wouldn't. I kissed my grandmother's papery cheek again. I closed the door softly behind me. I loved Nana, but I couldn't stand to be in that awful room.

When I went back out to the living room, Gable wasn't there. I knew where he'd be.

Gable was lying in the middle of my bed, passed out. As I saw it, that was the problem with caffeine. A little of it, and you had a nice buzz. Too much, and you were a goner. At least, that's how it was for Gable. I kicked him, not too hard, on the leg. He didn't wake up. I kicked him again, harder. He grunted a little and rolled onto his back. I figured I'd let him sleep it off. If worst came to worst, I'd sleep on the couch. Anyway, Gable was cute when he slept. Harmless, like a puppy or a little boy. I suppose I liked him best that way.

I took my school uniform from my closet and laid it out on my desk chair for the next day. I organized my bag and charged up my slate. I broke off a single piece of dark chocolate. The flavor was strong and woodsy. I rewrapped the rest in its silver foil and put it in my top drawer for safekeeping. I was glad I hadn't had to share it with Gable.

You're probably asking why Gable was my boyfriend when I barely wanted to share chocolate with him. The thing is, he wasn't boring. He was a little dangerous and, stupid girl that I was, I guess I found that sort of thing attractive. And—God rest your soul, Daddy—it could be said that I lacked positive male role models. Besides, sharing chocolate wasn't some casual thing: it really was hard to come by.

I decided to take a shower so I wouldn't have to do it in the morning. When I got out ninety seconds later (everyone's showers ran on timers because of how expensive water was getting), Gable was sitting cross-legged on my bed while stuffing the last of my chocolate bar down his throat.

"Hey," I said, my towel wrapped around me, "you went into my drawer!"

Chocolate was smudged on his thumb, index finger, and the inside corners of his mouth. "I wasn't snooping. I sniffed it out," he said in the middle of a bite. He paused chomping long enough to look up at me. "You look pretty, Annie. Clean."

I wrapped my towel tighter around myself. "Well, now that you're awake and you've had your chocolate, you should leave," I said.

He didn't move.

"Come on, then! Out!" I said this strongly, if not loudly. I didn't want to wake my siblings or Nana.

That's when he told me that he thought we should have sex.

"No," I said, wishing very much that I hadn't been so foolish as to take a shower while a dangerous, overcaffeinated boy lay in wait on my bed. "Absolutely not."

"Why not?" he asked. And then he said that he was in love with me. It was the first time a boy had ever told me that. Even as inexperienced as I was, I could tell he didn't mean it.

"I want you to go," I said. "We've got school tomorrow, and we both should get some sleep."

"I can't go now. It's past midnight."

Not that there were enough cops to enforce it, but midnight was the citywide, under-eighteen curfew. It was only 11:45, so I lied and told him he could still make it if he ran.

"I'll never make it, Annie. Besides, my parents aren't home, and your grandma will never know if I stay. Come on, be sweet to me."

I shook my head and tried to look tough, which was somewhat hard to do while wearing a yellow, flowered towel.

"Doesn't it count for anything that I just told you I love you?" Gable asked.

I considered this briefly before deciding that it didn't. "Not really. Not when I know you don't mean it."

He looked at me with big, dumb eyes like I had hurt his feelings or something. Then he cleared his throat and tried a different technique. "Come on, Annie. We've been together almost nine months. That's the longest I've ever been with anyone. So . . . Like . . . Why not?"

I gave him my list. One, I said, we were too young. Two, I didn't love him. And three, the most important of all, I didn't believe in sex before marriage. I was a mostly good Catholic girl, and I knew exactly where the type of behavior he was suggesting

8

would get me: straight to Hell. For the record, I very much believed (and believe) in Heaven and Hell, and not in an abstract way either. More about this later.

His eyes were a little crazy—maybe it was the contraband he'd consumed—and he got up from the bed and walked closer to me. He started tickling my bare arms.

"Stop that," I said. "Seriously, Gable, this isn't funny. I know you're trying to get me to drop my towel."

"Why'd you take that shower if you didn't want—"

I told him I'd scream.

"And then what?" he asked. "Your grandma can't get out of bed. Your brother's a retard. And your sister's just a kid. All you'll do is make them upset."

Part of me couldn't believe this was actually happening in my own house. That I'd allowed myself to be so witless and vulnerable. I hooked my towel under my armpits, and I pushed Gable away as hard as I could. *"Leo is not a retard!"* I yelled.

I heard a door open at the end of the hallway and then, footsteps. Leo, who was tall like Daddy had been (six feet five inches), appeared in my doorway wearing pajamas with a pattern of dogs and bones on them. Even though I had been handling things, I had never been so happy to see my big brother. "Hey, Annie!" Leo wrapped me in a quick hug before turning to my soon-to-be ex-boyfriend. "Hello, Gable," Leo said. "I heard noise. I think you should leave now. You woke me which is okay. But if you wake Natty that won't be good because she has to go to school tomorrow."

Leo led Gable to our front door. I didn't relax until I heard it shut and Leo had latched the chain.

"I don't think your boyfriend is very nice," Leo told me when he got back.

"You know what? I don't think so either," I said. I picked up Gable's discarded chocolate wrappers and crushed them into a ball. By Nana's standards, the only chocolate-worthy boy in my life was my brother.

The first day of school stunk more than most first days of school, and they tend to stink as a rule. Everyone had already heard that Gable Arsley and Anya Balanchine were over. This was annoying. Not because I had had any intention of staying with him after the foul he'd committed the night before, but because I'd wanted to be the one to break up with him. I'd wanted him to cry or yell or apologize. I'd wanted to walk away and not look back as he called my name. That sort of thing, right?

I have to admit: it was amazing how fast the rumors spread. Minors weren't allowed to have their own phones, and no one of any age could publish, virtually or otherwise, without a license or even send an e-mail without paying postage and yet gossip always finds a way. And a good lie travels a heck of a lot faster than the sad, boring truth. By third period, the story of my breakup had been carved in stone, and I hadn't been the one doing the carving.

I skipped fourth period to go to confession.

When I entered the confessional, I could see the distinctly female silhouette of Mother Piousina through the screen. Believe it or not, she was the first female priest Holy Trinity School had ever had. Even though these were supposedly modern times and everyone was supposedly enlightened, more than a few parents had complained when the Board of Overseers had announced her as their selection the prior year. There were some people who just weren't comfortable with the idea of a lady priest. In addition to being a Catholic school, HT was also one of the better schools in Manhattan. Parents who paid its exorbitant tuition did so with the understanding that the school wasn't allowed to change no matter how bad things got everywhere else.

I kneeled down and crossed myself. "Bless me, Mother, for I have sinned. It has been three months since my last confession . . ."

"What's troubling you, daughter?"

I told her how I'd been having impure thoughts about Gable Arsley all morning. I didn't use his name but Mother Piousina probably knew who I was talking about anyway. Everyone else at school did.

"Are you considering having intercourse with him?" she asked. "Because action would be an even greater sin than the thoughts themselves."

"I know that, Mother," I said. "Nothing like that. The thing is, this boy's been spreading rumors about me, and I've just been thinking how I hate him and I want to kill him or at least hurt him a little."

Mother Piousina laughed in a way that only somewhat offended me. "Is that everything?" she asked.

I told her that I'd used the Lord's name in vain several times over the summer. Most of the instances had occurred during the mayor's Great Air-Conditioning Ration. One of our "off days" had coincided with the hottest day in August. Between the 110-degree temperature and the heat generated by Nana's

11

many machines, the apartment had been a pretty close approximation of Hell.

"Anything else?"

"One more thing. My grandmother is very sick and even though I love her"—this was really hard for me to say—"sometimes I wish she would just die already."

"You don't want to see her suffer. God understands that you don't mean it, my child."

"Sometimes I have bad thoughts about the dead," I added.

"Anyone specific?"

"My father mainly. But my mother sometimes, too. And sometimes—"

Mother Piousina interrupted. "Perhaps three months is too long for you to go between confessions, daughter." She laughed again which annoyed me, but I continued anyway. The next one was the hardest to say.

"Sometimes I am ashamed of my older brother, Leo, because he's . . . It's not his fault. He's the kindest, most loving brother but . . . You probably know that he's a little slow. Today, he wanted to walk me and Natty to school but I told him that my grandmother needed him at home and that he'd be late for his job. Both lies."

"Is this your entire confession?"

"Yes," I said, bowing my head. "I'm sorry for these and all the sins of my past life." Then I prayed the Act of Contrition.

"I absolve you in the name of the Father, the Son, and the Holy Ghost," Mother Piousina said. She told me to say a Hail Mary and the Lord's Prayer as penance, which seemed a ridiculously minor punishment. Her predecessor, Father Xavier, really knew how to give a good penance.

I stood. I was about to open the burgundy curtain when she called to me, "Anya, light a candle for your mother and father in Heaven." She slid open the screen and handed me two candle vouchers.

"We're supposed to ration candles now," I grumbled. With the endless stupid coupons and stamps (weren't we supposed to be rationing paper?), the arbitrary point system, and the constantly changing rules, ration laws were incredibly annoying and impossible to keep up with. It was no wonder so many people bought goods on the black market.

"Look on the bright side. You can still have as much of the host as you want," Mother Piousina replied.

I took the slips and thanked Mother Piousina. For all the good lighting candles would do, I thought bitterly. I was pretty sure my father was in Hell.

After giving my vouchers to a nun with a wicker ticket basket and a box of votives, I went into the chapel and lit a candle for my mother.

I prayed that, despite having married the head of the Balanchine crime family, Mom somehow wasn't in Hell.

I lit a candle for my father.

I prayed that Hell wasn't so bad, even for a murderer.

I missed them both so much.

My best friend, Scarlet, was waiting for me in the hallway outside the chapel. "Nice work skipping Fencing on the first day, Miss Balanchine," she said, linking her arm through mine.

"Don't worry. I covered for you. I said you were having scheduling issues."

"Thanks, Scarlet."

"No problem. I can already see exactly what sort of year this is going to be. Shall we go to the caf?"

"Do I have a choice?"

"Yes, you could spend the rest of the school year hiding in the church," she said.

"Maybe I'll even become a nun and swear off boys forever."

Scarlet turned to study me. "No. Your face wouldn't be good in a habit."

On the walk to the dining hall, Scarlet filled me in on what Gable had been telling people, but I had overheard most of it already. The most important points were that he had broken up with me because he thought I might be a caffeine addict, because I was "kind of a slut," and because the start of a school year was a good opportunity for "taking out the trash." I comforted myself with the thought that if Dad had been alive, he probably could have had Gable Arsley killed. "So you know," Scarlet said, "I did defend your honor."

I was sure Scarlet probably had but no one ever listened to her. People thought of her as the crazy drama girl. Pretty and ridiculous.

"Anyway," she said, "everyone knows that Gable Arsley is a horse's backside. The whole thing'll blow over by tomorrow. Everyone's only talking about it because they're losers with no lives of their own. And also, it's the first day of school so nothing else has happened yet."

"He called Leo a retard. Did I tell you that part?"

"No!" Scarlet said. "That's pure evil!"

We were standing in front of the double doors that led into the dining hall. "I hate him," I said. "I really and truly hate him."

"I know," Scarlet agreed, pushing the doors open. "I never knew what you saw in him in the first place." She was a good friend.

The dining hall had wood-paneled walls and black-and-white linoleum tiles like a chessboard, which made me feel like a piece in a chess game. I saw Gable seated at the head of one of the long tables by the window. He had his back to the doors, so he didn't see me, though.

Lunch that day was lasagna, which I have always detested. The red sauce reminded me of blood and guts, and the ricotta cheese, of brain matter. I'd seen guts and brain matter for real so I knew what I was talking about. In any case, I wasn't hungry anymore.

Once we sat down, I pushed my tray toward Scarlet. "You want?"

"One's more than enough, thanks."

"All right, let's talk about something else," I said.

"Other than—"

"Don't you say that name, Scarlet Barber!"

"Other than the horse's backside," Scarlet said, and we both laughed. "Well, there's a most promising new boy in my French class. Actually, he kind of looks like a new man. He's all, I don't know, manly. His name's Goodwin but he goes by Win. Isn't that OMG?"

"What's that supposed to mean?"

"Um, it stands for something. Dad said it used to mean,

maybe, 'amazing'? Or something like that? He wasn't sure. Ask your nana, okay?"

I nodded. Scarlet's dad was an archaeologist and he always smelled like garbage because he passed his days digging up landfills. Scarlet went on about the new boy for a while but I wasn't really paying attention. I couldn't have cared less. I just nodded occasionally and pushed my repulsive lasagna around my plate.

I looked across the cafeteria. Gable caught my eye. What happened next is somewhat blurry to me. He would later claim that he hadn't, but I thought he sneered at me, then whispered something to the girl sitting to the left of him—she was a sophomore, maybe even a freshman, so I didn't know who she was—and they both laughed, and in response, I lifted my plate with the uneaten, though still scalding-hot lasagna (all food was required by law to be heated to 176°F to avoid the bacterial epidemics that were so pervasive), and then I was running diagonally across the black-and-white linoleum floor like a bishop gone mad and just like that Gable's head was covered with ricotta and tomato sauce.

Gable stood, and his chair toppled over. We were face-to-face, and it was like everyone else in the dining hall had disappeared. Gable started to yell, calling me a string of names that I won't bother to repeat here. I'd rather not type a whole long list of curse words.

"I accept your condemnation," I said.

He moved to punch me but then he stopped himself. "You're not worth it, Balanchine. You're scum like your dead parents," he said. "I'd rather just get you suspended." As he left the dining hall, he tried to wipe off some of the sauce with his hand, but it didn't do any good. The sauce was everywhere. I smiled.

At the end of eighth period, I was delivered a summons to appear in Headmaster's office after school.

Most everyone managed to avoid getting into trouble on the first day of school so there weren't that many people waiting. The door was closed which meant someone was already in the office, and a long-legged guy I didn't know waited on the love seat in the foyer. The secretary told me I should have a seat.

The boy was wearing a gray wool hat that he took off as I passed. He nodded, and I nodded back. He looked at me sidelong. "Food fight, right?"

"Yeah, you could call it that." I wasn't in the mood for making new friends. He crossed his hands on his lap. He had calluses on his fingers and despite myself, I found this interesting.

He must have seen me staring because he asked me what I was looking at.

"Your hands," I replied. "They're kind of rough for a city boy."

He laughed and said, "I'm from upstate. We used to grow our own food. Most of the calluses are from that. A couple are from my guitar. I'm no good; I just like to play. The rest I can't explain."

"Interesting," I said.

"Interesting," he repeated. "I'm Win, by the way," he said.

I turned to look at him. So, this was Scarlet's new boy? She was right. He certainly wasn't hard to look at. Tall and thin. Tanned skin and toned arms which must have come from the farming he'd mentioned. Soft blue eyes and a mouth that seemed more inclined to smile than to frown. Not my usual type at all.

He offered me his hand to shake, and I accepted it. "An—" I started to say.

"Anya Balanchine, I know. Everyone can't seem to stop talking about you today."

"Hmmph," I said. I could feel my face getting flushed. "Then you probably think that I'm crazy and a slut and an addict and a mafiya princess so I don't even know why you're bothering to talk to me!"

"I don't know about here, but where I'm from, we come to our own conclusions about people."

"Why are you here?" I asked him.

"That's an awfully big question, Anya."

"No, I meant here outside this office. What did you do wrong?"

"Multiple choice," he said. "A. A few pointed comments I made in Theology. B. Headmaster wants to have a chat with the new kid about wearing hats in school. C. My schedule. I'm just too darn smart for my classes. D. My eyewitness account of the girl who poured lasagna over her boyfriend's head. E. Headmaster's leaving her husband and wants to run away with me. F. None of the above. G. All of the above."

"Ex-boyfriend," I mumbled.

"Good to know," he said.

At that moment, Headmaster's door opened, and out came Gable. His face was pink and splotchy from where the sauce had hit him. His white dress shirt was covered in sauce, which I knew was probably bothering the heck out of him.

Gable scowled at me and whispered, "Not worth it."

Headmaster poked her head out the door. "Mr. Delacroix," she said to Win, "would it prove a terrible inconvenience to you if I saw Ms. Balanchine first?"

He consented, and I went into the office. Headmaster shut the door behind us.

I already knew what would happen. I was put on probation and assigned lunch duty for the rest of the week. All things considered, pouring the lasagna on Gable's head had still been completely worth it.

"You must learn to resolve these little relationship problems outside of Holy Trinity, Ms. Balanchine," Headmaster said.

"Yes, Headmaster."

It somehow seemed beside the point to mention that Gable had tried to date-rape me the night before.

"I considered calling your grandmother Galina, but I know she's been in poor health. No need to worry her."

"Thank you, Headmaster. I appreciate it."

"Honestly, Anya, I worry for you. This kind of behavior, if it becomes a pattern, could be damaging to your reputation."

As if she didn't know that I'd been born with a bad reputation.

When I left the office, my twelve-year-old sister, Natty, was sitting next to Win. Scarlet must have told her where to find me. Or maybe Natty had guessed—I was no stranger to the headmaster's office. Natty was wearing Win's hat. They'd obviously been introduced. What a little flirt she was! Natty was cute, too. She had long, shiny black hair. Like mine, except hers was stick-straight while I was stuck with untamable waves.

"Sorry about stealing your place in line," I said to Win.

He shrugged.

"Give Win back his hat," I told Natty.

"It looks good on me," she said, batting her eyelashes.

I took it off her head and handed it to Win. "Thanks for babysitting," I said.

"Stop infantilizing me," Natty protested.

"That's a very good word," Win commented.

"Thank you," Natty replied. "I happen to know lots of them."

Just to annoy Natty, I took her by the hand. We were almost to the hallway when I turned around and said, "My bet's on C. You're probably too smart for your schedule."

He winked—who *winked*? "I'll never tell."

Natty actually sighed. "Oh," she said. "I *like* that."

I rolled my eyes as we went out the door. "Don't even think about it. He's way too old for you."

"Only four years," Natty said. "I asked."

"Well, that's a lot when you're twelve."

We had missed our regular crosstown bus and, due to MTA budget cuts, the next one wasn't for another hour. I liked to try to be home when Leo got back from work and I decided that it would take less time for us to walk across the park back to our apartment. Daddy once told me how the park used to be when he was a kid: trees and flowers and squirrels, and lakes where people could canoe, and vendors selling every kind of food imaginable, and a zoo and hot-air balloon rides and in the summer, concerts and plays, and in the winter, ice skating and sledding. It wasn't like that anymore.

The lakes had dried up or been drained, and most of the surrounding vegetation had died. There were still a few graffiti-covered statues, broken park benches, and abandoned buildings, but I couldn't imagine anyone willingly spending time there. For Natty and me, the park was a half mile to be gotten across as quickly as possible, preferably before nightfall when it became a gathering place for just about every undesirable in the city. Incidentally, I'm not entirely sure how it got so bad, but I imagine it was like everything else in the city—lack of money, lack of water, lack of leadership.

Natty was pissed at me for making the crack about babysitting in front of Win, so she refused to walk with me. We were just across the Great Lawn (which, I suppose, must have had grass at some point) when she ran ahead about twenty-five feet.

Then fifty.

Then one hundred.

"Come on, Natty," I yelled. "It's not safe! You've got to stay with me!"

"Stop calling me Natty. My name is Nataliya, and for your information, Anya Pavlova Balanchine, I can take care of myself!"

I ran to catch up with her but by then she'd put even more distance between us. I could barely see her anymore; she was a tiny dot in a schoolgirl uniform. I ran even faster.

Natty was behind the glass section of the enormous building that used to be an art museum (now a nightclub) and she wasn't alone.

An incredibly skinny child, dressed in rags and, coincidentally, a decades-old Balanchine Chocolate Factory T-shirt, was holding a gun to my sister's head. "Now your shoes," he said in a squeak of a voice.

21

Natty sniffled as she bent down to unlace her shoes.

I looked at the child. The boy, despite being emaciated, seemed sturdy, but I was pretty sure I could take him. I scanned the area to see if he had any accomplices. No. We were alone. The real problem was the gun and so I considered the gun.

Now, what I did next might sound reckless to you.

I stepped between my sister and the boy.

"Anya! No!" my baby sister screamed.

My dad, you see, had taught me a thing or two about guns, and this kid's handgun didn't have a clip. In other words, no bullets unless there was one in the chamber, and I was betting that there wasn't.

"Why don't you pick on someone your own size?" I asked the boy. In point of fact, the boy was three inches shorter than Natty. Up close, I could see he was younger than I had thought— maybe eight or nine years old.

"I'll shoot you," the boy said. "I'll do it."

"Yeah?" I asked. "I'd like to see you try."

I grabbed his gun by the barrel. I thought about tossing it into the bushes, but I decided I didn't want him terrorizing any more people. I put it in my bag. It was a nice weapon. Would have done a heck of a job killing my sister and me. Had it been functional, that is.

"Come on, Natty. Get your stuff back from the kid."

"He hadn't taken anything yet," Natty said. She was still a bit teary.

I nodded. I handed Natty my pocket handkerchief and told her to blow her nose.

At this point, the would-be mugger had started to cry, too.

"Gimme back my gun!" He lunged at me, but the kid was weak with hunger, I'd guess, and I barely felt him.

"Look, I'm sorry, but you're gonna get yourself killed waving that broken gun around." This was true. I wouldn't be the only person who would notice he didn't have a clip and, likely as not, the type of person who noticed such a thing would shoot the kid between the eyes without a second thought. I felt a bit bad about taking his gun, so I gave him what money I had on me. Not much, but it'd keep the kid in pizza for a night.

Without even a moment's reflection, he took my offerings. Then he yelled an obscene name at me and disappeared into the park.

Natty gave me her hand, and we walked in silence until we were in the relative safety of Fifth Avenue.

"Why'd you do that, Annie?" she whispered as we were waiting for a walk signal. I could barely hear her above the city noise. "Why'd you give him all that stuff after he tried to rob me?"

"Because he was less fortunate than us, Natty. And Daddy always said that we have to be mindful of those who are less fortunate."

"But Daddy killed people, didn't he?"

"Yes," I admitted. "Daddy was complex."

"Sometimes, I can't even remember what he looked like," Natty said.

"He looked like Leo," I said. "Same height. Same black hair. Same blue eyes. But Daddy's eyes were hard and Leo's are soft."

Back at the apartment, Natty went into her bedroom, and I scrounged around for something for dinner. I was an uninspired chef but if I didn't cook, we'd all starve. Except for Nana. Her meals were delivered to her via tube by a home-health-care worker named Imogen.

I boiled exactly six cups of water per the package's instructions and then threw in the macaroni. At least Leo would be happy. Macaroni and cheese was his favorite.

I went to knock on his door to tell him the good news. There was no answer, so I opened it. He should have been home from his part-time job at the veterinary clinic for at least two hours, but his room was empty aside from his collection of stuffed lions. The lions looked at me questioningly with their dull plastic eyes.

I went into Nana's room. She was asleep, but I woke her up anyway.

"Nana, did Leo say if he was going anywhere?"

Nana reached for the rifle she kept under her bed, and then she saw that it was me. "Oh, Anya, it's only you. You scared me, *devochka*."

"Sorry, Nana." I kissed her on the cheek. "It's just Leo's not in his room. I was wondering if he said he was going anywhere."

Nana thought about this. "No," she said finally.

"Did he come home from work?" I asked, trying not to sound impatient. Clearly, Nana was having one of her less cogent days.

Nana considered this for about a million years. "Yes." She paused. "No." She paused again. "I'm not sure." Another pause. "What day of the week is this, *devochka*? I lose track of time."

"Monday," I told her. "The first day of school, remember?"

"Monday still?"

"It's almost over, Nana."

"Good. Good." Nana smiled. "If it's still Monday, that bastard Jakov came to see me today." She meant bastard literally. Jakov (pronounced Ya-koff) Pirozhki was my father's half brother's illegitimate son. Jakov, who called himself Jacks, was four years older than Leo, and I had never much liked him since the time he'd had too much Smirnoff at a family wedding and tried to touch my breast. I'd been thirteen; he'd been almost twenty. Disgusting. Despite this, I'd always felt a little sorry for Jacks because of the way everyone in my family looked down on him.

"What did Pirozhki want?"

"To see if I was dead yet," Nana said. She laughed and pointed to the cheap pink carnations that were sitting in a shallowly filled vase on the windowsill. I hadn't noticed them. "Ugly, aren't they? Flowers are so hard to come by these days, and that's what he brings? I suppose it's the thought that counts. Maybe Leo's with the bastard?"

"That's not nice, Nana," I said.

"Oh, Anyaschka, I would never say it in front of him!" she protested.

"What would Jacks want with Leo?" I had only ever known Jacks to ignore or show outright contempt for my brother.

Nana shrugged, which was difficult for her to do considering how little mobility she had. I could see that her eyelids had begun to flutter shut. I squeezed her hand.

Without opening her eyes, she said, "Let me know when you find Leonyd."

I went back into the kitchen to tend to the macaroni. I called Leo's job to see if he was still there. They said he'd left at four as usual. I didn't like not knowing where my brother was. He might be nineteen, three years my senior, but he was and would always be my responsibility.

Not long before my father was killed, Daddy made me promise that if anything ever happened to him, I would take care of Leo. I'd only been nine years old at the time, roughly the same age as that little mugger, and too young to really know what I was agreeing to. "Leo is a gentle soul," Daddy had said. "He isn't fit for our world, *devochka*. We must do everything we can to protect him." I'd nodded, not quite understanding that Daddy had sworn me to a lifelong commitment.

Leo hadn't been born "special." He had been like any kid, if not, from my father's point of view, better. Smart, the spitting image of Daddy, and best of all, the firstborn son. Daddy had even given him his name. Leo was actually Leonyd Balanchine, Jr.

The year Leo was nine, he and my mother had been driving out to Long Island to visit my maternal grandmother. My sister and I (ages two and six) had strep throat and had to stay behind. Daddy had agreed to stay with us, though I doubt it was much of a sacrifice as he'd never been able to tolerate Grandma Phoebe.

The hit had been meant for Daddy, of course.

My mother was killed instantly. Two shots through the windshield and straight through her lovely forehead and honey-scented chestnut curls.

The car my mother had been driving slammed into a tree as did Leo's head.

He lived, but he couldn't talk anymore. Or read. Or walk. My father had him sent to the best rehabilitation center followed by the best school for learning disabilities. And Leo certainly got a lot better, but he would never be the same. They said my brother would always have the intellect of an eight-year-old. They said my brother was lucky. And he was. Though I knew his limitations frustrated him, Leo managed a lot with the intellect he had. He had a job where everyone thought he was a hard worker, and he was a good brother to Natty and me. When Nana died, Leo would become our guardian—just until I turned eighteen.

I had added the cheese sauce and was considering calling the cops (for all the good that would do) when I heard the front door open.

Leo bounded into the kitchen. "You're making macaroni, Annie!" He threw his arms around me. "I have the best sister!"

I pushed Leo gently away. "Where were you? I was crazy worried. If you're going out, you're supposed to either tell Nana or write me a note."

Leo's face fell. "Don't be mad, Annie. I was with our family. You said it was okay as long as I was with family."

I shook my head. "I only meant Nana, Natty, or me. Immediate family. That means—"

Leo interrupted me. "I know what that means. You didn't say *immediate*."

I was pretty sure I had, but whatever.

"Jacks told me you wouldn't mind," Leo continued. "He said he was family, and you wouldn't mind."

"I bet he did. Is that the only person you were with?"

"Fats was there, too. We went to his place."

Sergei "Fats" Medovukha was my father's cousin and the owner of the speakeasy Gable and I had been at the night before. Fats was fat, which was less common in those days. I liked Fats as much as I liked anyone in my extended family, but I'd told him that I didn't want Leo hanging out at his bar.

"What did they want with you, Leo?"

"We got ice cream. Fats closed his place, and we went out for it. Jacks had . . . What do you call it, Annie?"

"Vouchers."

"Yeah, that's it!"

And if I knew my cousin, he'd probably made those vouchers himself.

"I had strawberry," Leo continued.

"Hmmph."

"Don't be mad, Annie."

Leo looked like he might cry. I took a deep breath and tried to control myself. It was one thing to lose my temper with Gable Arsley but behaving that way around Leo was completely unacceptable. "Was the ice cream good?"

Leo nodded. "Then we went . . . Promise you won't be mad."

I nodded.

"Then we went to the Pool."

The Pool was in the nineties on West End Avenue. It used to be a women's swimming club back before the first water crisis, when all the pools and fountains had been drained. Now, the Family (by which I mean the *semya*, or the Balanchine Family crime syndicate) used it as their primary meeting place. I guess they got the space on the cheap.

28

"Leo!" I yelled.

"You said you wouldn't be mad!"

"But you know you're not supposed to go to the west side without telling someone."

"I know, I know. But Jacks said that a lot of people wanted to meet me there. And he said they were family so you wouldn't mind."

I was so angry I couldn't speak. The macaroni had cooled enough to be eaten so I began to serve it into bowls. "Wash your hands, and tell Natty that dinner is ready."

"Please don't be mad, Annie."

"I'm not mad at *you*," I said.

I was about to make Leo promise that he would never go back there when he said, "Jacks said maybe I could get a job working at the Pool. You know, in the family business."

It was all I could manage not to throw the macaroni against the wall. Still, I knew it was no good getting mad at my brother. Not to mention, it seemed excessive to commit two violent acts with pasta in the same day. "Why would you want to do that? You love working at the clinic."

"Yeah, but Jacks thought it might be good if I worked with the Family"—he paused—"like Daddy."

I nodded tightly. "I don't know about that, Leo. They don't have animals to pet at the Pool. Now, go get Natty, okay?"

I watched my brother as he left the kitchen. To look at him, you wouldn't know anything was wrong with him. And maybe we made too much of his handicaps. It couldn't be denied that Leo was handsome, strong, and, for all intents and purposes, a grownup. The last part terrified me, of course. Grownups could get themselves in trouble. They could get taken advantage of. They could get sent to Rikers Island, or worse: they could end up dead.

As I filled glasses with water, I wondered what my *padonki* half cousin was up to and how much of a problem this was going to be for me.

I I. i am punished; define *recidivism*; tend to family matters

THE WORST PART OF LUNCH duty was the smock. It was red and tentlike and made me look fat and had a dry-erase sign vel-croed to the back that read ANYA BALANCHINE MUST LEARN TO CONTROL HER TEMPER. At first, you couldn't see the sign because of my hair but then they made me wear a hairnet. I didn't pro-test. The ensemble would have seemed incomplete without the hairnet.

While I collected my classmates' trays and glasses, Scarlet kept shooting me sympathetic looks which almost made the whole thing worse. I would rather have just served my time in a completely zoned-out state.

For obvious reasons, I saved Gable Arsley's table for last.

"I can't believe I ever went out with that," he said in a low voice that was still loud enough for me to hear.

Though several replies did occur to me, I smiled and said nothing. You weren't supposed to talk when you had lunch duty.

I pushed the cart with the trays to the kitchen, then I went back out to the cafeteria to eat my own lunch in the two minutes I had left. Scarlet had moved and was now sitting with Win. She was leaning toward him across the table, and laughing at something he said. Poor Scarlet. Her flirting technique could hardly be called subtle, and I had a sense that this approach wouldn't work with Win.

I didn't really want to sit down with them. I smelled like cafeteria fumes and garbage. Scarlet beckoned to me. "Annie! Over here!"

I trudged over to her.

"Love the hairnet!" Scarlet said.

"Thanks," I said. "I was considering wearing it full-time. The smock, too." I set down my tray and put my hands on my hips. "Probably needs a belt, though." I took off the smock and set it on the bench next to me.

"Anya, have you met Win?" Scarlet asked. She slightly raised her eyebrow to let me know that he was the one she'd been telling me about.

"In the principal's office. She was busy getting herself in trouble," Win said.

"Story of my life," I said. I started eating the vegetable potpie in what I hoped was a somewhat ladylike fashion. Even though I was sick of smelling the stuff, I was still famished.

As the bell rang, Win and Scarlet left, and I concentrated on speed-eating. I noticed that Win had forgotten his hat on the table.

Just as the second bell rang, Win returned to the cafeteria.

I held out the hat to him.

"Thanks," he said. He was about to leave but then he sat down in the chair across from me. "Felt rude to leave you here all alone."

"It's fine. You're late." I took one last forkful. "Besides, I like my own company."

He crossed his hands over his knee. "I've got independent study this period anyway."

I looked at him. "Suit yourself." Scarlet was into him and there was no way I would ever go for a guy she was into, no matter how nice his hands were. If there was one thing my dad had taught me, it was the importance of loyalty. "How do you know Scarlet?"

"French," he said, and he left it at that.

"Well, I'm done now," I informed him. It was high time for Win to be on his way.

"You forgot something," he said. He removed the hairnet from my hair, his thumb gently grazing my forehead, and my curls spilled out. "The hairnet's nice and all, but I think I prefer you without it."

"Oh," I said. I felt myself blush and so I ordered myself to stop blushing. This flirtation was starting to annoy me. "Why did you move here anyway?"

"My dad's the new number two in the DA's office." It was well-known that DA Silverstein was basically a puppet—too old and ailing to be effective. Being the second-in-command was actually like being the first-in-command but without the annoyance of having to run in an election. Things must have been pretty bad for them to have brought in someone from Albany. An outside hire implied a major regime change. In my opinion, that could only be a good thing as the city couldn't get much worse. I didn't remember exactly what had happened to the old number two, but it was probably the usual: he'd been incompetent or a thief. Possibly incompetent *and* a thief.

"Your dad's the new top cop?"

"He thinks he's gonna clean everything up," Win said.

"Good luck to him," I said.

"Yeah, he's probably pretty naïve." Win shrugged. "Calls himself an idealist though."

"Hey! I thought you said your people were farmers," I said.

"My mother is. She's an agricultural engineer specializing in irrigation systems. Basically a magician who grows crops without water. My father used to be the Albany DA, though."

"That's . . . You lied!"

"No, I only mentioned what was relevant to your question, which, if you recall, was how did I get my calluses? And I certainly did not get my calluses because my dad's the DA."

"I think you didn't say anything because you knew who my father was, and . . ."

"And?" Win prompted me.

"And maybe you thought I wouldn't want to make friends with a guy whose family is on the opposite side of the law from my family."

"Star-crossed lovers and all of that—"

"Hold on, I didn't say—"

"I take it back. And I apologize if I misled you in any way." Win looked a bit amused with me. "That's certainly a good theory, Anya."

I told Win I had to get to class which, in point of fact, I did.

I was already five minutes late for Twentieth-Century American History.

"See you around," he said as he tipped his hat.

On the board, Mr. Beery had written *Those who don't remember history are doomed to repeat it.* I wasn't sure if this was meant to be inspirational, thematic, or a joke about making sure to study.

"Anya Balanchine," Mr. Beery said. "Nice of you to join us."

"I'm sorry, Mr. Beery. I had lunch duty."

"Thus, Ms. Balanchine provides us with a walking example of the societal problems of crime, punishment, and recidivism. If you can tell me why this is so, I won't send you back to Headmaster's office for a late pass."

I'd only had Mr. Beery for one day so I couldn't completely tell if he was serious or not.

"Ms. Balanchine. We're waiting."

I tried not to sneer when I answered, "The criminal is punished for his or her crimes, but the punishment itself leads to more crimes. I was punished for fighting by being given lunch duty, but the lunch duty itself made me tardy."

"Dingdingdingdingding! Give this woman a prize," Mr. Beery said. "You may take your seat, Ms. Balanchine. And now, boys and girls, can anyone tell me what the Noble Experiment refers to?"

Alison Wheeler, the pretty redhead who would likely be our class's valedictorian, raised her hand.

"No need for any hand-raising in my classroom, Ms. Wheeler. I like to think of us as being in discussion."

"Um, yes," Alison said, lowering her hand. "The Noble Experiment is another name for the first prohibition, which lasted from 1920 to 1933 and banned the sale and consumption of alcohol in the United States."

"Very good, Ms. Wheeler. Any brave soul wish to hazard a guess as to why I've chosen to start the year with the Noble Experiment?"

I tried to ignore the fact that all my classmates were looking at me.

Finally, Chai Pinter, the class gossip, offered, "Because of, maybe, how chocolate and caffeine are today?"

"Dingdingdingdingding! You aren't quite as dull a lot as you look," Mr. Beery proclaimed. For the rest of the period, he lectured about Prohibition. How temperance people believed that banning alcohol would magically solve everything that was wrong with society: poverty, violence, crime, etc. And how the temperance movement succeeded, in the short run at least, because it allied itself with other more powerful movements, many of which didn't care about alcohol one way or the other. Alcohol had been a pawn.

I wasn't an expert on the chocolate ban as it had happened before I was born, but there were definite similarities. Daddy had always told me that there was nothing inherently evil about chocolate, that it had gotten caught up in a larger whirlwind involving food, drugs, health, and money. Our country had only chosen chocolate because the people in power needed to pick something, and chocolate was what they could live without. Daddy once said, "Every generation spins the wheel, Anya, and where it lands defines 'the good.' Funny thing is, they never know that they're spinning it, and it hits something different every time."

I was still thinking about Daddy when I became aware of Mr. Beery calling my name. "Ms. Balanchine, care to weigh in on the reason the Noble Experiment ultimately failed?"

I narrowed my eyes. "Why are you asking me specifically?" I would make him say it.

"Only because I haven't heard from you in a while," Mr. Beery lied.

"Because people liked their liquor," I said stupidly.

"That's true, Ms. Balanchine. A bit more, though. Something from your personal experience perhaps."

I was starting to loathe this man. "Because banning anything leads to organized crime. People will always find a way to get what they want, and there will always be criminals willing to provide it."

The bell rang. I was glad to be out of there.

"Ms. Balanchine," Mr. Beery called to me. "Stay a moment. I'm worried we may have gotten off on the wrong foot here."

I could have pretended I hadn't heard him I suppose, but I didn't. "I can't. I'll be late for my next class, and you know what they say about recidivists."

"I'm thinking of asking Win to come out with us this Friday," Scarlet said on the bus ride back from school.

"Ooh, Win," Natty said. "I like him."

"That's because you have excellent taste, Natty darling," Scarlet said, kissing Natty on the cheek.

I rolled my eyes at both of them. "If you like him so much, you should ask him out by yourself," I told Scarlet. "Why do you need me to come with you? I'll only be a third wheel."

"Annie," Scarlet whined, "don't be dense. If it's just me and him, I'll be the weird girl who asked him out. If you're there, it's more casual and friendly." Scarlet turned toward my sister. "Natty agrees with me, right?"

Natty paused to give me a look before nodding. "Once everything is going well, you two should have a signal that means it's time for Annie to leave."

"Something like this," Scarlet said. She winked in a ridiculous and cartoonish way that contorted half her face.

"Really subtle," I said. "Win'll never notice that."

"Come on, Annie! I have to stake my claim before someone else does. You have to admit that he's completely perfect for me."

"Based on what?" I asked. "You barely even know him."

"Based on . . . Based on . . . We both like hats!"

"And he's pretty," Natty added.

"He *is* pretty," Scarlet said. "I swear, Annie, I will never ask you for anything ever again."

"Oh, all right," I grumbled.

Scarlet kissed me. "I love you, Annie! I was thinking we'd go to that speakeasy your cousin Fats runs."

"Yeah, that might not be such a great idea, Scar."

"Why not?"

"Haven't you heard? Mr. Completely Perfect's dad is the new top cop."

Scarlet's eyes grew wide. "Seriously?"

I nodded.

"I guess we'll have to pick somewhere legal, then," Scarlet said. "That pretty much eliminates just about everything fun."

The bus stopped on Fifth and the three of us walked the remaining six blocks to my apartment. Scarlet was coming over to study as she often did.

We entered the building and walked past the empty doorman cubicle (after the last doorman had been killed and his family had sued, the apartment board decided that they couldn't afford to pay a doorman anymore) and we rode the elevator up to the penthouse.

Scarlet and Natty went into my bedroom while I checked on Nana.

Imogen, Nana's nurse, was reading to her. "To begin my life with the beginning of my life, I record that I was born (as I have been informed and believe) on a Friday, at twelve o'clock at night. It was remarked that the clock began to strike, and I began to cry, simultaneously."

Even though I wasn't much of a reader, Imogen had a sweet voice that lulled me, and I found myself standing at the door to listen for a while. She read until the end of the chapter (which wasn't very long), then closed the book.

"You're here for the start of this one," Imogen said to me. She held up the paper novel so that I could see the title: *David Copperfield*.

"Anyaschka, when did you get here?" Nana asked. I walked over to her and kissed her cheek. "I wanted something with more action," Nana said, wrinkling her nose. "Girls, guns. But this was what she had."

"It gets more exciting," Imogen assured her. "You must be patient, Galina."

"If it takes too long, I'll be dead," Nana replied.

"Enough with the gallows humor," Imogen reprimanded.

I took the book from Imogen and held it up to my face. The dust stung my nose. The aroma was salty and a bit sour. The cover of the book was disintegrating. There hadn't been new books printed (on account of the cost of paper) for as long as I had been alive, maybe longer. Nana once told me that when she was a girl there used to be huge stores filled with paper books. "Not that I ever went to any bookstores. I had better things to do," she'd say with longing in her voice. "Ah, to be young!" These days, most everything was digitized. All the paper books had been pulped and recycled into essentials like toilet tissue and money. If your family (or school) happened to be in possession of a bona fide paper book, you held on to it. (By the way, one of the goods the Balanchine *semya* dealt in was black market paper.)

"You can borrow it if you like," Imogen said to me. "It really does get more exciting." My grandmother's home-health-care worker was an avid paper book collector, which seemed ridiculously old-fashioned to me. Why would a person want all those dirty paper carcasses around? Still, the books had value for her, so I knew it was a sign of respect that she would offer one of them to me.

I shook my head. "No, thanks. I have a ton of reading for school." I preferred reading on my slate, and I wasn't much into fiction anyway.

Imogen checked my grandmother's machines one last time before she bid us good night.

"I suppose you found Leonyd," Nana said after Imogen had left.

"I did." I paused, uncertain whether to trouble Nana with the story of where (and with whom) Leo had been.

"He was at the Pool with Pirozhki and Fats," Nana said. "I asked him this morning."

"Well, what's your opinion?"

Nana shrugged her shoulders, which made her cough. "Maybe it's a good thing. It's nice that family has taken an interest in your brother. Leo's too much among us women. He could stand for some male companionship in his life."

I shook my head. "I don't have a good feeling about this, Nana. Jakov Pirozhki is not exactly trustworthy."

"Still, he's family, Anya. And family takes care of family. That's how it's done. That's how it's always been done. Besides, Fats, at least, seems a decent enough sort." Nana coughed again, and I poured her some water from a pitcher on the nightstand. "Thank you, *devochka*."

"Leo said something about getting a job at the Pool."

Nana's eyes widened for a moment and then she nodded. "He didn't tell me that part. Well, there have certainly been made men that were far more simpleminded than Leo."

"Like who?"

"Like . . . Like . . . Like . . . I've got it!" She smiled triumphantly. "Like Viktor Popov. He was of my generation. Six feet ten inches, three hundred and fifty pounds. Would have been one hell of a football player, if he could have remembered the rules. The other guys called him Viktor the Mule to his face and the Donkey behind his back. When they needed someone to move the stuff from the back of the truck, they'd call the Mule every time. It doesn't matter how high-tech things get, sometimes you need a guy who's good with manual labor."

I nodded. Nana was making some sense. For the first time since Leo had gone missing, I felt my stomach muscles unclench a little. "What happened to Viktor the Mule anyway?"

"That's not the important part."

"*Nana.*"

"He got shot in the head. Bled to death. A real shame." Nana shook her head.

"Not exactly a good end, Nana. And Leo's not exactly the Mule's body type," I said. My brother was tall, but he was thin as paper.

"My point is, *devochka*, that it takes all kinds to run the business. And your brother's a big boy now."

I gritted my teeth.

"Anyaschka, you're too much like your father. You want to control the whole world and everyone in it, but you can't. Let whatever this is—and it's likely nothing—play out. If we need to intervene later, we will. Besides, Leo would never leave the clinic. He loves the animals too much."

"So we do nothing?"

"Sometimes that's the only thing to do," Nana said. "Although . . ."

"Yes?"

"Get yourself a bar of chocolate from the closet," she ordered.

"Chocolate doesn't solve everything, Nana."

"It solves a whole heck of a lot, though," she said.

I went into her closet. I pushed past the coats to open the safe. I moved the gun out of the way. I took a chocolate bar: Balanchine Special Dark. I put the gun back. I closed the safe.

Something wasn't right.

One of the guns was missing. My father's Smith & Wesson.

"Nana?" I called.

She didn't answer. I went back into her bedroom. She was already fast asleep.

"Nana," I repeated, shaking her shoulder.

"What?" she sputtered. "What?"

"One of the guns is missing," I said. "From the safe. Daddy's gun."

"Were you planning to use it tonight? Take the Colt instead." Nana chuckled and that turned into a choke, so I gave her water. "Imogen probably moved it. I think she mentioned something about cleaning or it not being safe to keep the weapons in one place or . . . I'm sorry. I can't remember." Her face looked sad and confused for a moment, and I wanted to cry. She smiled. "Don't worry so much, darling. You can ask her tomorrow."

I kissed my grandmother's cheek, then I left. On the way back to my room, I passed Leo's. His door was shut but I could see light coming from the crack at the bottom. He must have gotten home while I'd been talking to Nana. I looked at my watch: 4:10, slightly early for my brother to be back from work.

I knocked on the door.

No answer.

I knocked again.

Still no answer. I put my ear against the wood. I could barely make out muffled sobs.

43

"Leo, I know you're in there. What's wrong?"

"Go away!" Leo said, his voice thick with tears.

"I can't do that, Leo. I'm your sister. If something's the matter, I need to know what it is so I can help."

I heard the sound of Leo fastening the lock.

"Please, Leo. If you don't open this right now, I'll have to pick the lock. You know I can." I had done it many times after Leo had locked himself in his room both by accident and on purpose.

Leo unlocked and opened the door.

His eyes were bloodshot, and trails of snot were coming out his nose. When he cried, my brother looked about six years old. His face turned pink and clenched up like a rose or a fist.

I put my arms around him, which made Leo cry even harder. "Oh no, Leo, what happened? Is it something with Jacks?"

Leo shook his head. After perhaps thirty more seconds of tears, Leo managed to tell me the cause of his distress. He couldn't look me in the eye, but he finally said that he had lost his job at the veterinary clinic.

"Don't worry, Leo." I rubbed his back the way he liked. When he had calmed down somewhat, I asked him to explain what had happened. It turned out that the veterinary clinic had been shut down. After Leo had gotten back from lunch, someone from the New York City Department of Health had shown up for an unscheduled inspection. The clinic had been cited for fifty-one violations, most of them having to do with cleanliness, and had been ordered to immediately cease operations.

"But it was clean," Leo said. "I know it was clean. It was my job to keep it clean, and I do a good job. Everyone says I'm a good worker, Annie."

"It's not your fault," I assured my brother. This sort of thing happened every day. Clearly, someone at the clinic hadn't been paying off the right person at the Department of Health. "Here's my prediction, Leo. I bet you anything the clinic will reopen in a couple of weeks and you'll be back at work in no time."

Leo nodded, but his eyes were unconvinced. "They sent away the animals, Annie. You don't think they'll hurt them, do you?"

"No." A couple of years ago there'd been a move to ban all pets from the city, but there were protests and it didn't fly. Some people still thought nonworking animals were a waste of our limited resources. Quite honestly, I wasn't sure what would happen, but there was no use telling Leo that. I made a mental note to call Leo's boss, Dr. Pikarski, to see if there was anything I could do to help.

Leo said he was tired so I tucked him into bed and told him I'd wake him for dinner. "I didn't cry in front of them at work," he said. "When it happened, I wanted to cry but I held it in."

"You were very brave," I said.

I turned off his light and closed the door.

When I got back to my room, Natty and Scarlet were monopolizing the space on the bed. I wasn't in the mood to kick out my little sister so I just sat on the floor.

"Everything all right?" Scarlet asked.

"The usual," I replied. "Family drama."

"Well, Natty and I were actually very productive," Scarlet

said. "We came up with a list of potential places to take Win on Friday night."

"Seems a bit premature, seeing as he hasn't even agreed to go with us yet," I said.

Scarlet ignored me and held out her hand, which was where the list was written:

1. Little Egypt
2. The Lion's Den
3. The Times
4. See a concert/show
5. Co . . .

Scarlet had sweated off half of number five. "What's that last one?"

"Co . . ." Scarlet squinted at her hand. "Comedy. Yeah, that was kind of lame anyway."

"Definitely Little Egypt," I told her.

"You're only saying that because it's close to your house," Scarlet said.

"What of it? It'll be interesting if he's never been there. Plus, you're planning to ditch me anyway, right?"

"True," she said. "If all goes well."

By the time Scarlet left, it was nearly five o'clock and I had yet to even consider my homework. The same was true for Natty. "Scat," I ordered.

Natty stood up. "You should tell her," Natty said.

"Get started on your homework," I said. I sat down at my desk and took out my slate. "I should tell who what?"

"Scarlet. You should tell Scarlet that you like Win."

I shook my head. "I don't like Win."

"Well, then, you should tell her that he likes you."

"You don't know that," I said.

"I was there yesterday. *I saw*," Natty said.

I turned to look at my sister. "Scarlet saw him first."

"That's stupid."

"And I just broke up with someone so . . ."

"Uh-huh." Natty rolled her eyes. "It's gonna be trouble if you don't tell her."

"What do you know? You're a little kid," I said. I honestly had no idea why I'd been entertaining this line of discussion for so long.

"I know some things, Annie. Like, it's not every day a supercute boy comes along that doesn't care who our family is. Mostly, you end up with dummies like Gable. And Win likes you which is practically a miracle. You're not exactly the easiest person in the world to like, you know."

"Go! Study! Now!" I ordered. "And close my door!"

Natty scurried to the door but before she shut it, she whispered, "You know I'm right."

Other than the respective textures of our hair, the main difference between Natty and me was that she was a romantic and I was a realist. I couldn't afford to be a romantic—I'd had to take care of her and Nana and Leo since I was nine years old. So, yeah, I wasn't blind. I saw that Win probably liked me, and I can truly say that I didn't care. He didn't even know me; he probably just had a thing for brunettes or C-cup breasts or my particular pheromones or blah, blah, blah, whatever dumb thing made anyone like anyone. Romance was a complete waste anyway. My mother had felt romantic about my father, and look where that got her—dead at thirty-eight.

This isn't to say I couldn't imagine that there were probably a few nice things about falling in love.

I was about to start my homework when I remembered that I needed to call Dr. Pikarski for Leo.

I picked up the phone. (We used phones sparingly because of how heavily they were taxed and the long-held belief in my family that our lines were being tapped.) I dialed Dr. Pikarski's home number. I liked her. I had spoken to her several times in the process of securing the position at the clinic for Leo in the first place, and she had always been straight with me. More important, she'd always been good to Leo. I felt like I owed her one.

Her voice was clearly stressed when she answered the phone. "Oh, Anya," she said, "I suppose you've heard. The guy from the DOH seemed to have it in for us!"

I asked Dr. Pikarski for the name of the DOH employee. "Wendel Yoric," she said, and then I had her spell it. My family still had some friends spread across the various government agencies, and I hoped I could speed the process along a bit.

After I hung up with Dr. Pikarski, I called my family's attorney, Mr. Kipling. (Two phone calls in one day!) Mr. Kipling had been the family's lawyer since before I was born. My father told me that I could always count on Mr. Kipling, and Daddy didn't say that about nearly anyone else.

"So, you want me to cut this Mr. Yoric a check?" Mr. Kipling asked after I had explained the situation.

"Yes," I said. "Or, you know, an envelope filled with cash."

48

"Of course, Anya. It was just a term of art. I have no plans to literally cut anyone at the Department of Health a check. Incidentally, it still might take a couple of weeks to sort this out," Mr. Kipling said. "So, hold tight, Anya. And tell Leo to hold tight, too."

"Thanks," I said.

"How's junior year treating you?" Mr. Kipling asked.

I groaned.

"That good?"

"Don't ask," I said. "I got in a fight the first day but it wasn't my fault."

"Sounds like Leo. Leo, Senior, I mean." Mr. Kipling had gone to high school with Daddy. "How's Galina?"

"Good days and bad days," I said. "We're all getting by."

"Your father would be proud of you, Annie."

I was about to say goodbye when I decided to ask Mr. Kipling what he knew about Jakov Pirozhki.

"Small-time guy who wishes he were big-time. Won't happen, though. No one in the organization really takes him seriously, especially his own father. And since his mother wasn't, you know, Yuri's wife, Jacks is pretty much dogged by questions of whether he's even a real Balanchine. I pity the kid to tell you the truth." Yuri, by the way, was Yuri Balanchine, my father's half brother and my uncle. He'd taken over the family after Daddy's murder. Mr. Kipling changed the subject. "Have you decided what colleges you're applying to?"

I sighed.

"The offer still stands for me to be your escort on your college tour."

"Thanks, Mr. Kipling. I'll keep that in mind." If I even went on such a thing, I'd probably take Leo with me.

"It would be my pleasure, Anya."

I hung up the phone. Talking to Mr. Kipling always managed to make me feel less lonely and more alone at the same time. I sometimes imagined that Mr. Kipling was my father. I imagined what it would be like to have a father who had a respectable profession like a lawyer. I imagined what it would be like to have the kind of father who took you on college tours. The kind of father who was still alive. Even before Daddy died, I sometimes imagined asking Mr. Kipling to adopt me.

But Mr. Kipling already had a daughter. Her name was Grace and she was studying to be an engineer.

I had finally opened my History reading when there was a knock at the door. It was Leo. "Annie, I'm hungry," he said.

So I put away my slate and went to tend to my family's needs.

I I I. i confess; contemplate mortality & teeth; lure a boy under false pretenses; disappoint my brother

I WENT TO CONFESSION Friday morning before school.

If you were wondering, my father wasn't Catholic. He, like everyone in the Balanchine family, had been born into the Eastern Orthodox faith. Not that Daddy was observant anyway. I never saw him in a church except for my and my siblings' christenings, or family weddings. Of course, my mother's funeral, too. I certainly never heard him mention God.

My mother was the Catholic, and she talked about God regularly. Actually, she said she talked to Him. She'd even wanted to be a nun when she was little but, obviously, that hadn't worked out for her. One might even say she'd gone in the complete opposite direction, marrying the head of a notorious crime family and all. But my point is, I was a Catholic because of my mother. Sure, I wanted to believe in the possibility of an afterlife and of redemption and salvation and reunion and maybe, most important, a forgiving God. But when I chose Holy

Trinity School (and yes, I had been the one to choose it for me and Natty), it was not God I was thinking of. It was my mother and what she would have wanted. And when I went to church and smelled incense burning in the priest's vessel, I felt close to her. And when the worn velvet brushed my knees in the confessional, I knew she had felt the same thing. And when I sat in a pew and looked up at the pietà bathed in soft, colored light, I almost saw her sometimes. And there was nowhere else in my life that this even came near to happening. For this reason, I knew I could never entirely walk away from the Catholic faith.

There were, of course, things that bothered me about my faith, but they seemed a small price to pay when you considered what it gave me in return. So what if I would be a virgin until I was married? Gable had never even had a chance.

"How many days has it been since your last confession?"

"Four," I said, and then I recited my sins, which if you've been paying any attention you ought to know already. Bribery, wrath, a few repeats from Monday, etc. I was assigned another minor penance, which I accomplished in time to make it to first period: Forensic Science II. This was my favorite subject, partly because I found it interesting and partly because it was the only thing I took that seemed relevant to the crime-ridden world I lived in and partly because I was better at it than anything else. I had inherited my aptitude. Sometime after she'd given up on her ambition to become a nun and before she'd married the Godfather, my mother had been a crime scene investigator for the NYPD. That was how she'd met Daddy, of course.

It was my second year having Dr. Lau, and she was by far the best teacher I'd ever had in school. (She'd been my mom's first FS teacher, too, and she was old though not as old as Nana. Fifties or sixties.) I appreciated that she wouldn't tolerate any squeamishness, no matter how disgusting what we were studying was. Even if it was a week-old chicken corpse or an ominously stained mattress or a menstrual pad. "Life is messy," Dr. Lau was fond of saying. "Deal with it. If you're judging it, you're not really seeing it."

"Today and for the next several days, you'll all be dentists!" Dr. Lau announced gleefully. "I have seven sets of teeth, and there're thirteen of you. Who wants to be odd person out?"

I was the only one to raise my hand. It might seem weird but I actually liked working with the evidence by myself.

"Thanks for stepping up, Annie. You'll have a partner next time." She nodded toward me and then began distributing trays with teeth in them. The assignment was pretty straightforward. Using only the teeth, we were to come up with a detailed profile of the person in life (e.g., Had he or she been a smoker?) and based on this, come up with a likely narrative for cause of death.

I put on a fresh pair of rubber gloves and began to contemplate my teeth. They were small and white. No fillings. A bit of asymmetric wear on the right molar as if the person had ground his or her teeth in sleep. The teeth seemed delicate—not like a child's but somehow feminine. I noted my findings on my slate: Wealthy. Young. Stress. Female?

Almost could have been describing myself.

Dr. Lau put a hand on my shoulder. "Good news. We found a partner for you, Annie."

It was Win. Mr. Too Smart for His Classes had transferred out of Forensic Science I into FS II.

"Can't seem to stop running into you," he said.

"Well, it's a very small school," I replied. I showed him my slate screen. "I've not gotten very far. I like to spend time thinking at the beginning."

"Makes sense," he said. He put on a pair of gloves, a gesture I appreciated in a potential lab partner, then he pointed to the backs of her bottom teeth. "Look, the enamel's damaged."

I leaned over. "Oh!" I hadn't looked at the back yet. "She must have been throwing up."

"She must have been sick," he said.

"Or making herself sick," I added.

"Yes." Win nodded. He lowered his head so that he was eye to teeth. "I think you're right, Anya. Our girl was making herself sick."

I smiled at him. "Her whole life story right here, waiting for us to read it."

He agreed. "It's sad when you think about it, but also kind of beautiful."

It was a strange thing to say, I suppose. But I knew what he meant without having to ask. All these teeth had once been in real, live people. They had talked and smiled and eaten and sang and cursed and prayed. They had brushed and flossed and died. In English class, we read poems about death, but here, right in front of me, was a poem about death, too. Only this poem was true. I had experienced death, and poems hadn't helped me one bit. Poems didn't matter. Evidence did.

It wasn't even 8:00 a.m. yet. Pretty early for such deep thoughts.

Still, that's what I loved about forensic science.

I wondered if Win had ever had someone close to him die.

The bell rang. Win gently put away the teeth, marking the tray with a piece of tape that read BALANCHINE DELACROIX—DO NOT TOUCH!!! I slipped my slate into my bag.

"See you at lunch," he said.

"I'll be the girl in the hairnet," I replied.

For my physical education elective (fourth period), I was in Advanced Fencing. The "advanced" designation did not speak particularly to my skill but to the fact that I had completed two previous years of fencing. The sport was kind of ridiculous when it came down to it. Despite being an "advanced" fencer, if I were ever in mortal danger I wouldn't use one iota of fencing knowledge. I'd use a gun.

Scarlet was my fencing partner and, though she filled out the outfit nicely, she and I were equally clueless fencers. The thing was, she could actually strike a series of plausible offensive poses, and I had the knack for striking appropriate, corresponding defensive postures. I'm reasonably sure that Mr. Jarre, the fencing master, saw through us, but he didn't really care. We bolstered the head count in Advanced Fencing, which meant that the class wouldn't get canceled.

After warm-ups, which included lunging and stretching, we broke off into pairs.

Scarlet and I fenced (sort of) and talked (mostly).

"So it's Friday, which means we have to ask Win today," she reminded me.

I groaned. "Seriously, just ask him yourself. I'll come, but . . ."

Scarlet tapped my shoulder lightly with the foil. "A touch!"

I yelled, mainly for Mr. Jarre's benefit. Then I staggered several steps backward.

"It'll sound more casual if you're there. Stop by about five minutes before lunch is over," she said. "And, Anya, my love, if you think of it, take off the hairnet."

"Funny," I said. I launched my foil into her hip.

"Ow," she said. "I mean, a touch!"

It was the last day of lunch duty, and I think I can say I was finally getting the hang of it. I knew how to pick up multiple trays without getting anything in my hair or on myself, and I knew how to serve Gable's table with a sarcastic "Y'all come back now" smile.

As I picked up Gable's tray, he said, "Hope you learned your lesson."

"Oh, I did," I said. "And thank you so very much for teaching me." I dropped the tray onto the cart so that a little bit of lunch (ground tofu with mysterious red sauce in a bun—Asian Delight?) splashed on his face. "Sorry," I said, and then I rolled my cart away before he had a chance to respond.

I unloaded the trays onto the dish-cleaning belt at which point the head lunch lady gave me permission to eat my own lunch. "Good work, Anya," she said. I know it was just lunch duty but I was still glad that she thought I had done a good job. Daddy always said that once you'd committed (or were committed) to something, you had to honor it all the way.

Scarlet was sitting with Win and several of her friends from the drama club. I sat down next to Scarlet and said my line. "So are we still going to Little Egypt tonight?"

"What's Little Egypt?" Win asked, which was, conveniently enough, exactly what he was supposed to ask.

"Oh, it's kind of dumb," Scarlet replied. "It's this nightclub that the city opened in the northern part of that abandoned museum on Fifth. There used to be a collection of Egyptian stuff there, which is why they call it Little Egypt." There were similar nightclubs in various abandoned structures across the city. They were a modest but steady source of revenue for the government, which was usually on the verge of a total financial collapse. "It's lame, but kind of cool if you haven't been there before and, I don't know, *j'adore le discothèque*!" (You will recall that Win and Scarlet had French together.)

I said my next line. "You could come with us if you want."

"I'm not sure I'm much of a nightclub person," Win conceded.

Scarlet and I had prepared for such a response.

"A lot of nightclubs in Albany?" Scarlet teased him.

He smiled. "Well, we used to go on hayrides sometimes."

"Sounds fun," Scarlet said with a flirtatious dash of sarcasm.

"A lot of hayrides in New York City?" he asked.

Scarlet laughed. I could tell she was about to have her way with Win.

We arranged to meet at my apartment—it was the closest to the club—that night at eight.

When I got back from school, the first thing I did was check on Leo, but he wasn't home. I told myself not to worry, that there was probably a simple explanation for his absence. I went into Nana's room. She was sleeping, but Imogen was sitting in the leather wing chair we kept by the bed, the chair that used to be Daddy's. Three fresh pink carnations sat in the vase on the windowsill: Nana had had a visitor.

I waved to Imogen. She put her finger to her lips to indicate that I should be quiet. Imogen had been Nana's nurse since I was thirteen, and she sometimes forgot that I was hardly a little girl prone to stomping into rooms where my grandmother was sleeping. (Not that I ever had been.) I nodded and beckoned Imogen into the hallway. Draping her book over the worn arm of the burgundy chair, she rose and closed the door gently behind her. I asked her if she knew where Leo was.

"Out with your cousin," Imogen informed me. "Galina said it was fine."

"Did they say where they were going?"

"I'm sorry, Annie. I honestly wasn't paying attention. Galina had a rough afternoon." She shook her head. "For a swim, maybe? No, that doesn't make any sense." Imogen frowned. "But I swear it was something to do with swimming."

Of course. The Pool.

"Did I do wrong not to stop Leo?"

"No," I told her. The truth was, it was neither Imogen's job nor her place to watch my brother. That was my job, a job made even more challenging by the fact that, in order to preserve his feelings, I had to act like I wasn't watching him at all. Also, I did have school to attend. I thanked Imogen, and she went back to reading her book in Daddy's chair.

I was about to head across town to claim Leo when he came through the door. He was out of breath and flushed. "Oh," he said when he saw me, "I was trying to beat you home. I didn't want you to worry, Annie."

"Too late," I said.

Leo gave me a hug. He was damp with sweat, and I pushed him away. "You're smelly," I told him. Leo hugged me even tighter. It was a game with him. I knew he wouldn't let go until I said I loved him. "Okay, Leo. I love you. I love you already! Now tell me where you were."

"You'll be proud of me, Annie. I was out getting a new job!"

I raised an eyebrow. "Imogen said you were at the Pool."

"That's where my new job is, Annie. Just until they reopen the clinic. It pays better than the clinic, too," Leo said.

I cleared my throat. "What kind of a job?" I asked softly so that Leo wouldn't hear how angry I was.

"Maintenance things. Cleaning the floors and stuff. Jacks says they need a guy, and I'm real good at that sort of thing, Annie. You know I am."

I asked Leo how he had become aware of such an opportunity, and he told me that Cousin Jacks had stopped by the apartment to visit Nana that morning. (This explained the fresh carnations.) Jacks had been surprised to find Leo home in the middle of the day so Leo had told him the story of the clinic getting shut down. Jacks then mentioned that they were looking for a maintenance guy at the Pool and that Leo would be perfect if he was interested in making some "easy money" before the clinic reopened.

"Easy money? Were those his exact words?" I asked.

"I—" Leo shook his head. "I'm not sure, Annie. Even after

59

the guy at the Pool offered me the job, I told him I'd have to talk to you and Nana first. That was the right thing to do, wasn't it?"

"Yes. But the thing is, Leo, our relatives, I mean the guys who work at the Pool, aren't always the nicest sort of people to be hanging out with."

"I'm not so stupid, Annie," Leo said in a harder voice than I'd ever heard him use. "I'm not so stupid as you think. I know what our family does. I know what Daddy used to do, too. I got hurt because of what Daddy used to do, remember? I know it every day."

"Of course you do, Leo. I know you're not stupid."

"I want to pull my weight, Annie. I feel bad that I don't have a job right now. If Nana dies and I don't have a job, they could take you and Natty away. And Cousin Jacks is a real nice guy, Annie. He told me you don't like him, but that was only because you'd heard something he said wrong."

I snorted. Nice Cousin Jacks had gotten wasted and put his hand on my boob. Nothing to mishear there. "I don't think so, Leo." I looked at my brother. He was wearing gray pants that were too big on him through the waist (they had been Daddy's) and a white T-shirt. Even though he was wiry, his arms were muscular from all the lifting they had him do at the clinic. He looked capable. Powerful, even. Not like someone who needed to be protected. Certainly not like someone whose little sister lay awake in bed worrying about him.

Leo's eyes were like Daddy's ice-blue ones with some of the ice thawed out. They were looking at me with hope. "I really want to do it, Annie."

"Let me talk it over with Nana, okay, Leo?"

Leo exploded. "I'm a grownup! I don't need you to say yes! You're a kid! I'm the big brother! I don't want you in my room anymore!" Then he pushed me toward the door. It wasn't a hard push but I still fell a couple of steps backward.

"I'm going to talk to Nana about it," I repeated. As I stepped over the threshold, Leo slammed the door behind me.

There was a good chance the ruckus had roused Nana, so I went back to her room. She was indeed awake. "How are you, darling?" she asked. "I heard yelling."

I kissed her cheek, which smelled of baby powder and bile, and then I looked over toward Imogen. I shook my head ever so slightly to let Nana know I didn't want to discuss family business in front of the nurse.

"Well, I should go." Imogen put her book in her bag. It was the end of her workday anyway. "I guess you found Leo," she said.

"Yes," I said with a half laugh. "In the hallway."

"Always the last place you look," said Imogen. "Take care, Anya. Sleep well, Galina."

After Imogen had closed the door, I told Nana where Leo had been and about the job. "So, what do you think?" I asked.

Nana laughed, which made her cough. I poured her some water, then held the straw to her lips. A few drops spilled out onto the maroon silk coverlet and to my eye these looked almost like blood. I repeated the question. "What do you think?"

"Well," said my grandmother in her desiccated voice, "I can already tell what you think. Your nostrils are flared like a race-horse's and your eyes are as bloodshot as a drunk's. You mustn't let your face show so much of what you feel. It's a weakness, my darling."

"So?" I asked.

"So, pfft," she said.

"Pfft?"

"Pfft. Jacks is family. Leo is without a job. Family takes care of family. Pfft."

"But, Leo—"

"But nothing! Not everything is conspiracy. I used to always have to say that to your father, too."

I decided not to point out the obvious—that Daddy had been right to be paranoid. He'd been shot to death in his own home.

Nana continued. "It's nice that anyone's taking an interest in your brother. Because from the Family's point of view, your brother is a *muzhik*, a nothing. He's like a woman or a child. No one would bother with him."

And yet Jacks was bothering with him for some reason.

"Anya! I can see your furrowed brow. I only meant no one will shoot your brother or get him in any kind of trouble. It wouldn't be honorable. These men at the Pool used to be your father's captains and foot soldiers. And one of the best things about your father, God rest his soul, was that he took care of people. They loved your father, and they respected him in life, and they do what they can to honor him in death. This is the reason Jacks finds a job for your brother. You do understand that, don't you?"

I unfurrowed my brow.

"Good girl," she said, patting me on the hand.

"Maybe I should go talk to Jacks at least?" I suggested. "Make sure everything's aboveboard."

Nana shook her head. "Let it be. If you go down there, it

will only humiliate Leo. He will lose face in front of the other men. And besides, Pirozhki himself is a nobody, and no threat to anybody."

She had a point. "I'll tell Leo at dinner that you said he should take the job," I said.

Nana shook her head. "In two years, you'll be in college and I'll be—"

"Don't say it!" I yelled.

"Fine, my dear, have it your way. I'll be elsewhere. My point is, isn't it best that you let Leo come to some decisions on his own, Anyaschka? Let him be a man, my darling. Give him that gift."

As a peace offering, I made macaroni and cheese for the second time that week. I told Natty to go get Leo, but he wouldn't come to dinner. I brought the bowl to Leo's door. "Leo, you should eat," I said.

"Are you mad?" he whispered. I could barely hear him through the wood.

"No, I'm not mad. I'm never mad at you. I was just worried before."

Leo opened the door a crack. "I'm sorry," he said. His eyes filled with tears. "I pushed you."

I nodded. "It's okay. It wasn't very hard."

Leo's mouth and eyes clenched shut in an effort to stop himself from crying. I stood on my tiptoes so that I could stroke his back. "Look, I brought you macaroni."

He smiled a little. I handed him the bowl, and he started scooping the yellow tubes into his mouth. "I won't go work at the Pool if you don't want me to."

"The truth is, I can't stop you, Leo," I said, somewhat ignoring Nana's advice. "But once the clinic reopens, I think you should work there again. They need you. And—"

He hugged me while holding the bowl, and a few macaroni tubes fell to the floor.

"And if anyone at the Pool makes you uncomfortable, you should quit."

"I promise," he said. He set the bowl on the floor, picked me up, and spun me around the way our father used to.

"Leo! Put me down!" I was laughing so he spun me around a couple more times.

"Let's go out tonight! You and me and Natty," he said. "You don't have school tomorrow, and I've got vouchers so we can get ice cream."

I told him that I wished I could but that I was supposed to go out with Scarlet.

"I love Scarlet," Leo said. "She can come, too."

"It's not that kind of thing, Leo. We're going to Little Egypt."

"I like Little Egypt," Leo insisted.

"No, you don't. The one time you went, you said how noisy it was. You got a migraine and had to leave after five minutes." This was the truth—the head trauma had left Leo quite sensitive to noise.

"That was a long time ago," Leo insisted. "I'm better now."

I shook my head. "Sorry, Leo. Not tonight. Just Scarlet and me."

"You never want me to go anywhere with you anymore!

I . . ." Jesus, Leo was on the verge of tears again. He turned to look out the window. "You're ashamed of me."

"No, Leo. It's not that." I put my hand on his shoulder, but he shrugged it off. Maybe he was right. Maybe it was a little bit that. But only a very little bit. Mainly, I just didn't think I could manage babysitting my brother in a crowded nightclub and hooking up Scarlet and Win at the same time. "Scarlet's got this guy she likes, and you shouldn't be mad at me because I barely even want to go to that stupid place myself," I explained.

Leo was silent.

"You're killing me here. Trust me, I'd much rather be spending the night with you and Natty." This much was true. "Can't I please have a rain check?"

He turned his head and gazed at me with eyes as dull as his stuffed lion's plastic ones. "Sure, Annie," he said. "Another time."

I V. i go to little egypt

As I STOOD IN FRONT of the mirror readying myself for the evening, my thoughts kept returning to Leo and how I might have handled things better. I picked up my tweezers and plucked a stray hair from my eyebrow.

The doorbell rang. Natty called, "I'll get it!"

"Thanks! It's only Scarlet!" Scarlet and I had agreed that she would arrive a half hour before Win so that we could, I don't know, strategize or something. "Tell her to come in the bathroom. I'm just plucking my brows."

"Don't overpluck, Annie!" Natty scolded. "You always overpluck."

I heard her run down the hallway to the door. "Annie says to go in the bathroom," Natty said as she opened the front door. "Oh, you're not Scarlet."

A male voice laughed. "Should I go in the bathroom anyway?" Win asked. "Seeing as she's only plucking her eyebrows."

I tightened my bathrobe around my waist and went out to our foyer, where Natty the flirt had already appropriated Win's hat. "You're early," I accused him.

"Great building," he said casually, as if he hadn't even noticed that I was annoyed. "The marble staircase in the lobby. The gargoyles out front. A bit spooky, but it's got a ton of character."

"Right," I said. "So, you were supposed to be here at eight o'clock."

"I must have gotten the time wrong. A million apologies." He bowed a tiny amount.

I don't like when plans change. "Well, I'm not ready yet, so what am I supposed to do with you now?"

"I'll take care of him," Natty volunteered. I looked over at my sister. Win's hat was kind of cute on her. It was a darker, sturdier fabric than the one he wore at school. Other than that, he was still wearing what he'd worn earlier in the day—that is to say, his school uniform—though he'd rolled up the sleeves of his dress shirt.

"Different hat," I observed.

"Yes, Anya. That would be my evening hat." He said this in a sort of self-deprecating way, but he leaned a bit toward me when he said it. His scent was woodsy and clean.

"All right, Natty," I said. "You may as well offer the early bird a drink." I turned to go back to my bedroom.

"Your eyebrows look great, by the way," he called. "At their current level, I mean."

The doorbell rang. Scarlet.

"Seems everyone's early tonight," Win commented.

"No," Natty volunteered. "Scarlet was supposed to get here early."

"Really?" Win asked. "Now, this is interesting."

I ignored him and turned to answer the door.

Scarlet kissed me lightly on the cheek so as not to leave a lipstick trace. Her outfit was classic Scarlet: a black lace corset and men's wool pants and a ton of her signature red lipstick. She had also somehow managed to procure a single white lily for her blond hair.

"That flower smells amazing," I told her, and then I whispered, "He's already here. He got the time wrong or something."

"Oh, that is so incredibly annoying," Scarlet said. She stowed her overnight bag in the foyer closet, then put on a smile and went into the living room. "Hi, Win! Love the hat, Natty."

I went to my bedroom to find something to wear other than my old bathrobe. Nana once told me that, in her day, the way we dressed was called vintage. New clothing production had all but ceased a decade ago, and a sartorial concoction like Scarlet's required a lot of effort and planning. Unlike my best friend, I hadn't put any thought into my outfit for that evening. I threw on an old dress of my mother's—red jersey, short and swingy but with a modest neckline. It had a hole in the armpit but I wasn't planning on doing a lot of hand-raising anyway. On my way back to the living room, I knocked on Leo's door to say good night and to make sure there weren't any hard feelings between us. He didn't answer so I pushed it open slightly. The lights were out, and he was buried under the covers. I gently closed the door behind me and went to join my friends.

"Oh," Natty said when she saw me, "you look pretty!"

Scarlet whistled at me, and Win saluted.

"Knock it off. You guys are embarrassing me," I said, though, if I'm totally honest, I did enjoy their compliments. "We may as well go to Little Egypt now."

Win removed his hat from my sister's head and we were on our way.

It was only a five-minute walk to the club but it took twice as long because of Scarlet's shoes, which were stilettos and not necessarily the greatest for walking. By the time we got to Little Egypt, the line to get in extended past the long flight of marble steps that led into the building. Little Egypt was pretty much the only thing going in this part of town.

Scarlet flagged down the bouncer. "Can my friends and I please go in? Pretty please."

"What'll you give me if I let you, blondie?" the bouncer wanted to know.

"My undying gratitude," Scarlet replied.

"Back of the line," he said. We had just started walking down the stairs when the bouncer called, "Hey, you! Red dress." I turned. "Annie, right?"

I made a face. "Who wants to know?"

"Nah, it's not like that. I used to work for your pops. Good man." He unhooked the velvet rope, waved the three of us inside, then reached into his pocket and thrust a bunch of drink tickets at me. "Toast to the old man, okay?"

I nodded. "Thanks." This sort of thing happened pretty

often, but it was still nice. Daddy had had a lot of enemies but even more friends.

"Be careful in there," the bouncer warned. "It's crazy tonight."

The bar was below a sign that said INFORMATION. Another sign, bolted to the front of the counter, listed admission prices from back when Little Egypt used to be a museum. We traded in our tickets for beers. There was only one kind and it wasn't particularly savory: a fizzy, amber pond scum. Why would someone ruin perfectly good water for this? "Bottoms up," Scarlet said.

"What's that phrase mean exactly?" Win asked.

Scarlet shook her head. "You ask a lot of questions," she said. She took his hat off his head and placed it on her own. I felt sad for Scarlet because she was using the same move my little sister had.

I took a sip of my beer and in my head, I toasted Daddy. Nana said that kids used to get in trouble for drinking when she was young and teen drinking had been illegal. Now you could get alcohol at any age as long as the person supplying it had the right permits—it was no harder to come by than ice cream and significantly less hard than getting, say, a ream of paper. It seemed incredibly strange to imagine that people had ever cared so much about alcohol. Maybe the illegality had been the enticement, I don't know. I'd rather have water any day. Alcohol made me fuzzy when my lifestyle required me to be sharp.

We left the bar and headed to the dance floor. The music was appropriately deafening and someone had brought in strobe lights, but you could still feel that the original intent of this place hadn't been nightclub. Even packed with a thousand people, all the stone made it incongruously cool inside. There were marble pedestals everywhere and girls in underwear-like clothing were dancing atop them. If you walked a bit farther, you came upon a shallow, intricately tiled pool that was roughly the size of a ballroom, and a mosaic fountain under a mural depicting a bucolic villa by the water. Both the pool and the fountain were, of course, completely drained and badly in need of a renovation that I knew would not be forthcoming. For a second, I closed my eyes and tried to imagine what it must have looked like when it was a museum. At some point, I became aware of Win standing next to me. His gaze was fixed on the mural and I wondered if we were thinking the same thing.

"Stop daydreaming, you two," Scarlet yelled. "There's dancing to be done!" She grabbed my hand, then Win's, and pulled us into the middle of the dance floor.

Scarlet danced next to me for a while and then she danced over to Win. I sort of danced by myself (making sure to keep my arms down so as not to reveal the hole in my dress or inadvertently make it larger) and observed Scarlet and Win. Scarlet was quite a good dancer. Win, uh, wasn't. He hopped around like an insect or something. His moves were comical.

He hopped over to me. "Are you laughing at me?" he said, leaning down to my ear. The music was so loud he needed to do this in order to be heard.

"No, I swear." I paused. "I'm laughing with you."

"But I'm not laughing," he said, and then he was laughing. "Notice you don't move your arms much yourself."

"You found me out," I said. I held up my arm. As I did this, I became aware of a person across the dance floor, a person who shouldn't have been there at all. Leo.

"Jesus Christ," I muttered. I turned to Scarlet. "Leo's here. I have to go deal with him. You'll be okay?"

She squeezed my hand. "Go," she said.

As I pushed my way through the undulating bodies, I told myself to calm down, act casual, and try not to make a scene.

When I finally got to Leo, he was surrounded by a group of sleazy girls, all older than me. I wasn't shocked. Leo was good-looking and on the rare occasions he went out, usually had a full wallet—he couldn't help but attract this sort of thing. If he couldn't always keep up his end of the conversation, well, I guess a certain kind of girl wouldn't notice that or even care if she did.

I wedged my way between Leo and one of the skanks. "Hey!" she yelled. "Wait your turn."

"He's my brother!" I yelled back.

"Hi, Annie," Leo said, as if it were the most natural thing in the world that we should run into each other.

"Hi, yourself," I said. "Thought you were staying in tonight."

"I was," he admitted. "But right after you left, Jacks stopped by and said we should go out."

"Jacks is here?" I asked, thinking it might be a good time to have a word with my increasingly present, increasingly annoying cousin.

"Yeah." Leo pointed to the edge of the pool, where Jacks was sitting with an oddly tanned redhead who seemed to be laughing at everything he said. Cousin Jacks always had a pretty girl by his side, and in general, women seemed to find him attractive, though I personally didn't get his appeal. He was short and very slim. His legs were too long for his torso. Before Jacks's mother became a prostitute, back when dancing was something people could do for a living, she had been a professional ballerina, and I suppose Jacks took after her. Jacks's eyes were green like mine, except his were always darting around the room to see if there was someone better he could be talking to. He had letters tattooed on his knuckles that read VORY V ZAKONE, which I knew translated to "thieves in law."

I looked at my brother. He was sweating a bit, and I wondered if his head was hurting him as it sometimes did in noisy places, or if I was being overly protective and he was just hot from dancing. "Leo, are you feeling okay?" I asked.

"I'm fine," he said.

"Don't worry, baby sister," one of the sleazy girls said to me. "We'll take care of your brother." She laughed and took Leo by the hand.

I ignored her and said to Leo, "I'm going to talk to Jacks and then I'm going home. Walk me back, okay?"

Leo nodded.

"I'll come find you when I'm done with Jacks," I told him.

On the steps of the pool, Jacks was busy groping the redheaded girl. She didn't seem to mind.

"Why, if it isn't Little Orphan Annie Balanchine all grown up!" Jacks greeted me. He slapped the redhead's thigh, then waved her away with a flick of his wrist. She didn't even have the dignity to look offended. Jacks stood up and kissed me on the cheek. I kissed him on his cheek but I didn't let my lips make contact with his flesh. "It's good to see you, Annie."

"Yes," I said.

"How long has it been?"

I shrugged, but I knew exactly how long it had been. "So, I suppose I should be thanking you for helping with Leo's work situation," I said.

Jacks waved his hand. "Leo's a good kid, and you know I'd do anything for your daddy. Don't mention it."

I looked Jacks in the eyes. "I have to mention it, cousin, because it wouldn't be right to accept such a favor without knowing what the giver expects in return."

Jacks laughed and took a swig from a silver flask that he kept in his pants pocket. He offered some to me, but I declined. "You're paranoid, kid. Not sure I blame you considering what your upbringing's been like."

"Daddy told me that he didn't want Leo working in the family business in any capacity," I said. (Maybe those hadn't been Daddy's exact words but I felt confident that was what he would have wanted.)

Jacks took a moment to consider this information. "Big Leo's been gone a long time, Annie. Maybe he didn't know what your brother's abilities were when he made such a pronouncement."

"Abilities?" I repeated. "What do you know of Leo's abilities?"

"Maybe you're too close to see it, but your brother's not the same kid who got hurt all those years ago. You got him cooped up half the day with the old lady and the other half the day at that dumb animal job." He pointed to Leo, who was dancing with the same sleazy girls. "He's thriving here. Someone needs to air the kid out once in a while."

Maybe he was right, but it still didn't explain what Jacks gained by helping Leo. I decided to put it to him point-blank. "So, what's in it for you?"

"Like I said, I'd do anything for your old man."

"Daddy's dead," I reminded him. "Helping Leonyd's son's not gonna buy you any favors."

"Real cynic, you. Actually, Annie, helping your brother does buy me something. It makes me look better to the other men in the family. Maybe the connection to your father puts a little residual shine on me, too. God knows I could use that."

He was finally making sense. "All right."

"There's a good little girl," Jacks said, looking me up and down. "You ain't so little anymore, cousin."

"Thanks for noticing." I turned to find my brother. At that moment, an alarm wailed. Lights began to flash, and an official-sounding voice blared through a bullhorn: "Everyone out! This establishment is being shut down by order of the New York Police Department and the New York City Department of Health. Patrons must evacuate now! Stragglers will be arrested!"

"Someone must not have paid off the right person," Jacks said to me. "Wasn't like this when Big Leo ran New York."

I went to find (Little) Leo but I couldn't find him anywhere and the momentum of the crowd began pushing me toward the exit. It was move or be trampled. I lost Jacks, which was fine with me, and I didn't see Scarlet or Win either.

Finally, I was outside on the steps where I could breathe again. I took a second to clear my head before looking for Leo.

Someone tapped me on the shoulder. It was one of the slutty girls Leo had been dancing with. Outdoors in the night, she looked more innocent though. "You're the sister, right?" she asked.

I nodded.

"Something's wrong with your brother."

V. i regret having gone to little egypt

SHE LED ME ACROSS THE steps to the south side of the building, not far from where Natty had been held up a scant four days prior. My brother was writhing on the ground like an insect under a magnifying glass on a sunny day.

"What's wrong with him?" the slutty girl asked. Her voice sounded a bit repulsed, and the only thing that stopped me from shoving her was that she had, at least, been decent enough to come and find me.

"It's just a seizure," I said. I was about to yell at someone to please protect his head from hitting the unforgiving marble stairs when I noticed someone already was.

Win held Leo's head in his lap. "I know it's not ideal," Win said when he saw me. "But we couldn't get him to a softer surface, and I didn't want him to bang his head."

"Thank you," I said.

"Scarlet spotted him," Win told me. "She's looking for you right now."

I thanked him again.

I took my brother's hand and squeezed it. "I'm here," I said. I looked into his eyes. The convulsions had stopped, which meant it was over. He'd had seizures on and off since the accident though it had been a fairly long time since his last one. I was guessing the blinking lights or the loud music had set it off this time. "You're fine."

Leo nodded but he didn't look convinced.

"Can you walk?" Win asked him.

"Yes," Leo replied. "I think so."

Win introduced himself as he helped Leo to his feet. "I'm Win. I go to school with Anya."

"Leo."

Scarlet rejoined us. "Oh God, Annie, I was looking every-where for you! I'm so glad you found us!" Scarlet threw her arms around Leo. "I was so worried about you," she said to my brother. There were tears in her eyes.

"Don't worry. I'm fine," Leo said to Scarlet. I could tell Leo was embarrassed that Scarlet had seen him that way. "It's nothing."

"Well, it sure didn't look like nothing," Scarlet said. "Poor Leo."

"We should get moving," Win said.

He was right. There were cops everywhere and curfew was approaching. Best to be on our way.

Leo's gait was a bit wobbly so Scarlet stood on one side of

him, clutching his arm, and Win on the other. I walked behind them. The slutty girl was nowhere to be found. Same with Jacks.

Our little caravan was slow and unsteady, and the trip back to the apartment took considerably longer than the trip there. By the time we got back, it was past city curfew, so Win had to call his parents to let them know he was spending the night at my place.

Scarlet went to the bathroom to deal with a few fairly intense blisters from her shoes, and I went to put Leo to bed. I helped him change out of his clothes, which were soiled from the seizure, and into his pajamas.

"Good night," I said, kissing my brother on the forehead. "I love you, Leo."

"You don't think Scarlet saw?" Leo asked as I turned off the light.

"Saw what?" I asked.

"That I . . . peed."

"No. I doubt she noticed. And it wasn't your fault. And even if she did, she loves you, Leo."

Leo nodded. "I'm sorry if I ruined your night, Annie."

"Please," I said. "My night was awful before you even entered the picture. You made things more interesting."

I popped my head into Natty's room. Even though she was twelve, she still looked like a baby when she slept.

I went into the bathroom, where Scarlet was applying a bandage to one of her blisters. "Before you even say anything,

Miss Balanchine, it was totally worth it," Scarlet said. "I looked completely amazing."

"You did," I agreed. "Why don't you bring some blankets out to Win in the living room?" I suggested.

Scarlet smiled. "That boy," she said in a strange, vaguely Spanish accent. "He is not for me."

"But you do both like hats," I said.

"I know." She sighed. "And he is adorable. But, alas, no"— she returned to her weird accent—"how you say? No chemistry, senorita."

"I'm sorry," I said.

She switched to French. *"C'est la vie. C'est l'amour."* She removed her makeup with a cloth. "You should bring out the blankets, Anya."

"What are you saying?" I asked.

"I'm saying that I won't mind if you bring the blankets to Win."

"I'm not into him," I protested, "if that's what 'bring the blankets' means."

Scarlet kissed me on the cheek. "Well, I don't know where you keep the bedclothes anyway."

I went to the hallway and took an extra set of linens out of the closet for Win.

In the living room, he had taken off his dress shirt but was still wearing his pants and a plain white undershirt.

"Thank you again," I said to him.

"Is your brother okay?" Win asked.

I nodded. "Embarrassed mainly." I set the linens on the couch. "These are for you. Bathroom's in the hallway. Second

80

door after my room and before Natty's and Leo's but if you hit my dying grandmother's room, you'll definitely know you've gone too far. Kitchen's right over there but it's basically empty. You're here on a Friday, and I can only bring myself to haggle for rationed products on the weekend. Well, good night."

He sat down on the couch and his face was illuminated by the table lamp. I could see he had a red mark on his cheek that would likely be black-and-blue by the next day. "Oh no! Did Leo do that?"

He touched his cheek. "He elbowed me, I think, while he was having his—it's a grand mal seizure, right?"

I nodded.

"My sister used to have seizures, too," he said. "So, right. The elbow. It didn't hurt very much when Leo did it, so I was hoping there wouldn't be a mark."

"I should get you ice."

"It's fine."

"No, the mark'll be less," I insisted. "Wait here."

I went into the kitchen and took a bag of frozen peas out of the freezer, which I brought to him in the living room. He thanked me and pressed the bag against his cheek. "Stay a minute. I can't go to sleep while I'm holding these peas to my face."

I sat down in the overstuffed crimson velvet chair that was next to the sofa. I wrapped my arms around a turquoise chinoiserie pillow—my shield, I suppose. "Bet you're sorry you ever came out with us," I said.

He shook his head. "Not exactly." He paused to rearrange the peas a bit. "Seems to me there's always something interesting happening whenever you're around."

"Yeah. I'm trouble."

"I don't believe that. You're just a girl with a heck of a lot on her plate."

The way he said it was so sweet, I almost believed him. I certainly wanted to believe him. "Before. You mentioned your sister used to have seizures. Did she ever stop having them?"

"Yes." He paused. "She died."

"I'm sorry."

He waved his hand. "Long time ago. I'm sure you've got a whole novel's worth of sad stories, too."

Of course, nobody was much interested in novels back then. I stood up and set the pillow back on the chair. "Good night, Win."

"Night, Anya."

Around 5:00 a.m., I woke to the sound of screams. I never allowed myself to sleep very deeply, so it only took me a second to figure out that the screams were down the hall and coming from my sister.

When I turned on the light, Scarlet was sitting upright in her sleeping bag. Her eyes were drowsy and terrified.

"It's just Natty. She's probably having another one of her nightmares," I told Scarlet as I got out of bed.

"Poor Natty. Do you want me to come with you?"

I shook my head. I was used to handling Natty's bad dreams. Natty had been having them since Daddy's death nearly seven years ago.

Win was in the hallway. "Can I help?"

"No," I told him. "Go back to bed." I was annoyed that he

was there at all. People knowing your private business gave them power over you.

I went into Natty's room, shutting the door on Win.

I sat down on Natty's bed. She was tangled in the sheets and sweaty. The screams were weaker now, but she still hadn't woken up. "Shhhhh," I said. "It's only a bad dream."

Natty opened her eyes and immediately started to cry. "But, Annie, it felt so real."

"Was it about Daddy?" Natty's typical nightmare centered on the night Daddy had been killed. It had happened in this same apartment, and we had both been home at the time. She had only been five years old; me, nine. Leo had been at boarding school, something for which I am very grateful. One person shouldn't have to be an eyewitness to the murder of both parents.

The killers came while Daddy was working. Not only had Natty and I been home, we'd been in the room with him. No one saw us because we'd been playing at Daddy's feet, concealed by the frame of his massive mahogany desk. He heard the intruders before he saw them. Daddy tilted his head toward us ever so slightly and put his finger to his lips. "Don't move" had been his last words, right before he was shot in the head. Even though I was still a child I knew enough to clamp my hand over Natty's mouth so that no one could hear her sobs. And though no one was there to clamp a hand over my own mouth, I didn't cry either.

They shot Daddy once in the head and three times in the chest and then they ran out of the house. From my position under the desk, I didn't see who did it, and the police still consider the crime unsolved. Not that they investigated it very much. I mean, Daddy had been a notorious crime boss—from their point of view, his murder was only a matter of time, an occupational hazard, et cetera. On some level, maybe they even thought the murderers had done them a favor.

"Was it about Daddy?" I repeated.

She looked at me with haunted eyes. "No, it was about you."

I laughed. "You might as well tell me about it. You'll feel better saying it out loud and then I'll be able to tell you how silly you're being."

"It was like the night Daddy was killed," she said. "I was under the desk when I heard the intruders come in. But then I noticed that you weren't with me. And I started looking every-where for you—"

I interrupted her. "That's easy. It's a metaphor. You're scared of being alone. You're probably having anxiety about me going to college. But I already told you, there's no way I'll leave New York, so you shouldn't worry about that."

"No! You didn't listen to the rest. Just as the intruders come in, I look up and you're seated in Daddy's chair. You're Daddy! And then I watch as they shoot you in the head." She began to cry again. "It was so awful, Annie. I saw you die. I saw you die."

"That's never going to happen, Natty," I said. "Not that way, at least. What did Daddy always tell us?"

"Daddy said a lot of stuff." Natty sniffled.

I rolled my eyes. "What did Daddy always tell us about why we would be safe?"

"He said that no one touches the families."

"That's right," I told her.

"But what about what happened to Mom and Leo?" Natty asked.

"That was a mistake. The hit was meant for Daddy. Mom and Leo were just in the way. Besides, all the people who planned it are gone."

"But—"

"Natty, it would never happen like that today. No one is trying to kill any of us because none of us is actively involved in the family business anymore. There's no reason to bother with us. You're being ridiculous!"

Natty thought about what I'd said. Her brow furrowed and she pulled her lip up to her nose. "Yes, I guess you're right. I feel sort of silly now."

Natty lay down in bed and I pulled the sheet up to her chin.

"Did you have a good time with Win?" Natty asked.

"I'll tell you about it tomorrow." I lowered my voice. "He's still here."

"Annie!" Her eyes grew wide and delighted.

"It's a long story and probably a lot less exciting than the one I suspect you're concocting, Natty. He's only using our couch."

I was just about to turn off the light and leave when Natty called to me. "I hope Win didn't hear me screaming," she said. "He'll think I'm such a baby."

I promised her I'd explain without telling him too much of our business, and Natty smiled. "Incidentally, you're not a baby because you have nightmares, Natty. Something terrible happened to you when you were little, and that's why you have them. It isn't your fault."

"You never have them," she pointed out.

"No, I go around pouring spaghetti sauce over boys' heads," I said.

Natty laughed. "Good night, brave Anya."

"Sweet dreams, Natty." I blew her a kiss, then closed her door.

I went into the kitchen and poured myself a glass of water. When I was in kindergarten, the teachers had taught us this incredibly lame water-conservation song called "Think Before You Drink," and I guess it stuck with me because to this day, I couldn't run a tap without mentally calculating the cost of eight ounces. Lately, I'd been thinking of that song a lot because, as the person who was responsible for our housekeeping budget, I'd noticed that the per-milliliter rate had begun to creep up with each monthly bill. Daddy had left us with plenty of money, but I still tried to keep track of such things.

I finished the first glass then had another. Thank God water wasn't a rationed commodity. I was desperately thirsty and, although I'd tried to play it off as nothing, Natty's dream had left me uneasy.

There were two things I didn't tell Natty.

First, I would kill anyone who tried to hurt her or Leo.

And second, I wasn't brave. I had bad dreams, too. More nights with than without. Unlike Natty, I had mastered the art of screaming inside my head.

Out in the living room, I could hear Win stirring. "Sorry we're all so noisy," I called.

Win came into the kitchen. "Not a problem," he said. "Curfew lifts at six so I can start heading home soon anyhow."

In the predawn light, I could see that his cheek was pretty swollen from where Leo had elbowed him. "Your poor face!" I exclaimed.

He looked at his reflection in our chrome toaster. "My dad's gonna think I was fighting." He smiled.

"Will he be mad?"

"He'll probably find the whole thing character-building or some such," he replied. "He thinks I'm too soft."

"Are you?" I asked.

"Well, I'm not my father, that's for sure." He paused, then continued. "Wouldn't want to be."

The oven clock turned to 6:00. "I'll walk you out," I said.

At the door, there was an awkwardness between us and I didn't quite know how to say goodbye. He had seen too much and knew too much about me. There were kids I'd gone to school with for years who knew less about my personal life. I'd dated Gable for close to nine months, and he hadn't known a thing about Leo's seizures or Natty's nightmares. He wouldn't have wanted to know either—in a way, disinterestedness was one of Gable's best qualities.

"What is it?" Win asked.

I decided to tell the truth. "You know too much about me."

"Hmm," he said. "The smart thing to do would probably be to have me killed."

I laughed. You might think that sort of kidding would offend me, but from Win, it didn't. In a way, it was worse when my background went unacknowledged. "No," I told him, "my dad would have considered that move to be premature. He would have told me to wait and see if you're trustworthy first."

"Or I could tell you all my secrets," Win said. "You wouldn't have to worry about me talking because you'd have enough information to ensure my silence. We'd be in it together."

I shook my head. "It's an interesting theory but I think I'll go with the wait-and-see approach."

"Not very bold," he said.

I told him that I wasn't very bold. That, appearances to the contrary, I was deeply old-fashioned.

"Yes," he said, "I can see that about you. Shame, because I don't think I would have minded you being the keeper of my secrets. I don't have that many friends in this town yet."

Standing in that hallway, I could definitely see how it might be nice to kiss him. How I could gently plant one on his bruised cheek and then work my way to his mouth. But this wasn't in the cards. So, I cleared my throat and apologized again for the insanity of the previous night.

"Anytime," he said as he turned to walk down the hall.

I don't know why, but I watched him walk away. Maybe I wanted a last look at what I was missing? As he got in the elevator, I called out, "Good night, Win!"

"Actually, it's morning!" he said as the elevator doors closed.

Scarlet left after lunch. "Thanks for going along with my doomed plan to seduce Win," she said as I waited with her for the elevator. "You're a really good friend, you know." She cleared her throat and then she spoke quickly. "It's okay with me if you go for him. He obviously likes you."

"Maybe," I said. "I'm not exactly looking for a boyfriend right now."

"Well, when you are, I wanted you to know that I'm not some stupid girl. Our friendship's not gonna be destroyed if you end up going for Win. I know how hard you have it, Annie—"

"Please, you don't have to say any of this, Scar!"

"I do. You need to know how important you are to me. And that I'd never get in your way over a boy that didn't like me back anyway. You deserve a really nice boyfriend—not necessarily Win, but definitely not someone like Gable Arsley either."

"Scarlet! You're being absurd."

"I deserve a nice boyfriend, too," Scarlet said just before the elevator swallowed her up.

The rest of Saturday was quiet, and I was finally able to make a dent in some of my schoolwork, which included reading a massively long article on teeth. The one thing I learned was that Win was probably right about the wear to the enamel. Our subject had been sick, and based on the amount of damage, she'd probably been sick for a very long time. I thought about calling him to say he was right about the teeth, but then I changed my mind. The information would keep until Monday, and I didn't want to give him the wrong idea.

VI. i entertain two unwelcome guests; am mistaken for someone else

On SUNDAY, WE HAD TWO visitors, and I could have gladly done without either of them.

The first was Jacks. He showed up after I'd gotten home from church, and he didn't call ahead.

I opened the door. "What do you want?"

"Is that any way to greet family?" Jacks was carrying a one-cubic-foot wooden crate. "And here I am making a special trip just for Galina. She said she was running low on Balanchine Special Dark."

"You know you're not supposed to carry that stuff out in the open," I admonished him. I took the box, then basically chucked it into the foyer.

"Worried I'll get arrested?"

"It's sloppy," I told him.

Jacks shrugged.

"Well, I'll give the chocolate to my grandmother," I said in a tone meant to indicate that he should feel free to leave.

"Aren't you going to invite me in?"

"No," I said. "Leo's resting as is Nana. There's no one here who wants to see you, Jacks."

"Why so angry, cuz? I thought you and I were finally making some progress back at Little Egypt."

I narrowed my eyes. "We were. Then you pulled your disappearing act."

Jacks asked me what I was talking about.

"I mean, you basically abandoned Leo!"

"Abandoned him? Stop being such a schoolgirl!" Jacks shrugged, which seemed to be his favorite gesture. "They were shutting down the club. Everyone had to get out. I assume Leo made it home fine, right?"

I realized then that Jacks didn't know anything about Leo's seizure and I debated whether to tell him: Would it convince Jacks to leave my brother alone, or would it reveal weaknesses to a person I didn't particularly think I could trust? I decided to keep my mouth shut. "Yeah, he made it home. No thanks to you. Personally, I like to make sure I leave with everyone I came with."

He shook his head. "You're way too protective." He paused to look me in the eyes. "But I get it. Life's made you the way you are, am I right, cuz? You and me are both creatures of circumstance."

"Thanks for bringing the chocolate by," I said.

"Fresh off the boat. Tell Leo that they'll be needing him down at the Pool on Wednesday," Jacks said.

"Could you make it next week instead? Leo caught some sort of cold. Wouldn't want to pass it to everyone in the *bratva*." I tried to pass this last part off as a joke. This was a mistake, by the way. I never joked with Jacks so, of course, my joking had aroused his suspicions. Daddy always said a person had to present a consistent character in business and that any changes in tone or manner should be carefully considered. "Be intentional," he would say. "Lapses won't go unnoticed by your friends and especially not by your enemies." The funny thing was, I hadn't understood half of what Daddy meant at the time he was saying this stuff to me. I'd just nod or say, "Yes, Daddy." But now that I was older, his words came back to me all the time, much more often and easily than Daddy's face did.

Jacks looked at me curiously. "Sure, Annie. Tell Leo next Monday's fine."

The second visitor showed up at eleven o'clock at night, far too late for a Sunday. He didn't call either.

I saw Gable through the peephole and after everything that had happened only one week earlier, I decided against opening the door. "Go away," I hissed.

"Come on, Annie," Gable said. "Let me in."

I made sure the chain was on the door before cracking it open. "No. I honestly don't think that's a good idea," I said. "You need to start heading home if you're going to make curfew anyway."

"Look, just let me in. I feel dumb standing in the hallway," Gable said, leaning his face into the crack of the door. We were so close, I could smell the coffee on his breath. "Don't worry," he continued. "There's no hard feelings from my side about what happened. You were upset I broke up with you. I can totally understand that."

"That's not what happened!" It was like he didn't even realize he was lying.

"The specifics are beside the point, Annie. I just stopped by to tell you that I want to stay friends. I still want you in my life."

"Fine!" I said. "Now go home!" How had I tolerated this loser for so long?

"How about a bar of chocolate for the road?" Gable asked.

I shook my head. So that's what "staying friends" really meant, I guess.

"Come on, Annie. I'll pay you."

"I'm not your dealer, Arsley." Out of the corner of my eye, I saw the fresh crate Jacks had brought over. I tore open the lid and pulled out two bars. I slipped the bars through the space between the door and the frame. "Enjoy," I said as I closed the door.

I could hear him tearing open the wrapper before he even got into the elevator. He was such a pig. Not for the first time, I considered the notion that a significant part of Gable's attraction to me had been based on my access to chocolate.

I picked up the case and carried it to the safe in Nana's room. I had just unpacked the last bar when I heard Nana call my mother's name. "Christina!"

I didn't answer. I assumed Nana was having a nightmare.

"Christina, come here!" she said.

"It's not Christina, Nana. It's Annie, your granddaughter." Mistaking me for my mother was getting to be a more and more frequent occurrence for Nana. I walked over to her bed and

Nana took my hand. Her grip was unusually strong. With my other hand, I flipped on the light. "See, Nana, it's me."

"Yes," Nana said. "I can see that it's not Christina now." She laughed. "I'm glad you're not Christina O'Hara. I never liked that slut mick, you know. Told Leo not to marry her, that she was trouble. She was a cop. The whole thing made him look weak. Stupid, love-struck little boy. Such a disappointment he turned out to be."

Yes, I had heard all this before. I reminded myself it was the combined effect of drugs and illness, not my grandmother.

"I hope you never have to face a disappointment like that, girl," she continued. "It's . . . It's . . ." A tear fell onto her cheek.

"Oh no, Nana, please don't cry." I could see Imogen's novel on the windowsill. "Would you like me to read to you?"

"No!" she yelled. "I can read myself! Stupid whore, what makes you think I can't read myself?" She tore her hand away from mine and though I don't think it was intentional, she ended up slapping my cheek with the back of her hand. For a moment, I couldn't move. It's not that the pain was much of anything, but still . . . She had never struck me before. No one in my family had. I had been in fights at school, but this was so much worse.

"Get out of my room! Do you hear me? I don't want you in my room! Leave now! *Leave!*"

So I turned off the light and I left. "Good night, Nana," I whispered. "I love you."

VII. i am accused; make matters worse

By MONDAY MORNING, I was definitely ready to go back to Holy Trinity. Compared to my home life, school was a vacation.

Scarlet had saved a place for me at lunch. Win was there, too—I guess we were the only people he knew. "Bet you're glad to be out of that hairnet!" Scarlet called.

"Nah," I said. "I was kind of getting used to it. Lunch duty, too. I was thinking I should go find Arsley and pour another bowl of . . . What's on the menu today anyway?" I looked at Win's lunch tray. Lunch was a whitish blob with a chunky brownish sauce and a side of purplish blob.

"Thanksgiving in September," Win reported. "Not particularly good for pouring over boyfriends' heads." He took a forkful of whitish blob. "Too starchy. It'd stick to the tray and then he'd be able to dodge."

"Yeah, you're probably right. I should shoot some over, slingshot-style, instead." I looked across the cafeteria to where

Gable usually sat. He wasn't there. "Oh, well. Arsley isn't here anyway."

"He wasn't in homeroom either," Scarlet reported. "Maybe he's sick?"

"Skipping more like," I said. "I saw him last night and he was fine."

"Did you?" Scarlet asked.

"It wasn't like that. He wanted—" I stopped myself. With Win's father being the unofficial top cop, I really wasn't sure it was that great an idea to mention the family business.

"What did he want?" Scarlet asked. Win and Scarlet were both waiting for me to finish.

"Sorry," I said. "I was thinking about something that happened with Nana. To talk. All he wanted was to talk."

"Talk! That's not like Gable. What did he want to talk about?" Scarlet asked.

"*Scarlet.*" I raised an eyebrow. "About closure. And stuff. I'll tell you later. Win doesn't want to hear any of this."

Win shrugged. "I don't mind."

"Well, I don't want to talk about it," I said, standing up from the table. "Besides, I should claim my Thanksgiving blobs before they get cold."

I didn't see Scarlet (alone) again until Fencing the next morning.

"So what did you talk about with Gable?" she whispered as we were stretching.

"Nothing," I whispered back. "He wanted chocolate. I couldn't say it in front of Win."

"Gable is such a tool belt!" Scarlet yelled. "I honestly can't believe him sometimes!"

"Ms. Barber," said Mr. Jarre. "Let's keep it down during stretching, shall we?"

"Sorry, Mr. Jarre," Scarlet said. "Seriously," she whispered to me. "He is just loathsome. By the way, he wasn't in homeroom again."

"Why?" I asked.

"Beats me," she said. "Probably off drowning kittens or something." Scarlet giggled. "Why are the cute ones always such sociopaths?"

"Win doesn't seem like too much of a sociopath," I replied without thinking.

"Oh, *really*? So, you think he's cute, do you? At least you're admitting it now."

I shook my head. Scarlet was incorrigible.

"Admitting it is the first step, Annie."

I was in FS II on Wednesday morning when I heard the news that Gable Arsley was in the hospital.

Chai Pinter, who always seemed to know everyone's business, made a special trip to my lab table to tell me. "Did you hear about Gable?" she asked. I shook my head, and of course she was delighted to tell me. "Well, apparently, he fell ill on Monday morning, but his parents didn't think it was anything serious. They just told him to stay home. And then he was, like, throwing up all day Tuesday, but they still thought it was stomach flu or something. When it didn't stop by Tuesday night, they finally took him to the hospital. And he's still there! Ryan Jenkins even heard he had surgery!" Chai looked over-the-moon at the prospect of one of our peers having possibly had surgery. "But I don't know if that's true. You know how people make stuff up."

I did.

"I figured you might know more than me about Gable's condition, since you guys went out for such a long time. But I guess not," Chai said cheerfully.

Dr. Lau clapped her hands to start class, and Chai returned to her seat.

The lecture was something about the different ways illnesses can affect the manner in which a body decays, but I couldn't really pay attention. It's not that I particularly cared about Gable, but the news was still shocking. And I couldn't help but wonder whether I had been the last person to see him Sunday night. And if that were true, I couldn't help but wonder if that coincidence was going to cause problems for me down the road. Or sooner. I couldn't afford any more problems. I was probably being paranoid, but . . . Life really had taught me that smart people anticipated the worst. That way, there was time to make a plan. At some point, Win whispered, "Are you okay?"

I nodded, but I wasn't okay. I wanted to go call Mr. Kipling. Like, right then. I decided that it probably wouldn't be a good idea for me to be seen running the heck out of class to call my lawyer. So, I sat in my seat, and I folded my hands in my lap, and I looked at Dr. Lau, and I didn't hear one word she said.

Win whispered, "Can I help?"

I shook my head, annoyed. What could he do? I needed quiet and time.

98

As soon as the bell rang, I started walking straight to the phone booths that were in front of the main office. I needed to call Nana and I needed to call Mr. Kipling. I moved briskly, but I made sure not to run.

Before I got there, I felt a hand on my shoulder. It was Headmaster. "Anya," she said, "these people need to have a word with you." When I turned, I was not particularly surprised to see several police officers standing behind her. They weren't wearing uniforms—plainclothes detectives, I'd guess—but I could smell the policeness of them all the same.

"Headmaster," I said, "how long is this going to take? I have an English test. *Beowulf*." Down the hall, I could see my peers looking curiously at me. I did my best to ignore them. I needed to concentrate.

"Don't worry about any of that. I'll see to it that you're able to make it up," she said, placing a hand on my back. "Officers, let's move this discussion to a more private location."

On the brief walk to the office, I was trying to decide whether to assert my right to refuse questioning without a lawyer present. Because I really would have felt better with Mr. Kipling in the room, and yet, I knew how these things worked—requesting his presence too soon could make me seem guilty. Even though it was my right, if I asked for Mr. Kipling, they could demand to question me at the police station instead of at school. That would definitely be worse. Calm down, Anya, I told myself. Wait and see what happens first.

There were three police detectives—a woman and two men. The woman was in her thirties with short, frizzy blond hair.

(Despite my predicament, I couldn't help but think she could benefit from a few hair-product vouchers.) She introduced herself as Detective Frappe. The two men looked nearly identical (crew cuts, doughy faces), only one had on a red tie (Detective Cranford) and the other a black one (Detective Jones).

Detective Frappe seemed to be the boss, as she did most of the talking. "Anya, you'd really be helping us out today if you answered a few questions."

I nodded.

"I assume you've heard about Gable Arsley," Frappe said.

I carefully considered my reply. "People have been talking but the only thing I know for sure is that he's been absent from school," I said.

"He's in the hospital," Frappe said. "He's very sick. He might even die. That's why it's very important that you tell us everything you can."

I nodded. "Can I ask a question?"

Frappe exchanged a look with Cranford. Cranford nodded slowly, so maybe he was the boss. "I don't see why not," Frappe said.

"What's wrong with him?" I asked.

Frappe exchanged another look with Cranford. Cranford nodded again. "Gable Arsley has been poisoned."

"Oh," I said. "Poor Gable. Jesus." I shook my head. "I apologize for my language, Headmaster. It's just so shocking."

"How does that make you feel?" Frappe asked.

I thought shaking my head and taking the Lord's name in vain and saying it was shocking had pretty much expressed that, but . . . "I feel bad, of course. Until recently, he was my boy-friend."

"Yes, Headmaster told us that. That's why we specifically wanted to talk to you, Anya."

"Yes."

"He broke up with you?"

If I hadn't mentioned it before, Jones was taping the whole conversation, and I didn't want it "on the record" that Gable Arsley had broken up with me. "No," I said.

"You broke up with him?"

"You could say the decision was mutual," I said.

"Care to elaborate?"

I shook my head. "It's sort of personal."

"This is important, Anya."

"The thing is, I really don't want to say it in front of her." I looked at Headmaster. "It's, well, vulgar," I added. "And embar-rassing."

"Go on, Anya," Headmaster said. "I won't judge you."

"Fine." I could see where this was going. I figured that, not knowing enough facts about Gable's poisoning and how they did or did not implicate me, it could be worse for me to start lying or concealing things now. "Gable Arsley wanted to sleep with me, and when I told him no, he tried to anyway. The only thing that stopped him was that my brother came into the room."

Cranford leaned over to Frappe and whispered something in her ear. I thought I could see his lips form the shape of the word *motive*. The round hole of *m-o*, and his tongue darting out on *t-i* only to hastily retreat on *v-e*. *Motive*. Duh, of course I had motive.

"Would you say you were mad at Gable Arsley?" Cranford asked this one.

"Yes, but not because he tried to sleep with me. I was mad because he lied to everyone about what happened. That's why I poured the lasagna over his head. I assume you've already heard about that, but if not, I'm sure Headmaster will be more than willing to fill you in." I paused. "Let me be clear about one thing, Detectives. I did not poison Gable Arsley. And if you want to ask me anything else, you'll have to do so with my attorney present. You probably know who my father was, but my mother was a cop and I know my rights." I stood up. "Headmaster, may I have a pass to go back to class now?"

The hallway was empty but I couldn't be sure I wasn't being watched. I made like I was going to English but then I walked right past the classroom door. I went outside into the courtyard. It finally felt like fall. Normally, the change of season would have made me happy.

I crossed the courtyard and went into the church. Then I went into the secretary's office. It was empty as I knew it would be—the secretary had been fired last week. I picked up the phone, entered the code that gave you an outside line (don't even think of asking me how I knew this), and dialed home. Leo answered.

"Are you alone?" I asked him.

"Yes, my head still hurts, Annie," Leo said.

"Is Imogen there?"

"Not yet."

"Is Nana awake?"

"No. What's wrong? Your voice is weird."

"Listen, Leo, some people might show up at the house very soon. I don't want you to be scared."

Leo didn't say anything.

"Leo, I can't hear you when you nod. We're on the phone."

"I won't be scared," Leo said.

"There's something very important I need you to do," I continued. "But you can't tell anyone about it, especially the people who might show up at the house."

"Okay," Leo said, not sounding at all certain.

"Take the chocolate from Nana's closet and throw it down the incinerator."

"But, Annie!"

"This is important, Leo. We could get in trouble for having it."

"Trouble? I don't want anyone to get in trouble," he said.

"No one will. Now, don't forget to push the fire button. And don't let Nana see you do it."

"I think I can do it."

"Listen to me, Leo. I might be home late tonight. If that happens, call Mr. Kipling. He'll know what to do."

"You're scaring me, Annie."

"I'm sorry. I'll explain everything later," I said. "I love you."

I crossed my fingers that Leo would manage to get rid of the chocolate before the cops arrived.

I hung up the phone, then I dialed Mr. Kipling. "The cops came to my school today. Someone poisoned my ex-boyfriend, and they think I did it," I said as soon as he came on the line.

"Are you still at Holy Trinity?" Mr. Kipling asked after a brief pause.

"Yes."

"I'll come right down and meet you there. Hold tight, Anya. We'll get this sorted out."

At that moment, the door to the secretary's office opened. "Found her!" Detective Jones yelled. "She's on the phone!" Then he turned to me. "We're going to need to take you down to the precinct for further questioning. Your boyfriend just slipped into a coma. They think he might die."

"Ex-boyfriend," I said quietly.

"Anya?" Mr. Kipling said. "Still there?"

"Yes, Mr. Kipling," I replied. "Could you meet me at the police station instead?"

I wasn't scared of police stations. Still, I wasn't exactly thrilled to be detained in one either. Though I'd grown up in the presence of criminals, I'd certainly never been accused of a crime.

The cops led me into a room. The back wall was a mirror so I assumed people were watching me from the other side of it. There was one overhead fluorescent light, and the heat seemed to be turned on even though the weather didn't call for it. The cops sat on one side of the table; me on the other. They had a pitcher of water. No beverage for me. Their chairs were cushioned; mine, a folding metal one. It was obvious that the intent of the room was to make the accused (me) uncomfortable. Pathetic.

The detectives were the ones from school: Frappe and Jones, though Cranford was out. As usual, Frappe did most of the talking.

"Ms. Balanchine," she began, "when's the last time you saw Gable Arsley?"

"I won't answer any questions until my attorney, Mr. Kipling, arrives. He should be here—"

At that moment, Mr. Kipling came through the door of the interrogation room. He was completely bald and slightly pudgy, but he had the kindest (albeit rather bulging) blue eyes. He was sweating and scant of breath, and I had never been so happy to see anyone in my life. "Sorry, I'm late," he whispered to me. "The car was stuck in traffic, so I got out and ran." Mr. Kipling turned his attention to the two detectives. "Is it really necessary to drag a sixteen-year-old girl with no prior record into a police station? To me, this seems excessive. As does the extreme temperature of your thermostat!"

"Sir, this is an attempted murder investigation, and Ms. Balanchine's treatment has been entirely appropriate," Frappe said.

"Debatable," said Mr. Kipling. "Questioning a minor at school without either a guardian or counsel present seems a bit borderline to me. Personally, I can't help but wonder why the NYPD's insisting on calling a kid with an upset stomach an attempted murder investigation."

"That kid's in a coma. He may die, Mr. Kipling. I'd like to continue questioning Ms. Balanchine as time is of the essence here," Frappe said.

Mr. Kipling nodded.

"Ms. Balanchine, when is the last time you saw Gable Arsley?" Frappe asked.

"Sunday night," I said. "He came over to my apartment."

"Why did he come over?" Frappe asked.

"He said he felt bad about what had happened between us and that he wanted us to still be friends."

"Anything else?" she asked. "Was there any other reason he came over?"

I could see where this was going.

The chocolate.

Of course, it was the chocolate. It was always the chocolate. I had only wanted Leo to destroy it because it was illegal to have it in your possession and I hadn't wanted to cause any trouble for my family if the cops should decide to search our place. But what if the police thought I had poisoned Gable with chocolate? Then it might look like I had instructed my brother to destroy evidence. I should have thought of this before. I should have thought things through better, but there really hadn't been time. Everything had happened so quickly.

And, in my defense, Gable Arsley wasn't exactly a Boy Scout. He was a wealthy glutton and a habitual connoisseur of contraband substances. Who knew what he had gotten himself into? Plus, I had no reason to doubt the integrity of Balanchine chocolate. Though I had lived with chocolate being illegal my whole life, I had never once worried about it being poisoned. Daddy had always been so vigilant about quality control, but then, Daddy hadn't been running Balanchine Chocolate for a very long time.

"Ms. Balanchine," Frappe repeated.

The only thing to do was be honest. "Yes, there was another reason. Gable wanted to know if I had chocolate."

"Did you?"

"Yes," I said.

Frappe whispered something to Jones.

Mr. Kipling said, "Before you two go getting all excited, I'd like to remind you that the Balanchine family has ties to the chocolate import-export business. They produce a line of chocolate bars under the name Balanchine Special, which are available in Russia and Europe where chocolate is still legal. It's only natural that some of the product ends up here on occasion, so I don't find it unusual that Ms. Balanchine should be in possession of chocolate."

"It is if the person she gave it to ended up poisoned," Jones remarked.

"Oh, you talk too now?" Mr. Kipling asked. "Even if Mr. Arsley was poisoned, what proof do you have that the poison came from the chocolate? The poison could have been on or in anything."

Frappe smiled before she said, "Actually, we know with 100 percent certainty that the chocolate was the source of the poison. When Ms. Balanchine set out to poison Mr. Arsley, she gave him two bars of chocolate."

"Your girl was nothing if not thorough," Jones said.

"She gave him two bars of chocolate, but Mr. Arsley only ate one," Frappe continued. "His mother found the other bar in his room, and it was immediately sent to the lab where it was found to contain a massive amount of Fretoxin."

"You know what Fretoxin does to a person, Anya?" Jones asked. "Starts with a stomachache. You don't even feel that sick."

"Poor kid probably thought he had the flu," Frappe interjected.

"But wait, it gets better," Jones continued. "Delay getting treatment too long and ulcers start to form in the stomach and intestines. Your liver and spleen shut down, then other organs fail, too. Meanwhile, cysts have started sprouting up all over the skin. Ultimately, your body can't take it anymore. You'll either have a fatal heart attack or maybe sepsis from the many infections that are raging inside of you. It's a total system-wide shutdown, and the sad part is, you won't care. You'll be praying to God to end it."

"You'd have to really hate a person to do that, wouldn't you?" Frappe asked.

"Just the way you hated Gable Arsley," Jones finished.

"I don't know how that got in there! I would never poison Gable!" I yelled. But even as I was yelling, part of me knew it was pointless. This wasn't getting fixed today.

After they took my fingerprints and picture, I was locked in an isolated cell in the police station. This accommodation was only for the night. The next afternoon, a juvenile court judge would decide what to do with me while I awaited trial for the attempted murder of Gable Arsley and the lesser charge of possession of an illegal substance. Mr. Kipling thought they'd probably just send me back to my house with a tracker embedded in my shoulder as I didn't have any prior offenses. "Maybe you'll have to stay with me and Keisha for a bit if the judge doesn't think your grandma's up to watching you." Keisha was Mr. Kipling's wife.

"She wouldn't mind that?"

"No. She'd love it. She misses our daughter something

terrible. So, hold tight, Anya," Mr. Kipling said to me from outside my cell. "This *will* get straightened out, I promise."

I nodded, but I wasn't convinced. "You should know," I whispered, "Jacks Pirozhki was the one who gave me the tainted chocolate."

Mr. Kipling promised that he would look into it. "Let's wait to tell the police about Pirozhki until we have more information. They're obviously convinced it's you so we have to be careful. We don't want to accidentally give them more ammo."

"I also had Leo destroy the rest of the chocolate," I whispered. "It was stupid. I wasn't thinking. I was worried about them searching the house and finding the contraband."

Mr. Kipling nodded. "I know. Leo called me. The police were banging on the door just as Leo had gotten into Galina's closet. There wasn't time for him to do it."

"That's good," I said. "I'm glad I didn't inadvertently make my brother an accessory to whatever this is." My voice broke a tiny bit on the word *this*. I could feel a tightness in my throat that felt like the beginning of tears. I didn't let myself cry, though.

"Don't worry, Anya," Mr. Kipling said. "This absolutely will get straightened out. I'm sure there's a logical explanation for everything."

I looked at Mr. Kipling. His eyes were bloodshot and his face was pale, even a bit green. "Are you feeling all right?" I asked.

"Just tired. It's been a long day. Now, don't you go worrying about me. I want you to try to get a good night's sleep, or as good a night's sleep as it's possible to have in a police station."

He gestured toward the metal bed with the paper-thin mattress and the scratchy wool blanket.

"Pillow doesn't look so bad," I said. It didn't. It was surprisingly plump.

"That's my girl," Mr. Kipling said. He stuck his hand through the bars and brushed my cheek with his index finger. "I'll see you tomorrow, Annie. At the courthouse. I'm stopping by your apartment now just to make sure Leo, Natty, and Galina have everything they need."

The cops had neglected to take my platinum-gold cross necklace. I unclasped it and handed the necklace to Mr. Kipling. It had been my mother's and I didn't want to somehow end up losing it or for someone to steal it from me. "For safekeeping," I said.

"I'll bring it back to you tomorrow," he promised.

"Thank you, Mr. Kipling. For everything." And by everything, I meant not even asking if I was innocent. He assumed I was. He always thought the best of me. (Maybe that was his job, though?)

"You're very welcome, Anya," he said as he left.

And then I was alone.

It was odd to be alone. At home, there was always someone demanding my time or attention.

I might even have enjoyed the sensation had it not occurred in a jail cell.

The next morning, a police officer drove me to court. Even though I didn't know what awaited me there, I definitely remember feeling glad to be out of that cell. It was sunny, and on the

110

ride over I was optimistic about everything. Maybe Mr. Kipling was right. Maybe there was a logical explanation for everything. Maybe this would end up being little more than a vacation from school. The worst that would happen is I'd have a ton of makeup work.

When I got to the courthouse, Mr. Kipling wasn't there. I'd usually known him to be early for such matters, but I wasn't that worried.

Frappe was in the courtroom, and another woman who I assumed was the prosecutor. At 9:01, the judge came in. "Ms. Balanchine?" She looked at me, and I nodded. "Do you know where your attorney is?"

"Mr. Kipling said he'd meet me here. Maybe he was caught in traffic?" I suggested.

"Is your guardian here?" the judge asked. "I'm aware that your parents are dead. Perhaps your guardian could call your attorney?"

I told her that my guardian was my grandmother and that she was confined to bed.

"Most unfortunate," the judge said. "I suppose we could proceed without an attorney, though, as you are a minor, I'd rather not. Perhaps we should postpone?"

At that moment, a boy who didn't seem much older than me came into the courtroom. He was wearing a business suit. "I'm sorry I'm late, your honor. I'm Mr. Kipling's colleague. Mr. Kipling has had a heart attack and won't be able to come to court today. In his absence, I'll be representing Ms. Balanchine. I'm Simon Green."

As soon as he arrived at the table, he offered me his hand.

"Don't worry," he whispered. "Everything will be fine. I'm not as young as I look and I actually know more about criminal matters than Mr. Kipling does anyway."

"Will Mr. Kipling be all right?" I asked.

"They don't know anything yet," Simon Green said.

"Ms. Balanchine," the judge asked, "are you comfortable with this arrangement? Or shall I postpone?"

I considered the question. The truth was, I was not one bit comfortable with this arrangement and yet postponing seemed like an equally bad idea—I didn't relish another night in jail or somewhere worse. If the matter was postponed, they wouldn't send me to Rikers Island, but there was a good chance I'd be sent to a juvenile facility while everything was sorted out. And it would be difficult to mind Natty, Leo, and Nana from a juvenile facility. "I'm fine with Mr. Green," I said.

"Good," said the judge.

The prosecutor recited the evidence they had against me, and the judge nodded a great deal, as did Simon Green. The attorney concluded by giving her recommendations for what she thought should be done with me. "Ms. Balanchine should be sent to Liberty Children's Facility while she awaits trial."

I waited for Mr. Green to object but he said nothing.

"Detainment seems a bit excessive in a juvenile case," said the judge. "The girl hasn't been convicted of anything yet."

"Ordinarily I'd agree," said the prosecutor. "But you must consider the severity of the crime and the fact that the victim may die. Also, there's a family history of criminal behavior"—I was starting to hate this woman—"which suggests that the suspect may pose a flight risk."

I nudged Simon Green. "Aren't you going to say anything?" I whispered.

"We're listening right now," Simon Green whispered back. "I'll talk more after I've heard everything."

The prosecutor continued. "I'm sure you know that the father was notorious crime boss Leonyd Balanchine, which probably suggests that Anya Balanchine is rather well connected—"

"Excuse me, Your Honor," I said.

The judge looked at me for a moment, as if she were trying to decide whether or not to discipline me for interrupting. "Yes?" she said finally.

"I don't see what my family has to do with me. I have no prior record, and I haven't been convicted of anything yet. If I were sent to Liberty Children's Facility, this would pose an incredible hardship for me."

"Do you mean missing school?" the judge asked.

"No." I paused. "I'm sort of responsible for watching my sister. My grandmother is sick, and my older brother's health is . . ." What was the best word here? "Delicate."

"I'm sorry to hear that," said the judge.

"What Ms. Balanchine describes is exactly my point," the prosecutor interjected. "This ailing grandmother is the girl's sole guardian. If you allow Anya Balanchine back to her own home, it sounds as if she'll be entirely unsupervised."

The judge looked at me, then at Simon Green. "Can you speak to her home situation?" she asked Simon Green.

"Uh, I'm sorry . . . I only got on this case today and . . . and . . ." Simon Green stammered. "My expertise is more criminal law, not family law."

"Well, I need more time to think and to find someone who does know something about this," said the judge. "In the meantime, I'm going to send Ms. Balanchine to Liberty Children's Facility. Don't worry, Ms. Balanchine. It's just until we get everything sorted out. Let's meet back here in a week."

The judge banged the gavel, and then we had to leave the courtroom.

I sat down on a marble bench outside the courtroom and tried to come up with my next move. I heard the prosecutor say something about arranging my transport to Liberty from here.

"I'm sorry, Anya," Simon Green said to me. "I very much wish I'd had more time to prepare."

In a way, it had been my fault. If only I'd kept my mouth shut about needing to take care of Nana, Natty, and Leo! By mentioning my situation, I'd only made things worse. In my defense, it really hadn't looked like Simon Green knew what he was doing. Someone needed to say something.

"Anya," he repeated. "I'm sorry."

"There isn't time for that," I said. "I need you to do a couple of things for me. There are people I need you to call. Mr. Kipling will have the numbers. There's a woman named Imogen Goodfellow. She's my grandmother's home-health-care worker. Call her and tell her that she needs to stay at the apartment full-time. Tell her that we'll pay her time and a half for the extra hours."

Simon Green nodded.

"Do you need to note this somewhere?" I asked. I could not have had less faith in this man.

"I'm recording it," he said, removing a device from his pocket. "Please, continue."

Daddy would never have stood for recording conversations, but there wasn't time for me to worry about that. "Scarlet Barber goes to school with my sister and me. Tell her that she needs to accompany Natty to and from school."

"Yes," he said.

"Finally, I need you to call my brother, Leo. Tell him that I don't want him to take the job at the Pool because I need him to watch everyone at home. I doubt he'll put up an argument but if he does, tell him . . ." I could see the prosecutor and a social-worker type walking toward me and I lost my train of thought. There wasn't much time.

"Yes?"

"I don't know what to tell him. Come up with something that makes sense."

"Yes, I can manage that," Simon Green said.

The social worker came up to me. "I'm Mrs. Cobrawick," she said. "I'll be transporting you to Liberty."

"Ironic name for a jail," I said, making a semi-joke.

"It's not a jail. Simply a place for children in trouble. Children like yourself."

Mrs. Cobrawick was one of those overly earnest types. "Yes, of course," I said. Jail was where I'd be going later if they tried me as an adult and if I didn't manage to get acquitted of poisoning Gable Arsley. I nodded toward Simon Green. "I'll be hearing from you?"

"Yes," he assured me. "I'll come see you this weekend."

I watched as he walked away. "Mr. Green!" I called out.

He turned.

"Please give Mr. Kipling my best wishes!"

And then it happened. My voice broke on the word *wishes*, and I started to cry. Nothing else could make me do it, but somehow the thought of Mr. Kipling in the hospital made me feel lonelier than I'd ever felt in my life.

"There, there," said Mrs. Cobrawick. "It won't be so bad at Liberty."

"It isn't that—" I started to say, but then I changed my mind. At the very least, my passing display of weakness hadn't been in front of anyone I knew.

"I always find it's the hardest cases that shed the most tears," Mrs. Cobrawick commented.

Let this Mrs. Cobrawick think what she wanted. Daddy always said you only explained things to the people that actually mattered.

VIII. i am sent to liberty; am also tattooed!

MRS. COBRAWICK AND I RODE the ferry to Liberty Children's Facility. The view from the boat did not necessarily encourage me: several low-rise gray concrete structures, bunker-like with few windows, surrounded a pedestal. Atop the pedestal was an enormous greenish pair of women's feet in sandals and the bottom of her skirt, both made of what I'd guess was aging copper. I think my father had once told me some story about what had happened to the rest of the statue (maybe it had been scrapped for parts?) but at that moment, I couldn't remember it, and the torsoless woman seemed ominous to me. There was something inscribed on the base of the pedestal but the only words I could make out were *tired* and *free*. I was the former though not the latter. The whole island was surrounded by a chain-link fence, which, I could tell from the coiled structures at the top, was electrified. I told myself that I wouldn't be there long.

"Back when my mother was a girl, Liberty used to be a tourist attraction," Mrs. Cobrawick informed me. "You could climb up the woman's dress and the base was a museum."

What hadn't been? Half the places in my neighborhood used to be museums.

"What you said back at the courthouse? Liberty is not a jail," Mrs. Cobrawick continued. "And you shouldn't think of it as such. We're very proud of Liberty and we like to think of it as a home."

I knew I should probably keep my mouth shut, but I couldn't help replying. "What's the electrified fence for then?"

Mrs. Cobrawick narrowed her eyes at me, and I could tell my question had probably been a mistake. "It's to keep everyone safe," she said.

I didn't comment.

"Did you hear me?" Mrs. Cobrawick asked. "I said, the fence is there to keep everyone safe."

"Yes," I replied.

"Good," Mrs. Cobrawick said. "For the record, it's polite to show some acknowledgment when a person's answered a question you've asked."

I apologized and told her I hadn't meant to be rude. "I'm tired," I explained, "and a bit distracted by what's been happening."

Mrs. Cobrawick nodded. "I'm glad to hear that. I was worried your rudeness was a sign of poor breeding. I'm well versed in your background, Anya. Your family history. It wouldn't come as a surprise to me if you lacked certain refinements."

I could tell she was baiting me, but I wouldn't take it. The boat was docking at the island, and I'd be quit of this woman soon.

"The truth is, Anya, your stay here can be easy or it can be difficult," she said. "It's completely up to you."

I thanked her for the advice, making sure not to sound sarcastic.

"When I heard about your situation this morning, I specifically offered to transport you myself, though normally such responsibilities fall well below my purview. You could say I had an interest in you. You see, I went to college with your mother. We weren't friends per se but I often saw her on campus, and I'd hate to see you end up like her. I've found that early intervention can make a world of difference in borderline cases."

I took a deep breath and bit my tongue. I mean I literally bit it. I could taste the blood in my mouth.

The boat had stopped, and the captain called for everyone going to Liberty Children's Facility to disembark. "Well," I said, "thanks very much for taking me over."

"I'm coming in with you," she said.

I had assumed she worked at the court, not at Liberty, but, of course, this had been foolish of me. I wondered how she had known that I'd be sent to Liberty, considering how quickly the hearing had progressed. Had my fate been decided before I even arrived at court that morning?

"I'm the headmistress here," Mrs. Cobrawick told me. "Some people call me the warden behind my back," she added with a strange smile. "Though don't you go being one of them."

Once we were off the dock, my hostess led me to a concrete room marked CHILDREN'S ORIENTATION, where a skinny blond girl in a lab coat and a man in yellow coveralls were waiting for me. "Dr. Henchen," Mrs. Cobrawick said to the blond girl, "this is Anya Balanchine."

"Hello," Dr. Henchen said, looking me up and down. "Do I process her as long or short term?"

Mrs. Cobrawick considered the question. "We're not entirely sure of that yet. Let's say long term to be on the safe side."

I have no idea what short-term might have been like, but long-term orientation was one of the most humiliating experiences of my life to that point. *(NB: This is foreshadowing, dear readers—more and deeper humiliations to come . . .)* "I do apologize, Miss Balanchine," Dr. Henchen had said in a polite if curiously emotionless voice. "In the last several months, we've had a rash of bacterial outbreaks so, in order to avoid this, our intake procedure has become rather intense. Especially for long-term residents who will be exposed and expose themselves to the general population here. This won't be very pleasant for you." Still, I was unprepared for what came.

I was made to strip and then I was hosed down by the male attendant with scalding hot water. After that, I was soaked in an antibacterial bath that stung every part of me and then what I'd guess was a delousing solution was placed in my hair. The final part was a series of ten injections. Dr. Henchen said they were mainly to protect against flu and sexually transmitted diseases, and to relax me, but, at that point, my mind was elsewhere. I've always been able to do that—separate my brain from the awful thing happening at the moment.

Whatever they gave me must have knocked me out because I woke up the next morning in the upper bunk of a metal-framed bed in an extremely stark girls' dormitory. My arm hurt where they had repeatedly injected me. My skin was raw. My stomach, empty. My brain, fuzzy. It took a moment to even remember how I'd gotten here.

The other inmates (or whatever term of art Mrs. Cobrawick had invented for us) were still asleep. There were narrow windows—not much more than slits—along the sides of the room and I could make out a bit of predawn light. Of my many concerns, the most immediate was breakfast and what it would consist of.

I sat up in bed and took a moment to establish that I was wearing clothes as, last I remembered, I had been naked. I was glad to find that I was clothed. A navy-blue cotton jumpsuit—not particularly stylish but better than the alternative. In sitting up, I became aware of an odd pain on my right ankle, almost like a fire-ant bite. I looked down and discovered that I had been tattooed. A tiny bar code that presumably linked my person to my nascent criminal record. (This was common practice. Daddy had had one, too.)

An alarm went off, and the room became chaos. A stampede of girls charged toward the door. I got out of bed and debated whether or not to follow. I noticed that the girl in the bunk below me wasn't joining the frenzy so I asked her what was happening.

The girl shook her head and said nothing. She held a notepad toward me. The notepad was suspended from a leather cord that was tied around her neck. On the first page was written *My name is Mouse. I am mute. I can hear you but I will have to write my reply.*

"Oh," I said. "Sorry." I didn't know why I was apologizing.

Mouse shrugged. The girl was certainly tiny and quiet—Mouse was a good name for her. I'd guess she was about Natty's age though her dark eyes made her look older.

"Where's everyone going?"

Shower room, she wrote. *1 x per day. H_2O on for 10 sec. Everyone at once.*

"Why aren't you going then?"

Mouse shrugged. I would later learn this was her all-purpose way of changing the subject, especially useful when a subject was too complex to be expressed concisely. She let the notepad drop and held out her hand for me to shake, which I did.

"I'm Anya," I said.

Mouse nodded and picked up her notepad. *I know*, she wrote.

"How?" I asked.

On the news. She held up her pad, then wrote some more: *"Mob Daughter Poisons Boyfriend with Chocolate."*

Wonderful. "Ex-boyfriend," I said. "What picture are they using?"

School uniform, Mouse wrote.

I'd been wearing school uniforms as long as I'd been going to school.

Recent, she added.

"By the way, I'm innocent," I said.

She rolled her dark eyes at me. *Everyone here's innocent*, she wrote.

"Are you?"

Not me. I'm guilty.

We hadn't known each other long enough for me to ask her

122

what she had done so I changed the subject to matters more pressing. "Anywhere to eat in this place?"

Breakfast was oatmeal. It was surprisingly edible or maybe I was just hungry.

The cafeteria at the girls' reformatory was pretty much like the cafeteria at my high school: i.e., a hierarchy of seating with more influential cliques/gangs occupying the "better" tables. Mouse seemed to be gangless as she and I ate alone at what must be said was the least desirable table in the place—back of the room, as far away from the windows as you could get, next to the garbage. "Do you eat here every day?" I asked.

Mouse shrugged.

Aside from being mute, she seemed normal enough. I wondered if the reason she was alone was out of choice or because the others were ostracizing her on account of her handicap or simply because she was new to Liberty like me. "How long have you been here?"

She put down her spoon to write *198 down. 802 to go.*

"One-thousand-day sentence. That's a long time," I said, though this really was an idiotic comment to have made. One look in Mouse's eyes and you could see exactly how long a thousand days was.

I was about to apologize for having said something so daft when an orange plastic cafeteria tray hit Mouse in the back of the head. A bit of oatmeal spattered onto Mouse's hair and face.

"Watch yourself, Mouse," said the girl holding the tray. The sarcastic voice belonged to a tall, rather striking (in both senses of the word) girl with long, straight, black hair. She was flanked by a corpulent blonde and a petite, but sturdy girl with a shaved

123

head. Shaved Head had a series of tattoos where her hair should have been. The tattoos consisted of words in a rather mesmerizing, swirling, paisley design.

"What are you looking at?" Shaved Head asked.

Your amazing tattoos, I wanted to say, but I decided against it.

(Aside: Seriously, though, you can't tattoo words on your scalp without having the reasonable expectation that someone might try to read them.)

"What's wrong, Little Mousey? Cat got your tongue?" asked the one holding the tray.

The blonde replied, "She can't hear you anyway, Rinko. She's, like, deaf."

"No, she can't talk. There's a difference, Clover. Don't be ignorant," said Rinko. She leaned over so that she was up against Mouse's cheek. "She hears every little thing we say. You could talk if you wanted to, couldn't you?"

Mouse, of course, said nothing.

"Aw, I was trying to see if I could fool you," Rinko continued. "There ain't a damn thing wrong with that tongue of yours. But you're just sitting back, aren't you? Judging all of us, thinking you're better when you're really the lowest of the low."

"Baby murderer," hissed the tattooed one.

Mouse didn't move.

"Aren't you gonna write me a love note?" Rinko said, pulling the pad that hung around Mouse's neck.

"Hey!" I yelled. The group looked at me for the first time. I switched to a more humorous tone and said, "How can she write you a note when you're holding her notebook?"

"Look, Mouse made a pretty new friend," Rinko said. She

studied my face. "Hey, I know you. You should come sit with us."

"I'm fine where I am, thanks," I said.

Rinko shook her head. "Listen, you don't know how it works around here yet so I'll pretend you didn't say that. Mouse ain't your friend, and you're gonna need friends around here."

"I'll take my chances," I said.

Clover, the blonde, lunged toward me. Rinko waved her hand, and Clover obeyed. "Leave her," Rinko demanded. "You and me are gonna be great friends," she said to me. "You just don't know it yet."

After Rinko and company were out of earshot, Mouse wrote me a note: *Don't be stupid. You don't owe me anything.*

"True," I said. "But I don't like bullies."

Mouse nodded.

"You know, even though you're small, you should still try to defend yourself. Those kinds of people prey on people that they perceive to be weak."

Her eyes told me I wasn't telling her anything she didn't already know.

"Why do you put up with it then?"

She considered my question for a second then wrote *Because I deserve it.*

Liberty had classes during the week, but Saturday was visiting day. Though I had several visitors that Saturday, the rule was that you could only see one person at a time.

The first person was Simon Green. I asked him how Mr. Kipling was faring, to which he replied, "He's stable." Apparently,

Mr. Kipling was still on a ventilator and unavailable for consultation. "Unfortunately," Simon Green added.

And it *was* unfortunate. Though I was worried for Mr. Kipling, I was equally worried for myself and my family.

"Per your instructions, I made all the calls, Anya," Simon Green said. "Everything is arranged. Ms. Goodfellow agreed to stay. Ms. Barber will take your sister to and from school. Your brother, for the moment, is not taking the job at the Pool. I also spoke to your grandmother . . ." Simon Green's voice trailed off. "Her mind seems to be . . ."

"Going," I finished.

"You're the one running the show, aren't you?" Simon Green asked.

"Yes," I answered. "And that's why I never would have poisoned Gable Arsley. I couldn't afford to take such a risk."

"Let's talk about Mr. Arsley for a moment," Simon Green said. "Do you have any theories as to how the poison got in the chocolate?"

"Yes. Jacks Pirozhki delivered the box to my house. I believe the chocolate was intended for my immediate family. Gable got in the way."

"I know Jacks Pirozhki. He's a nobody, a nonentity in the Balanchine organization. He's considered good-natured and essentially benign," Simon Green replied. "Why would he want to poison you and your siblings?"

I told him how Pirozhki had been hanging around my brother for weeks and how he had been the one to set up Leo with the job at the Pool. "Maybe he thought murdering the children of Leonyd Balanchine would be some sort of symbolic gesture? Raise his profile among Daddy's enemies."

Simon Green considered this, then shook his head. "Doubtful. But his behavior's still very suspicious and I'll definitely have a word with Mr. Pirozhki. Would you like to hear the case the State has against you?"

Here were the main points:

1. I had given Gable Arsley not one, but two bars of poisoned chocolate.
2. I had committed a prior act of violence against him (the lasagna incident).
3. I had been heard making threats against him.
4. I had a motive (I was a woman angry for being either dumped or assaulted, depending on whose story you believed).
5. I had asked my brother to destroy evidence.

"Where did they get that last part?" I asked.

"When the cops arrived at your apartment, Leo was moving the chocolate out of your grandmother's closet. Your brother never admitted anything but his behavior seemed suspicious. Of course, they confiscated the whole lot."

"The only reason I asked him to move the chocolate was because I didn't want Nana to get in trouble for possession!" I said.

"She won't," Simon Green promised. "They're pinning the possession charge on you as well. But don't worry about that, no one goes to jail or juvenile hall for possession of chocolate.

"Anya, something about this smells off to me. And despite my poor performance in court on Thursday, I will get to the bottom of it," Simon Green assured me. "You will be exonerated and back at home with Galina, Natty, and Leo."

"How did you come to work for Mr. Kipling?" I asked.

"I owe him my life, Anya," Simon Green said. "I would tell you the story but I wouldn't want to betray Mr. Kipling's confidence."

I could respect that. I took a moment to consider Simon Green. He had very long legs and arms and in his suit he looked almost like a daddy longlegs spider. His skin was very pale, as if he spent his days not just indoors, but underground. His eyes were more green than blue, and they seemed thoughtful. No, intelligent. I allowed myself to feel ever so slightly encouraged that this person was on my side.

"How old are you anyway?" I asked.

"Twenty-seven," he said. "But I graduated top of my class at law school and I'm a quick learner. However, Mr. Kipling's business is complex, to say the least, and I apologize for not knowing more about your situation. I only became his associate last spring."

"Yes, I think he may have mentioned that he was taking someone on," I said.

"Mr. Kipling is very protective of you, and he was planning to introduce us after I had worked for him a year. We'd both hoped that I might replace him someday, but neither of us had any inkling it would happen so soon."

"Poor Mr. Kipling."

Simon Green looked down at his hands. "Though I don't wish

to make excuses for myself, I think some of my incompetence in court can be attributed to my shock at the sudden turn in Mr. Kipling's health. I do apologize again. How are they treating you?"

I told him I'd rather not discuss it.

"I want you to know that my first priority is getting you out of here." Simon Green shook his head. "If I'd done a better job, they never would have sent you here to begin with."

"Thank you, Mr. Green," I said.

"Please. Call me Simon." I still preferred Mr. Green.

We shook hands. His grip was neither too strong nor too weak, and his palms were dry. Not to mention, the man knew how to apologize properly. "You have visitors besides me. I should let you get to them," Simon Green said.

My other visitors that afternoon were Scarlet and Leo, but I almost wished that neither had come. Having visitors was exhausting. They both wanted to be reassured that I was fine, and I wasn't up to the task. Scarlet told me that Natty had wanted to come, but Scarlet had discouraged her. "Win, too," she added. Her instincts had been right on both counts. "Your picture's all over the news," she informed me.

"I heard," I replied.

"You're famous," she said.

"Infamous more like."

"Poor darling." Scarlet leaned in to kiss me on the cheek, and a guard yelled, *"No kissing!"*

Scarlet giggled. "Maybe they think I'm your girlfriend. Your lawyer's kind of cute, by the way," she said. She had apparently met him in the waiting area.

"You think everyone's cute," I said. I didn't care that my lawyer was cute; I only cared that he would be effective.

After my visitors had left, Mrs. Cobrawick approached me. She was much more dressed up than she had been yesterday. She was wearing a tight beige dress and pearls and makeup and her hair was pulled into a style I think is called a French twist. "As a rule, the girls are only allowed two visitors, but I made a special exception for you," Mrs. Cobrawick said.

I told her that I hadn't known that and I assured her it wouldn't happen again.

"No need, Anya. A simple thank-you would suffice," Mrs. Cobrawick replied.

"Thank you," I said. However, I was not in the least comfortable with being indebted to this woman in any way.

"I saw your brother here earlier. I had heard he was simple but he seemed perfectly normal to me," Mrs. Cobrawick commented.

I didn't wish to discuss Leo with this woman. "He does well," I said.

"I can see this subject makes you uncomfortable, but I am your friend and you should feel at liberty to discuss this or any other matter with me. How did you find orientation?"

Was orientation her word for what had happened to me on Thursday? "I found it pretty medieval," I said.

"Medieval?" She laughed. "You're a strange one, aren't you?"

I said nothing.

A woman with a camera walked by and asked, "Photograph for our donor newsletter, Mrs. Cobrawick?"

"Oh, my! Well, I suppose one can never escape the demands

of the public." Mrs. Cobrawick put her arm around me. The flash went off. I hoped I looked halfway decent, though I doubted it. I knew how these things worked. The picture would be sold, and I suspected it would only be a matter of days, if not hours, before this image ended up on the news right alongside my school photo.

"How much do you think you'll get for it?" I asked.

Mrs. Cobrawick fidgeted with her string of pearls. "Get for what?"

I knew I should probably stop, but I continued. "The picture," I said. "Of me."

Mrs. Cobrawick looked at me with slit eyes. "You're a very cynical young lady, aren't you?"

"Yes," I said. "I probably am."

"Cynical and disrespectful. Perhaps those are things we can begin to work on while you're here. Guard!"

A male guard appeared. "Yes, ma'am."

"This is Miss Balanchine," Mrs. Cobrawick said. "She has led a very privileged lifestyle and I think she could benefit from spending some time in the Cellar."

Mrs. Cobrawick walked away, leaving the guard to deal with me. "You must have really pissed her off," he said once she was out of earshot.

I was led down several flights of stairs into the basement of the building. It smelled putrid, a winning combination of excrement and mold. Though I could not see anyone, I heard moans and scratching, punctuated by an occasional scream. The guard left me in a tiny, dirt-covered room with no light and little air. There wasn't even space to stand. You could only sit up or lie down, like in a dog kennel.

"How long will I be in here?" I asked.

"Varies," said the guard as he closed the door and locked me in. "Usually until Mrs. Cobrawick thinks you learned your lesson. I hate this job. Try not to lose your mind, girl."

Those were the last words spoken to me for a very long time.

The guard had given me good advice, which turned out to be nearly impossible to follow.

In the absence of visual information, your mind invents all manner of intrigue. I felt rats running across my legs and cockroaches on my forearms and I thought I smelled blood and I lost feeling in my legs and my back hurt and I was just plain scared.

How had I even ended up here?

I had nightmares too awful to describe. Natty getting shot in the head in Central Park. Leo slamming his head over and over again on the steps at Little Egypt. And me, always behind bars, unable to act.

Once, I woke up because I heard someone screaming. It only took me a minute or so to figure out that it was me.

Although I doubt this had been Mrs. Cobrawick's point, I did learn something about insanity while I was down there. People go crazy, not because they are crazy, but because it's the best available option at the time. In a way, it would have been easier to lose my mind because then I wouldn't have had to be there anymore.

I lost track of time.

I prayed.

I lost track of time.

Everything smelled like urine.

I suppose it was mine, but I tried not to think about that.

The only human contact I had was when a stale dinner roll and a metal cup with water would be slipped through the panel in the door. I didn't know at what intervals the rolls were coming.

Four rolls passed.

Then five.

On the sixth roll, a different guard opened the door. "You're free to go," she said.

I didn't move, unsure if the guard was a hallucination.

She shined a flashlight at my face and the light hurt my eyes. "I said, you're free to go."

I tried to push my way out, but I found that I couldn't move my legs. The guard pulled me out by my arms, and my legs woke up a little.

"Just need to sit down," I croaked. My voice didn't sound like me. My throat was so dry it was hard to speak.

"Come on, honey," the guard said. "You'll be okay. I'm taking you to clean yourself up and then you can leave."

"Leave?" I asked. I had to lean on the guard. "You mean, I can leave the Cellar?"

"No, I mean leave Liberty," she said. "You've been exonerated."

I X. i discover an influential friend & then, a foe

My conservative estimate for how long I'd been in the Cellar would have been a week though I wouldn't have been surprised to hear it had been a month or even longer.

In reality, it had only been seventy-two hours.

Turned out that a lot had been happening in that time.

The climb up from the basement was far more exhausting than the climb down had been. It seemed strange that being confined to sitting and lying positions could be so physically debilitating, and I felt a newfound empathy for Nana.

The guard, who told me her name was Quistina, led me to a private shower. "You need to clean yourself up now," she said. "There are people waiting to speak to you."

I nodded. I still felt so unlike myself that I couldn't even be bothered to ask who was waiting for me or how all this had come about.

"Is there a time limit on the shower?" I asked.

"No," said Quistina. "Take as long as you need."

On the way into the shower, I caught sight of myself in the mirror. I looked feral. My hair was matted and filled with knots. My eyes were bloodshot and the dark circles under them were more like bruises. There were actual bruises and marks up and down my arms and legs. (Not to mention that tattoo on my ankle.) My nails were ragged and bloody—I hadn't even been aware that I had been digging at the ground, but that was the only explanation. I was coated in dirt. Once I was actually in the shower, I became aware of how truly terrible I smelled, too.

As it wasn't on my dime, I took a very long shower. Possibly the longest shower of my life.

When I got out, my school uniform was on the bathroom counter. Someone had laundered it and even shined my shoes.

Upon putting on my clothing, I realized that I must have lost some weight. The skirt that had fit perfectly a few days earlier was now a couple of inches too big in the waist and rested on my hips.

"Mrs. Cobrawick would like to see you before you go," Quistina said.

"Oh." I was not eager to encounter that woman again. "Quistina," I asked, "would you happen to know why I'm being released?"

She shook her head. "I don't really know the specifics or if I'm even supposed to talk about it with you."

"That's okay," I said.

"Although," she whispered, "on the news, they said people all over town were ending up in the hospital with chocolate poisoning, so . . ."

"Jesus," I said, and then I crossed myself. This news meant that the Fretoxin contamination had been in the supply. It hadn't just been Gable. He'd likely been the first because my family got our chocolate before everyone else. The question wasn't whether I had poisoned Gable but who had tainted the entire shipment of Balanchine Special. These kinds of cases could take years to solve.

I'd been using Mrs. Cobrawick's private bathroom and according to Quistina, she was waiting for me in her sitting room, which was down the hall.

Mrs. Cobrawick was wearing a formal black dress as if she were in mourning. She was perched on the edge of an appropriately severe black parsons chair. The only sound in the room was the tapping of her nails against the glass coffee table.

"Mrs. Cobrawick?"

"Come in, Anya," she said in a tone that was markedly different from the one she'd last used with me. "Have a seat."

I told her that I'd rather stand. I was exhausted but relieved to be ambulant again. Besides, I didn't exactly relish a lengthy visit with Mrs. Cobrawick and standing would discourage such a possibility.

"You look tired, dear. And it's polite to sit," Mrs. Cobrawick said.

"I've spent the last three days sitting, ma'am," I said.

"Is that meant to be some sort of dig?" Mrs. Cobrawick asked.

"No," I replied. "It's a statement of fact."

Mrs. Cobrawick smiled at me. She had a very broad smile— all her teeth showed and her lips disappeared. "I see how you're going to play this now," she said.

"Play this?" I asked.

"You think you've been treated badly here," Mrs. Cobrawick said.

Hadn't I? I thought.

"But I simply wanted to help you, Anya. It looked as if you might be here a very long time—there was so very much evidence against you—and I find that it makes everyone's time easier if I'm stern with the new arrivals up front. It's my unofficial policy, really. That way, the girls will know what's expected of them. Especially those who've had as privileged a background as you've had—"

I couldn't listen to this any longer. "You keep mentioning my privileged background," I said. "But you don't know me, Mrs. Cobrawick. Maybe you think you know things about me. What you've read in the newspapers about my family and such, but you really don't know the first thing."

"But—" she said.

"You know, some of the girls here are innocent. Or even if they're not innocent, whatever they've done is in their past and they're just trying to do their best to move on. So, maybe you could treat people based on your own experiences with them. Maybe that might make a good unofficial policy." I turned to leave.

"Anya," she called. "Anya Balanchine!"

I didn't turn back around but I heard her coming after me. A couple of seconds later, I felt her clawlike hand on my arm.

"What?"

Mrs. Cobrawick clutched my hand. "Please don't tell your friends at the DA's office that you were treated badly here. I don't need any trouble. I was . . . I was foolish not to consider how well connected your family still is."

"I don't have any friends at the DA's office," I said. "Even if I did, getting you in trouble is pretty much at the bottom of my list of things to take care of. What I'd most like is to never see you or this place again in my life."

"What about Charles Delacroix?"

Win's father? "I've never met him," I said.

"Well, he's waiting for you outside. He's come to personally escort you back to Manhattan. You really are a very fortunate girl, Anya. To have such powerful friends and not even know it."

Win's father was to meet me in the Exit Room, an area that was reserved for those leaving Liberty. The Exit Room was more elaborately decorated than any other place in the facility with the possible exception of Mrs. Cobrawick's quarters. There were overstuffed couches, brass lamps, and framed black-and-white photographs of immigrants arriving at Ellis Island. Mrs. Cobrawick waited with me. I would have very much preferred to wait alone.

Though I might have expected such a powerful man to have an entourage, Charles Delacroix had arrived alone. He looked like a superhero without the cape. He was taller than Win, and his jaw was broader as if he spent his days eating trees or rocks. His hands were large and powerful but much softer than Win's. No farming for Charles Delacroix.

"You must be Anya Balanchine," he said cheerfully. "I'm Charles Delacroix. Let's ride on the ferry together, shall we?"

His manner was such that it seemed as if there was nothing he'd rather be doing than taking some mafiya daughter on a boat ride back to Manhattan.

Mrs. Cobrawick piped up. "We are so very honored to have you visiting our facility, Mr. Delacroix. I am Evelyn Cobrawick, the headmistress here."

Charles Delacroix offered her his hand. "Yes. How rude of me. Pleasure to meet you, Mrs. Cobrawick."

"Perhaps you'd like a tour of the facility while you're here?"

"No time for that today, I'm afraid," Charles Delacroix said. "But we really must reschedule."

"Please do," said Mrs. Cobrawick. "I'd love for you to see Liberty. We are very proud of our humble institution. Truth be told, we think of it more like a home." Mrs. Cobrawick punctuated this comment with a modest laugh.

"Home?" Charles Delacroix repeated. "Is that what you call it?"

"Yes," said Mrs. Cobrawick. "It might seem silly to you, but I do think of it that way."

"Not silly, Mrs. Cobrawick, but perhaps a tad disingenuous. You see, I was raised in an institution like this one. Not a reformatory, but an orphanage. And trust me, those confined to the walls of such a place do not think of it as a home." Charles Delacroix turned his gaze to me. "But you're in luck. For I have Miss Balanchine as a traveling companion and I imagine she will be able to attest to the qualities of Liberty on the boat ride back."

I nodded, but said nothing. I would not give Mrs. Cobrawick any more fodder. I crossed my arms, which made Charles Delacroix notice that one of the injection sites was inflamed and oozing pus. "Did this happen to you here?" he asked me in a gentle tone.

"Yes." I pulled the sleeve of my dress shirt down. "But it doesn't hurt much."

His eyes moved down my arm to my hand and to the raw and worried skin of my fingertips. "And this I presume."

I said nothing.

"I wonder, Mrs. Cobrawick, if these are the kinds of injuries that children sustain in a home." Charles Delacroix took my arm in his. "Let's do schedule that tour, Mrs. Cobrawick. On second thought, perhaps I'll drop in unannounced."

"Your predecessor never had any problem with the way I ran Liberty," Mrs. Cobrawick called.

"I am not my predecessor," Charles Delacroix replied.

Once we were on the boat back to Manhattan, Charles Delacroix said to me, "Dreadful place. I'm glad to be out of there. I imagine you are, too."

I nodded.

"Dreadful woman, too," he continued. "I've known Mrs. Cobrawicks all my life. Small-minded bureaucrats in love with their tiny bit of power." Charles Delacroix shook his head.

"Why don't you do something about Liberty then?" I asked.

"I suppose I'll have to someday. But the city has so many serious problems and I frankly don't have the resources to deal with everything at once. Liberty is a fiasco. That woman is a fiasco. But they are, at the very least and for the time being, contained fiascoes." Mr. Delacroix stared over the railing of the ferry. "It's called *triage*, my dear."

140

Triage was something I understood very well. It was the organizing principle of my entire life.

"I want to apologize for the fact that you were sent to Liberty at all. This was a mistake. People in my office got overexcited at the idea of a teenage poisoner, and they became positively histrionic at the idea of that criminal being the daughter of Leonyd Balanchine. They mean well, but they're . . . It took a couple of days, but you've been completely cleared, of course. Your attorney, Mr. Green, was remarkably vocal in your defense. Incidentally, the young man . . . Gable is it?"

I nodded.

"He's taken a turn for the better. He'll have a long recovery ahead of him, but he's definitely going to make it."

"I'm glad to hear that," I said weakly. I felt anesthetized, unlike myself.

"You go to school with my boy?" Charles Delacroix asked.

"Yes," I said.

"Win thinks very highly of you," he said.

"I like him, too," I replied.

"Yes. I was afraid of that." Charles Delacroix turned to look me in the eyes. "Listen, Anya—do you mind if I call you Anya?"

"No."

"So, Anya, I can tell you're a very levelheaded young lady. How do I know this? Back at Liberty, you could have taken the opportunity to destroy Mrs. Cobrawick in front of me. You didn't. You were thinking about your next move. Getting out of that place. I admire that. Street smarts, I guess you'd call it, something my son lacks. And I can see why Win would like you.

You're very attractive and your background is exciting to say the least. But you can never be my son's girlfriend."

"Come again?"

"I can't have you dating Win. We're both practical people, Anya. We're both realists. So I know you'll understand me. My job is very difficult. The truth is, no matter how hard I try to clean up this city, I still may fail." Charles Delacroix lowered his head, as if the weight of his responsibilities was too much to bear.

"Let me begin again. Do you know what they called my predecessor, Anya? The Cookie-Jar Prosecutor, a moniker she received because she had her crooked hands in so many people's pockets, including—I would be remiss not to mention it— Balanchine Chocolate."

"I don't know anything about that."

"Of course not, Anya. Why would you? You have the last name; you don't write the checks. And my predecessor's *interests*, to put it politely, were broad. Here's how it works. Rationing and well-meaning—if pointless—bannings beget black markets, and black markets beget poverty, pollution, and, of course, organized crime, and organized crime begets corruption, and all this has turned our government into a place where cookie-jar bureaucrats of every stripe can thrive. It is my personal mission to root these bureaucrats out. I will not be known as a cookie-jar prosecutor. But if my son begins dating the daughter of Leonyd Balanchine, the notorious chocolate boss, it will have the appearance of impropriety. It will be a hit to my credibility. I can't afford to take such a hit. This once-magnificent city can't afford for me to take such a hit. It isn't your fault, and I very much wish the world were a different place. The people—they're prejudiced, Anya. They rush to judgment. I'm sure you know this better than anyone."

"Mr. Delacroix, I'm afraid you've misunderstood. Win and I are just friends."

"Good. I was hoping you'd say that," Win's father replied.

"Besides, if you don't want me to date Win, why don't you forbid him?" I asked. "You're his father, not mine."

"Because if I forbid him, he'll only want you more. My son is a good boy, but he's contrary, romantic, and idealistic. His life has been too easy. He's not practical like you and me."

The ship horn sounded. We were about to dock.

"So, do we have an agreement?" Charles Delacroix asked me. He held out his hand for me to shake.

"My father always said that you shouldn't make an agreement unless you know exactly what you're going to get out of it," I said.

"Good girl," Charles Delacroix said. "I admire your spirit."

The boat arrived at the dock. I could see Simon Green waiting for me on the shore. With what energy I had left, I ran to him and away from Charles Delacroix.

Someone I didn't know called out, "It's her! It's Anya Balanchine!"

I turned toward the voice and was temporarily blinded by a lightning storm of camera flashes. Once my vision returned, I could see a blue police barricade to the right of where Simon Green stood. Behind the barricade were at least fifty reporters and paparazzi, all shouting questions at once.

"Anya, look over here!"

Despite myself, I did.

"Anya, how was Liberty?"

"A vacation," I replied.

"Any plans to sue the city for wrongful imprisonment?"

I felt Charles Delacroix put his arm around me. Another wave of flashbulbs.

"Please, people. Miss Balanchine has been very brave and helpful, and I imagine she'd just like to get home to be with her family. You can talk to me all you want, of course," Charles Delacroix said.

"Mr. Delacroix, any leads on how the chocolate supply was contaminated?"

"The investigation is still active. That's all I can say for now," Mr. Delacroix said. "What I can tell you is that Miss Balanchine is 100 percent innocent."

"Mr. Delacroix, regarding District Attorney Silverstein's health. No one's seen him in public for weeks."

"I don't make it a practice to comment on my boss's health," Mr. Delacroix replied.

"Should you be considered the acting district attorney?"

Mr. Delacroix laughed. "When I've got an announcement to make, you'll be the first to know."

While Mr. Delacroix continued to talk to the press, I was able to slip away.

Simon Green had a private car waiting for me. This was a real luxury back then—most everyone took public transportation or walked—and I appreciated the gesture. The last time I had ridden in a private car had been when Gable and I went to prom and before that, for my father's funeral. "I thought you'd want some privacy," Simon Green said as he held the door open for me.

I nodded.

"I'm sorry. I wasn't counting on that circus. On that level of interest in you."

"Charles Delacroix probably wanted the photo op," I said, as I slipped into the leather seat.

"Yes, you're probably right," Simon Green agreed. "Though he seemed like a very nice man when I was arranging the details of your release on the phone this morning. Once I was able to get through to him myself, that is."

"He was about what you'd expect," I said.

The car had started moving. I rested my head on the window.

"Mr. Kipling told me to return this to you." Simon Green placed my cross into my palm.

"Oh, thank you," I said. I put the chain around my neck, but when I went to clasp it, my fingers were too tired to work the tiny mechanism.

"Here! Let me," Simon Green said. He lifted my hair, his fingertips grazing the back of my neck. "There," he said. "You must be exhausted, Anya. I brought food if you're hungry."

I shook my head. "Maybe some water?"

Simon Green handed me a thermos with water. I drank it down in one gulp. Some of it spilled out the side of my mouth, and I felt bad at the waste.

"You were thirsty," Simon Green commented.

"Yes, I—" Suddenly, I knew I was going to throw up. I pressed the button that rolled down the window, and I managed to aim most of it outside the car. "I'm sorry," I said. "I shouldn't have had so much to drink at once. I'm kind of dehydrated."

Simon Green nodded. "Don't apologize. Once all of this is settled, I'm going to personally file a complaint about your treatment at Liberty."

I couldn't think about any of that, so I changed the subject. "How did this come about?" I asked. "My release, I mean."

"Over the weekend, more and more cases of Fretoxin poisoning started appearing at city hospitals. I think the number ended up being in the low hundreds, and so it became clear the contamination was in the supply."

I nodded.

"Still, I wasn't able to get anyone at the DA's office to listen to me. Mr. Kipling is the one with the friends—both in your family and in law enforcement. People were mistrustful of me. And despite the fact that you're Leonyd Balanchine's daughter, no one in the Balanchine organization was willing to help either. Not that they wouldn't have helped eventually, but the timing was most unfortunate. The Balanchines had a five-alarm fire of their own to deal with—the poison was in their chocolate."

"You must have been very persistent," I said. "Thank you."

"Well, actually, Anya, I can't take all the credit. There was one stroke of good luck. You go to school with a boy named Goodwin Delacroix, I believe?"

"Win."

"Several times, I had spoken to your friend Scarlet Barber about your situation. And it was Scarlet, I believe, who went to Win, who—"

"Went to his father. Yes, that makes sense."

"And from that point on, the ball started rolling. The problem had been your name, you see. Though you're, of course, unconnected to a supply-wide poisoning, you still carry the Balanchine name and I think the DA's office was reluctant to release a Balanchine in the middle of this circus. It took a personal connection—"

I yawned. "Excuse me."

"Perfectly fine, Anya. You're tired. I've never understood what's so rude about yawning anyway."

"I'm not that tired," I insisted. "I'm just . . ." My eyelids were fluttering shut. "I'll have to thank Scarlet when I go back to school . . . And Win, too . . ." I yawned again and then I fell asleep.

X. i convalesce; receive visitors; hear news of gable arsley

WHEN I WOKE, I WAS IN MY OWN BED and it was almost as if the whole ordeal had never happened.

Almost, I say, because Natty lay beside me and Leo was dozing in my desk chair. These were not our usual sleeping arrangements.

"Are you up?" Natty whispered.

I told her that I thought I was.

"Imogen said we should let you rest," Natty reported. "But Leo and me didn't want to miss it if you woke up so we've been staying in here mostly."

"What day is it?" I asked.

"Thursday," she said.

I had slept for two days. "Shouldn't you be in school?"

"I already went. It's night." Make that two and a half days.

Leo stirred in his chair. "Natty, you shouldn't talk! You'll wake—" And then he saw me. "Annie!" Leo jumped into bed and wrapped his arms around me. "Oh, Annie, I missed you so much!" He kissed my forehead and my cheeks.

I laughed. "I missed you, too."

When I reached up to embrace Leo, I noticed that my arm was attached to an IV. "What's this?" I asked.

Apparently, Imogen had declared me malnourished and dehydrated. "Poor Annie," said my sister.

The next day, I wanted to go back to school—I was so behind—but Imogen wouldn't let me. "You're still too weak," she said.

"I'm feeling much better," I assured her.

"You'll feel even better on Monday," was Imogen's reply.

I reminded her that she was Nana's nurse, not mine. Imogen did not find this argument in the least compelling. "Go back to bed, Annie."

Instead of doing that, I decided to see how Nana was faring.

I went into Nana's room and kissed her on the cheek. She immediately recognized me, which I took to be an encouraging sign. Maybe she was having one of her good days.

"Hello, Anyaschka," Nana said. She squinted at me. "You're looking very thin."

"Don't you remember? Imogen told you that I was being questioned about a crime."

"A crime? No, that doesn't make any sense. That wasn't you. That was your father," Nana replied.

"They thought I had poisoned a boy named Gable Arsley."

"Gable Arsley! That sounds like a made-up name. I've never heard of such a person." Nana waved her hand to dismiss me.

"He was my boyfriend," I said. "You met him once." I stood

to leave. Nana seemed agitated and I didn't want to end up with another slap across the face.

"Annie?" Nana said.

"Yes."

"Did Leo take that job at the Pool?"

I was surprised that she remembered. My grandmother's mental health was more and more of a puzzle to me. I sat back down. "Not yet," I replied. "We've all been kind of occupied here."

"Good, good. Because I've been thinking about it," Nana said. "I'm not sure it's such a great idea."

As I had nothing better to do, we debated the merits of Leo taking a job at the Pool for a while. No new ground there. Then I really did start to feel tired, so I told Nana I had to go.

"Have a bar of chocolate, darling," Nana said. "And be sure to share it with someone you love."

There was nothing in the world I wanted less than chocolate and I knew the police had confiscated our entire supply anyway. Still, I went into the closet and pretended to retrieve a bar for Nana's sake.

Friday night, Scarlet was allowed to visit, and this was a welcome distraction. While I appreciated how concerned Imogen, Leo, and Natty had been for my health, their solicitude made me feel like an invalid. I needed someone to behave normally around me.

"So, what's been happening at Holy Trinity?" I asked after Scarlet had made herself at home on my bed.

Scarlet laughed. "Are you kidding? You're the only thing that's been happening. You and Gable."

"That's just great," I said.

"Seriously, it's all anyone can talk about." Scarlet crossed her legs. "With my inside information, I've basically been the most popular girl in school."

"Congratulations."

"Yeah, I'm sure I made a lot of lasting friendships in the last nine days," Scarlet said. "You've got a ton of competition now."

I thanked Scarlet for taking Natty to and from school. And then I thanked her for telling Win to go to his father.

"Win? I had nothing to do with that. Win went to his father on his own," Scarlet said.

"But you must have had something to do with it," I insisted.

"We talked about you, of course," Scarlet said. "But he didn't tell me he was going to his father and I didn't ask him to. I thought about it—oh, don't look so surprised, Annie! Your silly best friend does think things through on occasion. I thought about it, but I didn't do it because I wasn't sure if it would potentially make things worse for you."

"So why did Win do it then? We barely know him."

Scarlet rolled her eyes. "I'm sure you can come up with a reason."

This was annoying to me. I didn't like owing Win anything. I especially didn't like owing Win after the conversation I'd had with his father.

"Enough with the furrowed brow! It's not some great mystery. He likes you, Annie. The only thing he wants is his lab partner back. And maybe a thank-you. And maybe a date to Fall Formal."

I sighed.

"Oh, poor Annie, the really cute new boy likes her," Scarlet teased me. "Her life is so, so tragic." She flopped dramatically on the bed.

"I was in a reformatory, you know," I reminded her.

"I know," she whispered. "I was only teasing you." Her big blue eyes filled with tears. It was easy to make Scarlet cry. "I'm so sorry about everything that happened to you. It's really terrible. I can't even imagine. I was just trying to make you laugh."

I did laugh. Her expression was sweet and apologetic.

"When I came in the room, I couldn't believe how weak you looked. Natty had warned me, but . . . Was it horrible?" Scarlet asked.

I shrugged. I had no interest in rehashing my time at Liberty for Scarlet or anyone else. "I got a tattoo." I pushed down my sock and showed her the bar code on my ankle.

"That is very hard-core," Scarlet replied.

I pulled my sock back up. "How's Gable doing?"

"He'll live, I guess," Scarlet said. "Chai Pinter heard that he had to have skin grafts on his face. The Fretoxin made parts of his skin fall off or something."

"Oh, God."

"Well, Chai isn't always the most reliable source. I don't even know where she's getting her information half the time. I think she makes most of this stuff up. What Headmaster is saying is that Gable won't be back to school until next term at the earliest. He's in a rehab facility somewhere upstate," Scarlet said. "He really did almost die, Annie."

"Do you think I should send a card?" I asked. "Or go visit?"

Scarlet shrugged. "Gable was horrible. He was horrible to you. And sick Gable is probably even more horrible." She shrugged again. "But if you must, I suppose I could come with you. You shouldn't go alone."

"Well, I didn't mean tomorrow. Maybe in November?" I had a ton of schoolwork to catch up on and I had plenty of my own problems right here.

Leo came in. "Hi, Scarlet! Natty said you were here." Leo gave Scarlet a hug. "You look pretty!"

Scarlet was wearing sweatpants and a T-shirt, which was very dressed down for her. Her blond hair was loose and tangled. She didn't have on any makeup either. Maybe that was what Leo found pretty? Scarlet had an excellent complexion, but it was usually covered up. "Why thank you, Leo!" Scarlet said. "To tell the truth, I wasn't feeling very pretty, but after your compliment, now I do."

Leo blushed. "You always look pretty, Scarlet. I think you're maybe the prettiest girl in the world."

"Hey!" I said.

"You're sister-pretty," Leo said to me. "Scarlet is *prettyyyyyy* . . ."

Scarlet and I both laughed, causing Leo to blush even more.

"Imogen says you should leave now, Scarlet," Leo relayed. "Annie needs to sleep."

"All I've been doing is sleeping!" I protested.

"She said you would say that," Leo continued. "She said to ignore you."

Scarlet stood up and kissed me on the cheek. "I'll come for you on Monday morning so we can go to school together." On the way out of my bedroom, she kissed Leo on the cheek, too. "Thanks for the compliment, Leonyd."

Sunday afternoon, my uncle and Nana's stepson, Yuri Balanchine (aka the head of the family), stopped by the apartment. Uncle Yuri was only about ten years younger than Nana and had a limp that I think Daddy had said was from a war injury. The limp must have gotten worse since the last time I'd seen him, as now he was confined to a wheelchair.

Uncle Yuri visited Nana occasionally, but on that day, he wasn't there to see her. He was there for me.

Uncle Yuri always smelled of cigars and his voice was scratchy from years of smoking. He was flanked by several bodyguards; Jacks, his son by the prostitute; and Mikhail Balanchine, his "real" son and heir. Uncle Yuri instructed them to wait in the hallway. Mikhail piped up. "Dad, can I stay?"

"No, Mickey, you leave, too," Uncle Yuri said. "I have a private matter to discuss with my niece."

I sat on the sofa.

"Little Anya," Uncle Yuri said, "you've gotten to be quite the beauty. Come closer. Let me look at you, my darling." I leaned forward, and he stroked my cheek with his hand. "I can remember the day you were born. How proud your papa was!"

I nodded.

"Leonyd—God rest his soul—thought you were the most beautiful baby alive. I didn't see it myself, but now it's clear he knew what he was talking about." Uncle Yuri sighed. "I'm sorry I don't come to see you and Galina more often. This apartment has many sad memories for me."

"For all of us," I reminded him.

"Yes, of course," Uncle Yuri said. "How thoughtless of me. For you even more than me. But today, I come about another matter. I wanted to discuss the incident with the young man."

"Gable Arsley, you mean?"

"Yes," Uncle Yuri said. "I wanted to apologize for not intervening last week. The connection to Balanchine Chocolate made most of our contacts in law enforcement run cold. Had I intervened, I worried that you might become a pawn to the DA's office. The man in charge there is new, and we do not yet know if he is a friend to us."

He was talking about Win's father. "It worked out in the end," I said.

"I want to assure you that you were never far from my thoughts. You are the daughter of Leonyd Balanchine, and you would not have been left to rot in prison."

I nodded, but said nothing. These were nice words, but only that.

"I can tell exactly what you are thinking. Nice words from the old man, but what good do they do me now?" Uncle Yuri leaned in closer. "I can tell you are a bright girl. You have sharp eyes like your father."

"Thank you," I said.

"You keep everything inside like him. You don't give away too much. I admire that," Uncle Yuri said. "I admire that restraint in someone so young."

I wondered if he would still be saying that if he'd seen me with the lasagna on the first day of school.

"I am ashamed," Uncle Yuri continued. "I feel that this family has failed you. I feel that I personally have failed you." Uncle Yuri lowered his head and then he lowered his voice. "I want you to know that there are larger forces at play here. Dark things beyond my control. I must get to the bottom of this matter with the chocolate, and then I can work on making amends with you. Your siblings as well."

He held out his hand for me to shake, which I did. "I like you, Anya Balanchine. It's a shame you are not a boy."

"So I could be dead at forty-five like my father, you mean?" I asked in a low voice.

Uncle Yuri didn't respond. I wasn't sure if he had even heard me. "Would you mind wheeling me down the hall to Galina's room? I'd like to visit with my stepmother before I depart."

On the trip down the hall, he asked me how Nana was faring.

"Depends on the day," I replied. "Uncle Yuri, there was talk of my brother coming to work at the Pool."

"Yes, I had heard something about that," Uncle Yuri said.

"I'd rather he didn't."

"You're worried that we will corrupt him?" Uncle Yuri asked. "You have my word that the only thing that will happen to your brother is the receipt of a nice paycheck for an easy day's work. We will take care of him. He will never be asked to do anything dangerous or be put in harm's way. I had heard he had lost his job. Giving him a temporary one is the least we can do, yes?"

Uncle Yuri certainly made me feel better about the whole matter than Jacks had. And considering how delicate Nana's condition seemed and how potentially delicate my legal situation was, it would definitely be better for Leo to at least have the appearance of being gainfully employed. Not to mention, I had no idea when the situation at the animal clinic would resolve itself, especially now that Mr. Kipling wasn't able to work on it. (How was he anyway?) Uncle Yuri and I had reached Nana's room. I opened the door and called out, "Nana, are you sleeping?"

"No, Christina, come on in," she said.

"It's not Christina," I said. "It's Annie. And guess who I've got with me? Your stepson, Yuri!"

I wheeled Yuri into the room. "Ugh," Nana said to him. "Yuri, why have you gotten so old? And so fat?"

I happily slipped out the door.

Mickey Balanchine was standing in the hallway outside Nana's room. "You probably don't remember me but I'm your cousin," he introduced himself.

"Who isn't?" I joked.

"It's true. Every time I meet a girl I like, I have to check and see if she's related to me first," Mickey said. Mickey Balanchine was on the short side, only an inch or two taller than me. His hair was so blond it was almost white and his skin was equally fair except for the freckles across his nose and cheeks. In contrast to his skin and hair, he was dressed entirely in black. His suit was very well tailored and even looked new. Though I can't say for sure, his boots may have had little heels on them to make him look taller.

"I've been wanting to meet you for some time," Mickey said. "Now that you're all grown up, I mean. When I was a teenager,

157

I used to run errands for your father. I've been in this apartment on many occasions. I've even seen you naked, little Anya." He pointed down the hallway to the bathroom. "Right in that room. Your mother was giving you a bath. I accidentally walked in."

That was too much information.

"So," Mickey continued, "what did you and the old man talk about?"

Nothing, I thought, but that was none of Mickey's business. "I suppose if it concerned you to know, he would have told you himself," I said.

At that moment, Jacks came down the hallway. "What's going on here?" he asked.

"Just having a conversation with my cousin," Mickey replied.

"She's my cousin, too," Jacks said.

"Maybe," Mickey said.

"What's that supposed to mean?" Jacks asked. "What are you trying to say, Mikhail? That I'm a bastard?" His eyes were blazing and I swear I could smell the testosterone coming off him. He lunged at Mickey, but Mickey stood firm. It became obvious to all of us that Jacks didn't have the *yaytsos*.

"Oh, Jackie, relax!" Mickey said. "You're embarrassing yourself in front of my cousin."

"Annie, could I have a word with you?" Jacks asked.

"Speak," I said.

"Alone," Jacks specified.

"It seems no one wants to talk in front of Mikhail today," Mickey commented.

I ignored him. I have never responded to that sort of childishness. Besides, I had things I wanted to say to Jacks, too. "Let's go out on the balcony," I said.

The balcony was just off the dining room. You could see Central Park and even part of Little Egypt. It must have been a nice view once.

My cousin got right into it. "Look, Anya, I'm sorry about the chocolate. I had no idea it had been laced. I honestly thought I was doing Galina a favor by bringing it over."

"I appreciate you saying that," I told him. "Because here's how it looks to me: you brought that chocolate over extra early to ensure that my whole family died from eating it."

"No!" Jacks said. "I have no interest in poisoning any of you! What could that possibly gain me?"

"I have no idea, Jacks. But it's how it looks to me."

Jacks ran his fingers through his hair. "You probably know this without my having to say, but I'm low in the organization. No one tells me about anything. I had no more warning than you that that chocolate was poisoned. You have to believe me!"

"Why do you care if I believe you?" I asked.

He lowered his voice. "Because things are changing in the Family. The chocolate scare was just the beginning. The perception—and I'm not saying I agree—but the perception is that Yuri is weak. I think the poisoning was the move of a rival family."

"Like who?"

Jacks shrugged. "I'm only speculating here but it could be the Mexicans or the Brazilians. Even the French or the Japanese. Any

159

of the big players in the black market chocolate biz. There's not enough information to narrow it down. My point is, you could bring heat on me, Anya. You haven't, I don't know why, but I appreciate it. And I wanted you to know that I would never do anything to hurt you or your siblings."

"Thanks," I said. The truth was, I believed that Jacks hadn't been trying to poison us, but only because he was too weak to organize (or even be informed of) such a large operation. The second truth was, I wanted to move on from all of this and the less I heard from my relatives the better.

"So we're friends?" Jacks said, offering me his hand. I shook it only because it would have been more awkward not to. Jacks was not my friend. It had certainly not escaped my notice how scarce he had made himself during my legal troubles. Such behavior didn't exactly seem friendly to me.

After my relatives had left, I spent the rest of the day doing homework and before I knew it, Sunday was over. Around nine o'clock, I heard the phone ring. Natty knocked on the door. "It's Win," she said.

"Tell him I'm asleep."

"But you aren't!" Natty said. "And he called yesterday, too."

I stood up from my desk and flipped off my light. "I am sleeping, Natty. See."

"I love you, Annie, but I don't approve of you right now," she said. I heard her return to the kitchen. I could barely make out the sound of my little sister lying for me.

I lay down in my bed and pulled the blanket up to my chin. The night air felt like fall.

I knew that nothing Charles Delacroix had said to me really mattered.

And yet, I also knew that it did.

Daddy always said that an option that you know to have a bad outcome is only ever a fool's option, i.e., not an option at all. And I liked to think that Daddy hadn't raised a fool.

X I. i define *tragedy* for scarlet

Aт school, i was handled with kid gloves. As I'd been cleared of any involvement with Gable Arsley's poisoning, the administration feared that they had bungled my situation—for starters, by allowing the cops to question me on campus without calling Nana or Mr. Kipling first—and I think they were worried that I would either sue them or, even worse, start telling tales that would be damaging to their heretofore spotless reputation as the best private school in Manhattan. My teachers were emphatic that I should take as much time as I needed and, overall, my return to academic life was easier than I had anticipated.

Win was already in FS II when I got there. He didn't mention that he'd called me twice or that I'd met his dad, if indeed Charles Delacroix had deigned to speak to him about me. He didn't mention anything about my absence, except to say, "I had to present on our teeth without you."

"How'd that go?" I asked.

"Good," he said. "We got an A minus."

Coming from Dr. Lau, that really was a good grade. She was tough. "Not bad," I said.

"Anya," Win started to say, but then Dr. Lau began class. I wasn't in the mood for more pointless small talk with Win anyway.

I was granted a one-month excuse from Advanced Fencing, which I appreciated. I lacked the stamina for even pretend bouts. The administration granted Scarlet a one-month excuse so that she could keep me company. Further proof of how contrite the school was.

Scarlet used the extra time to prepare for her upcoming *Macbeth* audition. "You're reading all the lines with me. Why don't you try out, too?" Scarlet asked. "You could be Lady Macduff or Hecate or . . ."

The truth was, I didn't really have a good reason not to except that I was tired and I didn't exactly feel like putting myself out there after my picture had been plastered all over the news for a week.

"You can't just stop everything because of what happened," Scarlet said. "You have to keep moving forward. And you still have to apply to college next year one way or the other. Your extracurricular activities are definitely somewhat lackluster, Annie."

"What? Being the daughter of a celebrated criminal doesn't count as an extracurricular activity?"

"No," Scarlet said. "A case could be made for poisoning your ex-boyfriend however."

But she was right. Of course she was right. If he'd been alive, Daddy would have said the same thing. Not the extracurricular part. I mean, the part about moving forward.

"Have it your way," I said.

Scarlet tossed me an ancient paper-book copy of *Macbeth*.

We read lines until the period was over and then we went to lunch, where Win was waiting for us at our usual table.

Scarlet told me to sit, that she had promised Imogen she would get both our lunches. "Oh, come on," I said. "I'm not that weak."

"Sit," she ordered. "Make sure she sits, Win."

"I'm not a dog!" I protested.

"Will do," he said.

"She sure is bossy," I commented.

Win shook his head. "I must admit," he began, and then he paused. I sincerely hoped he wasn't going to bring up his father or some other subject I wasn't keen on discussing. Maybe he sensed my discomfort. "I must admit," he repeated, "I underestimated your friend. Scarlet seems like this silly girl when you meet her, but she's got a lot more grit than that."

I nodded. "The best thing about Scarlet is how loyal she is."

"That is important," he agreed.

Even though Win would never be my boyfriend, I realized that I did want him for my friend. And if we were going to be friends, it was rude of me not to acknowledge the part he'd played in my release from Liberty. Even if we weren't going to be friends, it was rude. "I should have thanked you before," I said. "For talking to your dad, I mean."

"Is that meant to be you thanking me now?" Win asked.

"Yes," I said. "Thank you."

"No problem," Win said. He started unpacking his lunch from his bag. (I guess he didn't want to eat the school option.) His meal consisted of various vegetables, including a roasted sweet potato and a long white one that resembled a carrot.

"What's that one?"

"A parsnip. My mother's trying to grow them in Central Park."

"Sounds dangerous," I said.

"You want to try it?"

"No, it's your lunch."

"Come on," he said. "It's sweet."

I shook my head. My stomach was still wonky and I didn't want to throw up all over the table. (Though maybe not such a bad idea, as it would have decisively settled the idea of Win and me as a couple . . . I don't think a person can feel romantically attracted to you after you've vomited on him.) Win shrugged. He took two oranges out of his bag.

"Oranges!" I said. "We haven't had those here since I was a kid. Where did you get them?"

"Mom's trying to grow those, too. She got a license to start a grove on the roof of our town house. It's not producing anything yet. These are samples from Florida. Here, take one."

"No thank you." I didn't want to owe him any more than I already did.

"Suit yourself," he said.

"I really am grateful for what you did."

"Don't mention it," Win said.

"But I have to mention it," I insisted. "It wouldn't be right not to because now I owe you."

"You don't like owing people, do you?" he asked.

I admitted that, all things considered, I would rather not be in anyone's debt.

"Well, here's the thing. I didn't have to do anything except ask my father. And trust me, Anya, there are plenty of drawbacks to being my father's son and relatively few perks. While you could certainly say that there are"—he paused—"things my father owes me, that's not the reason he helped you anyway. He intervened because he agreed with me that your situation was unjust."

"But—"

"But we're even, Anya. You don't owe me anything. Though I did end up doing the lion's share of the work on the project for FS II."

"Sorry about that."

At that moment, Scarlet returned with lunch. She slammed the trays on the table. "Ugh, lasagna again!" she called. "And no Gable Arsley to pour it over!" Neither Win nor I laughed, though I did smile a little. "Hmm, maybe it's still too soon for Gable Arsley jokes."

In my room that night, I noticed that Win had put one of the oranges in the zipper section of my backpack. I set the orange on my desk. Even with the peel on, it made my whole bedroom smell sweet. Though I knew it probably wasn't a good idea, I decided to call Win. I told myself that if Charles Delacroix answered, I'd hang up. Luckily, Win answered.

"You left something in my bag," I said.

"Yeah, I was wondering what happened to that orange," Win said. "I guess you may as well have it then."

"Oh, I'm not going to eat it," I told him. "I'm never going to eat it. What I love is the scent. Oranges remind me of Christmas. My dad used to have a business associate who sent him a crate of oranges every Christmas from Mexico. None of us ever ate them." I was rambling, and this was embarrassing, not to mention expensive. "I should go."

Win asked, "You want to know the real reason I tried to help you?"

"I'm not sure."

"Well, you probably already know it but maybe it needs to be on the record," Win said. "It's because I'd like to get to know you better. That was gonna be hard to do with you locked up at Liberty."

"Oh . . ." I felt myself blushing. "I really should go. I shouldn't even have called you. See you at school." And then I hung up the phone.

In the morning, Jacks came to the house to get Leo for his first day at work. Leo was still getting dressed so I went to talk to Jacks in the living room.

"If anything happens to him . . ." I said.

"I know, little cousin, I know. Don't you worry about Leo."

I asked Jacks what kinds of things they were planning to have Leo do there.

"Cleaning. Getting lunch for the men. Nothing that intense," Jacks assured me. "You made quite an impression on the old man, by the way."

"You mean Uncle Yuri?"

"He said he'd marry you. If you weren't related. And if he were fifty years younger. Et cetera. Et cetera."

"That's a lot of very important *if*s, Jacks."

"What I mean is, he was impressed with you," Jacks said. "As am I."

I told him that I had to get to school.

I walked down the hallway. I knocked on my brother's door, and he told me to come in. "Annie, I'm late! Help me pick a tie."

"Let me see," I said.

Leo held up a solid-pink tie and then a violet floral-patterned one.

"Maybe no tie? I don't think it's going to be that kind of job."

Leo nodded and set the ties on the bed.

"You can call me at school if anything goes wrong. I'll come get you," I reminded him.

"I don't need my baby sister coming to get me!"

"Don't be mad, Leo. I didn't mean anything by it," I said. "I just wanted to remind you that if anyone asks you to do anything that you're uncomfortable with, you don't have to do it. There will always be other jobs."

"I'm late!" Leo grabbed his messenger bag from the floor. He kissed me on the head and on both my cheeks. "See you tonight. I love you, Annie!"

"Leo," I called. "One of your shoes is untied!" He didn't hear me. At least, he didn't turn around. I resisted the urge to run after him.

That night, Leo brought flowers (yellow roses) for Nana

and a pizza for the rest of us. When he came through the door, he seemed taller than he had that morning, and I noticed that both his shoes were tied, too. I couldn't help but wonder if I'd been wrong about the job at the Pool.

"How was it?" I asked after we'd all sat down to dinner.

"It was fine," he said, and in a style uncharacteristic of my brother, he left it at that.

Thursday, Scarlet and I auditioned for *Macbeth*. Auditions were held in Mr. Beery's office. Everyone had to go in one at a time. You were supposed to tell Mr. Beery what part you'd like to play, then read a bit of it.

Scarlet wanted to play Lady Macbeth, of course. "Unless Mr. Beery's up for gender-blind casting, but I doubt it. I'd make a good Macbeth, don't you think?"

"You should tell him that," I suggested. "But you'd probably have to cut your hair."

"I'd do it!" Scarlet said. "For Macbeth, I'd do it!"

Scarlet went in first, and I went in after she came out.

I read a bit of Lady Macduff. Her part wasn't that big. Her main scene is her talking to her kid and then she gets murdered a scene or two later and it's supposed to be very sad. She gets to scream "Murder!" when the murderers show up, which seemed fun and like a satisfying sort of thing to do. I'd rather have been a witch but Scarlet thought Lady Macduff was the better part for me. ("She'll definitely have the better costume," Scarlet had insisted.)

"Not bad," Mr. Beery said when I was done. "Though I'm disappointed you're not reading for Lady Macbeth, too."

I shrugged. "I relate more to Lady Macduff."

"Just read a little," Mr. Beery insisted.

"I would rather not," I replied.

"Come on, Anya. It wouldn't be disloyal to your friend to try reading a bit of it for me. I believe your background could unearth exciting things for the part."

I shook my head. "I have absolutely no interest in playing Lady Macbeth, Mr. Beery. And your statement that my 'background' would 'unearth exciting things' is offensive. I assume you're saying this because I've known murderers. But the truth is, I've been in situations almost exactly like Lady Macduff's, not like Lady Macbeth's. I don't relate to Lady Macbeth's ambitions or anything about her. I have no ambition, Mr. Beery, except to get through high school. And, if you offered me the role of Lady Macbeth, I would turn it down. I'm not saying this as some sort of reverse psychology either. The only reason I'm going out for this play in the first place is because I said I would keep my friend company."

"Ms. Barber doesn't have your spark, Anya. She doesn't have your fire!" Mr. Beery objected.

"I think you're mistaken about Scarlet, Mr. Beery." I had known people like him my whole life. People willing to embellish me (for better or worse) because of my family history. In a way, Mr. Beery wasn't that far from Mrs. Cobrawick.

"Very well, Ms. Balanchine," Mr. Beery said. "List will be up tomorrow."

When I left, Scarlet was waiting for me in the hallway.

"You were in there a long time," she said.

"Was I?" I replied.

170

"How'd it go?" she asked.

I shrugged. "Okay, I guess."

"Well, he spent a lot of time with you," Scarlet said, "and that's always a good sign."

The next day, the cast list was posted on the door of the school theater. Scarlet got Lady Macbeth like she wanted. Though I wouldn't have been surprised to have been passed over entirely, I was cast as Hecate.

"Who's Hecate again?" I asked Scarlet.

"Chief witch," she replied. "It's a good part!"

I hadn't read for that role but this turn of events suited me just fine.

We were still going over the cast list when Win came up to congratulate us.

"Chief witch," he said to me. "That's the most important of all the witches."

"So I've been told," I said.

"You've got to keep those other witches in line," he said.

"I think I'm up to it." I'd been keeping witches (and a lot worse) in line my whole life.

And that was my week. No one was arrested. No one died. I was chief witch. If none of my problems had disappeared or improved, none had gotten markedly more severe either. All things considered, not bad.

Friday night was Scarlet's sixteenth birthday so I got my cousin Fats to give us the back room at his speakeasy. On account of my legal problems and the state of Gable's health, we decided to keep the guest list small—a few of Scarlet's drama friends,

Natty, and that would be that. I wasn't planning to serve coffee or chocolate or anything, but I still wasn't sure if we should invite Win or not. As this wasn't a surprise party, I discussed the matter with Scarlet. (Incidentally, I don't believe in surprise parties. I don't like to be surprised and I'm not sure that anyone does.) So, back to Win. "He knows what your family does, Annie," Scarlet said. "It's not this big secret. I say we definitely invite him."

I hadn't told Scarlet about my conversation with Win's father. In point of fact, I hadn't mentioned it to anyone. It was too embarrassing, I suppose. "You ask him if you want," I told Scarlet.

Scarlet considered this, then shook her head no. "I've already made enough of a fool of myself around that boy, thank you very much. You do it."

"Fine," I said. "Do you mind if I ask Leo, too?"

"Of course not!" Scarlet said. "Why would I mind? I love your brother."

In a way, that was sort of the problem. It had become increasingly apparent to me that Leo liked my best friend as more than a friend, and I didn't want him to end up with a broken heart. Scarlet flirted with everyone but I was worried that Leo might not understand that.

"What about your lawyer?" Scarlet asked.

"Mr. Kipling? He's still in the hospital."

"Not Mr. Kipling! The young one. Simon, is it?" Scarlet said.

I told Scarlet that he wasn't that young.

"How young isn't he?"

"Twenty-seven," I said.

"That's not that old either. That's only eleven years older than me."

"You're getting as bad as Natty," I said.

Scarlet's mouth slipped into a pout. "Well, I don't like any of the boys my own age."

I shook my head at her. "You're hopeless," I said.

"And the ones I do like don't like me back."

Natty and I got to Fats's place early to set up the back room. Fats's place had wrought-iron tables and chairs and a big wooden bar across the back. Vintage advertisements for alcohol hung on the wall in heavy gilt frames. Supposedly, they only served wine but the place reeked of coffee beans. Coffee was a hard smell to get rid of, and it was my favorite scent in the world. Both my parents had loved the stuff. Before it was banned, they had always kept a pot on the stove.

Fats offered to help us. "How you been, kid?" Fats asked while we shifted tables and chairs into the back room.

I showed him my ankle tattoo.

"Now you're really a Balanchine," Fats commented.

I sighed. "Leo's working at the Pool."

"Heard that, too," Fats said.

"You had something to do with it, didn't you?" I asked. Hadn't Leo told me that Jacks and Fats had been the ones that first took him to the Pool?

Fats shook his head. "Pirozhki asked me to introduce him to Leo so I did."

"Why did Pirozhki want to meet Leo?"

Fats shrugged. "Think he said something about wanting to know more of the family."

This seemed like a suspicious response, like Fats was hiding something. I would have called him on it, but at that moment, Scarlet showed up. She was wearing a strapless red taffeta ball gown and a headband with a peacock feather in it. Natty trailed behind her. "Doesn't Scarlet look pretty?" Natty said.

"Amazing," I agreed. While it was true that Scarlet looked amazing, she also looked slightly insane.

"I brought something for you to wear, too," Scarlet said. "I knew you wouldn't have changed." She was right; I was still wearing my school uniform. Scarlet pulled a black, sequined, drop-waisted dress out of her bag. It was not the kind of thing that I would wear and I told Scarlet so.

"Come on, it's my birthday. And I want you to be sparkly," Scarlet insisted.

"Fine," I said. "If you want me to look ridiculous. You're early, by the way." Scarlet had told me she was planning to arrive fifteen minutes late in order to make a grand entrance.

"I didn't want you to have to do everything by yourself," she said. "I'll leave and then I'll come back later to make my entrance."

The party was a success. Scarlet's outfit was much admired. (Mine was, too.) I busied myself with the music and keeping everyone fed and watered. I liked having something to do, and I wasn't in the mood for conversation anyway.

At the end of the night, I had Leo and Natty escort Scarlet home, and I stayed after everyone had left to put the tables and chairs back in their rightful places and to thank Fats.

"Here," Win called. "Let me help you with that." He took the chair I was carrying and set it in a stack with the others. "I can finish that for you."

"I thought you'd gone," I said. I was not entirely thrilled to find myself alone with him, but if he wanted to move chairs, so be it.

He went over to his hat, which was hanging on a brass hook on the wall. "I left my hat," he said as he put it on his head.

"Sometimes I think you go around leaving your hat everywhere on purpose," I grumbled.

He stacked the last of the chairs. "Now, Anya, why would you think that?"

I didn't answer. Win walked over to me. He held out his palm. In the middle of it was a single black sequin from the dress Scarlet had lent me. "You lost this," he said.

I giggled, slightly embarrassed to be leaving bits of myself behind. "I'm shedding."

"I did abandon my hat on purpose," he admitted. "It's hard to ever get you alone, and there's something I've been wanting to ask you . . ." And then he invited me to the Fall Formal. "I know, it's kind of childish, but, well, I have to go. I'm the entertainment. Me and these guys are playing music, so . . ."

"Guys playing music? You mean, you're in a band?" I asked.

"No, we're not a band yet. Just a couple of guys come together for the purpose of entertaining at the Holy Trinity Fall Formal. I hate when people have been together, like, two minutes and they're all, *We're a band!*" This was said incredibly quickly and with a great deal of gesturing. I guess he was nervous. He took his hat off his head, as if to give his hands something to do.

"So, yes, I'm definitely going. With or without you," he said. "But I'd rather it be with." He smiled at me, and his blue eyes went soft and shy. Had I been a different kind of girl with a different kind of life, I would have maybe kissed him right there.

"So, Anya, what do you say?"

"No," I replied firmly.

"Okay," he said, putting his hat back on his head. "Just so I know, is it the dance or is it me?"

"Does it matter?" I asked.

"Yes, because if you don't like me, I'll stop bothering you," Win said. "I'm not the type of person to linger where I'm unwanted."

I considered this question. If I was very honest with myself, I didn't want him to stop bothering me and yet it was the only sensible solution. "It's not you," I lied. "I just don't think with Arsley in the hospital and how complex my personal life is, I should be seeing anyone at the moment. Triage, you know?"

"I understand, but that sounds like bull," he said. Then Win left, making sure to take his hat with him this time.

In that moment, I liked Win more than I ever had before. I appreciated that when something sounded like bull, he said so.

I let myself feel good and sorry for myself, but only for a second. Daddy always said that the most useless of all human emotions was self-pity.

On Monday, Win was cordial with me in FS II, but he didn't sit with us at lunch. Instead, he ate with some of the guys who were not technically a band. Scarlet asked me if anything had happened between me and Win, so I told her.

"What is wrong with you?" Scarlet asked. Her voice sounded surprisingly angry.

"Nothing," I said. "Maybe it's not that great an idea for me to have a boyfriend right now. Gable is still in the hospital, you know."

"What does Gable have to do with anything? You've been flirting shamelessly with Win ever since school started!"

"That's not true!"

Scarlet rolled her eyes. "I, on purpose and very selflessly I might add, stopped going for Win because I thought my very best friend was in love with him."

"It isn't a good time, Scarlet."

Scarlet shook her head. "I don't understand you at all." She concentrated on eating her lasagna (again!) and so I did the same.

"What's so great about being in a couple anyway?" I demanded of Scarlet. "Get your own boyfriend if you think they're so important."

"That was mean," she said. Scarlet shook her head at me, and I immediately regretted the second half of my comment. Even though Scarlet was beautiful and loyal, she was also considered slightly odd and, consequently, she rarely got asked out. Nana, when she was still herself, used to say that Scarlet was one of those girls who would be far more appreciated when she was older.

"I'm sorry," I said. "Scarlet, I'm sorry. I didn't mean it."

Scarlet didn't reply. She picked up her tray and left me to eat alone.

All through play rehearsal that afternoon, Scarlet wouldn't speak to me and she didn't wait for me at the end of rehearsal either. I hated that I had hurt Scarlet's feelings so I stopped by her apartment on the way home from school to apologize again. Scarlet lived on the top floor of a six-story walk-up. It was quite a climb, which was why we usually hung out at my house where the elevator was mostly reliable.

"Apology accepted," Scarlet said. "I decided I'd probably overreacted once I got to the hallway, but by then I'd already stormed off and it seemed embarrassing to storm back. By the way, it's not that everyone has to be in a couple! You clearly like Win, and he clearly likes you. It's simple, or it should be."

I looked at Scarlet. "Nothing is simple."

"Then explain," she said. "Please explain."

"All right," I said. "But you have to promise never to repeat this to anyone. Not to Natty. And especially not to Win." Scarlet promised, so I told her what Charles Delacroix had said to me about how no son of his could ever date a girl like me.

"That's awful," Scarlet said.

"I know."

"It is awful," Scarlet continued. "But I don't actually see why it matters."

"It's his family," I said, "and family matters more than anything."

"Yes, but it's Win's family, so if he wants to piss off his father, that should be his choice, don't you think?" Scarlet asked.

"Maybe," I said. "But when you think about it, it's not as if I'm going to marry Win or like I'm even in love with him, so what's the point? There are millions and billions of people in the world to get with, so why bother with the one whose father is very powerful and dead set against me?"

Scarlet considered this statement. "Because it might be fun. And it might make you happy. So, what's the harm if it probably won't last anyway?" Scarlet kissed me on the cheek.

As I mentioned about one hundred pages ago, Scarlet was a romantic. Daddy used to say that calling a person a romantic was just another way of saying he or she acted without regard for consequences.

"Scarlet, I can't," I said. "I wish I could, but I can't. I have to think about Natty and Nana and Leo. Imagine if Charles Delacroix decided to retaliate against me."

"Retaliate! That's ridiculous and paranoid!"

"Maybe, maybe not. Win's father struck me as . . . Well, I guess you'd call it ambitious. It wouldn't be outside the realm of possibility that he could call the authorities on my family to get me out of the picture."

"You sound crazy, Annie," Scarlet said. "There's no way that would ever happen."

"Listen, I'll tell you one scenario I thought of. Charles Delacroix knows that Natty and I don't have a real legal guardian at the moment. Nana's not good. She's really lost it, Scar. Leo is . . . Leo is what he is. What if Mr. Delacroix called Child Protective Services on us? What if I ended up back at Liberty or someplace like it, only forever? And Natty could end up there, too! My point is, Win's just not worth it to me."

Scarlet's eyes filled with tears.

"Why are you crying?" I asked.

Scarlet waved her hand in front of her face in a manner that struck me as almost comical. "The way that boy looks at you! And he doesn't even know why you're . . . I wish I could tell him."

"Scarlet, don't go getting any ideas."

"I would never betray your trust. Never!" Scarlet blew her nose on her sleeve. "It's so tragic."

"It's not tragic," I assured her. "This is nothing. Tragedy is when someone ends up dead. Everything else is just a bump in the road." For the record, that was something Daddy used to say, but I'm pretty sure Shakespeare would have agreed, too.

XII. i relent; make an adequate witch

DESPITE THE FACT that neither of us had dates, Scarlet wanted to go to the Fall Formal and so we did. I would have preferred not to, but as Daddy might have said, that was the price of friendship.

The theme of the dance was "Great Romances," or some such nonsense. There were projections of supposedly great couples from the past on the walls of the gym. Romeo and Juliet, Antony and Cleopatra, Hermione and Ron, Bonnie and Clyde, etc. I don't think most of them met a particularly good end, but I suspect this was an irony that entirely bypassed the event's organizers.

I was not surprised to discover that Win was there with Alison Wheeler. Though Alison and I were not friends, there was no animosity between us and we had gone to school together for years. She was pretty verging on very pretty, with a willowy frame and long red hair out of a storybook. It showed good taste on his part, and I was glad to see he had gotten over me so quickly. No one else had asked me to the Fall Formal, by the way. I suppose they were justifiably worried about ending up like Gable Arsley.

Toward the middle of the night, Win's band set up to perform. (They were only to play during the DJ's break.) I asked Scarlet if she wanted to leave.

"No, that would be rude," she said. "He's still our friend so let's listen to at least one of his songs and then we can go."

They started with a cover of a really old song called "You Really Got a Hold on Me." Win had a deep, husky singing voice, and he played guitar well, too.

"He's good," Scarlet said.

"Yes," I said.

"Do you want to go now?" she asked. "I waved to him so I know he saw that we stayed."

I shook my head.

The nameless "band" did a couple of original songs, and I liked those even better than the cover. The lyrics were clever and even poetic. Win was talented. There was no doubt about that.

I found myself very much wishing that we had left. It would have been easier not to have known that Win was talented.

They played a fifth and final song. It was a ballad, but not too sappy. I thought Win might have looked at me, but then he made a lot of eye contact with everyone. He seemed entirely comfortable onstage.

The band took their bows, and the DJ came back on to spin a couple more songs. I was glad that it was over. I felt hot and ill. I needed to get outside for some fresh air.

"Let's go," I said to Scarlet.

At that moment, one of the boys from the play asked Scarlet to dance. I didn't want to be mean so I told her I would wait.

Scarlet made her way to the dance floor. It was a fast song, and she danced with considerably more skill than her partner. I was glad the dance hadn't been a total bust for her. Behind Scarlet, I spied Win dancing with Alison Wheeler. She was wearing a knee-length white dress that really complemented her skin tone and her hair. She looked elegant and very grown-up. Win had taken off his tie and rolled up his sleeves, and I guess he must have been a bit hot from performing, because his short hair was curled into ringlets around his ears in a way I had never seen before. I don't know why, but I found those ringlets to be ridiculously sweet and irresistible.

As I was on the verge of a useless bout of self-pity, I decided to go over to the buffet table to get a tumbler of fruit punch.

A different song came on at some point, a slower one, and that was when I felt a hand on my shoulder.

"Miss Balanchine," Win said.

I turned around. His eyes were bright and almost sheepish.

For some reason, having heard his music made me feel awkward around him. "I'm glad you came over. I really liked . . . You play well." Not my most eloquent moment, to say the least.

"Dance with me," Win said. "I know I'm probably making a fool of myself. You're probably thinking, how many times do I have to reject this guy? Can't he take a hint?"

I shook my head.

"But somehow I don't even care. I see you in your red dress, standing by the punch table, and something in me wants to keep trying. I think, she is a person worth knowing."

"You're here with someone else," I pointed out.

"Alison? Alison's a friend," he said. "My parents have known her parents for years. I'm doing her a favor. Her dad doesn't like her boyfriend so I'm keeping them off his trail."

"That's not how it looked to me," I said.

"Come on," Win said. "Dance with me. There's only half a song left. What harm can it do?"

"No," I said, and then because I didn't want him to think badly of me, I added, "I wish I could, but I can't."

I walked out of the gymnasium and into the hallway to get my coat. Scarlet would have to find her way home without me. Win followed me.

"What does that mean?" he asked. "I don't understand you."

I couldn't get my arm in my left sleeve for some reason. "Here," he said, "let me help." He leaned across my body and guided my arm into the sleeve.

"I don't want your help," I said, but it was too late. I felt somehow outside my body. I knew no good would come of it, but I rose up and kissed him on the mouth.

His lips were sweet and salty. It took a second for them to respond to mine. But dear God, when they did!

"I'm sorry," I said. "I shouldn't have done that."

"That's a terrible thing to say," Win said.

And then I ran out the front doors of the school and into the brisk November air.

The weird thing was, I had meant to run out by myself, but somehow I had grabbed Win's hand.

We ended up back at my apartment.

We kissed for a while in the living room, and if I'm honest

184

(God forgive me!), I wouldn't have minded if it had gone further. But I wasn't that kind of girl and, thankfully, Win wasn't that kind of boy either.

We stayed up all night talking about nothing in particular.

And then the sun came up, and because I liked him as much as I did, I knew I had to talk about something very particular with him: i.e., his father.

"I like you," I said.

"Good," he said.

"I want to tell you a story," I said.

He said he liked stories, and I replied maybe not this one. And then I told him about the day I met his father.

Win's eyes narrowed and their color seemed to change from a clear blue sky to twilight just before a hurricane. "I don't give a damn what he thinks or says, Anya," Win said.

But I doubted that was true. "I care what he thinks," I said. "I have to." I explained how I didn't want any heat brought down on my family. Unlike Scarlet, Win didn't say I was being ridiculous for thinking that was a possibility. "So that's why we can't be together."

Win considered this. "I'm really sorry he said that to you, but screw my father. Seriously, screw him," he said. "What I do is none of his business."

"But it is, Win. I see his point."

Win kissed me then, and for the moment at least, I stopped seeing Charles Delacroix's point.

It was nearly 7:30 a.m. Still clad in her pajamas, Natty emerged from her bedroom. "How was the dance, Annie?" Then she noticed Win. "Oh!"

"Hi," he said.

"He was just leaving," I said.

Win stood, and I pushed him toward the door.

"Let's go see my father right now," Win said in a tone that I couldn't quite identify as serious or joking.

"And tell him what?"

"That our love is too strong for him to suppress it!"

"I don't love you yet, Win," I told him.

"Ah, but you will."

"I have a better idea," I said. "Let's keep this a secret until we know if it's serious. Why sound the alarms if we don't even end up liking each other all that much anyway?"

"Hmmph," Win said. "I think you might be the least romantic girl I've ever met."

"I'll take that as a compliment." I laughed. "I'm just being practical."

"Fine," he said. "Practical it is."

The elevator came, and he was gone, and, truthfully, I felt the least practical I'd ever felt in my life.

Inside the apartment, Natty was waiting for me. "What was that?" she asked.

"Nothing," I said.

"It sure looked like something," said my little sister.

"You're imagining things," I told her. "Now what do you want for breakfast?"

"Eggs," she said. "And a love story if you've got one, Annie. A really sappy, romantic one with tons of kissing and stuff."

I ignored her. "Eggs it is."

"Have you told Scarlet?" Natty asked.

"No, because there's nothing to tell," I said.

"It sure looked like something," Natty repeated.

"You already said." I cracked two eggs and began to scramble them. Natty was still looking at me expectantly. Her eyes were moist and shiny as a dog's, and something about the sweet anticipation of her expression made me want to laugh and confess. Life hadn't been easy for Natty either—everything that had happened to me had happened to her, too. It was a beautiful thing how innocent and generous she still was, how much she cared if her older sister was having a romance. "I like him, all right?"

"You *looove* him!"

I poured the eggs into the pan. "And you have to promise that you won't tell anyone. Not Nana or Leo or Scarlet or anyone!"

"I liked him from the first time I met him," Natty said happily. "What was kissing him like?"

"How do you know I even kissed him?"

"I just do," Natty said. "You look all pink and . . . and kissed. You've got to tell me. He's got those soft-looking lips."

I laughed. "It was good, okay?"

"That is not very descriptive," Natty said.

"Well, that's all you're going to get." As I put her eggs on the table, I noticed a bruise on her right forearm. "What's that?"

"Oh," she said. "I don't know. I probably banged it in the night."

"Does it hurt?"

Natty shrugged. "I had a nightmare, only a little one. I didn't even have to wake you up. Maybe I hit it against the wall? When are you going to see Win again?"

"Maybe never. Maybe he won't ever call. Boys sometimes act like they like you and then never call, Natty."

At that moment, our phone rang. It was Win.

"You got home fast," I said.

"I ran," he said. "I wanted to talk to you before you changed your mind about things. Can I see you tonight?"

Part of me thought it might not be such a great idea to see Win again so soon, but that part of me was curiously mute. "Yes," I said. "Come over tonight."

"I want to take you somewhere," he said.

"Where?" I asked.

"It'll be a surprise."

I told him that I still thought it would be a good idea if we kept our relationship a secret.

"I know and I agree," he said. "But you don't have to worry. Where I'm taking you, no one will know us."

We rode the subway out to the farthest stop in Brooklyn, which was Coney Island. When we got off the train, there was a weathered boardwalk and an ominous cluster of nonoperational amusement park rides that looked like colorful spiders.

"Oh, I know this place!" I said. My parents had taken me and Leo here the summer before it had been closed by the city. (Something to do with an infectious outbreak. Or maybe it had been power-grid issues. I had been too young to remember.) "Nothing runs anymore."

"Not quite nothing," he said, taking my hand. He led me down the boardwalk. I could hear voices in the distance, and I could see that a small kiddie Ferris wheel was lit up.

"Someone reported this to the DA last week," Win said. "These people built an illegal generator and have enough power to run a different ride every Saturday. My dad doesn't care about them. The city has bigger problems. You've heard his stump speech."

"I have. Unfortunately. But I will say that he did seem like he wanted to make a difference."

"The only thing he wants is self-advancement."

The ride operator greeted us. "I just need to warn you that this ride has not been inspected and you may get, for lack of a better word, killed."

Win looked at me. I shrugged.

"So long as you know," the operator reiterated.

"Not a bad way to die," Win said. I agreed.

Win gave the operator money, and we got on the Ferris wheel. I'd never been on one before. We sat side by side, though it was actually a sort of tight squeeze as this particular ride had been built for children, and, though I'm reasonably petite, my behind is generously sized. I was self-conscious about the way my rear was pushing into his, but then he put his arm around my shoulders to make more room, and I stopped thinking about my butt.

It was peaceful on the Ferris wheel. It took forever to get started because the operators waited until the whole thing was loaded to run it. The November air was cold and I could smell something burning in the distance. Win had put on aftershave and it was minty, though not quite strong enough to cover the scent of burning.

I didn't much feel like talking, and Win seemed to understand that.

At some point, the wheel made it to the top. I could see water and darkness and land and beyond that the skyline of Manhattan, where I had spent my whole sad life. I wished I could stay up there forever. Everything awful happened on land. There was safety in elevation.

"I wish I could stay up here forever," Win said.

I leaned over and I kissed him. The metal basket we were in began to sway and squeak.

The only person I told was Natty. I didn't even tell Scarlet. Scarlet was much occupied with being Lady Macbeth. (Hecate turned out to be a far less demanding role.) If she noticed that Win had begun eating lunch with us again, she didn't remark on it. In addition to the play, Scarlet was busy with a romance of her own—Garrett Liu, who was playing Macduff.

At school, Win and I made sure never to be seen alone. Scarlet was usually with us, and I never waited for him by his locker or anywhere else.

Win and I were still lab partners in FS II, and this was probably the most exquisitely torturous hour of my day. I wanted to touch him, to hold his hand under the lab table, to write him a note, but I never did. I knew that our relationship could not continue if our peers started to know about it or to talk about it. Once that happened it would surely get back to Win's father, and I didn't think our silly teenage love affair would survive that.

So, it was torture.

Yet, for as long as it went on, the keeping of the secret was sort of thrilling in its way.

The school day before the opening night of *Macbeth*, Scarlet had to go to an additional rehearsal so Win and I were left at the lunch table by ourselves. It would have been strange for us not to eat together as everyone knew that was where he usually sat. Still, I suggested that we go eat with his friends in the band, but he thought it would be better if we just stuck to the usual routine.

That lunch seemed to stretch on forever. Being with him and yet not with him was unpleasant. To be alone and yet not alone. We spoke of the play, his band, the weather, our plans for the holidays, and other safe subjects, as if fearful that discussing anything more interesting would reveal more than we wished to reveal. The wooden tables were narrow, and at some point, I felt his knee push up against my knee. I moved my knee, but his knee followed. I shook my head, only slightly, and narrowed my eyes. At that moment, Chai Pinter from our FS II class sat down next to Win. "Hi, Win," she said. "Annie." She began to chatter stupidly about some concert she and her set of friends were going to over the holidays. I could barely pay attention because she kept touching Win a lot. I mean, a lot. One moment, her hand was on his hand. The next, it was on his shoulder. The next, she was brushing his hair behind his ear. It was all I could do not to reach across the table and strangle her with my bare hands. I took a deep breath and coaxed myself back from the dark side.

"So do you want to go?" she asked. "Because I've got an extra ticket. I mean, it's a big group of us, so it's not like a boy-girl thing . . . I mean, unless you want it to be?"

Was this happening? Was I watching someone ask my boyfriend, albeit my secret boyfriend, on a date in front of me? I wondered if perhaps we had done too good a job of covering our tracks. Again, I had an impulse to reach across the table, only this time it was Win I wanted to grab. I wanted to kiss him on the mouth in front of everyone and mark him as mine, mine, mine.

"No, sorry," Win was saying. "It's a really nice invitation but my girlfriend wouldn't like it."

"Oh," Chai said, "you mean Alison Wheeler? She said that was just a friends thing."

"No. From my old school. It's long-distance." Win lied so easily that I almost wondered if he actually did have a girlfriend at his old school. At that moment, the bell rang, and Win stood to leave. "See you around, Chai." He nodded at me. "Annie."

"Long-distance girlfriend, huh?" Chai said to me. "Well, those never last."

"I don't know," I muttered. Then I grabbed my books and tore out of the cafeteria. I ran down the hall and in the direction of Win's sixth period, which had changed to English. I knew I could be late to my own sixth period because that was Beery, and Beery was in the theater, finishing the play. I tapped Win on the shoulder. "Excuse me," I said. "Could I have a word with you?"

He nodded, and I led him into a storage closet that was next to the school theater, and then I kissed him. *Kissed* sounds so much more tame than what it was. I pressed my body up against his, and then I stuck my tongue in his mouth as deep as it would go, and then I put my arms around him. "I'm tired of this being a secret," I said.

"I know," he agreed. "But you said that this is the way it has to be."

When we left the closet, the halls were empty. Sixth period had started.

The theater door swung toward us, and Scarlet emerged.

"Oh hey," she said. "Where did you guys come from?" She seemed a bit distracted, which I imagine was because of opening night.

"We were in there," Win replied, indicating the closet. The hallway was a dead end, so there was really no other place we could have come from.

"Why were you in there?" Scarlet asked. She didn't seem suspicious, just curious.

"Because Annie wanted to run through her lines and it was the only space where we could be alone," Win lied. Wow, I thought, he's quite good at this. But then, I could easily imagine several scenarios in which Win would need to lie to a father like Charles Delacroix.

"Why didn't you tell me you were having trouble remembering your lines? I would have run through them with you," Scarlet insisted.

"No, you're busy being the lead. I'm just a witch. I didn't want to bother you." I was no slouch at lying myself.

"Chief witch," Scarlet said. "I'm so proud of you, Annie. I could explode!" And she was proud of me, I could tell, and for whatever reason, this nearly made me want to cry. Because despite the circumstances of my life, I had had no shortage of love. My sister loved me. My brother loved me. Nana loved me. It even seemed that this boy, this Goodwin Delacroix, loved me. But proud of me? I was unaccustomed to anyone being proud of me. Most anyone who might have been proud of me had died long ago.

I should devote a word or two to the play. It was a school play, maybe slightly better than most because Mr. Beery expended significant time and effort into making us not be terrible and because the school was, as I have mentioned, well-funded. Scarlet was the best one. (You probably guessed I would say this, but it doesn't make it not so.) As for my role? The best thing I can say for myself is that I was the only witch who did not have to wear a wig. My dark, curly hair was deemed witchy enough, and, looking back, I'm not sure that my hair wasn't the sole reason I was given the role of Hecate.

XIII. i tend to an obligation (ignore others); pose for a picture

Over christmas break, Win and I took the train to Albany to visit Gable Arsley in the rehab center. I had told Win that I was fine to go by myself as it might be strange for my new secret boyfriend to accompany me on a visit to my badly injured ex-boyfriend. Win argued that he knew the area better than me, and I relented. Whatever. It was a long train ride, and the Hudson River, murky and shallow, didn't make for much of a scenic view anyway.

Christmas Eve, Gable had sent me a message asking me to come. I suppose Christmas had put him in a contemplative mood or maybe he was lonely. He had written that he had had a lot of time to think since he'd been ill and he knew he'd behaved badly toward me. His doctors thought he might be ready to return to school soon, and he'd like to know that everything was all right between us before that happened.

I had visited the Sweet Lake Rehabilitation Center before

because Leo had been briefly sent there after he'd been injured. It was a nice place, as much as any of these types of places can be considered nice places. I've visited my share of hospitals and rehabilitation centers, and the main thing that terrifies me about them isn't anything you see there, but the scent. The chemical-cleanser smell, sweet and awful, covering up illness and weakness and death. Ironically, there was no lake by Sweet Lake, just a big cavern of dirt where a lake or pond must once have been.

"Do you want me to come in with you?" Win asked when we got to the lobby. We were far enough away from home that we felt we could hold hands, but now I didn't want to in case Gable's parents or siblings or friends were nearby.

I shook my head. "No," I said. "I'll be fine."

"I think I should go with you. Isn't he the same boy who tried to force himself on you?"

I shrugged. "Honestly, Win, I don't know who he is anymore, but my gut tells me that you in the room will only make him"—I searched for the right word—"irritated. Besides, I'm tough. I've been taking care of myself for years."

"I know you're tough. That's one of the things I like best about you. I just want to make life easier for you sometimes."

"You do," I said, and then I kissed him quickly on his nose. I'd meant to leave it at that, but then I kissed him again, on the mouth.

Win nodded. "All right, tough girl. I'll be waiting out here for you. If you're gone more than a half hour, I'm coming in after you."

I gave my name to the receptionist at the desk and she gave me Gable's room number, 67, and pointed me down a corridor.

196

I knocked on the door.

"Who is it?" I heard Gable say.

"It's Anya," I said.

"Come in!" His voice sounded odd in a way that I could not quite pinpoint.

I opened the door.

Gable was seated in a wheelchair that faced the window. He rolled around, and I saw his face. The texture was pocked in some places and still raw in others, and a strange patch of skin was sewn from his left cheek to the corner of his mouth—it was this skin graft that was slightly impeding his speech. There were bandages around some of his fingertips. And his body looked extremely thin and weak. I wondered why he was in a wheelchair and so my eyes drifted down to his thighs, then to his knees, then to his foot. Yes, foot—there was only one of them. The right one had been amputated.

Gable watched me look at him. His gray-blue eyes were still the same. "Do you find me repulsive?" Gable asked.

"No," I said honestly. The circumstances of my life had not allowed me the luxury of being squeamish around injury.

Gable laughed—a tinny, flat sound. "Then you're a liar."

I reminded Gable that I had seen worse things in my life.

"Yes, of course you have," Gable said. "The truth is, I repulse myself, Annie. What do you say to that?"

"I can understand why you would feel that way. You've always cared so much about appearances. Like that day at school . . . I know you hated having the spaghetti sauce on your shirt more than anything else"—I paused to look at Gable and he nodded and, oddly, even smiled a little at the remembrance—"but how you are now . . . No one can deny that you are much changed, but I suspect it isn't as bad as you think."

Gable's laugh came out as a wretched bleat. "Everyone says I shouldn't say such things, but not you. This is why I love you, Annie."

I did not feel the need to reply. He was still a liar.

"For a long time, I wished I had died," Gable said. "But not anymore."

"That's good," I replied.

"Come closer," Gable insisted. "Come sit on the bed."

Through our exchange, I had been standing by the door. Even though Gable was confined to a wheelchair, I was still wary of him. Bad things happened when the two of us were alone.

"I won't bite," he said, kind of like a dare.

"All right." As there were no available chairs, I walked to the bed and sat down.

"Do you know why I lost my foot? Sepsis. I'd never heard of it. It's when the body starts shutting down and attacking itself. I also lost three fingertips." He waved his damaged hand toward me. "But they say I'm lucky. I'll walk again and even dance. Don't I look like a lucky, lucky boy?"

"Yes, you do." I thought of Leo and my mother and my father. "You look like someone who survived something awful."

"I don't want to look that way," Gable said. "I detest survivors." He spat out the word *survivors*.

"My father used to say that the only thing a person needed to be in life was a survivor."

"Oh, spare me the pearls of wisdom from the criminal! Do you think I have any desire to hear anything your father had to say?" Gable asked. "The whole time I was with you, it was *Daddy this* and *Daddy that*. Your father's been dead a million years. Grow up, Anya."

"I'm leaving," I said.

"No, wait! Don't go, Annie! I'm unfit for company and I'm sorry." Gable's voice was whiny and babyish. I suppose I pitied him.

"The thing is, you're still handsome," I said. And he was. His skin would heal. He'd learn to walk again and then he'd be the same old awful Gable, hopefully a tiny bit kinder and more empathetic than the previous version.

"Do you think so?"

"Yes," I assured him.

"You're a damned liar!" Gable roared. He rolled himself toward the window. "I've thought of you every day, Annie," Gable said in a quiet voice. "I waited every day for you to come on your own, but you never did. I thought you would have, considering you had some role in my fate, but you never did."

"I'm sorry, Gable," I said. "We weren't exactly on the best of terms when it happened but I did mean to come. I don't know if you heard but I was sent to Liberty. And then I was ill myself for a while. And then I just lost track of time, I suppose. I should have come."

"Should have. Would have. Could have. Didn't."

"I really am sorry."

Gable said nothing. He was still facing the window. After several seconds of silence, I heard him sniffle.

I walked over to him. There were tears running down his ruined face.

"I treated you so badly," Gable whimpered. "I said terrible things about you. And I tried to make you . . ."

"It's forgotten," I lied. I'd never forget what Gable had almost done, but he had been punished enough.

"And you loved me! The way you used to look at me. No one will ever look at me like that again."

I hadn't loved him, but it seemed cruel and beside the point to mention that now.

"And you were my only real friend. None of those other people meant anything to me. I'm ashamed," he said. "Can you ever forgive me, Annie?"

He was truly pathetic. I decided that I could indeed forgive him, and then I told him so.

"I'll need friends when I'm back at Trinity. Can we be friends?"

"Yes, of course."

He reached out his "good" hand for me to shake and then I shook it. He pulled me toward him and the move was so unexpected that I stumbled into him. That was when he kissed me on the mouth. "Gable, no!" I stood and pushed his wheelchair away from me hard enough that the back handles banged against the window.

"What?" he asked. "I thought we were going to be friends again."

"I don't kiss my friends on the mouth," I said.

"But you leaned into me!" he sputtered.

"Are you mad? I tripped!"

I turned to walk away and, with surprising speed and force, Gable aimed his wheelchair at me. I was knocked over onto his hospital bed. At that moment, Win ran into the room and pushed Gable's chair away from me.

"Get off of her!" Win yelled.

Win raised a fist toward Gable's face.

"Don't! You'll hurt him," I said to Win.

Win lowered his arm.

"Who the hell is this?" Gable asked.

"My friend," I replied.

"The kind of friend you kiss on the mouth, I'm betting," Gable replied. "Yes, now this makes sense. What's your friend's name? You look familiar."

Win and I exchanged looks.

"My name is Win, but you can think of me as Annie's friend who doesn't like men that force themselves on women."

Then we left.

I didn't speak to Win until we were on the train home.

"You shouldn't have burst in like that," I said.

Win shrugged.

"I had it under control," I assured him.

"I know you did, lass. You're the toughest girl I know."

"'Lass'? Where did that come from?"

"I don't know. I just felt the urge to call you that. Does it bother you?"

I thought about his question. "It's kind of girly but, no, I guess not." I put my head in the crook of his arm. "Were you waiting out there the whole time?"

"Yes, I suppose I was."

"Gable will figure out who you are, and once he does, everyone will know about us," I said.

"Maybe it won't be so bad?" Win said. "I wouldn't care if people did know. Besides, Gable could decide to keep the information to himself."

"Why would he do that?"

"Well . . . to blackmail us or something?"

"Maybe." But I knew that blackmail wasn't Gable Arsley's style. Blackmail required planning, patience. Gable was all impulse.

When we got off the train in New York City, the paparazzi were waiting for us. "Hey, kids! Look over here! Smile!"

"I guess Gable figured it out," Win whispered to me.

"Anya, is that your boyfriend?"

"He's my friend from school," I yelled out. "We're lab partners."

"Yeah, right."

The pictures were everywhere by the next morning. They'd gotten one of us kissing as we left the train. The headlines were all something like "Star-Crossed Lovers? *Bratva* Princess and Asst. DA's Son Find Love in the City."

Win called me in the afternoon.

"Are you calling to break up?" I asked.

"No," he replied, a bit amused. "My dad wants you to come to dinner tonight."

"Was he angry?"

"He never asked me not to date you. He asked you, remember?"

"So, you mean he's mad at me? I think I'd rather not come, thanks."

"Are you scared? That's not like you."

I asked him what time I should be there.

"Seven," Win replied. "I'd come get you if you didn't mind another photo session," he joked.

"Why do you sound so damn happy?"

"Hmm. I suppose I'm sort of glad people know you're my girlfriend."

"What should I wear?" I asked gruffly.

"I'm partial to that red dress of yours," he said.

I put on my trusty red dress and took a bus to Win's house. It was a much nicer apartment than the salary of the assistant DA (or the DA for that matter) could afford. Either Win's mother had made a killing in farming (possible), or there was family money.

Charles Delacroix opened the door before I even had a chance to ring the bell. He'd been waiting for me. He seemed significantly smaller inside this apartment than he had that day at Liberty and on the boat. It was as if he had the ability to expand or contract as the situation required. "You're looking well, Anya. Much better than the last time we met."

"Yes. I'm feeling better," I said.

"Win is with my wife procuring some essential missing ingredient for dinner. Why don't you come into my study. We'll talk and wait."

I followed him into the study, which had red walls and rugs and mahogany shelves filled with paper books.

"You collect books?"

Charles Delacroix shook his head. "My wife's father did."

203

That settled that. Win's mother was the one with the money. On Mr. Delacroix's screen was one of the articles about Win and me.

"The truth is, I orchestrated this," Charles Delacroix admitted. "I wanted us to meet alone, so I'll cut to the chase here. Win tells me he's in love with you. Is that right?"

I nodded.

"And you're in love with him? Or are you too practical for such indiscretions?"

"We haven't known each other very long," I began, "but I think I might be."

Charles Delacroix rubbed his neck with his skinny, uncalloused fingers. "All right, then. It is what it is." He sighed. It seemed as if he were going to continue speaking, but he said nothing. Instead, he poured himself a drink from a crystal decanter.

"Is that it?" I asked.

"How rude of me. Would you like a drink, too?"

I shook my head. "I meant, is that all you have to say about the matter?"

"Listen, Anya, I advised you against dating Win, and it would probably make my job simpler if you'd gone in a different direction here. But I'm not such an ogre. If my son's in love . . ." Charles Delacroix shrugged. "We are where we are. I like you, Anya. And I'd be the worst sort of hypocrite if I held your parentage against you. We, none of us, can escape the circumstances of our births. Now, if you decide to marry Win, that might be another story. My advisers tell me that my campaign—my theoretical campaign, I mean, and mind you, nothing's been decided yet about that—can handle Win dating you, but marrying you, they weren't so sure."

"I promise you, Mr. Delacroix, I'm not planning to marry anyone anytime soon."

"Good!" Charles Delacroix laughed and then his face grew solemn. "Did Win ever tell you about his older sister, Alexa? She died when she was about your age now. I don't like to speak of it."

I nodded. I could understand not wanting to speak of things.

"My point is, despite what I said to you that day on the ferry, I want my only living child to be happy, Anya. But I also want him to be safe. The one thing I ask is that if you ever think my boy's in danger because of any of your familial associations, please come to me. Do we understand each other?"

"Yes," I said.

"Good. And, of course, if you ever commit any legal indiscretions, I will have to prosecute you to the fullest extent of my office. I can't be seen to show you favoritism." This was said in as friendly a manner as it's possible to say such things, so I told him that I understood.

Win and his mother arrived home then. "Charlie!" a woman's voice called out.

"We're in the study!" Mr. Delacroix called back.

Win and his mother entered the room. She had long ink-black hair and light green eyes and was about my mother's height and build. "I'm Jane," she said. "You must be Anya. My, you're very pretty."

"You . . ." And then I had to stop because I felt as if I might cry. "You remind me of someone I used to know."

"Oh, well, thanks, I guess. I suppose I should ask you if it was someone you liked or someone you didn't like." She laughed.

"Someone I liked," I said. "Someone I miss very much." I knew it was an awkward thing to say but I didn't want to tell her that she reminded me of my mother.

After dinner, Win walked me home. The paparazzi had left for the night, or maybe they'd simply gotten bored of the story. Win wanted to know if his father had been awful to me. I told him that he hadn't been. "He mainly wanted to make sure that I wouldn't get you killed."

"What did you say?" Win asked.

"I told him I'd try not to, but I couldn't make any guarantees." And then we were back in my room.

We didn't have sex, or even get particularly close, but I'd be lying if I said the thought hadn't crossed my mind. I could feel myself opening up toward him like a rose in a hothouse.

I just couldn't, though. I thought of my parents in Heaven or Hell and I thought of God. Daddy once said, "If you don't know what you believe, Annie, you'll be a lost soul." I realized something very important that night. It had been easy to resist losing my virginity to Gable because I had never really wanted him. In other words, there had never been much temptation. It was far more challenging to stick to my principles where Win was concerned.

That night, Win asked me about sex, like what my beliefs were, etc. And I told him that I didn't want to have sex until I was married. Without missing a beat, he nodded and said, "So let's get married."

I hit him. "You're that desperate to have sex?"

"No," he said. "I've had sex."

"I'm sixteen! And we barely know each other."

He held my chin in his hand and looked in my eyes. "I know you, Anya."

He might have been serious, but I made a joke of it. "You'd probably marry me just to annoy your father."

He grinned. "Well, that would certainly be a bonus."

"Why don't you like him?" I asked. "He seems all right."

"In five-minute doses," Win muttered. "I imagine you've noticed that he's pretty ambitious."

"Sure. My father was, too. In the opposite way though. But I still loved him."

"He . . ." Win began, and then he stopped. "I admire Dad. He came from nothing. He was raised in an orphanage. Both his parents were killed in a car accident, but he lived. He thinks I'm soft, but who can compete with that?" He looked at me. "Oh, right. You can, can't you? My poor, brave girl." He kissed me on the forehead.

I told him that I didn't want to talk about me. "Why does he think you're soft?"

"Because I got in some trouble a long time ago . . . Boring kid stuff. I'd tell you but it's embarrassing."

"Now you have to tell me!"

"No, I'm ashamed, lass, and it's not very interesting anyway. It was after my sister died, and it was the lowest I've ever been. The point is, my dad thought it was weakness, and that my mother indulged my weakness."

"Do your parents get along?"

"Dad says the only person who's ever loved him is my mother . . ."

"She seems nice," I said.

"She is. But Dad? He cheats on her. She ignores it, but I can't. I mean, how can I respect a man like that?" Then he asked me if my father had ever cheated on my mother.

Despite my father's many failings, it was impossible to imagine him ever behaving in such a way. I told him that I didn't know for sure, that I'd been too young to know, but I doubted it. "He believed in marriage," I said.

"So does my dad but that doesn't stop him from acting the way he does," Win said. "I would never treat you that way, Annie."

I knew that without him having to say it. Win was perfect in his way.

I could go on and on about Win, but personally, I'm sickened by that sort of thing. Daddy always said that if a person had a bout of good fortune, that person would do best to keep it to herself. Win felt like the best stroke of luck I'd had for a very long time. (Insert finger in throat if you'd like . . .) But yes, I was happy for a time. I was the kind of girl I usually hate, and I realize that the only reason I ever hated those girls in the first place was because I envied them. Clichéd? Yes, undoubtedly, but it also happened to be true.

(*Aside: Still, you may find yourself asking What of Leo's job? What of the contaminated chocolate supply? What of the tattoo on Anya's ankle? What of Nana's health and Natty's nightmares? Just because Annie has a delicious new boyfriend, she can't possibly think that's a good excuse to go around ignoring everything and everyone else in the world.*

The truth is, there were most definitely things that fell through the subway grates, but, at the time, I wasn't paying attention. Even when I consider all that was to happen in the months that followed, I would not take back those dumb and happy, sweet and foggy, endless, numbered days.

Correction: Once, I thought about that tattoo on my ankle. We were in my bedroom, and Win's lips were on it. He said it was "kind of cute," then sang me a song about a tattooed lady.)

XIV. i am forced to turn the other cheek

I HADN'T TALKED TO SCARLET for all of winter break, which was probably the longest we'd gone without communication in the entire history of our friendship. I didn't see her until Fencing our first day back. During stretching, she didn't bring up my relationship with Win, but then, she barely spoke to me. I could tell she was angry and that I was going to have to make amends.

"So," I joked after we'd broken off into pairs. "Maybe you heard? I've gone and got myself a fella."

"Yeah. I felt as if I hadn't seen you in ages, but at least now I know why," Scarlet said, thrusting her foil toward me. "Of course, I wish I hadn't had to read it! Nice pictures, by the way." She thrust her foil at me again, and the movement had more weight behind it than was typical of our bouts.

"Double touch!" I yelled.

"So?"

"So, we each score a point," I told her.

"Oh. How do you know that?" Scarlet was out of breath.

"Because we've been taking fencing for two and a half years."

Scarlet laughed. "I really should learn something about fencing one of these days." She lowered her foil. "Seriously, why didn't you tell me?"

"Because you were busy with the play and your new boyfriend—"

"That's over," Scarlet said. "It was a production romance. At least, that's what he said when he ended it. But that's the life of the theater, I suppose."

I told her I was sorry. "You should have called," I said.

"I wanted to, but by then I'd heard about you and Win, and I was pissed about that, so I didn't. Annie, I wasn't so busy that I wouldn't have wanted to know about you and Win. We ate lunch together every day, and we saw each other at rehearsal every other day, and we rode home on the bus together every day, and we—"

"I know. I'm sorry. I honestly decided I wasn't going to tell anyone. I thought it would make things easier."

"But my point is, you were lying to me every time you saw me. That day outside the supply closet? I totally believed you, and you played me for a fool. And I would never do that to you. You're my best friend."

She was right. I should have told her. "I really am sorry."

Scarlet sighed. "Apology accepted," she said.

As we were changing out of our fencing attire, Scarlet turned to me. "Can I just say? I know your life is difficult, much more difficult than mine has ever been, even when you consider the fact that I can't seem to keep a boyfriend to save my life. But, it's not the easiest thing in the world being your best friend either. And I think I've been there for you through a lot of bad times, haven't I?"

I nodded.

"So, when something good happens to you, I'd like to know about it. I'd like to be there for some of the happy times, too."

Scarlet's words made my cheeks burn with shame. I had behaved thoughtlessly.

When we got to lunch, Win was already at our table. "Gable Arsley's back," he said. Scarlet and I turned to look at Gable. We weren't the only ones looking either.

Gable was waiting in the lunch line in his wheelchair, his backpack draped over one of the handles. He had a glove over the hand with the mangled fingers and a baseball cap pulled low over his still raw-looking face. I watched as Gable struggled to get food on his tray, using only one hand and at a serious height disadvantage. "Why isn't anyone helping him?" Win asked.

"Because he was a bully," I said.

"Because he never had anything nice to say about anyone," Scarlet added. "And he isn't exactly a gentleman either."

"I'd go over, but I don't think the guy would want to see me again after our last meeting," Win said.

"Why should you go?" I asked. "He ratted us out to the whole world."

"We don't know that for certain," Win said.

"And he kind of tried to force me to have sex with him."
Maybe I had seen too many hard things in my life, but I found
Win's sympathy for Gable annoying.

"He's awful, Annie, but I just don't know how he's going
to wheel that chair and carry a tray," Scarlet said. As she said
that, Gable began to wheel himself away from the line with his
tray balanced precariously on his lap. The food slipped over—
coincidentally, it was the same lasagna I'd poured on his head all
those months ago—and the sauce spattered on his pants before
landing on his shoes, one of which must have contained a pros-
thetic foot. Gable yelled a curse word, and I actually heard several people in the cafeteria laugh. The boy—and yes, in that
moment, he was restored to that for me—looked at a complete
loss as to what he should do next.

"Enough," I said. It was starting to feel deeply unchristian
to let him sit in the middle of the cafeteria, and I didn't want my
parents, wherever they were, to have to be ashamed of me. "I'm
going over."

"We'll come with you," Win and Scarlet said.

I stood up from the table. "Arsley, come eat with us!" I called.

For a moment, Gable looked as if he might say something
rude, but then he shook his head and smiled at me. "Promise you
won't try to poison me, Balanchine!" Gable said, sounding like
his old self.

A few people in the cafeteria laughed at his joke.

"I'll be your food tester," Scarlet called out.

"I'm holding you to that," Gable said.

Scarlet walked over to Gable and wheeled him to our table.

Win went to the lunch line and got him another tray of food. I went to the bathroom and used all the quarters Scarlet and I had to get Gable enough wet paper towels to clean himself up.

Once we were seated again, Gable commented, "This is the last place in the world I want to be sitting. With Mobster Daughter, Stupid Fedora, and Lady Drama."

I kept my mouth shut.

"We're thrilled to have you, too," Win said.

Gable struggled to reach his shoes and legs with the paper towels. I had to draw the line at helping clean him up. Luckily, Scarlet volunteered.

"No," Gable said. "It's fine."

"I'm happy to," she said as she bent over to wipe up his shoes.

"It's," I heard him whisper—"embarrassing to be this way."

"No," she said. "It's just life."

I saw him wince as Scarlet blotted a spot on his pant leg. "Are you in much pain?" Scarlet asked.

"Some," he said. "But it's manageable."

"All done," she said brightly.

Gable took Scarlet's hand, and I could feel the hairs on the back of my neck stand up. "Thank you," he said. "Really."

Scarlet pulled her hand away. "You're welcome."

"Hey, Arsley," I said. "You know I'd never let Scarlet date you, right?"

"You aren't her mother," Gable said. "And I wasn't that bad to you."

"Um, you were the worst boyfriend in the world, but let's not go into that." I tried to say this lightly. "We're only letting you sit here because you're gimpy and we feel bad for you. But if you sitting here's gonna lead to you wooing Scarlet, you can go wheel yourself back to the middle of the cafeteria right now."

"You're an ass, Anya," Gable said.

"And you're a sociopath, Gable," I replied.

"Takes one to know one," he said.

I rolled my eyes.

"Honestly, Anya, I was only thanking her," Gable said.

"Well," Win said, "I've got an idea. Let's agree to make this the sort of lunch table where we keep our hands to ourselves."

I didn't see Scarlet again until the bus ride home, though I'd been worrying about her all afternoon. The problem was that Scarlet loved hard-luck cases and wounded things. (Probably one of the reasons why she'd been such a good friend to me and mine.) People like Scarlet tend to get taken advantage of, especially by people like Gable Arsley.

"You know, you can't go out with Gable Arsley," I said as we rode through the park to the east side.

Natty was with us, and she wrinkled her nose and asked, "Why would Scarlet ever go out with him?" Gable had never enjoyed much popularity in my family.

"I wouldn't," Scarlet said. "I just felt bad for him today." Scarlet described to Natty what had happened at lunch.

"Oh," Natty said, "I would have felt awful for him, too."

"That's because you and Scarlet are a couple of softies. Just because he's hurt doesn't mean he's not the same old horrible person inside."

"You either have no faith in me or you think I'm dumb,"

Scarlet said. "I remember what he did to you. And I'm not so desperate that I'd drop all my principles for your one-handed, one-legged, badly disfigured ex-boyfriend!" Scarlet giggled. "Oh, that's awful! I shouldn't be laughing." She covered her mouth.

Natty and I laughed, too.

"You have to admit. It is sort of ridiculous what happened to Gable," Scarlet added.

"It is ridiculous," I replied. My whole life was ridiculous.

"But, for argument's sake," Scarlet said, as the bus reached her stop, "don't you think having such a medical trauma would change a person?"

"*No!*" Natty and I yelled.

"I'm kidding, darlings." Scarlet shook her head. "How can you be so gullible, Annie?" She kissed me on the cheek. "See you tomorrow," she called as she got off the bus.

Once Natty and I were home, Imogen told me that Nana needed me, so I went into her room.

Nana had actually seemed somewhat better in the last couple of weeks. At least, she hadn't mistaken me for my mother.

I bent down to kiss Nana's cheek. There were yellow roses in a turquoise vase on the windowsill. Someone had been by to see her.

"Pretty," I commented.

"Yes, they're not bad. My stepson brought them by today," Nana said. "Take them to your room if you like, Annie. They're wasted on me. They make me think of my funeral, which . . ."

I waited for her to continue, but she didn't. "Imogen said you wanted to see me," I said finally.

"Yes," Nana said. "You must do something for me. Yuri's

son Mickey is getting married next month. You, Leo, and Natty need to go to the wedding on my behalf."

Family weddings were not my favorite. And Mickey was getting married? It might have been my imagination but I was reasonably certain he had been flirting with me the last time we'd met. "Where is this wedding?"

"At the Balanchine compound in Westchester."

Even though it was just a bunch of houses and stables and a mostly dried-up lake, I hated that place. Natty and I had lived there in the weeks after my father had been killed and it only had bad associations for me.

"Do we have to go?" I whined.

"Is it such a hardship? I wish I could go, but I don't have legs to take me there. Besides, you can bring your little boyfriend . . ." she said mischievously.

"How do you know about him?" I asked.

"I still have ears. Your sister told me. She thinks you're going to marry him, but I said that my Anya is far too young and far too practical for marriage, no matter how head over heels she is."

"Natty is absurd."

"So you will go to the wedding?"

"If I must," I said.

"Good. Bring your boyfriend to meet me someday, too. Maybe the day you go to the wedding? Yes, it's settled." Nana nodded, then reached for my hand. "I feel clearer lately," she said.

"That's good."

"But I'm not sure how long it will last. And I want to set this house in order," she continued. "You are sixteen years old now?"

217

I nodded.

"Which means if I died tomorrow, your brother would become your guardian."

"But you won't die," I reminded her. "The machines will keep you alive until I'm old enough."

"Machines fail, Anyaschka. And sometimes—"

I cut her off. "I don't want to discuss this!"

"You must listen, Anya. You are the strongest one, and you need to hear. I need to know that we have discussed these matters. Though Leo will technically be the guardian, it has been arranged with Mr. Kipling and his new associate—I am forgetting his name—that you will be the only one with access to the money. This will make it so that Leo cannot make any decisions alone. Do you understand?"

I nodded impatiently. "Yes, of course."

"Your brother may be angry when he finds out, and I am sorry for that. He is damaged, but he is not without pride. Still, it is the only thing to be done. The real estate will be placed in a trust that stipulates that it cannot be sold until you are eighteen, too. And when you turn eighteen, guardianship of Natty will transfer from Leo to you as well."

"Fine, fine. But the doctors say the machines will keep you alive until I'm eighteen, if not longer. I don't know why we have to discuss this now."

"Because life can be unexpected, Anya. Because lately I have noticed increasingly long periods where I am not myself. You cannot say that you don't notice these, too?"

I admitted that I had noticed.

"Well, I am sorry for anything I may have said to you during these times. I love you, Anya. I love each of my grandchildren, but you most of all. You remind me of your father. You remind me of me."

I didn't know what to say.

"The loss of one's body is one thing. The loss of one's mind is more than can be tolerated. Remember that, my dear one." Then she told me to take a bar of chocolate, and as I always did, I went into her closet and pretended to take a bar, although there hadn't been any chocolate in Nana's closet for months. This time I was surprised to find a single bar in the safe. Uncle Yuri must have brought it.

"Share it with your new boyfriend!" she called as I closed the door.

In my bedroom, I found myself stroking the bar of chocolate. It was Balanchine Special Dark, my favorite. Daddy used to melt it down to make hot chocolate for Natty, Leo, and me. He would heat milk over the stove top, then he'd chop up the chocolate bar into small pieces so that it would melt into the milk. I considered going into the kitchen to make some myself, but decided against it. Even though I had heard that the supply was clean again, I had lost my taste for chocolate in the months since I'd been arrested.

The doorbell rang so I went to answer it. I looked through the peephole, and there was Win.

"Come in," I told him. Out of habit, I looked around before I kissed him.

"What's that?" he asked.

I was still holding the candy bar and I told him how Nana had given it to me and how she always told me to share it with someone I loved.

"So?" he said.

"Oh no. Definitely not gonna happen." Had he already forgotten the tribulations of the last boyfriend I shared chocolate with?

"Fine," he said. "Besides, I tried chocolate once and I didn't really like it."

I rolled my eyes. "What kind did you try?"

He named a brand which was pretty much the bottom of the barrel quality-wise. Daddy used to have a name for that stuff: rat turd. Daddy had been very particular about his chocolate. "That's not even chocolate," I told Win. "It barely has any cacao in it."

"So, give me some of the real stuff then," he said.

"I would but I promised your father I'd keep you out of the way of illegal activity." I slipped the bar into the pocket of my cardigan and then I took his hand and led him into the living room. "So, I need to ask a favor of you." I told him about the family wedding in Tarrytown.

"No," he said. He smiled and crossed his hands over his knees.

"No?"

"That's what I said, isn't it?"

"Well, why not?"

"Because I still haven't gotten over your rejection of my invitation to the Fall Formal and I'm a person who holds a grudge. Am I meant to do everything you say, Anya? If I did, wouldn't you lose respect for me?"

He had a point, I suppose. "You seem to have made up your mind."

"Yes, I have." Then Win laughed. "I'm disappointed! Aren't you even going to try to reason me into it? Aren't you going to try to make me an offer I can't refuse?"

"It's not going to be very fun and I barely want to go myself," I said.

"Is this your pitch?"

"My family is a bunch of hooligans," I continued. "One of my cousins will probably get superdrunk and end the evening by trying to touch my boob. I'm just hoping no one tries to touch Natty's or I'll seriously have to deck someone."

"I'll go," he said. "But I want to try your chocolate first."

"Are those your terms?"

"It's your family business, isn't it? I can't go to this wedding without being informed, can I?"

"Well played, Win." I stood up. "Follow me."

I set rice milk on the stove top to heat. I took the chocolate out of my pocket, then I checked the date just to make sure it wasn't from last fall. I unwrapped the silver lining and smelled it to confirm. (Did Fretoxin even have a scent?) I lowered the heat once the milk began to boil, then added a little bit of vanilla and sugar, stirring the milk until the sugar dissolved. I chopped up the chocolate into fine pieces and whisked it through the hot milk until the chocolate was more or less melted. Finally, I ladled the mixture into two cups and sprinkled cinnamon over the top of each. Daddy had always made it look so easy.

I set one cup in front of Win. He moved to pick it up, but I pulled it back. "Last chance to change your mind."

He shook his head.

"Aren't you worried about ending up like Gable Arsley?"

"No." He drank at an even pace until he finished. Then he set down the cup and didn't say anything.

"Well?" I asked.

"You're right. It's definitely not what I had before."

"But did you like it?"

"I'm not sure," he said. "Let me have yours."

I pushed my cup over to him. He drank more slowly this time, contemplatively, even. (Is it possible to drink contemplatively?) "It's not what I expected it would be. It's not sweet. It's too substantial to be called sweet. It's probably not to everyone's taste, but the more I drink it, the more I like it, I think. I can see why they banned this. It's very . . . intoxicating."

I walked over to his side of the table and sat in his lap. And then I kissed him. I ran my tongue over his lips, and I could taste the cinnamon. "Do you ever wonder if the only reason you like me is because it irritates your father?" I asked.

"No," he said. "No, you're the only one who wonders that. I like you because you are brave and far too substantial to ever be called sweet."

It was a ridiculous thing to say, but nonetheless, I felt my insides becoming warm and I knew I was probably flushed. I wanted to take off my sweater. I wanted to take off other things. I wanted to take things off him.

I wanted him.

I wanted him, but I couldn't.

I got off of his lap. Though the kitchen was sweltering, I re-tied and tightened the belt of my boiled-wool cardigan. Then I pushed up my sleeves and went over to the sink. I began to wash out the pan I'd used to heat the milk. I must have used three times the amount of water that the job required, but I needed to steady myself.

He came up behind me and set his hand on my shoulder. I jumped, I was still so wound up. "Annie, what's wrong?" he asked.

"I don't want to go to Hell," I said.

"Me neither," he said. "And I don't want you to go there either."

"But lately, when I'm with you . . . I find myself rationalizing things. And we haven't even known each other that long, Win."

Win nodded. He took a dish towel that was hanging over the oven-door handle. "Here," he said. "I'll dry that for you."

I handed him the pan. Pan-less, I felt more vulnerable. I missed having a weapon.

"Anya, I'm not going to lie. I'd really like to sleep with you. I think about it. The possibility of it, I mean. I think about the possibility of it fondly and often. But I'm not going to force you to do anything."

"It's not you I'm worried about, Win! It's me!" It was embarrassing to talk about how much I feared losing control of myself when I was around him. I felt feral, savage, violent even, unlike myself. It disturbed me and shamed me. I hadn't been to confession in months.

"I'm not a virgin, Annie. Do you think that means I'm going to Hell?" he asked.

"No, it's more complicated than that."

"Explain it, then."

223

"You'll think it's stupid. You'll think I'm provincial, super-stitious."

"No, I could never think that. I love you, Annie."

I looked at him and though I wasn't sure he really knew what love was—how could he? His life had been too easy—I decided that I trusted him. "When my father died, I made a deal with God that if He just kept all of us safe, I'd be good. I'd be better than good. I'd be pious. I'd honor Him. I'd be in control of myself and everything else."

"You are good, Annie. No one can say you haven't been good," Win said. "You're practically perfect."

"No, I'm so not perfect. I lose my temper all the time. I think bad thoughts about almost everyone I know. But I try my best. And I couldn't say that anymore, if . . ."

Win nodded. "I understand." He was still holding the dried pan, so he handed it to me. His smile was a bit lopsided. "I won't let you sleep with me, no matter how much you're begging me to," he joked.

"Now you're making fun of me."

"No, I'd never," Win said. "I take you and all things related to you very seriously."

"You're not being serious now."

"I assure you, I'm being deathly serious. Go ahead and try to sleep with me right now. Do it. Even if you stripped down to nothing, I'd push you away like you were on fire." There was still mirth in his voice. "From now on, we're in one of those old books. You can kiss me, but that's it."

"I don't think I like you right now," I said.

"Good. Then the plan's working."

Win had to get home, so I walked him to the door.

I leaned over to kiss him, and he pulled back and offered me his hand. "Only on the hand from now on," he said.

"You're being extremely annoying."

I kissed his hand and then he kissed mine. He pulled me close so that his lips were near my right ear. "You know how we could solve all this?" he whispered. "We really could get married."

"Stop saying that! You sound absurd, and I don't even think you mean it. Besides, I'd never marry you," I told him. "I'm sixteen, and you're a slut, and you can't stop saying preposterous things!"

"True," he admitted. He kissed me on the lips and then I closed the door.

I arranged for Imogen to stay with Nana while the rest of us went to the wedding.

Win came to the house so we could all take the train together. Before we left, I asked him if he wouldn't mind meeting my grandmother. Even though I was fairly over-the-moon about Win at that point in time, I was still self-conscious introducing people to Nana. Her behavior was erratic to say the least and though my family was used to her appearance, she was more than a bit ghoulish (bedridden, mostly bald, bloodshot eyes, yellowish-green skin, rotten-smelling) to those who didn't know her. I wasn't embarrassed by her, but I felt protective of her. I didn't want strange eyes on her. I warned Win what to expect before we went in.

I knocked on the door. "Come in, Anya," Imogen whispered. "She told me to wake her before you left. Wake up, Galina. It's Annie."

My grandmother woke. She coughed for a while and then Imogen slipped a straw into her mouth. I looked over at Win to see if he was repulsed by poor Nana, but his eyes betrayed nothing. They looked, if anything, as kind as usual, and slightly concerned.

"Hi, Nana," I said. "We're about to leave for the wedding."

Nana nodded.

"This is my boyfriend, Win," I said. "You said you wanted to meet him."

"Ah yes." Nana looked Win up and down. "I approve," she said finally. "I approve of your looks, I mean. I certainly hope there is more to you than your pretty face. This"—she nodded toward me—"this one is a very good girl, and she deserves more than a pretty face."

"I agree," Win said. "Nice to meet you, too."

"Is that what you're wearing to the wedding?" Nana asked me.

I nodded. I had on a dark gray suit, which had been my mother's. Win had brought me a white orchid, and I had pinned it to my lapel.

"It's a bit severe, but the cut flatters your figure. You look lovely, Anyaschka. I like the flower."

"Win gave it to me."

"Hmmph," she said. "OMG, the young man has taste." She turned her attention to Win. "Do you know what OMG stands for, young man?"

Win shook his head.

Nana looked at me. "Do you?"

Scarlet's word. "Amazing or something," I replied. "I always meant to ask you."

"Oh my God," Nana said. "Life used to move much more quickly when I was a girl. We needed to abbreviate just to keep up."

"OMG," Win said.

"Would you believe that I looked like Anya once upon a time?"

"Yes," Win said. "I can see that."

"She was prettier," I said.

Nana told him to come closer, and Win obeyed. She whispered something in his ear, and Win nodded. "Yes," he said. "Yes, of course."

"Have a good time, Anyaschka. Dance with your pretty boyfriend for me, and give everyone my best."

I leaned down to kiss her on the cheek. She grabbed my hand and said, "You have been a wonderful granddaughter. An honor to your parents. God sees everything, my darling. Even and maybe especially what the world does not. I wish that I could have been stronger for you. Always remember that you are powerful beyond measure. This power is your birthright. Your only birthright! Do you understand? I need to know that you understand!"

Her eyes were teary, so I told her that I did understand though, in point of fact, I didn't. Her speech seemed rambling and incoherent, and I assumed she was beginning another one of her less lucid periods. I didn't want her to slap me in front of Win and Imogen. "I love you, Nana," I said.

"I love you, too," she said, and then she started to cough. The coughs seemed more violent than usual, almost as if she were choking. "Go!" she managed to yell.

Imogen massaged my grandmother's chest with her palm, and Nana's coughing subsided somewhat.

I asked Imogen if she needed my help.

"We're fine, Annie. Her lungs have been bothering her from the cold. It's very ordinary for someone in your grandmother's condition." Imogen continued to work on Nana's chest.

"Get out of here!" Nana yelled between coughs.

I grabbed Win's hand and we left.

I whispered to him, "I'm sorry. Sometimes she gets confused."

Win said he understood and that there was no need to apologize. "She's old."

I nodded. "It's hard to imagine ever being that age."

Win asked what year she was born, and I told him 1995, that she'd be eighty-eight that spring. "Before the turn of the century," Win said. "Not many people that age left."

I thought of Nana as a little girl and as a teenager and as a young woman. I wondered what type of clothes she wore, what books she read, what boys she liked. I doubt she thought she'd outlive her only biological son, that someday she'd be an old woman in a bed—powerless and confused and a little grotesque. "I don't ever want to be that old," I said.

"Yes," Win agreed. "Let's stay young forever. Young, stupid, and pretty. Sounds like a plan, don't you think?"

The wedding was elaborate as was typical of my family. Golden table linens, a band, and someone had even managed to obtain (read: bribe someone for) additional flower and meat vouchers for the occasion. The bride's dress was too big through the waist, but her veil was intricately embroidered and even looked new. Her name was Sophia Bitter, and I knew nothing about her. In terms of looks, it's mean to say, but she was remarkable only in her plainness. She had limp brown hair, a long horsey nose, and she couldn't have been much older than me. When she said "I do," it was with an accent of some kind. Her mother and sisters wept for the entire length of the ceremony.

Natty was seated at the kids' table among our cousins. Leo was placed with several of his colleagues from the Pool and their wives and girlfriends. Win and I were at a table of loose ends— not a family table, not children, just people who didn't fit in anywhere else.

Win went to get drinks, and since my shoes were my mother's and thus a size and a half too tight for my freakish size ten feet, I decided to stay behind. A man across the table from me waved, and I waved back, though I wasn't sure who he was. He was Asian and in his twenties. He was probably a member of another chocolate family.

He walked around the table and sat next to me. He was very handsome, with longish black hair that kept falling into his eyes. He spoke English with a bit of a British accent though he wasn't British. "You don't remember me, do you? I met you and your sister when you were children. Your father had a meeting with my father at our country house in Kyoto. I showed you our gardens. You liked my cat."

"Snowball," I said. "And you are Yuji Ono. Of course I remember you." Yuji shook my hand. He was missing the pinkie on his right hand, but the rest of his fingers were long and extremely cold. "Your hands are like ice."

"You know what they say. Cold hands. Warm heart," Yuji said. "Or is it the reverse?"

The summer before I turned nine, the summer before Daddy died, he had taken us with him on business to Japan. (This was before international travel had become so difficult because of both cost and worries about disease.) Daddy very much believed in the benefits of travel for young people, and he also hadn't wanted to leave us alone after my mother's murder. One of the people we visited was Yuji Ono's father, who was the head of the Ono Sweets Company and the most powerful chocolate dealer in Asia. Incidentally, I had had a huge crush on Yuji Ono though he was seven years older than me. Fifteen at the time; now, I suppose, twenty-three.

"How is your father?" I asked.

"He passed away." Yuji lowered his eyes.

"I'm sorry. I hadn't heard."

"Yes. It was very tragic, though he wasn't murdered like yours. Brain cancer," Yuji said. "It seems you don't follow these things, Anya, so I'll tell you. I am the head of Ono Sweets now."

"Congratulations," I said, though I wasn't at all sure if this was the right thing to say.

"Yes, it was much for me to learn in a very short time. But I was luckier than you. My father was still alive to teach me." Yuji smiled at me. He had a sweet smile. There was the slightest gap between his front two teeth, and it made him look more boyish than he was.

"You came a long way for a Balanchine family wedding," I observed.

"I had other business, and I am a friend of the bride as well," he said, and then he changed the subject. "Dance with me, Anya."

I looked over to the drinks line—Win was about halfway through. "I'm here with someone," I said.

Yuji laughed. "No, I didn't mean that way. I'm practically married myself, and you're far too young for me. Forgive me, but I still see you as the little girl you were, and I feel almost paternal toward you, I suppose. I think my father would want me to dance with you. Your boyfriend can't possibly object to old friends like me." He offered me his hand, and I took it.

The band was playing a slow number. Though I didn't feel in the least romantic toward him, dancing with Yuji was no hardship either. He was a good dancer and I told him so. He said that his father had made him take lessons when he was a kid. "When I was a child, it seemed an incredible waste of time," he said, "but now I'm glad for the skill."

"You mean because women like it?" I asked.

A tap on my shoulder. I expected Win, but it was my cousin Jacks. "Do you mind if I cut in?" he asked Yuji.

"It's up to Anya," Yuji replied.

Jacks was flushed and his eyes were overly bright. I very much hoped he wasn't drunk. Still, I decided to consent because it seemed that if I didn't my cousin would make a scene. "Yes, it's fine," I said.

Jacks took my hand, and Yuji left. His palm was damp and a bit greasy even. "Do you know who you were dancing with?" Jacks asked me.

"Yes, of course," I said. "Yuji Ono. I've known him for years."

"Well, then, do you know what they're saying about him?" Jacks asked me.

I shrugged.

"There are people who think he's the one who orchestrated the contamination of the Balanchine chocolate supply."

I considered this. "What would be his interest in doing that?"

Jacks rolled his eyes. "You're a smart girl, Anya. Figure it out."

"You were so keen to cut in on me. Why don't you just tell me yourself?"

"The Kid—that's what they call Yuji Ono, Junior, to distinguish him from Yuji Ono, Senior—the Kid's eager to prove himself. Everyone thinks the Balanchine organization is weak. What better way for the Kid to make his mark than by destroying the Balanchine business in North America?"

I nodded. "If people think that, why's he at the wedding then?"

"He says he didn't have anything to do with the contamination, of course. His presence is a gesture meant to show that we believe that, too. I've got to tell you, Anya. It doesn't exactly look good for you to be dancing with him, though."

First, I laughed because I wanted him to know that his opinion didn't matter to me. Then I asked him, "Why?"

"People will think you've made some sort of alliance with him."

"Who are these *people*, Jacks? The same people who rose to my defense when I was hauled into prison a few short months ago? Tell these people that Yuji Ono has been my friend for years and I'll dance with who I like."

"You're making a spectacle of yourself," Jacks said. "Everyone was watching you. You might think that you're unimportant but you're still Leonyd Balanchine's oldest child and you mean something to these people."

"That is unbelievably rude! What about my brother, Leo? Doesn't he count? You're the one who's always telling me not to underestimate him."

"I'm sorry, Anya. I didn't mean it that way. I—"

At that point, another tap on my shoulder: this time, Win wanting to cut in, thank God.

I shrugged Jacks off and gladly moved over to Win. The other song had ended, and a slower one had begun. I hadn't even noticed because I'd been distracted by my argument with Jacks.

"I didn't think you liked to dance," Win said.

"I don't." I was annoyed over Jacks's comments and I wasn't in the mood for conversation.

"You're very popular," Win continued. "When you were dancing with that black-haired man, I wondered if I should be jealous."

"I hate these people," I said as I buried my head in Win's chest. His coat smelled like cigarettes. Although Win didn't smoke (no one really smoked anymore because of how much water it took to grow tobacco), the coat must have once belonged to someone who had. The scent made me a little sick but I still kind of liked it. "I hate being dragged into this. I wish I had never been born. Or that I had been born someone else entirely."

"Don't say that," Win said. "I'm glad you were born."

"And my shoes hurt," I grumbled.

Win laughed gently. "Should I carry you?"

"No, just don't make me dance anymore." The song was over, so we went back to the table. Yuji Ono wasn't there, and someone else occupied what I'd thought was his seat.

Because we could not make it back to the city by curfew, we had arranged to stay the night in Tarrytown in one of the carriage houses on the compound property. I bunked with Natty, and Win was meant to share a room with my brother. Leo went to hang out with Jacks and some of the other unmarried guys from the Pool, so I put Natty to bed, then went to keep Win company. Win was something of an insomniac so I knew he'd be awake. I was the opposite, by the way. I pretty much always fell asleep as soon as my head hit the pillow. And, if I hadn't felt bad for dragging Win to this awful wedding, I would have happily curled up next to Natty and gone right to sleep. The combination of the travel and my uncomfortable shoes had exhausted me.

It might seem silly but I made sure to wear my pajamas and a bathrobe I found hanging in the closet. Despite our multiple conversations about waiting, Win and I had had more than a few close calls. So, bathrobe and pajamas it was.

Win was lying on the bed, strumming an out-of-tune guitar he'd found on the premises. It was missing a string and there was a hole in the side. He smiled when he saw me in my getup. "You look cute," he said. I sat in the only chair in the room. I curled my knees up to my chest and rested my head on them. I yawned. Win suggested I lie down on the bed, but I shook my head no. Win continued to strum the guitar, and the radiator came on. The heat made me even sleepier, but also, um, hot. I took off the bathrobe.

"This is ridiculous. Use the bed. I won't try anything, I swear," Win said. "I'll wake you when Leo gets back."

I nodded. I lay down on the other side of the bed, and I drifted off.

An hour or so later, I woke. Win was asleep with the guitar across his chest. I picked up the guitar and laid it down on the floor. And I couldn't help myself. I kissed him.

He stirred, then woke, then kissed me back.

I wanted to feel my skin against his skin, so I reached my hands up under his T-shirt.

And before I knew it, my pajamas were off. This happened so quickly that in retrospect, it seemed silly that I had thought pajamas would be a significant barrier to anything. And I was asking him if he had something. Me, Anya Balanchine, mostly good Catholic girl. I could scarcely believe the words had come out of my mouth.

Yes, he said, he did. "But only if you're sure, Annie?"

My body was, even if my mind wasn't. "Yes," I sputtered. "Yes, I am. Just put it on already."

And then there was a scream in the other room. Natty was having another nightmare.

"I have to go," I said, pulling myself off him.

Because there was no time, I left my pajamas on the floor and threw on the bathrobe.

As I walked to the other room, I felt hot and flushed and altogether ashamed that I had let it get so far. That scream had saved me, really.

Natty was already awake when I got there. Her face was pink and tearstained.

I took her in my arms. "What was it this time?" I asked.

"Nana," Natty whispered. "I was in the apartment, and Nana was dead. Her face was gray like stone. And when I went to touch her, her fingers started to fall off, and then she was just sand."

The content of this nightmare was not unique, and though a large part of my brain was busy thinking about what had almost happened with Win, I was still able to comfort Natty. "Nana *will* die someday, Natty," I said. "We have to be prepared."

"I know that!" Natty yelled. "But Nana dying was only the beginning. When I went into your room, you were lying on your bed, and your skin was gray like Nana's. And then I went into Leo's, and he was the same way. I was the only one left." Natty began to weep.

"Leo and I aren't going to die, Natty. Not anytime soon, at least. We're young and healthy."

"So were Daddy and Mommy," Natty replied.

I pulled Natty even closer to me, and Win seemed miles away. "Our lives won't be anything like theirs. You'll see. Everything I do, every thought I have, is about protecting us, and especially you, from that sort of life."

Natty nodded though her eyes seemed doubtful.

I tucked her into bed. As I was about to get in next to her,

I remembered that I wasn't wearing my pajamas. I would have to sleep in this moth-eaten flannel bathrobe. I hoped I wouldn't get body lice or something awful. Then again, maybe that would be a good lesson about remembering to keep my pajamas on.

Uncharacteristically, I couldn't get to sleep. I lay awake thinking about my sister, and whether I should arrange for her to talk to someone. And then I thought about what Win and I had been doing (or about to do) in the moments before Natty's nightmare. Though I was basically a good Catholic, I didn't consider myself a spiritual person. Still, I couldn't help but wonder if Natty's scream had been a sign of some sort. God, or maybe my dead parents, telling me to stop. Or was this reading too much into things? Natty had nightmares regularly, after all, and they didn't necessarily mean anything. And who is to say I wouldn't have stopped things with Win myself? Win and I had been nearly as close before, and I had always put the brakes on without need of any higher intervention.

And yet the timing certainly gave me pause.

My skin was itchy from the bathrobe. For a while, I tried to ignore the itch, but then I couldn't help it. I gave in. I scratched my calf until it bled.

I heard a gentle knock at the door: Win. He was carrying my pajamas, which he had folded up. Win was gentlemanly that way. Gable, for instance, would have thrown my discarded clothes at me in a rumpled ball.

So as not to wake Natty, I went out to the hallway. "Thank you," I said. "I'm sorry," I added.

Win shook his head.

"No. I *am* sorry. I don't want to keep doing this to you. I want . . ." It was embarrassing to say this next part out loud. "The thing is, my body and my mind don't always agree on what to want."

Win kissed my cheek. "Well, normally, that would be incredibly annoying, but luckily for you, I'm crazy about you."

For now, I thought.

"What? You're furrowing your little brow. What're you thinking?"

"For now," I said. "You're crazy about me for now."

"Forever," he insisted. "I mean it."

Win was probably the nicest boy I had ever known, and it was a nice thing to say. Though I didn't believe him, I knew he believed himself and I didn't want to hurt his feelings. I tried not to let the doubt show on my face.

I kissed him on the lips, making sure to keep my tongue in my mouth where it belonged. I closed the door and returned to the room I was sharing with Natty. I took off the bathrobe and slipped into my pajamas. Then I got back into bed next to my sister. She cuddled into my side and placed her arm around my waist.

"Did I interrupt something with you and Win?" she whispered.

"Nothing important," I told her. I decided that it hadn't been.

"I do like him," Natty said dreamily. "If I ever have a boyfriend, which seems pretty doubtful, I'd want him to be exactly like Win."

"I'm glad you approve," I replied. "And for the record, Natty, I'm pretty sure you'll have a million boyfriends some day."

"A million?" she asked.

"Well, as many as you want."

"I'd settle for one," she said. "Especially if he were as nice as yours."

XV. we mourn again; i learn the definition of *internecine*

WE DIDN'T GET BACK TO THE CITY until Sunday after lunch. Win went to his apartment straight from the train station—his apartment was fairly close to Grand Central—and Leo, Natty, and I made our way back to ours. I was eager to be home. I was sleepy and hungry and I had a ton of schoolwork. Besides which, being away always made me anxious.

As the weather was unseasonably warm for February, Leo and Natty wanted to walk from the train station instead of taking the bus. I had wanted to take the bus in order to expedite the trip, but I had been overruled.

We were nearly halfway home when I began to feel an inexplicable and almost painful need to be back in the apartment. I quickened my pace.

"Slow down," Natty called. "You're walking too fast for us."

I turned my head over my shoulder and suggested we race. We had just reached the anachronistically named Museum Mile, which, along the park side, was a fairly straight shot back to our apartment.

"Come back, Annie," Leo said. "It's not fair if you have a head start."

I backtracked to where Natty and Leo were standing.

"On your mark," I said, "get set, go!"

Natty, Leo, and I raced up the sidewalk. Leo was in the lead, with Natty not far behind. I was last but I liked that position. Easier to keep my eye on my siblings.

Though we were panting and red faced, we got home in less than ten minutes. The exertion had quelled my anxiety, too.

"Take the stairs?" Leo joked.

"Good one, Leo," I said, pushing the elevator button.

In contrast to the mild day outside, it was unusually cold inside the apartment. A draft was coming from the living room, so I went to close the windows. In the living room, I found Imogen seated on the sofa and the disquiet I had felt earlier immediately returned.

"Something's wrong," I said.

Imogen shook her head. "Where are Natty and Leo?"

"In their rooms," I told her.

"Sit down," she said, and I knew this instruction could only mean one thing.

"I'd rather stand," I insisted. "If you're going to tell me Nana is dead, I'd rather stand."

"She died last night. There was a power failure, and the backup generator didn't work for whatever reason. By the time the power came back on, it was too late. I'm sure she didn't suffer much."

241

"How do you know?" I asked.

"How do I know what?" Imogen replied.

"That she didn't suffer much! How can you possibly know?" Imogen said nothing.

"You don't know! Maybe it was horrible! While you slept, maybe she choked and gasped and her skin felt like fire and she thought her eyes would pop out of her head and she prayed for it all to be over . . ."

Imogen reached out to put her hand on my arm. "Please, Annie, don't do this."

"Don't touch me!" I pulled my arm away. I could feel my old rage returning. I slipped into it easily, like a tailored suit. "Your whole job was to make sure that those machines kept running! You've failed miserably! You're a failure and an idiot and a murderer!"

"No, Annie. Never," Imogen protested.

Leo came into the room. "Annie, why are you yelling at Imogen?" he asked.

But I couldn't be bothered to address my brother. I was in that angry fugue state. "Maybe someone paid you to unplug Nana's machine?"

Imogen began to cry. "Annie, why would I ever do that?"

"How should I know? People will do all sorts of things for money. And my family has many enemies."

"How can you say these things to me? I loved Galina just as I love you and your entire family. It was her time. She told me as much. I know she told you, too. Or at least, she tried to."

"Nana's dead?" Leo asked in a panicked voice. "Are you saying that Nana is dead?"

"Yes," I said. "She died last night. Imogen let her die."

"That isn't true," Imogen replied.

"Get out of our house," I ordered her. "And don't ever come back."

"Please, Anya. Let me help. You have to make arrangements for the body. You shouldn't have to do this alone," Imogen pleaded.

"Just get out," I said.

She stood there, but didn't move.

"Leave already!"

Imogen nodded. "Her body is still in her bed," she said before she finally left.

Leo was sobbing quietly, and I went up to him. I put my hand on his shoulder. "Don't cry, Leo."

"I'm crying because I'm sad. Not because I'm weak or stupid."

"Of course you are. I'm sorry."

Leo continued to cry, and I said nothing. In point of fact, I felt nothing except the embers of my rage mixed with anxiety over what my next steps should be. At some point, Leo began speaking again but I was so distracted that I had to ask him to repeat what he'd said. He had wanted to know if I'd meant everything I'd said to Imogen.

I shrugged. "I don't know what I meant. I'm going in to look at Nana. Do you want to come?"

Leo shook his head.

I opened the door to Nana's room. Nana's eyes were closed and her gnarled hands were laid peacefully across her chest. I assumed Imogen had done that.

"Oh, Nana." I took a deep breath and kissed her wrinkled cheek.

I became aware of the sound of whispering. Nana and I weren't alone. Natty was kneeling by the window at the side of the bed, her head bowed in prayer.

Natty raised her head. "I just came in to tell her about the wedding . . . And . . . She's dead." Her voice was small and childish, still barely above a whisper.

"I know."

"It's like my dream," Natty said.

"No one's turned to sand that I can see," I said.

"Don't make fun," Natty admonished me. "I'm serious."

"I'm not making fun. We all died in your dream, didn't we? And in reality, Nana is the only one who's dead. You knew this would happen someday. I told you as much last night." And in that moment, I began to realize just how ridiculous and wrong the things I'd said to Imogen had been. I regretted my behavior and I wondered why my first response to anything was rage. Sadness, worry, fear—all of those emotions came out as rage for me. Maybe if I'd been braver in that moment, I would have cried.

"Yes, I knew she would die," Natty admitted, "but part of me never really believed it."

I suggested that we pray for Nana together. I took Natty's hand and kneeled down by the side of the bed.

"Say something out loud for her," Natty implored me. "That thing they read at Daddy's funeral."

"You remember that?"

Natty nodded. "I remember a lot of things."

"Jesus said to her, 'I am the resurrection and the life; he who believes in Me, will live even if he dies, and everyone who lives and believes in Me will never die . . .'" I stopped. "I'm sorry, Natty, that's all I know by heart."

"No, that was it," she said. "That was enough. It's so beautiful, isn't it? And it means she isn't really dead. Not in any important way at least. It makes me feel so much less afraid somehow. Even less alone." There were tears in her eyes.

"You aren't alone, Natty. I'll always be here for you. You know that." I wiped the tears from her cheeks.

"But, Annie, what will we do now? You aren't old enough to take care of us yet. Will Leo, then?"

"Leo will be our guardian, yes. And I'll go on taking care of everything else just as I always have. As far as you're concerned, nothing will change, I swear." This, I realized, was how parents ended up lying to children. They promised certainties when all they had were pretty speculations. I prayed to God this would go down smoothly. "In fact, I should really go call Mr. Kipling right now to begin making arrangements." There was so much to do. If I didn't begin right away, the burden of it all might paralyze me. I took Natty by the hand and led her out of the room. I closed Nana's door gently behind us. I went into my bedroom and immediately picked up the phone.

Mr. Kipling had only recently returned to work after his heart attack. "Anya," he said, "I have Mr. Green on the phone. He'll be listening in from now on. It's a precaution I'm taking in case I should have a recurrence, though I have no reason to believe this will be so."

"Hello, Simon," I said.

"Hello, Ms. Balanchine," Simon Green replied.

"What can we do for you today?" Mr. Kipling asked.

"Galina is dead." I kept my voice cool.

"I'm sorry for your loss," Mr. Kipling said.

"I am, too," Simon Green added.

"She was very old." It had already begun to feel as if I were speaking of someone I had barely known.

"While I'm very sorry for your loss, I also want to reassure you, Anya. As you are well aware, everything has been arranged to make this transition as simple as possible for you and your siblings." Mr. Kipling then said that he and Simon Green would come immediately to the apartment. "Is Leo with you?"

"Yes," I said.

"Good. He'll need to be in on these discussions."

"I'll make sure he stays put. Should I call the funeral home?"

"No, no," Mr. Kipling said. "We'll arrange that."

I hung up the phone.

I had felt as if there were a million things I needed to do, and yet, for the moment, it seemed there was nothing but to wait for Mr. Kipling and Simon Green to show up.

I wanted something to do.

I thought about calling Win, but the truth was, I didn't really want him around. This was a time for family.

I lay down on my bed.

Oh, Nana. How many times had I wished that your suffering would be over, that you would die. And how many times had I prayed for the opposite, that you might live forever or at least until I was old enough to be Natty's legal guardian.

And here it was, that day. And I felt nothing except perhaps guilty that I felt nothing. Maybe I had seen too many hard things in my life. But then, so had Leo and Natty, and they both had cried. What was wrong with me that I could not muster a tear for my grandmother, who I had loved and who I know had loved me?

The doorbell rang, which was just as well. I didn't wish to continue along this line of thought anymore.

I went to answer it: Mr. Kipling and Simon Green, of course. They had made exceptionally good time.

Mr. Kipling, who I once would have described as stout, had lost a great deal of weight since his heart attack. In his present manifestation, he looked a bit like a teddy bear with the stuffing removed.

"Annie," said Mr. Kipling. "Again, I am so very sorry for your loss. Galina was a magnificent woman."

We went to the living room to sit down. Leo was still there. He hadn't moved since Imogen had left.

"Leo," I said.

He looked at me blankly. His eyes were nearly swollen shut from crying. He didn't remotely resemble the confident man I'd seen in the last several months, and this worried me. Come on, Leo, I thought.

I continued. "Mr. Kipling and Mr. Green are here to discuss what happens now that Nana has passed."

Leo stood. He blew his nose on an already soggy handkerchief, then said, "Okay, I'll just go to my room."

"No," I said. "You need to stay for this. You're a very important part of everything that's about to happen. Come and sit next to me."

Leo nodded. He pulled his shoulders back and walked over

to the sofa and sat down. Simon Green and Mr. Kipling sat in the two armchairs across the coffee table from us.

First, we made plans for Nana's funeral. This was simple as Nana had left clear written instructions: *No open casket, no expensive coffin, no chemical preservation, no fancy marker, though I would like to be next to my son in the family plot in Brooklyn.*

"Do you want there to be an autopsy?" Simon Green asked me.

"Simon, I don't think that's necessary," Mr. Kipling disciplined. "Galina had been sick for many years."

"Yes, well . . ." Simon Green said. "What did lead up to her ultimate passing?"

I described what Imogen had said about the power failure.

"Why didn't the backup generator come on?" Simon Green persisted.

"I don't know," I said.

"You trust this Imogen, right?" Simon Green asked. "No one could have gotten to her. Maybe paid her off or something? Someone who might have had a good reason for wanting Galina Balanchine dead."

"Who would have wanted Nana dead?" Leo asked, his voice a bit quivery.

"Simon, you're being absurd and inappropriate." Mr. Kipling shot Simon Green a warning look. "Imogen Goodfellow has worked for this family for years. She is as loyal and fine a worker as there is. As for the circumstances of Galina's death? There is no mystery here. She was incredibly sick. It's amazing she endured as long as she did. In the weeks leading up to her death, she and I had had several discussions about the inevitability of her condition and she even confessed to me that she suspected her time would be soon, that she had even begun to hope for such a time."

"She told me the same thing," I said. I looked at Leo. "She did."

Leo nodded. Then he nodded again. Finally, he said, "But it wouldn't hurt anything to have a . . ." When Leo was upset, he sometimes lost language. "What he said"—he pointed at Simon—"the thing where they find out why she died? Then we would know for sure, right?"

"An autopsy, you mean?"

"Yes, an autopsy," Leo repeated. "Annie always says that it is better to have more information than less."

I admitted that I had only been chorusing Daddy.

Mr. Kipling patted my brother on the hand. I winced, because there had been a time, and not too long ago either, when Leo couldn't bear to be touched by anyone who wasn't immediate family. But Leo was fine. He barely seemed to register the touch. "Actually, Leo, though usually I couldn't agree more with your sister and your father about the power of information, in this instance, there are things having an autopsy could hurt. Would you mind if I explained to you what they are?"

Leo nodded, and Mr. Kipling laid out his argument. "Your grandmother is dead. And nothing is going to change that fact. There is no reason to believe she died of anything but old age and the cumulative effects of her illness. But, if this family authorizes an autopsy, it will seem as if we've had reason to believe that there was another possible cause to her death. It will seem as if we believe there is more to this story, and that is the last thing this family needs."

Leo nodded. "Why?"

"Because you and your sisters cannot afford the exposure. You are certainly aware that, as the only sibling who is over eighteen, you are becoming Natty and Annie's guardian?"

"Yes," Leo said.

"If the living arrangements of your family become a matter of public interest, Child Protective Services could try to take Natty and Annie away from you, Leo. You are very young and people are aware of your medical history. The authorities could send Natty and Annie to foster care, if, for some reason, you were deemed an unfit parent."

"No!" Leo yelled. "No! Never!"

"Well, don't worry, Leo. I'm going to do everything in my power to make sure that never happens," Mr. Kipling said. "And this is why I'm advising you to make no moves that bring any unwanted attention to your immediate family. The folks at social services are entirely overwhelmed. No one will care about your living arrangements unless you give them reason to."

There was a pause.

"Yes . . . What you say . . . This makes sense to me," Leo said finally.

"Good," said Mr. Kipling.

"Do you think Leo should give up his job?" I asked.

"I don't want to do that!" Leo roared.

"He's still working at the Pool," I explained.

Mr. Kipling ran his fingers through the invisible hair on his bald head. "Ah yes. I never did resolve that situation at the animal clinic, did I? I apologize, Anya. My heart attack—but it's really inexcusable on my part. Mr. Green, would you make a note?"

Simon Green obeyed and said nothing. Indeed, he hadn't said a word since suggesting the autopsy. His expression reminded me of a basset hound.

"Do you enjoy your work at the Pool?" Simon Green asked my brother.

"Yes," said Leo. "Very much."

"What kind of things do they have you do?"

"I get lunch for the men. And I get snacks and drinks, too. And I drop off the laundry."

"And they treat you well?"

"Yes."

"I absolutely understand your concern, Anya, but I don't think Leo should quit his job at the Pool," Mr. Kipling concluded. "Even with the taint of organized crime, it is better that he appear to have been consistently employed." Mr. Kipling looked in my brother's eyes. "You must promise never to do anything dangerous or illegal. You are the protector of Anya and Nataliya now. And you are extremely important."

Leo sat up straight and nodded solemnly. "I promise."

"Good," said Mr. Kipling. "In terms of administration of this household, most everything else will continue as it always has." Of course, I already knew this. Mr. Kipling was really speaking to Leo. "Your finances have been placed into a trust that I will manage until Annie is of age."

Leo didn't question these arrangements nor was he insulted by them, as Nana had feared he might be. He accepted all of it unquestioningly, and this was a relief. Despite Simon Green's gaffe, Mr. Kipling had done well in making Leo feel valued. We went on a while, discussing plans for Nana's modest service. Mr. Kipling was adamant that the wake shouldn't take place in our apartment, but that it needed to be at some private location where our mafiya relatives would feel comfortable paying their respects. "Mr. Green and I will come up with something."

We were just about finished with all the immediate business when the doorbell rang. It was the undertaker, come to take Nana's body to the funeral home. Leo excused himself to his bedroom. (I think he was a little afraid of Nana's corpse.)

"Why don't you go see if the undertaker needs any help?" Mr. Kipling said to Simon Green. Simon Green was being dismissed and he knew it.

Mr. Kipling was perspiring, so I suggested we go out onto the balcony.

"How is your health?" I asked him.

"Much better, thank you. I almost feel 62 percent normal. Keisha is watching everything I eat. She doesn't want me to accidentally end up getting something with flavor." He put his arm around my shoulders in a paternal way. "I know how much you loved Galina and how much she loved you. I know how sad you must be."

I didn't say anything.

"I worry about you. The way you keep everything inside, Annie. It's not healthy." Mr. Kipling laughed. "Though I don't know who I am to be giving health advice.

"Annie, there's something you and I haven't discussed. I hesitate to even bring it up, but I feel I must."

252

"Yes?"

"The Delacroix boy," Mr. Kipling said. Of course, he'd seen the news stories just like everyone else. "Silverstein has finally announced his retirement, which means that Charles Delacroix will surely declare his candidacy for DA any day now. And when he does, it will bring attention to him and everyone in his orbit."

Yes, I understood what he was getting at, and it was something I'd thought of many times myself. I'd said as much to Scarlet back in November. "You think I should end it with Win?"

"No, I'd never presume to tell you that, Anya. But the timing of things—of Galina's death and Leo becoming your guardian and Mr. Delacroix's political aspirations—might not be ideal. I wouldn't be a good adviser to you if I didn't at least pose the following question: Is this relationship worth the potential scrutiny?"

My brain said no.

But my heart!

"You don't have to answer right now," Mr. Kipling said. "We'll be in touch a great deal over the next several weeks."

Through the glass door, I could see Simon Green beckoning us back into the living room.

Mr. Kipling apologized for Simon Green. "He shouldn't have suggested the autopsy in front of your brother. Simon means well and he isn't without intelligence, but I'm afraid he still has much to learn."

Mr. Kipling and I went back into the living room, where the undertakers needed Mr. Kipling to sign some paperwork regarding the transfer of Nana's body. At the moment, Nana's body was on a gurney, enclosed in a black vinyl bag with a zipper that ran down the middle. Seeing her there, it occurred to me that no priest had given Nana last rites. I worried for her soul and mine.

"No one gave her last rites," I said to Mr. Kipling. "She told me she was dying, but I didn't listen! I could have gotten her a priest. It's all my fault."

"Annie," Mr. Kipling said gently, "your grandmother wasn't a Catholic."

"But I am!" I moaned. "And I don't want her to go to Hell!"

Mr. Kipling said nothing. We both knew that Nana had done some hard things in her life, and it wasn't worth pretending that it was otherwise. Galina Balanchine would have needed every possible advantage if she were to have any chance of making it to Heaven.

That night, after Nana's body had left for the funeral home in Brooklyn, after I'd served Leo and Natty macaroni, after I'd stripped the bed in Nana's room, after I'd confirmed with Mr. Kipling that the Pool was an acceptable location for Nana's wake, after I'd made Natty take a shower and put her to bed, after I'd given Leo an aspirin for a headache so bad it made him cry, after I'd prayed that Leo's headache wouldn't turn into a seizure, after I'd gone to bed myself, only to be woken by Natty having a nightmare, after I'd comforted my sister, after Leo called for me on my way back to my room (wanting me to please check and see that Nana's window was open and her door was closed), after I'd done that and gone to bed a second time, after all these things I'd done, it was quiet. It was quieter than I could remember the apartment having been in years and years. The machines that had kept Nana alive had been so noisy and yet I had grown used to the noise, I suppose. And it was this strange, new silence that seemed noisy to me now. I couldn't fall back asleep so I got out of bed and went into Nana's room. As long as Nana had been ill, the room had always smelled a bit sour to me, and now it smelled like nothing. How quickly that had happened!

The room had been Daddy's office before Nana had moved in with us. I don't think I've ever mentioned this before, but it was the room where Daddy was murdered. The first night Nana came to stay with us, I had thought she was going to sleep in Mommy and Daddy's old bedroom, but she told me that my parents' room would be my new room—I had been sharing with Natty to that point—and that she would use Daddy's office. Even though I was only nine, I didn't think it was right that she should have to sleep where her own son was murdered (there had still been bloodstains on the rug!), and I told her it wouldn't be a problem for me to bunk with Natty. "No, Anyaschka," she'd said. "If we don't use this room, it will forever be the place where your father died. It will be a memorial when what it needs to be is a room. It is never a good idea to keep a coffin in the middle of one's house, my darling. And besides, you are a big girl, and a big girl needs a room of her own." I didn't entirely understand what she was saying at the time, and I can remember even being a little angry at her. *Daddy died in that room!* was what I had wanted to say. *Show some respect!* But now I realized how much strength it must have taken for her to sleep there. Daddy had been her only biological child: though she hadn't let on, she must have been grieving, too.

I looked atop Nana's nightstand and then in the drawer to see if she'd left me a note. Nothing except pills and Imogen's copy of *David Copperfield*.

I sat down on the bare mattress. I closed my eyes and imagined Nana saying *Get a bar of chocolate and share it with someone you love.* I opened my eyes. No one would ever say those words to me again. No one would want me to have something sweet, just because. No one would care who I shared my chocolate with. There was less love for me in the world than there had been even twenty-four hours ago. I buried my face in my hands and I did my best to cry without making any noise—I didn't want to wake my siblings.

Nana had loved me.

She had really loved me.

And despite this, I was relieved that she was dead. (The truth of this made me cry even harder.)

I fell asleep in Nana's room that night.

I woke to the sunrise, which I couldn't see from my own west-facing bedroom. I could understand why Nana had liked this chamber. The closet was bigger than mine, and the morning light was spectacular.

Mr. Kipling and I had discussed the importance of sticking to the regular routine, and especially of Natty and me needing to attend school as usual. And so we did. We were swollen-eyed and unprepared, but we were there.

I told Scarlet in Fencing. She cried and said nothing particularly helpful.

I told Win at lunch. He wanted to know why I hadn't called or told him earlier. "I would have come," he said.

"There was nothing for you to do," I said.

"Still," he insisted. "You shouldn't have been alone."

I couldn't help thinking about my discussion with Mr. Kipling. I looked at Win, and I wondered if I should give him up. More to the point, I wondered if I *could* give him up. "Win, do me a favor. Don't tell your father about my grandmother dying yet."

"As if I would," he said. "I don't tell him anything."

"I know," I said. "But I don't want to end up a problem for your father to solve."

Win changed the subject. "When's the funeral?" he asked. "I'll go with you."

"There won't be a funeral, just a wake at the Pool this Saturday. Family only." I didn't think it was that great an idea that Win go with me.

"If you don't want me to come, you can just say, you know."

"It's not that . . ." Suddenly, I was exhausted. I'd slept very little, and I was having trouble being sensible.

"It's not as if I have nothing better to do than go to your grandmother's funeral," Win said.

"I'm tired," I said. "Can we discuss this later?"

"Sure," Win said. "I'll come over tonight. If I didn't manage to say so before, I am incredibly sorry about your grandmother." He kissed me, though not in a sexy way. Gentle. Tender. Then the bell rang, and he had to get to his next class. I watched him jog across the chessboard cafeteria floor. His hips were slim and his shoulders were square and broad. He moved gracefully, almost like a dancer. From behind, it was obvious to me how much of a boy he still was. Yes, he was a boy. He was just a boy. It wouldn't be easy, but I decided that if I had to, I could give him up. As a Catholic, I had learned early to accept renunciation as a part of life.

"Anya Balanchine?" Someone tapped me on the arm. It was one of Natty's teachers. I'd never had her. She was new, had only been teaching a year or two, and had the sort of cartoonish enthusiasm one might expect in someone so inexperienced. "I'm Kathleen Bellevoir! I was hoping I'd run into you today! Do you have a moment to talk about your sister? I'll walk you to your next class!" It was all exclamation points with this lady.

I nodded. "Sure. If Natty was a little off in class today, well, we recently had a death in the family, and—"

"I'm very sorry to hear that, but no, it's nothing like that. The opposite, in fact! I wanted to talk to you because of how well she's doing! Your sister has a gift, Anya."

A what? "A gift? What subject do you teach again?"

"Math," she said.

"Math? Natty has a gift . . . in math?" This was news to me.

"And science, though I don't have her for that subject. Listen," Miss Bellevoir said. "May I call you Annie?"

I shrugged.

"That's how Natty refers to you! She talks about you constantly!"

"Well, thanks for telling me about Natty's gift," I said.

"You see, there's this camp in Massachusetts for gifted children. Eight weeks in the summer. It's a chance for Natty to be

258

with other children like herself. She needs a sponsor and I'd be willing to accompany her."

"Why would you be willing to do that?"

"I . . . Only because I believe in Natty."

"What would you want for it?" I asked. "You must want something."

She blushed. "No. Nothing! Except to see Natty be as successful as she deserves to be."

I could not even begin to think about this. I had to worry about Nana's wake and social services and about a million other things.

Miss Bellevoir continued. "I sent in an application for her several months ago."

"You did what?" Who the hell did this woman think she was?

"I apologize if I overstepped. Your sister has a truly extraordinary mind, Annie. The most extraordinary mind I've come across in all my years of teaching."

How long had that been? Like, two years?

"Oh, you're probably thinking that I haven't been teaching very long. Let's add my years of being in school, too. Natty could be the person who solves the water problem, for instance. Or anything. Anything . . ." She sighed. "Listen, Annie, I do have a selfish reason for wanting to help your sister. Simply put, I'm tired of how awful things have gotten. Don't tell me you've never asked yourself why things are the way they are. Why we devote all our resources to trying to compensate for our lack of resources. Can you honestly remember the last time anyone in our society came up with anything new? Other than a law, of course. And do you know what happens to a society of old things? It withers and dies. We are living in the Dark Ages, and half the people don't even seem to know it. We can't go on like this forever!" Miss Bellevoir paused. "Forgive me. When I'm passionate, I sometimes end up sounding muddled. My point is that Natty is someone who could honestly do anything. Minds like hers are our only hope and, as her teacher, I wouldn't be doing my job if I let such a resource go to waste."

Natty had always gotten good grades, but this was ridiculous. "If she's so extraordinary, why hasn't anyone pointed this out to me before?"

"I don't know," Miss Bellevoir said. "Perhaps they were intimidated by your family. Or perhaps they saw Natty through a certain lens because of that."

"You mean they were prejudiced?" I clenched my jaw.

"But I *am* new, and I have fresh eyes. And I'm telling you now."

We were outside Mr. Beery's classroom. She told me she would send me more information. Miss Bellevoir was a busybody, but I decided that she wasn't a bad sort.

"I have to discuss this with my . . ." I almost said grandmother. "My brother and our attorney."

"Natty says that you make all the decisions in your family," Miss Bellevoir said. "That you're everyone's protector."

"She shouldn't say things like that," I said.

"Must be a lot of burden for one person," Miss Bellevoir said.

Truthfully, it annoyed me that someone else, some stranger,

had observed things in Natty that I had not. I felt as if I had failed my sister. "If Natty's such a genius, why didn't I ever notice?"

"It's hard to see things that are right in front of us sometimes," Miss Bellevoir said. "But I'm telling you, what she has is precious. And it needs to be encouraged and protected." Miss Bellevoir squeezed my hand. Then she winked at me and nodded as if we were conspirators.

I opened the door to the classroom. Miss Bellevoir waved to Mr. Beery to let him know that I had been with her. He nodded. "Nice of you to join us, Ms. Balanchine," he said.

"I was with Miss Bellevoir. Didn't you see?"

Mr. Beery said nothing.

"I mean, I saw you wave at her," I said. "So you must have seen."

"That's enough, Ms. Balanchine. Have a seat."

Instead of sitting down at my desk, I walked to the front of the classroom and put my face right up against his face. "I think you did see," I continued. "You just like being sarcastic. You enjoy belittling us, don't you? You enjoy the teeny tiny bit of power you have. You play us against each other so that you can win our favor. It's pathetic."

"You're being inappropriate," he said.

"And when I say *it's*, I actually mean *you*. You're pathetic," I replied.

I picked up my bag and began heading toward Headmaster's office.

Mr. Beery yelled, "Go! To! Headmaster!"

"I'm ahead of you there," I said.

Maybe I shouldn't have gone to school the day after Nana died after all.

Headmaster wasn't that tough on me on account of the death in my family. One day of suspension starting tomorrow. This could hardly be called a punishment. Just a chance for me to stay home. I probably should have done that in the first place. I had felt pretty sluggish all day.

Natty, Scarlet, Win, and I rode the bus back to my apartment.

Natty was wearing Win's hat. "Hey," I said, "did you guys know we happen to have a genius among us?"

"Well, I wouldn't say I'm a genius," Scarlet said. "Though I am pretty talented."

"Not you," I said. "Natty."

"I can believe it," Win said. "Her head's nearly as big as mine. Look how she fills out that hat."

Natty said nothing.

"So, what are you a genius at, kid?" Win asked.

"Math," Natty said. "And stuff."

"I never knew that," Scarlet commented.

"It's news to all of us," I said.

"Well, um, congratulations, I guess," Scarlet told Natty.

When we got to the apartment, Natty ran into her room and slammed the door. I didn't feel like going after her, but I did. I turned the knob, but it was locked.

"Come on, Natty. Let me in."

"Why did you embarrass me like that?" Natty yelled through the door.

"Why didn't you ever mention you were a genius?" I yelled back.

"Stop calling me that name!"

"What name?"

"Genius!"

"That's not a name. It's a compliment. So, why didn't you ever tell me? Why did I have to hear it from some dumb teacher who looks younger than me?"

"Miss Bellevoir is not dumb!"

"No, I'm the dumb one. I didn't even notice my own sister was a genius." I sat down in the hallway outside Natty's room. "I felt so stupid, Natty. It looked like I didn't know you very well or like I didn't care about you."

Natty opened the door. "I know you care about me," she said. "It's just . . . I didn't even know I was one. I thought everyone was like me. Until Miss B. said that they weren't."

"And when you figured it out, why didn't you mention it?"

"Because I didn't want to worry you. You'd just gotten back from that horrible place, Liberty. And I didn't want to cause any more problems for you. And you were all in loooooove with Win."

"But you being a genius? This should have been a good thing, right? Why would you think it was a problem?"

"I guess because you're always saying that we should keep a low profile at school. So, I try to keep quiet in class. I don't raise my hand too much. Half the time when I know the answer, I don't even say."

"You mean you've tried to act *less* smart?" The thought of my little sister trying so hard to be average was incredibly depressing.

My skull felt like it was pressing into my eye, so I placed my head in my hands for a moment. "But, Natty," I whispered, "that's not right."

"I'm sorry, Annie. I was only trying to help. I told Miss B. not to talk to you. That there was no point."

I raised my head slightly. My throbbing eye seemed to have resolved itself somewhat. "Do you want to go to this summer camp?" I asked.

"No," Natty said. "Maybe."

"What about your nightmares?" I asked. "I couldn't go with you, you know. I can't leave Leo. Besides which, I'm not exactly a genius."

"I don't know," Natty said. "I hadn't thought about that part."

"Well, we don't have to figure this out today," I said. "But you have to tell me these things, Natty. Especially now that Nana's dead. I know I'm not Nana or Mommy or Daddy, but I try my best."

"I know, Annie. I know everything you do for me. For Leo, too. I wish I was older so that I could help you more. I wish things weren't so hard for you." She put her skinny arms around me, and I couldn't help but think of what Miss Bellevoir had said about Natty being someone precious, someone who needed to be protected. I had allowed myself to be distracted over the last several months, and this was unacceptable, especially now that Nana was dead. I was responsible for this girl in my arms. In that moment, the magnitude of that hit me. Without me, she wouldn't live up to her potential. She might fall in with bad people—God knows, we were surrounded by those. Without me, she might even die. Or, if not die, fail to be the person she was meant to be, and that might be an even worse sort of death. I pulled my baby sister to me. I felt light-headed and breathless and like I might throw up. My chest was tight and I wanted to punch the wall. I realized that this was love, and it was awful.

All of a sudden, I really did have to throw up. I let go of Natty and ran down the hall to the bathroom. I made it to the toilet, but barely.

I threw up for the next ten minutes or so. When it was over, I noticed that someone was holding my hair back. I thought it was Natty, but when I turned around it was Win. I'd forgotten he'd come back with me after school.

"Oh," I said, lunging to flush the toilet. "You should go. I'm too disgusting."

"I've seen worse," he replied.

"Where's Natty?" As in, why wasn't she the one in here holding back my hair?

"She went to call Imogen."

Considering how my last conversation with Imogen had gone, I doubted she would come.

"You should go," I told him. "I don't want you to catch whatever horrible thing I've got."

"I never get sick," he said. "I have an excellent constitution."

"Bully for you," I grumbled. "Would you go already? I just want to be sick by myself, thanks." I got up off the bathroom floor. I felt a little unsteady, but Win took my elbow and led me to my room.

I collapsed into my bed and fell asleep.

* * *

When I awoke, Imogen was by my bedside. She had placed a cool washcloth on my forehead.

My brain throbbed against my skull. My eyes were watering and my vision was blurry. Colored spots floated across the room. My stomach rumbled with acid. My skin was insanely itchy. I felt like I was dying. "Am I dying?"

"You have the chicken pox, Annie. Natty was inoculated, but you and Leo never were because there were vaccine rations those years."

(Were you worrying I was pregnant? That I had had sex with Win and didn't tell you? I would never do that to you. Unlike some, I pride myself on being a very reliable narrator.)

Imogen continued. "Maybe you caught them at your cousin's wedding? Did you notice anyone looking sick?"

I shook my head. I went to scratch my face, but Imogen had put cotton gloves on my hands.

"I can't be sick. I have a wake to plan. And there's so much to do with Nana's death. And school. And Natty and Leo need me. And . . ." I sat up in bed. Imogen gently but firmly pushed me back down.

"Well, you won't be doing any of that until next week at the earliest."

"Why are you here?" I asked.

"Because Natty called me." She slipped a straw into my mouth. "Drink." I obeyed.

"No," I said. "I meant, why are you here after the horrible things I said to you?"

She shrugged. "I had time on my hands. I did just lose my

steady paycheck." She shrugged again. "You were upset," Imogen replied. "Drink more. You need fluids."

"I'm sorry," I said. "I'm really sorry. I have a lot on my mind."

"You're a good girl, and I accept your apology," Imogen said.

"I'm so tired," I said.

"Then sleep, baby." She stroked my hair with her cool, clean, dry hand. It felt comfortable and comforting. Maybe Nana's last moments had been like this. Maybe her death hadn't been so bad.

I closed my eyes, then I opened them again.

"Did you know Natty's a genius?"

"I suspected as much," Imogen replied.

I wanted to scratch but instead I said the secret horrible thing I'd been carrying in my heart since my conversation with Mr. Kipling. "I think I have to break up with my boyfriend." There it was.

"Why? He seems like a very nice young man."

"He is. He's the nicest young man I've ever known," I told her. "But a long time ago, his father warned me that if I dated Win my business would become his business. And now that Nana is dead, I'm worried that his father might try to interfere with us. You and I both know that if we went to court, Leo would never be proven a fit guardian." I coughed. My throat was so dry. Imogen pushed the straw into my mouth.

"The only way I can keep Natty and Leo and me safe is if we manage to fly below the radar until I'm eighteen."

"Hmm," Imogen said. She pushed the straw toward me again. "Drink."

I drank. "But if I'm not in a relationship with the son, the father will have no need to bother with me. With us."

"I see," Imogen said. She set the glass on the nightstand, apparently satisfied that I had had enough to drink.

I was beginning to be horribly itchy again. I moved to scratch my arm. Imogen pressed it down. "This will make you feel better," she said. She took a tube of lotion from the nightstand and began applying it to the welts that had sprouted on my skin. "You don't know for sure that the father will do anything," she continued. "Most parents want their children to be happy above all things."

I thought of Charles Delacroix that day on the way home from Liberty. I knew at least one parent who would do whatever he had to do to win, regardless of his child's happiness. I shook my head. "I don't know for sure what the father will do, but I think being with this boy puts us in danger. And as much as I"— Did I love Win? Did I really love him? Yes, I suppose I did—"love Win, I love Natty and Leo more. I can't put them in jeopardy for my silly high school love affair. If Nana were still alive . . . But I just can't risk it." I knew what I had to do. It wouldn't be easy, but I would do it. I moved to pull off my glove, but Imogen stopped me by taking my gloved hand in hers.

"Remember, high school love affairs aren't always so silly, Annie. And you can't do anything right now. Your sickness will give you a couple of days to think."

"I really miss Nana," I said. "I know most people saw her as some old woman in a bed, but I still really miss her." I was itchy and weak and my eyes began to tear. I missed having her to go over things with. I missed talking to her. It was inconceivable that I would never hear her voice again. "I just miss her," I said.

"Try not to speak. I miss her, too," Imogen said. "Would you like me to read to you a bit? It always helped your grandmother to sleep. I have one of my favorites with me." She held up her book so that I could see the title.

"Isn't that about an orphan?" I asked. I hated those kinds of books.

"You can't avoid orphan stories, child. Every story is an orphan story. Life is an orphan story. We are all orphaned sooner or later."

"In my case, sooner."

"Yes, in your case, sooner. But you are strong, and God never gives us more than we can bear."

I didn't feel strong. I felt like burying my head under the covers and never coming out. I was so awfully tired. "Read your story if you must," I told Imogen.

"Chapter one," she read. "There was no possibility of taking a walk that day. We had been wandering, indeed, in the leafless shrubbery an hour in the morning; but since dinner (Mrs. Reed, when there was no company, dined early) the cold winter wind had brought with it clouds so sombre, and a rain so penetrating, that further out-door exercise was now out of the question . . ."

Aside from trying not to scratch, I didn't do much of anything for the next five days. Because of my condition, I wasn't even able to attend Nana's wake. Scarlet and Imogen went with Natty in my place. I had told Scarlet to keep an eye out for Leo, too. (Scarlet had gotten lucky and managed not to catch my pox. Oddly, the only other person at school who had gotten them was Mr. Beery.)

I didn't feel particularly bad about not being able to go to Nana's wake. In theory, I understood wakes—they were about respect for the living as much as they were about respect for the dead. It was the emotional-displays-in-public-venues part that I had trouble with. At Daddy's funeral, for instance, I had felt observed, and by observed, I suppose I mean judged. It wasn't enough to be sad inside. You had to *look* sad for other people. While I was sorry to subject my brother and sister to such scrutiny, I was grateful that my pox had given me an excuse not to go. I had been to plenty of funerals in my sixteen years already.

I helped my siblings pick out wake clothes: an old black tie of Daddy's for Leo, an old black dress of mine for Natty. Just before noon, Imogen and Scarlet showed up to meet my siblings. Finally, I was alone with my red spots, which I did my best not to worry. Aside from being itchy and unattractive, I did not feel especially unwell. A touch after noon, the doorbell rang. It was Win, who I had not seen since the afternoon he'd discovered me on the bathroom floor. I still looked terrible. What was particularly annoying about that was how wonderful he looked. He was wearing a long olive-green coat that looked like it must have belonged to a soldier who had served in an arctic clime. His hair was a bit damp—he must have showered before coming over—and parts of it were even frozen into little spikes on account of how cold it was outside. And yes, the spikes were adorable. "I've brought something for you," he said after I'd let him in. He reached into his deep pockets and produced four oranges. "Your favorite."

I took one and pressed it up to my nose.

"My mother's rooftop experiments are starting to bear fruit," he joked. "This is called a Cara Cara orange. It's pink on the inside and incredibly sweet."

He moved to kiss me, and I moved away. "Aren't you afraid I'm contagious?" I asked.

He shook his head. "I've had them."

"Still, people do get chicken pox a second time. And—"

"I won't get them a second time," he insisted.

I moved even farther away from him. "How can you want to kiss me? I'm completely disgusting right now."

"Not completely," he said.

"I am. I've seen myself in the mirror and I know."

He laughed at me. "All right," he said finally. "I'm not here to force myself on you. I figured you'd want company while everyone else was at the visitation. Look, I'll even peel your orange for you."

I told him that I could peel my own orange.

"Not with those," he said, indicating the cotton gloves that Imogen had insisted I keep wearing. He put his hand over my gloved one and squeezed it. I became aware of my heart in my chest. I needed to end things with him.

We went into the living room. He sat down on the larger sofa, which was upholstered in brown velvet. I curled up next to him, resting my head against his ribs. He started to run his fingers through my hair, which annoyed me, but I didn't say anything. My hair is curly and prone to frizz, so I'd usually rather people didn't touch it. I was glad for the annoyance, which I found fortifying in a way. See, I thought, he isn't perfect. If I could focus on this one annoying thing he did, maybe I could end it.

I sat up on the sofa. Then I got up and moved to the red chair.

"What is it?" he asked.

I knew that it would be better to tell him that it wasn't working out, that we weren't compatible, that there wasn't always a reason for these things. Unfortunately, I didn't do this. "Win," I said. "You can't be my boyfriend right now." I laid out my case to him just as I already have to you: I really, really liked him (NB: I did not use the word love.) but my family was more important than my feelings, and now that my grandmother was dead, I couldn't risk having his father in my life, etc.

And then he talked me out of it. Or maybe I let myself be talked out of it. Maybe I wanted to be talked out of it. He told me that he loved me and I loved him and that was the most important thing. He told me that I didn't get to make this decision by myself. He told me that his father wouldn't bother with me and that he could control his father if his father ever tried to interfere with my family. (Even then, I knew this to be a ridiculous lie—I mean, I had met Charles Delacroix.) He told me that love was the only thing that really mattered in this world. (Another lie.)

But I was in a weakened state, and lies can sound awfully pretty when a girl is in love with the person telling them. The truth was, I couldn't, at that moment, bear the loss of Win, too.

We heard the front door open. It was only one o'clock, and

I hadn't expected everyone back for at least another hour. I walked to the foyer. Leo blazed past me, running straight to his room and slamming the door behind him. Imogen, Natty, and Scarlet stood in the hallway, taking off their coats.

"What happened?" I asked them, feeling guilty that I hadn't dragged my pox-ridden self to the wake. "Why are you back so early? What's wrong with Leo?"

Scarlet answered, "We aren't sure. We were all together, but Leo went off with some of the guys he works with at the Pool. I thought it would be okay. But the next thing I knew, there was yelling, and Leo had a black eye—"

"Wait," I said. "Leo has a black eye?"

"I should go put something on it." Imogen excused herself to the kitchen.

"Yes," Scarlet continued. "I didn't see it happen—none of us did—and he wouldn't say who did it. And then Yuji was telling all of us to get into a car."

"Yuji?" I asked. "Yuji Ono? He was there?"

"He's *here*," Natty added.

And that's when I noticed Yuji Ono standing in the doorway, wearing a black coat.

"I was still in the States, so I came to pay my respects," Yuji said.

"I . . ." I pulled my bathrobe tighter around myself and wished for a veil to pull over my head. "I hope you've had the chicken pox."

"Yes," he said. "I was warned."

Win was standing behind me. The foyer was getting incredibly crowded. Win held out his hand for Yuji to shake. "I'm Win."

"He's Annie's boyfriend," Natty added.

Yuji nodded. "I saw you at the wedding last weekend. Nice to meet you."

"Let's all go into the living room," I said.

"No," said Yuji, bowing his head slightly. "I must go. I wondered if you might have a moment for us to talk alone before I depart. I was hoping to see you at the funeral, but I didn't know of your illness."

"Yes, of course. I—"

"Annie!" Imogen called me from the hallway. "Can I speak to you?"

"Excuse me," I said. "I'll only be a second." I scurried down the hallway to Leo's room, where Imogen was standing outside, carrying a bag of frozen peas. "Your brother's locked himself in, and he won't open the door. I need you to pick the lock."

I knocked on the door. "Leo, it's Annie. Please let me in!"

No reply.

I removed the fine nail that we kept above the door frame for exactly this purpose, and began to work on the lock. Despite the fact that my mind was occupied with questions, it only took me fifteen seconds. I hadn't lost my touch. I took the peas from Imogen and told her I would go in by myself.

Leo was seated on his bed, facing the window. He wasn't crying, which I considered a good sign.

"Leo," I said softly, "you should put something on your eye."

He didn't reply, so I sat down next to him on the bed. I raised my arm to put the frozen peas on his face. He jerked his body away from me. "Annie, leave me alone!"

"Please, Leo. You don't have to talk. Just let me put this on your eye. With your medical history, I'd feel better knowing your head isn't swelling too much. I don't want you to have a seizure."

"Fine!" Leo grabbed the peas from me and held them up against his face.

"Thank you. You are very important to this family. To me," I added. "And you have to take good care of yourself."

At first, Leo didn't say anything. "This stings," he said, moving the peas from his eye and setting them down in his lap. I finally got a good look at his eye. The lid was swollen shut, and a pinkish-purple mark was spreading across his cheek. The skin was bleeding a little near his temple.

"Oh, Leo," I said. "Who did this to you?"

He pulled the bag up to his eye again. "I hit him first."

"Who? Who did you hit?" When he'd first been injured, Leo had had trouble controlling his anger, but this hadn't been a problem for years.

"Annie, I don't want to talk about it."

"I need to know who you hit in case I need to do something about it," I said. "It doesn't have to be a big deal, but we might have to apologize or, at least, talk to people, explain about your condition."

Leo threw the bag of peas at the window and the bag broke open. Peas rolled in every direction across the floor. "*Shut up, Anya!* You are not the boss of me and you don't know everything."

"Okay, Leo. You're right. Please, just tell me who you hit. I need to know."

"Cousin Mickey," he said.

You'll no doubt remember that Mickey was Yuri Balanchine's son and likely successor. Apologies would most certainly need to be made and, ideally, as soon as possible.

"Why, Leo? Did Mickey do something bad to you?"

Leo's gaze floated to the upper-right corner of the room. I peered up to see what was there, but I saw nothing. "It's his fault Nana's dead," Leo said finally.

"Come again?"

"If we hadn't been out of town for his stupid wedding, Nana wouldn't have died. She'd be here now, and I wouldn't be . . . Why did we even have to go to that wedding?"

"Nana wanted us to, remember? She thought it was important for us to show respect to the rest of the family."

Leo wrung his hands. "It's a lot of pressure. It's too much pressure. It's a lot of pressure."

"What is?" I asked.

"Being in charge of you and Natty. I miss Nana. I want Nana back. And Daddy!"

"Oh, Leo! You aren't alone in any of this. I'm here."

"But you're my little sister. I need to protect you."

I smiled. In a way, it was touching that he saw me that way. "Leo, I really can take care of myself. I've been taking care of myself for some time."

Leo said nothing.

"Can you lie down for me, Leo? I think it would be good if you rested."

Leo nodded. I loosened his tie and took off his bloodstained dress shirt, and then he lay down. "Do you think everyone is going to be mad at me?" he asked.

"Don't worry about any of that right now. I'll explain everything. Everyone understands how hard Nana's death has been on us."

I walked out of the room. Imogen was still standing in the hallway so I asked her if she wouldn't mind keeping an eye on Leo for me. "I had already planned on it," Imogen said.

Though Win, Natty, and Scarlet had gone into the living room, Yuji Ono had remained in the foyer.

As I retied my bathrobe, I wished very much that I'd gotten dressed that morning. "I'm sorry to have kept you waiting. I know you're in a rush."

Yuji waved his hand dismissively. "I'd like to speak to you in private," he said. "Can we be heard here?"

I suggested we go out onto the balcony. We walked through the living room, past the others, to get outside. Win looked at me questioningly, and I smiled slightly to let him know that I was fine.

"Why weren't you at the wake today?" Yuji asked after I'd closed the balcony doors behind us.

I told him that I'd been ill and that I'd feared infecting other people.

Yuji studied my face and this made me uncomfortable. As I was only wearing my bathrobe, I began to shiver so Yuji offered me his coat. I declined, but he insisted, taking the coat off and placing it over my shoulders.

"What happened to make Leo strike Mickey?" I asked.

"I am not sure I know. One moment Leo was speaking to his friend, Yuri's illegitimate son with the prostitute—I cannot remember the young man's name?"

"Jakov Pirozhki," I said. "Jacks."

"And the next moment, Leo was running across the room to deck Mickey. The reason I wanted to talk to you was because I was concerned that perhaps this Jacks has an unhealthy influence on your brother."

"It's possible, but I don't think Jacks put Leo up to striking Mickey Balanchine, if that's what you mean. I'm afraid one of our lawyers put the idea in Leo's head that, if we hadn't gone to the wedding, Galina would still be alive," I explained.

Yuji stretched out his hands, then took a deep breath and bowed his head. I could tell he was debating whether to speak his mind. "Anya, what I am about to say, I say with the greatest respect for you and for your family and especially for the relationship between our beloved fathers, now deceased." He paused to clear his throat. "It is time for you to set your house in order."

"What do you mean?"

"You have allowed things to get out of hand here, but it is not too late. I feel sure that your brother has come under the influence of Jakov Pirozhki. But it is more than this. The reason I made this trip to America was on behalf of the big-five chocolate families. Do you know who they are?"

I nodded. "The Balanchines here. You guys in Asia. The . . ." And here I paused. I honestly wasn't sure which families would be considered the other three.

"Yes, I was like you once," Yuji said. "I'd spent my whole life living in the shadow of this business without really knowing anything about it: in what climates chocolate thrives, what the factories look like, why it became illegal in parts of the world, the people who make their livelihoods growing and distributing it, the—"

"Enough," I interrupted him. I could tell I was being insulted. "Why should I know anything about it when I have no plans to ever work in it?"

"Yes," Yuji said, "I thought that once, and I, too, resisted. But, Anya, people like you and me, we don't get a choice. We were born into these destinies. You will be in chocolate whether you want to be or not. You are the oldest child of Leonyd Balanchine, and—"

"I am not! Leo is!"

"Leo was," Yuji insisted. "You are a smart girl, and I know you understand what I mean by this."

I said nothing.

"Can you honestly tell me that you consider it a wise strategy to have nothing to do with your family's business? Why were you in prison last fall? And why did your boyfriend end up poisoned and missing a foot? Why is your father dead and your mother? And so many in my family as well? Why is your brother the way he is? Anya, you are nearly a grown woman now, and it is time."

"Time for what?" I demanded.

"For you to accept your birthright and make the best of it," Yuji said.

"What about Yuri? And Yuri's son? Don't they run the Balanchines?"

"Not wisely. Not well. The other families perceive the weakness and the turmoil here. They see opportunities. And your uncle has made many enemies. He never should have become the head of the Balanchine family, and everyone knows it. Back when your father was killed, everyone thought your grandmother Galina would become the interim head of the Balanchine Family, but she opted to care for you and your siblings instead."

I had never known that.

"It's a very dangerous situation for you, Anya. More people will end up dead. Trust me. The Fretoxin poisoning will only be the beginning of it."

"I have responsibilities," I said. "The best way I can protect my family—by which I mean Natty and Leo—is by keeping all of us out of it."

Yuji looked me in the eyes. "If I understand correctly, chicken pox are only contagious before they scab. You could have been at Galina's wake today, but you chose not to be. It seems to me that you chose to spend the morning making out with your boyfriend instead."

"That isn't true."

"Isn't it, though?" Yuji asked.

"What do you want from me?" I asked.

"I'm here because I'm a friend of your family and that is why I was chosen to make a report to the other families on the dealings of the Balanchines since the poisoning debacle."

"What will you say?"

"I don't know yet," Yuji replied. "In my opinion, your family is on the verge of great internecine turmoil. On the one hand, what may be in the best interest of the other families is to allow this to occur, and once it's over, we'll all swoop in to divvy up the Balanchines' share of the market."

I wasn't sure what *internecine* meant. I'd have to look it up later.

"On the other hand, I believe that it is better for the chocolate business to have strong partners. Your father was a great leader. And I believe that you could be a great leader, too."

"You've become as warped as the rest of them. My father was no great leader. My father was a common criminal. A thief and a murderer."

"No, Anya, you're wrong. Leonyd Balanchine was a simple businessman, trying to make the best of a bad situation. Chocolate wasn't always illegal, and it could be legal again someday, too. Soon it may not even be about the chocolate."

"What *will* it be about?"

"This is a longer discussion, I'm afraid. Perhaps child labor. But I believe, as do many others, that it will be water. We are running out of it, and the person who controls the water supply will control the whole world."

"I can't do any of this!" I said. "I'm just a girl and I have to take care of my brother and sister. I'd like to finish high school, maybe even go to college. What you seem to be asking of me is impossible."

"Here is something my father always said to me that I will now repeat to you: 'Yuji, you can either be a bystander who lives his life in reaction to the decisions that others make, or you can be the leader who is making those decisions.' It may have lost a little something in translation from the Japanese, but you see my point. You say you want to protect your brother and sister above everything. I ask you, Anya: Of those two people my father named, which one do you think is better able, better prepared to protect his or her family? The one who is running around trying to avoid conflict? Or the one who knows there will be conflict and embraces it? Do you know what my father said is the best thing in life to be?"

I shook my head. Yuji was clearly passionate, but I wasn't sure I was completely grasping his point.

"The catalyst. In a chemical reaction, the catalyst instigates the change but is not changed itself."

"Your father is dead, Yuji," I reminded him. "As is mine."

At that moment, another Japanese man came out onto the balcony. This man was the most enormous person I'd ever seen in the flesh. He had a round belly and big arms like a sumo wrestler. He wore a black suit and his black hair was in a ponytail. He couldn't have been anything but one of Yuji's bodyguards. (He must have been waiting in the exterior hallway the entire time.) He spoke several sentences in Japanese, and Yuji replied in kind. Yuji bowed his head toward me. "I must go," he said in a much more formal manner. "I am leaving for Asia this afternoon. I have extended this visit as long as I could. Perhaps even longer than was wise. We won't be seeing each other again very soon. If you ever need to speak to me, please don't hesitate to call, though. Goodbye, Miss Balanchine. And good luck." He bowed his head again.

I walked him to the door, past Win and Scarlet and Natty again, and then I went into the bathroom to splash some water on my face before going back to the living room. I caught a glimpse of myself in the mirror. All my welts were scabbed over, and though I was feeling better, my physical appearance was at its most gruesome. Some tiny part of me felt vaguely embarrassed that handsome, twenty-three-year-old Yuji Ono had been forced to see me looking so ugly. I would rather have not seen anyone in this condition, let alone my childhood crush. Still, I realized now that it had been more than a mistake not to go to Nana's wake: it had been selfish and a sin. I should have anticipated that Leo might have reacted in such a way. Yuji had been right. Despite what I said before, it had not been a fear of infecting other people or poor health that had stopped me from going, but vanity.

It was a good lesson.

I went into my bedroom to put on clothes. Though I wouldn't have minded spending the rest of that day in bed, there were things yet to be done. I needed to go see Yuri and Mickey Balanchine to explain about my brother.

The doorbell rang. I thought it might be Yuji Ono, come back to tell me all the other ways in which I was failing, but it wasn't: it was Mr. Kipling and Simon Green. They had tied up the business at the wake and had come to check on Leo and the rest of us.

"Yes," I reported. "We're all fine enough. Leo is resting. And I'm on my way to make amends with Yuri and Mickey. Would either of you happen to know what the word *internecine* means?"

"Bloody," they replied in unison.

"It's a bloody conflict within a group," Simon Green continued.

"Something for a school report?" Mr. Kipling asked.

I shook my head.

"You look awful," Simon Green added unhelpfully.

"Thank you," I replied.

"No, I only meant, are you sure you're up to going out?" Simon Green asked.

"I'd rather not, but I don't think it can be put off," I said.

"Anya is right," Mr. Kipling said. "When small wounds are left untreated, they can fester and become far more serious injuries. We'll take you there, if you'd like."

"No," I replied. "I think it's best if I go alone. It'll seem less formal."

Mr. Kipling agreed that my instincts were probably right, but he insisted that he and Simon Green ride the bus with me to the Pool anyway.

XVI. i apologize (repeatedly); am apologized to (once)

As I mentioned before, the Pool was located on West End Avenue in the nineties, not too far from Holy Trinity. Though I tried to avoid going there, the Pool was beautiful in its way. Mosaic tiles lined the walls in gold, white, and turquoise. No one had swum there in years, but the whole place still smelled lightly of chlorine. And because all of it was underground, it was quiet and cool. Sound bounced around in unusual, unpredictable patterns. Daddy had chosen the space because it was cheap, easy to secure, and more convenient than the old offices in Williamsburg. I imagine it had also pleased him aesthetically. One of the main reasons I didn't like going there was because it reminded me so strongly of Daddy.

Fats was waiting in the lobby with Jacks. "I'd like to see Uncle Yuri and Mickey," I said. "Are they in?"

"Sure, kid," Fats said. "They're still in the offices. Sorry, but I'll have to frisk you before you go back there."

"Hope you don't get chicken pox," I replied as I held up my arms.

"Had the vaccination when I was a kid," Fats said as he ran his hands up and down my clothes. "All done. How you doing with the itching?"

"I've been trying to concentrate my scratching on one or two spots. I had this theory that if I scratched the heck out of one, I'd barely even notice the others."

"Yeah," said Fats. "How's that working for you?"

"Not great," I admitted.

I noticed that Jacks hadn't said anything since I'd come in. This silence didn't seem like him, and I was reminded of what Yuji Ono had said about Jacks being an unhealthy influence on my brother. "Hi, Jacks," I said.

"Nice to see you, Annie," Jacks said.

"So," I said, "what happened with Leo today anyway? I heard you were with him at the time."

Jacks ran his fingers through his hair several times. "You know your brother better than anyone. Sometimes stuff sets him off. I think he was sad over your grandmother so he took it out on Mickey."

"But why Mickey? Why not you?" I persisted. "Weren't you closer by?"

"Christ, Annie. I don't know. Mickey's an ass. Maybe he looked at Leo funny. Who the hell knows? I'm not my brother's keeper or your brother's either." Jacks turned to Fats. "Is it okay if I go now? I'm starving."

Fats nodded. "Yeah, but I got to get back to my establishment by eight, so don't be gone too long."

286

Jacks turned to me before he left. "Sorry if I was short with you, Annie. I've got a lot on my mind."

"Don't mind him," Fats said. "I think he's got his period." Fats pointed me toward the back. "You better get going if you want to talk to Mickey and Yuri."

Yuri's office was in the heart of the locker room. The whole front of the office was a glass window. This window in combination with a large convex mirror in the upper corner of the wall made it easy to see who was coming or going no matter where you stood in the office. Consequently, I didn't have to knock on the door. I was just waved in.

"Annie," Uncle Yuri said, rising to greet me. "Good to see you. We missed you at Galina's wake today. But I can see from your face that you are still unwell."

"I'm mainly better," I assured him. I kissed him on both of his cheeks because that was the protocol.

"Hello, Anya," Mickey said. Mickey was lurking in the corner of the room. I could see that he had a light bruise on his cheek. What he had done to Leo had been much more severe.

"You should be in bed," Uncle Yuri said. "What takes you from your bed, little Annie?"

"I'm here to apologize for my brother," I said. "Leo doesn't always think before he acts. I believe he was just emotional from the wake."

"Don't trouble yourself, child," Uncle Yuri said. "We know that Leo is"—he looked for a word—"sensitive, but we love him here."

I looked over at Mickey to see if he felt the same way. "I want you to know that I didn't do anything to provoke him,"

Mickey said. "And I feel awful about hitting someone"—now it was Mickey's turn to search for a euphemism for my brother—"like him. It's below me."

"Now kiss your cousin and make up," Uncle Yuri instructed Mickey.

"I've not had chicken pox yet," Mickey said. "No offense, Anya. Vaccines don't always work."

"None taken," I assured him. "Did you have a nice honeymoon?" I asked.

"We didn't go on one. I couldn't leave work," Mickey said. "Yuji Ono was in town, breathing fire down my neck, and we're still dealing with fallout from the Fretoxin poisoning all these months later, if you can believe that."

"Did you ever figure out who did it?"

Mickey shook his head. "Some of us are starting to suspect it was an inside job."

"Enough business talk," Yuri said. "Annie doesn't want to hear this."

I nodded and turned to Yuri. "Perhaps it would be best if Leo didn't work at the Pool anymore?" I suggested.

"There is no need for that," Uncle Yuri assured me. "He's an excellent worker, and what has happened is of no consequence. Tell Leo to take tomorrow off and we'll see him on Monday as usual." Uncle Yuri offered to pour me a cup of tea, but I told him that I was needed at home. "How are things now that Galina has passed?" he asked. "Are you and your siblings managing?"

I nodded. I wasn't sure if we were, but the last thing I wanted was my family's help.

* * *

288

When I got back to the apartment, everything was quiet. I could see a light under my sister's door, which usually meant she was studying. Though it wasn't part of her job description, Imogen was washing dishes. I went into the kitchen to talk to her.

"I made dinner," Imogen said. "And I gave your brother an aspirin."

"Thank you very much," I said. "You didn't have to do any of this."

Imogen turned off the water. "I care very much for you and your brother and sister, Annie. Even though Galina is dead, I still worry for you."

I nodded and suddenly I had what I thought was a very good idea. "I hope this won't offend you, but would you be willing to stay on for the next couple of weeks?" I asked her. "I know you're a health-care worker, not a nanny, but I could really use the help. And it might make things more normal for them." I gestured down the hallway toward where we slept. "Mr. Kipling will pay you the same amount you've always been paid."

"Only I won't have to deal with any bedpans." Imogen smiled at me.

"If you ever wanted to stay over, you could use Nana's room," I said.

"Sounds good, Annie. Honestly, I was hoping to be asked."

Though I am not much of a hugger, I hugged Imogen. She was holding her arms wide out to me, and it would have been rude not to.

She offered to heat up some dinner for me, but I declined. My stomach was still a bit wonky.

"Toast?" she offered.

289

I had to admit, that sounded good.

She cut off the crusts and set the toast on a pretty porcelain plate and then she sent me to bed.

When I went into my room, I found Win waiting for me. He was reading a book.

"Oh," I said. "I didn't know you were still here."

"You didn't say goodbye earlier," Win said, setting the book on the bed. (The book was one of Imogen's.) "I didn't know where you'd gone. I was just waiting to see if you'd been killed. Now that I see you aren't dead, I can leave." Win stood up. He was almost a foot taller than me. I felt small and wretched next to him.

"I'm sorry," I said. "It couldn't be avoided."

"'It couldn't be avoided'? Is that the best you can do for an apology?" He was smiling when he said this.

"I . . . My life is complex. I really am sorry."

Win furrowed his brow and then he kissed me. "You're forgiven."

"The only thing I've done today is apologize. I'm starting to feel like the sorriest person on earth."

"Don't be so hard on yourself," Win said. "I doubt you're the sorriest person on earth. Earth is a very big place."

"Thanks."

"I was starting to wonder if you'd run off with Yuji. Is that how you say his name?" Win asked.

"Yes."

"I was starting to be jealous."

"Don't be," I said. "Yuji is twenty-three. He's way too old for me."

"And you prefer me, right?"

"Yes, of course I prefer you. Stop being so silly, Win."

"Twenty-three isn't all that old," Win teased me. "By the time you're eighteen, he'll only be twenty-five."

"Funny. That's the exact same thing Natty once said about you. Except you're only four years apart from her."

"Does Natty have a crush on me?" Win asked.

I rolled my eyes. "Can't you tell? She's sort of obsessed with you."

Win shook his head. "That's cute."

The doorbell rang, and I went to answer it. I looked through the peephole. A man I'd never seen before carried a cardboard box wrapped in clear cellophane (the expensive kind that you didn't see much in those days because it wasn't recyclable). He was shorter than me with thin limbs that seemed suspicious in contrast with his round belly. I wondered if he was really fat or if all that padding concealed something nefarious: i.e., a weapon.

"Delivery for Anya Balanchine," he called.

"Who's it from?" I asked without opening the door.

"Didn't say," the supposed delivery man replied.

"One minute," I called back. I went to Nana's closet to retrieve Daddy's gun. I tucked it into the waistband of my skirt and returned to the foyer. I left the chain on and opened the door a crack.

"What is it?" I asked.

"If I told you, it'd spoil the surprise," the delivery man replied.

"I don't like surprises," I said.

"Come on, all girls like surprises," said the delivery man.

"Not me." I moved to close the door.

"Wait! It's flowers!" he said. "Just take them, will you? You're my last stop of the night."

"I'm not expecting any flowers," I told him.

"Well, that's how it works. People don't usually expect flowers."

He had a point.

"Sign here." The man held out the cardboard box and then gave me an electronic device to sign.

I told him that I'd rather not.

"Come on, kid. Stop making my life so hard. Sign here, will ya?"

"Why don't you do it for me?" I asked.

"Fine," he said. Then he muttered, "Kids these days ain't got no manners."

I took the surprisingly heavy box into the kitchen. I cut open the cellophane with a knife. Twenty-four yellow roses cut short sat in neat rows in a shallow square vase. They were the nicest flowers I'd ever been sent. I tore open the cream paper envelope with my name on it and read the message:

> Dear Anya,
>
> I apologize if I was hard on you today. You have experienced a very great loss and my behavior was little more than that of a thoughtless bully.
>
> I, of all people, know the sacrifices you make. Know that you are neither alone nor friendless.
>
> Your Old Friend (I hope),
> Yuji Ono

P.S. When I was still a boy, I once had reason to be in the depths of despair. Your father shared these words with me: Our deepest fear is not that we are inadequate, but that we are powerful beyond measure. These words have always stayed with me, which is why I now pass them on to you.

P.P.S. One of these days, perhaps you will have opportunity to return to Kyoto.

In order to fit all of that on the card, the writer had had to make his letters small and precise. Though I couldn't be sure, I thought it was Yuji's own handwriting—he could have stopped at the florist on the way to the airport—and this, along with the formal wording, were very great signs of respect to me. Beyond that, there was the gift of hearing something my father had said. I could hold on to that long after the flowers had died. I bent down to smell the roses. The scent was clean and peaceful, suggesting a place I had never been but should very much like to visit someday. I did not particularly care for flowers, but these were . . . I had to admit, these were lovely. I had just slipped the card into my pocket when Win came into the kitchen. He asked me who had sent me the flowers, and without knowing why, I lied.

"One of my relatives couldn't make it to Nana's wake," I explained.

"They look expensive," he commented. "I should go," he said. "I'm meeting up with some guys from the non-band."

"So soon?" I felt like I'd barely seen him.

"Anya, I've been here eight hours!"

After Win was gone, I sat down at the kitchen table across

from my roses, and I read the card again. I wondered why Yuji had been in the depths of despair. Had it been the death of his father? Or had it been before that? I remembered that he had been kidnapped as a boy. That was how he had lost his finger, though I wasn't sure of the specifics.

I read the card yet again. Is it going too far to say that his card made me feel seen? I had spent so much of my life trying to keep us unseen: i.e., alive and well. And yet someone had guessed. Someone had seen. Someone had apologized to me. And not just anyone, but someone uniquely positioned to know how things stood, who knew the game from the player side. Someone who had suffered as I had.

I was not alone.

I slipped the card back into my pocket and then I went to Nana's room to return the gun to her closet.

XVII. i make plans for the summer

THE FIRST THING I DID WHEN I got back to school was go to see Natty's teacher. While I was convalescing, I had come to a decision about the genius camp: namely, that Natty should go to it and that I should do everything in my power to make this happen. Upon hearing the news, Miss Bellevoir behaved in an expectedly ludicrous manner—hugging and kissing me, then loading me down with instructions and phone numbers and deadlines and costs. "We are now joined together in this noble quest," she said to me as I left. I did not want to be joined to her. I had more than my share of obligations as it was.

My conversation with Miss Bellevoir took longer than I had anticipated so I was five minutes late to Dr. Lau's FS II class. In general, Dr. Lau was relaxed about tardiness, especially mine, but on this day she lowered her glasses and said in a cement voice, "Ms. Balanchine, I'd like to have a word with you after class." Her tone was such that it made my classmates *ooh*. I took my seat next to Win and waited for the hour to end so that I could receive my punishment. I liked Dr. Lau and I was a good student, but this had certainly not been my strongest year academically. I'd missed nearly a month of school in total, and FS II was an especially hard class to make up, having as much of a lab component as it did.

The bell rang. I told Win to go on ahead. "Good luck," he said.

I walked slowly to Dr. Lau's desk. I resisted the urge to apologize for my absenteeism. It's a weakness to apologize before hearing what the other person's grievances are. You don't want to end up creating new grievances where there were none to begin with. (Another Daddy-ism, if you hadn't already guessed.) "Ah, yes, Ms. Balanchine," Dr. Lau said, "I'd like you to have a look at this."

She tapped the screen to send a file to my slate. I opened and then skimmed it:

TEEN CRIME SCENE ENRICHMENT SUMMER

JUNE 30–AUGUST 15, 2083
Washington, D.C.

Sponsored by the FBI and the National Society of Criminologists

Deadline: April 8, 2083

Teachers, only your best young criminologists need apply.
Students must be rising juniors and seniors, have completed
at least two (preferably three) years of forensic science

(crime scene processing, the handling of trace evidence, etc.),
and demonstrate extraordinary aptitude for the field.

Selection will be highly competitive.

I set down my slate and looked up at Dr. Lau.

"You've only had two years of forensic science, but they've been with me. I feel confident that two years with me stacks up to three years with most any other teacher," Dr. Lau boasted. "It's a solid program," she continued. "Lots of field research, which is not something I can provide for you here. And you'd get to spend the summer away with kids your own age. They have activities—ice cream socials and bowling and such. Not that this is the point. You have a mind for forensic science and this could be an important step for you, Anya."

The idea of visiting actual crime scenes was certainly appealing. But even more appealing than that was the possibility of spending the summer away.

The summer away. Other people spent summers away. Scarlet, for instance, had passed several of them at a theater camp in Pennsylvania. I spent summers here, watching my brother and sister and Nana. And I knew for a fact that Win wasn't doing anything this summer except filling out applications for college. There were worse ways to pass the summer than hanging out with my boyfriend, assuming I was able to keep him.

"I can't," I said finally.

"I thought you'd say that." Dr. Lau nodded. "I know a bit about your circumstances and I've prepared a counterargument. Would you like to hear it?"

I nodded.

"Then I will speak bluntly. Your grandmother is dead, so you don't have to watch her anymore. In all likelihood, Nataliya will be attending genius camp with Miss Bellevoir—"

I interrupted. "How did you know about that?"

"Teachers do talk, you know. Your brother, Leonyd, may be somewhat mentally disabled, but he is a grown man and you cannot babysit him forever. If anything, a summer away would be good practice for your inevitable separation from him." She paused to see how I was responding. I made sure to keep my face blank. "That deadpan will serve you well as a criminologist, Anya. My final point is that you haven't been accepted to the program yet. Despite the glowing recommendation I will surely write for you, they only accept one hundred students to the program, and you have a handicap, which is that you've only had two years of forensic science. In other words, you may as well apply now and decide later."

Her argument was well thought out and comprehensive. "Thank you," I said.

I put off my application until the last Sunday of Easter vacation. Mainly what tripped me up was the essay. There was a choice of five questions. After much deliberation, I picked the fifth: *What is the relation of forensic science to your life?* The writing did not come easily to me. It was such a personal subject, really. I wrote about my father being murdered and how the cops hadn't done a thorough job investigating the crime scene because they had assumed he was a criminal. And though it was true that my father had been a criminal, he had also been a father and a son. I wrote that all people, no matter their background or how obvious the circumstances of their crime look, are owed a thorough investigation. I wrote that even more than the victims, the survivors of a crime are owed the peace of mind of knowing what happened, so that they can get on with their lives. Forensic scientists weren't merely scientists for the dead, but, really, priests and therapists for the living, too.

Then I paid the postage, hit send, and, for the moment at least, managed not to feel as if I was betraying anyone.

The phone rang. I thought it might be Win, but it turned out to be Mr. Kipling. He said that he had some news for Leo. The animal clinic where Leo used to work had finally cleared up its health-code-violations situation, and would reopen on June 1. "I still don't know where the original tip came from," Mr. Kipling said, "but this is good news, right?"

"You have no idea!" I said. I told him about my application to Teen Crime Scene Summer and Natty's admittance to genius camp, and how much better I would feel knowing that Leo was back working at the animal clinic instead of at the Pool.

"A summer away would be good for you, Annie," Mr. Kipling said. "Just the thing to get you on the road to your first-choice college. Have you put any thought into that yet?"

"Um . . ."

"Well, there's still time for that. And, of course, the offer about the college tour still stands," Mr. Kipling said. "Maybe on the way back from your summer program even?"

"We'll see," I said.

"As I mentioned, the clinic won't reopen until the summer, and I'm not sure it's the best thing for any of you if Leo appears to be switching jobs too often or has too long a period of unemployment. Nothing that bad has happened to Leo at the Pool, right?"

"Aside from the punch, and it seems that was mainly his fault, not that I know of."

"So, perhaps we should leave well enough alone for the time being. Leo stays on at the Pool until the clinic reopens in June."

After I hung up the phone, I went down the hall to my brother's room to tell him the good news.

I knocked on Leo's door. He was lying on his bed, staring out the window. Though his eye was much improved, he seemed preoccupied and listless. I asked him a series of questions about his day to which I received a series of one-word replies.

"You seem tired, Leo," I said finally.

"I'm fine," he said.

"Is it your head?"

"I'm fine, Annie! Stop fussing at me."

"Well, I have good news for you," I said brightly. "I was on the phone with Mr. Kipling. He said the clinic will be reopening in the summer!"

Leo smiled for the first time in weeks. "Oh, that's so great!"

"Do you think you'd like to work there again?" I asked him.

Leo thought for a moment, and then he said, "I don't think I can."

I asked him why not.

"They need me at the Pool, Annie."

"They need you at the clinic, too. What about the animals, Leo?"

Leo pulled his mouth into an obstinate line and shook his head.

I wanted to yell *Why do they need you? A million guys can get the sandwiches but only one guy can be Natty's and my guardian. It isn't safe there, Leo! Look at your eye! And if I'm to even consider the possibility of going to Teen Crime Scene Summer, I'd like to know you're not going to get yourself shot!* But I didn't. Yelling was never an effective tactic with my brother. Besides, Leo's cheeks were already starting to flush and his lips had moved from a line to being pursed up like a pink carnation. I could tell he was on the verge of tears, so I decided to take another approach.

"Leo," I said. "I need your help."

"Help?" Leo said. "There's nothing I wouldn't do for you, Annie."

"I've been thinking about maybe going away for the summer. It's this silly little teen program for kids who are contemplating careers in forensic science. Do you think you'd be able to manage without me? Imogen could make your meals and Mr. Kipling would take care of the financial arrangements. And I'd make sure that you were able to call me whenever you wanted if you needed anything at—"

"I'm not a child, Annie. I'm a grown man."

"I know that, Leo. Of course, I know that. I just wanted to make sure you knew that everything was taken care of. For the next two years, you're Natty's and my guardian. You're very important now."

"Yes, I'm very important," he said in a tone that could almost be described as sarcastic. "I'm Anya Balanchine's very important older brother. I'm very, very important, and I need to sleep. Would you mind turning off the lights when you leave, Annie?" Something about this little speech did not sit well with me, and yet, I did not press. I decided it was as he said: he was tired, nothing more.

Leo rolled away from me. I kissed him on the side of the head, on the raised scar from where they'd had to slice into his head. He was not that much younger than Yuji Ono, and if not for that scar, he could even be Yuji Ono. Someone like him, I mean.

I kissed Leo a second time. "Good night, sweet prince," I said.

"Mommy used to say that," Leo said.

"Really?"

Leo nodded sleepily.

I didn't know what made me think of it or use it that night. Later, I'd learn it came from *Hamlet*, that some character had said it after Hamlet had died, and I'd wonder what Mom had been thinking, bidding her only son good night with such ominous words. About many things, though, I wondered what my mother had been thinking.

She died when I was six years old, so, in a way, she was like a fictional character to me, and a poorly drawn one at that. I knew she was a crime scene investigator, that she fell in love with my father, that she gave up her career for him, and that she died. I remembered that she was pretty (though what mother isn't to a little girl?), and that she smelled of a particular lavender hand

302

lotion. I wouldn't recognize the sound of her voice if you played me a recording nor could I recall a single conversation I ever had with her. Though I missed the idea of her, the idea of having a mother, I barely missed *her* at all. How could you miss someone you didn't know? Whereas Daddy . . . My brain was filled with Daddy, but you already know that about me.

So, it was strange for me to have any memory of my mother, even something as small as remembering what words she had used to bid Leo good night.

"Do you miss her?" I asked, sitting back down on his bed.

"Sometimes," Leo said. "My brain . . . I forgot a lot." Then he smiled at me. "But you look like her. This, I know. You're beautiful just like her." He touched my cheek with the back of his hand. Then he smoothed out the furrow between my brows. Then he wiped away the tear that must have fallen from my eye. "Go to camp, Annie. You don't have to worry about me anymore, I swear."

That night, I dreamed of Teen Crime Scene Summer. I dreamed of Scarlet in my bedroom, helping me decide what to pack. I dreamed of Natty and Leo and Win waving goodbye to me at the train station. I dreamed of my roommate, a skinny redhaired girl, offering me my pick of bunks. I dreamed of white chalk lines on the pavement and evidence in neat plastic bags. I dreamed of ice cream socials and excursions to museums, real ones with paintings inside. How old-fashioned these trips were, but still kind of fun. Best of all, I dreamed of all the people I would meet, how none of them would know anything about me. In New York, I was Anya Balanchine, daughter of a slain crime boss, but outside the state my family was far less famous. Hadn't

Nana once mentioned some other Balanchine from a century back? A choreographer, maybe? A dancer? Yes, I would say I was related to that one. "I'm Anya Balanchine. I come from a long line of ballerinas."

I could see it all so clearly.

XVIII. i am betrayed

THE NEXT DAY, Scarlet and I were getting changed after Fencing when she asked me about Win's and my plans for the prom. "Do you think you guys will go?" she asked.

I told her that we hadn't discussed it yet, but I didn't see why not. In general, Win liked that sort of thing. And since Fall Formal had been such a debacle, I was planning on asking him this time. "Why?"

"Well, it's only a month off, and I'm on the junior planning committee, so . . ." Her voice trailed off. "And the thing is, someone asked me," Scarlet said.

"Already? That's great!" I kissed her on the cheek. "Don't tell me. You got back with Garrett Liu."

"No . . ." she said.

"Who is it?" I teased. "Is it someone who goes to our school? Or some sexy older man?"

She didn't say anything.

"Who, Scarlet?" The longer she didn't speak, the more it began to occur to me what (or rather who) her silence might mean. "You can't mean—"

"It's a friends thing. And we've been thrown together so much since he's come back to school. It isn't romantic. *Obviously*. Gable's just someone to go with."

There. She'd said the name.

"Scarlet, you can't! He's awful. He's completely awful," I sputtered. I shook my head. There were no words. I couldn't even look at her.

"He's changed, I swear. You've seen Gable. He's different than he once was. How could he not be? After what happened to him, I mean. He lost his foot, Annie. I . . . I feel sorry for him, I guess."

"Is that it?" I asked. "You feel sorry for him?"

"I . . . Look, it's not like I'm Miss Popularity myself. No one ever asks me anywhere. They think I'm the . . . weird drama girl. Or Anya Balanchine's odd friend. I might be silly, but I know what people say. And what do you care anyway? You have Win."

"Scarlet, you know that's not the point! The point is"—what was the point?—"the point is, we're talking about the boy who practically tried to rape me the night before school started."

"I asked him about that. He said you misunderstood—"

"I did not misunderstand!"

"Listen a second, would you? He said you misunderstood, but only a little. That he wanted to have sex with you, but that he would never have forced himself on you, even if Leo hadn't shown up. Either way, he knows he was wrong. He was in the wrong. He shouldn't have gone into your bedroom that night.

He shouldn't have said the things he said after either. He knew you were a good Catholic girl—that's what he said, Annie, 'a good Catholic girl'—and that he never should have put you in that position. He knows he took advantage of your situation. He knows, Annie. And he's sorry. We spent hours talking about what happened between you two. I couldn't even consider going with him if I didn't believe he was really and truly contrite."

"He's lying, Scarlet. He's manipulating you." I tried to control my breathing. I was dangerously close to saying or doing something awful to Scarlet, and despite her current betrayal, she had been a very good friend to me.

"There's one other thing. I promised not to tell you this, but his parents wanted to sue your family over Gable's poisoning. But Gable talked them out of it. He said it was his fault for asking for the chocolate. He took all the blame and told them that the rest was an unfortunate accident—"

"*It was an accident!* How noble of him, Scarlet, admitting that what was an accident was an accident!"

"Yes, but Gable had and has a lot of medical bills, so even though it was his own gluttony that led to his poisoning—"

I interrupted her. "Listen to me, Scarlet. If you go to prom with Gable Arsley, we can't be friends anymore."

Scarlet shook her head. Her eyes filled with tears. "Gable said you would say that, but I thought he was wrong. Your life has been hard, but you are not the only person in the world who suffers, Annie. Gable has been suffering. All you have to do is open your eyes and look at him to see how much." She took a deep breath. "People do change."

"Gable Arsley has *not* changed."

"I was talking about me. I love you, Annie. I love your whole family. I love Leo and Natty and I would do anything for you, but I want to do something for me for a change."

"You consider going to prom with the gimpy boy something for you?" I said cruelly. "Perhaps you've set your standards a tad low, Scar."

"That remark was below you," she said. She picked up her schoolbag and left the locker room.

I used my last quarter to splash my face. I seriously felt like I might kill someone.

I went into the cafeteria. Scarlet must have already been in the lunch line. I didn't see Win, but across the chessboard floor of the cafeteria, I did see Gable Arsley.

At this point, the whole world went into slow motion.

I was running toward Gable.

I picked up a tray from one of the other tables.

"Hey! That's my food!" called Chai Pinter, but her voice sounded like she was under water.

Now I was running toward him carrying the tray, red sauce splashing in tiny spikes.

Suddenly, I was standing an inch in front of him. I was about to pour the lasagna over his head when I noticed his face. The ruined texture of it. The strange pinkish hue where the skin graft was. And farther down, the missing fingertips which, had they been there, might have pointed me toward his missing foot.

I felt Win's hand on my arm.

And then Scarlet was there, too. "Anya, leave him alone! Please, you have no idea how much pain he's in."

"Shh," Gable said to Scarlet. "It's fine."

I set the tray on the table in front of Gable.

I leaned down. It was the most intimate I'd been with Gable since that afternoon at the rehab center. My cheek was lightly brushing his cheek when I whispered in his ear, "You may have Scarlet fooled, but you and me have known each other too long, Gable. If anything ever happens to her, don't expect to live. You know who my family is and what they're capable of."

"I thought you were going to pour that lasagna over my head again," Gable cracked. "Just like old times."

I didn't reply. I wouldn't sit with Gable and Scarlet. Or speak to them either. I picked up Chai Pinter's tray and returned it to her.

"Sorry," I said.

"Ooh, is something happening between Gable and Scarlet?" Chai asked. "Are you totally mad?"

I walked away without answering. I sat down at a table that was as far away from Gable as possible. Win sat down across from me. He took an orange out of his bag and began to peel it.

"Did you know about this?" I asked him.

He shrugged. "Not for sure. I kind of thought something might be happening, but . . . I honestly thought they might just be friends."

"That's what Scarlet claimed, but still. It's the principle of the thing. She wants to go to prom with him. Can you imagine the absurdity of that?"

Win broke off a section of orange for me. "Prom, by definition, is sort of absurd, Annie. The tuxedos. The ball gowns. The punch bowl. I don't see how Scarlet going with Gable makes it any more absurd than normal."

"Whose side are you on here?"

"Yours," Win replied. "But also theirs," he added with a sigh. "One of the best things about your friend Scarlet is how compassionate she is. No one at our entire school likes Gable Arsley, Annie. Every single one of his old friends abandoned him. If we hadn't eaten lunch with him, he would have eaten alone. You know this. So, I can't help but think that if Scarlet can find it in her heart to be kind to Gable Arsley, who are we to stop her?"

"But she betrayed me, Win. How can I ever forgive that?"

Win shook his head. "I don't know what to tell you, Annie. She happens to be the most loyal friend you have."

For a guy whose father was a tough political operative, Win sure was naïve. Daddy used to say you could assume a person was loyal until the day she betrayed you. Then you should never trust her again.

"So I guess we won't be double-dating to prom?" Win joked.

"Technically I think it's too soon for that sort of joke," I told him. "And furthermore, I don't think I agreed to go with you yet." I was annoyed that he'd ruined my plan to ask him.

"But you will," he said. "I'm the only friend you have left."

I threw an orange slice at him.

Halfway through Mr. Weir's class, I was summoned to Headmaster's office. I assumed it was something to do with my lunchtime behavior. Either someone (Chai Pinter perhaps? Or Scarlet—who knew what she was capable of?) had reported me for running across the cafeteria like a madwoman or, alternatively, Gable himself had tattled about the threats I'd whispered in his ear. In any case, it was annoying. I hadn't done anything to anyone. Considering the circumstances, I thought I'd shown admirable restraint. "They're waiting for you," the school secretary said as I entered the foyer.

Who're they? I thought.

Two police officers were seated in front of Headmaster's desk. I recognized one of them from last fall when I'd been arrested. This seemed a bit excessive for what had happened at lunch. They couldn't arrest me for running across a cafeteria carrying a tray that wasn't mine. Could they?

"Hello, Anya," Headmaster said. "Have a seat."

I didn't.

"Detective Frappe," I said to the one I recognized. "You cut your hair."

"I had it relaxed," Frappe replied. "Thanks for noticing. So, let's get to it, shall we? You aren't in any trouble, Anya, but we do need to talk to you about something that's happened."

I nodded. My heart was beginning to flutter, and my stomach felt like there was an elastic band around it.

"Your brother, Leo, tried to kill Yuri Balanchine this morning with your father's gun."

I asked her to repeat what she had said. These words made no sense to me.

"Your brother shot your uncle with your father's gun."

"How did they know it was my father's gun?" I asked numbly.

"Your cousin Mickey was there, and he recognized it as such. Red handle. The words *Balanchine Special Dark* on the side."

If Mickey was right, it was the Smith & Wesson that had gone missing so long ago.

"You said 'tried to kill' Yuri. Does that mean Uncle Yuri is still alive?" I asked.

"Yes, but he's in serious condition. The bullet punctured his lung and he went into cardiac arrest," Frappe replied. "He's in the ICU."

I nodded. I didn't know if it would be better or worse for Leo if Yuri survived. "Is Leo alive?" I asked.

"Yes, but no one knows where he is. He shot once, then ran before anyone could stop him."

"Is he hurt?"

Frappe didn't know. "Your cousin Mickey shot defensively, but he wasn't sure if he hit him or not."

Poor Leo. He was probably so scared. Why had I ever allowed him to work at that place?

"Have any idea why your brother would have wanted to shoot Yuri Balanchine?" the other cop asked.

I shook my head.

"So, you'll get in touch with us if Leo tries to contact you? I think you'll agree that it'd be better for him if he ends up in our hands before he ends up in your family's."

I smiled and nodded and thought, *Like hell I'll turn Leo over to the police.*

The police left, but I couldn't move. Headmaster walked over to me. She placed her hand on mine. "Do you have anyone watching you at home? Leo was your guardian if I'm not mistaken? If there's no one to supervise you and your sister, I'll have to call Child Protective Services, Anya."

"Yes." And here, I stretched the truth. "We have a nanny. Her name is Imogen Goodfellow. She used to take care of Galina and now she watches us." I wrote down Imogen's phone number for Headmaster. Next, I asked her if Natty and I could take the rest of the day off in case Leo tried to go back to the apartment.

"Of course, Anya," Headmaster replied. "Be careful on your way home. There're already reporters out there."

I looked out the window. Sure enough, there was a hornet's nest of press standing on the sidewalk outside Holy Trinity.

Headmaster sent someone to get Natty from class and I asked if I could use the phone while I waited. I called Mr. Kipling and Simon Green. At the very least we would need a car to drive us home. I explained what had happened. For a moment, neither man spoke, and I wondered if the line had gone dead. "I'm sorry, Anya," Mr. Kipling said finally. "This news is truly beyond comprehension."

"Do you think Natty and I will need protection coming home?"

"No," Mr. Kipling said. "The family likely won't make any moves until Yuri's condition has stabilized. And even if they did, it's Leo they'll want to kill, not you."

When Natty arrived in the office, I told her about Leo. I expected her to cry, but she didn't. "Let's go light candles for Leo in the chapel," she said, wrapping her small hand around mine.

I agreed that it certainly couldn't hurt anything. "We'll need vouchers," I said.

But in my heart, I didn't think it would help much either.

* * *

For the next several days, Natty and I were like zombies. We ate, we slept, we bathed, we went to school. We did everything we were supposed to do in order to not appear as if we lacked supervision. But really what we did was wait for Leo to contact us.

I worried that he was dead. That Mickey had hit him and Leo was bleeding to death in an alley somewhere. I couldn't get a detailed account of what had happened because it wasn't safe for me to contact anyone in the family. I felt so isolated. I missed Scarlet. And I decided that it wasn't a good idea for Win to come visit either.

On the Friday after our fight, Scarlet came up to me. "I'm so worried about Leo," she said.

I ignored her. I wanted to talk to her, but I couldn't. As a confidant, I considered her to be compromised. She discussed me with Gable Arsley, after all. And who knew who he would tell?

I went to my classes, but the only subject that occupied me was why Leo had done it. I knew he'd punched Mickey because he'd thought he'd had something to do with Nana's death. Had Leo been going for Mickey and accidentally shot Yuri? I knew Jacks might have a few answers, but getting in touch with him wasn't an option at the moment.

I tortured myself by thinking about all the things I might have done to prevent this. I should have found out what had happened to Daddy's gun. I should never have let Leo go to work at the Pool. I should never have put the idea in Leo's head that Nana had been murdered. (He was so suggestible. For God's sake, of course she hadn't been murdered. She was practically a corpse already when she'd died.) I shouldn't have brought up the summer program. I shouldn't have put so much pressure on him

314

about being our guardian. I shouldn't have let myself be distracted by Win. I should have gone further to discourage Leo's relationship with Jacks. Anyway, I went on and on with these sorts of suppositions. I couldn't shake the feeling that this was my fault and that I had let Daddy down.

Monday morning, instead of going to Dr. Lau's class, I went into the chapel to pray. I couldn't concentrate. So many thoughts were bouncing around in my head.

I sat in a pew and crossed myself.

"Annie," a voice called in a hoarse whisper. I looked around the chapel. No one appeared to be here.

"In the middle," the voice called again.

I walked halfway down the aisle. Then I sat in another pew. Lying on the ground was Leo. I did not move to hug him though I wanted to. I focused my eyes on Jesus and kept my voice steady.

"I've been waiting for you," he said. "You don't say prayers as much as I thought you did. A school is a good place to hide. I get food in the cafeteria at night. Then I stay in the chapel all day. No one comes in here, and if they do, they think I'm some kid trying to skip class. When there's school chapel, I go to the theater. One day, I saw Scarlet kissing Gable Arsley, Annie. Did you know they were together? It makes me like her less. I knew they thought I would go back to the apartment, so I came here instead."

I wanted to cry. "Oh, Leo, that was very smart of you, but you can't stay here. Eventually, someone will see you. And then . . ."

"Pow! I'll be dead," he said rather cheerfully. Leo took the gun out of his waistband. Daddy's Smith & Wesson, like Mickey

315

had reported. I resisted the urge to take it from him. If the Balanchines showed up at school, Leo should have some ability to defend himself.

"Why did you do it, Leo?"

"There were a million billion trillion reasons." Leo sighed. "Because I'm the son of Leonyd Balanchine and I'm the rightful head of the family," he said. "Yuri is old and he's trying to set things up so that Mickey can be the next head. He's trying to steal my"—Leo struggled to find the right word—"my birthright.

"Also because Mickey is bad. He set up the Fre . . . Fre . . . Fre . . . chocolate poisoning to make his father look weak so that he could be the head sooner—"

"Wait, how do you know that Mickey set it up?" I asked.

"Because Jacks told me," Leo replied.

"What else did Jacks tell you?"

"That Mickey and Yuri made us go to the wedding so that they could kill Nana. Yuri controls the power and that's why the machines stopped."

"Leo! What sense does that make? Why would they want to kill Nana?"

"So I'd be too busy being a guardian to claim what is rightfully mine."

I put my head in my hands. My poor brother. "Oh, Leo, why would you even want to be the head of the family? It's a terrible job. Look what happened to Daddy."

Leo paused. "Because it was the only way to protect you and Natty from the people in our family."

"But Natty and I were fine until . . ."

"No you weren't. You were sent to jail last fall because of our family. You came home like a little broken doll, Annie. That's when I knew I had to do something. Daddy told me before he died that my job in life was to protect my sisters."

Stupid Daddy. He'd told me the same thing. "But, Leo, the best way to protect us would have been to stay out of it. Now they'll come for you. And if they find you, they'll probably kill you."

Leo slowly shook his head. "I know you think I'm dumb, Annie. That I'm like Viktor the Mule."

"Viktor the Mule?" Who the heck was Viktor the Mule? And then I remembered.

"You didn't know I was outside the door but I was. Nana said I was like him. That he was dumb and good for moving boxes. And you agreed. Dumb Leo. Just like Viktor the Mule."

"No, Leo, you misunderstood . . ." But he hadn't. He had heard exactly right.

"Everyone underestimates me, Annie. Just because I struggle with words and cry sometimes doesn't mean I'm an idiot. Just because I have seizures doesn't mean I'm weak and can't protect my sisters. Just because I was hurt doesn't mean I'm a worthless thing who never got better."

I wanted to scream, but I couldn't afford to attract attention to us. "Did Jacks explain this to you?"

"*No!* You haven't been listening, Annie. This is me. Maybe Jacks told me a couple of things about how the family works. But I did this myself, Annie. I did this for all of us."

Leo was delusional and dead wrong. He had been manipulated by Jacks, that much I knew. But it didn't change the fact

317

that Leo was now an attempted murderer. If the Family got to him, Leo would be killed. If the police got to him, Leo would be sent to prison, which could be even worse than death for a person like my brother.

I had to get him out of the country. But first I had to get him out of this school.

I crossed myself again and said a quick prayer.

I made Leo promise to keep alternating pews throughout the day to reduce the chance of being spotted. I gave him my school scarf to wrap around his head so that, if he was seen, he might be mistaken for someone else.

I left the chapel and went into the church secretary's office. The office was empty as they had yet to replace the secretary these many months later. I picked up the phone. It was nine at night in Kyoto. I didn't think it was too late to call, but even if it was, it couldn't be helped.

Yuji answered the phone in Japanese.

"Yuji, it's Anya Balanchine. I need a favor." I explained my situation. "I don't expect you to watch Leo, but I can't leave him in this country. He'll be killed and they'll be right to do it. Still, I can't let my brother die, can I?"

"Of course not," Yuji replied.

"I'm hoping that you'll be able to arrange a secret transport of some kind for Leo to Japan. Again, I know it would compromise you to have him in your home, so I was hoping you might find an institution of some kind where they could watch him. He's lost his mind. He has no sense of his abilities, of his limitations. I believe the associate you warned me about, Jacks, has been puffing him up, though to what end, I still don't know."

"I will arrange the transportation and a place for your brother," Yuji said.

"Thank you. Of course, I'll pay you for everything, but it can't be right now."

"Not a problem."

"I . . . It might seem a little disingenuous coming on the heels of me asking you for such an enormous favor, but I wanted to thank you for your flowers and especially for your note."

"Yes, of course, Anya. May I ask you a question?" he asked.

"Yes."

"Do you have any idea how and when you're going to get him out of your school? If it's as surrounded by media and police as you say, I mean. And since you obviously can't bring him back to your home either."

"There's this school dance coming up in two weeks. It's a big one. With catering and fancy clothes and lots of people coming in and out. I think I'll be able to get him out then, though I don't know exactly how yet," I said.

"It is my theory that he should go straight from your school to the transport. Less chance of anything happening to mess things up."

I agreed. We decided that we would talk in exactly two weeks, at which time Yuji Ono would give me the details of where Leo was to go. I would call him from the school. I couldn't be sure that our home line wasn't tapped.

"Thank you," I said for maybe the fourth time.

"It's my pleasure. Someday, and I hope this day will never come, I may call on you to return the favor."

Yes, I knew what that meant. "And, Yuji, make it as nice a place as you can find for Leo. He's done this horrible thing, but he's a gentle soul. He's just a child." My voice wavered a bit on *child*, betraying more emotion than I would have liked.

I went to Fencing. I hadn't spoken to Scarlet since she'd told me about Gable, so she was surprised when I cornered her in the girls' locker room.

"Scarlet, are you still on the prom committee?" I whispered.

"Oh, now Miss Balanchine decides to talk to me! Well, I don't know if I want to talk to you," Scarlet replied.

"Scarlet, I don't have time for this. I need you to help me with something important. And you have to swear you won't tell Arsley about it. If you tell Arsley, people could die or get hurt."

"I don't tell Gable everything, you know." Scarlet lowered her voice to a whisper. "Is it about Leo?"

I made sure no one was watching us or listening, then I nodded.

"What can I do?" she asked.

"He's here," I said. "At school. I've arranged for him to go far away, but I need to figure out a way to get him out of here. I was hoping to do it on prom night. I don't want anyone but us to know. I'm not going to tell Win or even Natty."

Scarlet nodded. "So, you still trust me even though I'm going to prom with Gable."

"What I believe," I said diplomatically, "is that you would never do anything to hurt Leo or Natty or me. You're my oldest friend, and I need your help."

Scarlet took that statement at face value. She hugged me. "I missed you so much!"

I hugged her back. I had missed her, too.

Scarlet and I whispered plans all through Fencing for the next week. We didn't resume sitting together at lunch, though. That way, no one would suspect she was helping.

Some of the plans we came up with were too elaborate. For example, build a piñata horse on wheels for decoration and have Leo ride in a cavern inside. Piñatas were overly complicated to build, requiring paper licenses and a knowledge of piñata-building, and they were totally inappropriate to the theme of the prom, which was "Hawaiian Paradise." What we ultimately decided on was very simple: hide Leo in plain sight. We reasoned that since many boys would be going into the dance in tuxedos, why couldn't Leo just walk out wearing one? At 9:30, about an hour into the dance, Leo would simply walk outside and get into a car. He'd look just like any other boy at the dance. Scarlet and I even arranged for Gable, Win, and Leo to rent the exact same tuxedo. Entirely unbeknownst to any of them, they'd assist in the illusion that Leo was another male student, indistinguishable from any other.

Funny story: about ten days before the prom, Win asked me if I still wanted to go. "You've been under so much stress," he said, "and I know I like these things more than you. I'd definitely understand if you wanted to sit this one out."

"No," I said. "I want to go with you. I think it's best for me not to wallow. To be out and about as much as possible." This was true, but what I failed to mention was that my brother's very survival depended on me attending that dance. I had never anticipated a formal event so much in my whole life.

The week of the prom, I called Yuji Ono as scheduled. He had arranged for Leo's transport as he'd said he would. "A car will take Leo to a boat that will take him to an island off the coast of Massachusetts. From there, I have arranged for a private plane to take him to Japan."

"And in Japan, what waits for him there?" I hesitated to even ask.

"I found a very suitable place for him. I think you will be pleased. It's a Shingon Buddhist monastery in the foothills of Mount Koya. There is a lake with fish in it and many animals. I recall you telling me that your brother has a soft spot for animals. The monks who live there are a peaceful people. They eat fish, but no other meats. And even better, the language barrier will not be a problem for your brother nor will you have to worry about the discretion of the community—most of the monks who live there are under a vow of silence. It is not a harsh lifestyle, and I believe the monks will be very kind to your brother, Anya."

I closed my eyes. I imagined Leo wearing a sun hat, fishing in a wooden *bekabune*. The sky and the water were so blue you could barely tell where one ended and the other began.

"It sounds like paradise. How do you know about such a place?" I asked.

"A long time ago, I once thought I should like to stay there myself," was Yuji Ono's reply.

* * *

322

After an endless week that included many secret discussions with both Scarlet and Leo, and my own private worries that Leo's hiding place might be discovered, the night of the prom finally arrived. Win bought me a corsage with a single white orchid to wear on my wrist. The orchid was lovely but in combination with my black dress the effect was a bit funereal.

"I didn't want to get you roses," Win explained. "Too clichéd for someone like Anya Balanchine."

"Have a good time, you two!" Natty called as she took our picture. She set down the camera. "I wish I was going."

"Here," Win said, setting his hat on Natty's head. "Take care of my hat for me."

We got to the dance at 8:30. I danced several dances with Win, then I excused myself to the ladies' room on the third floor where I was to meet up with Scarlet. Scarlet's job had been to bring the tuxedo and get Leo dressed.

"Is Leo in the tux?" I asked her.

"Yes," Leo answered for her, stepping out from one of the stalls. Leo looked so handsome and grown-up. I almost wished I'd brought my camera to take a picture for Natty, though the impossibility of this should be obvious.

"Doesn't he look handsome?" Scarlet asked.

"Yes." I kissed Leo on the cheek.

"Are you sure I shouldn't escort him to the car?" Scarlet asked. She placed a black hat on Leo's head so that his face was obscured. "Just in case someone out there recognizes you."

We'd gone back and forth on this point several times and decided that since everyone knew Scarlet had gone to prom with Gable Arsley, who was wheelchair-bound, it would be better for me to escort Leo to the car. Leo would probably be mistaken for Win, if anyone noticed us at all. "No, we'll be fine. It's only fifty feet to the car."

"Leo, are you ready?"

Leo offered me his arm and I hooked mine through it. "Goodbye, Scarlet," he called. "You look beautiful tonight. Don't let Gable Arsley be mean to you."

"I won't, Leo. I swear," Scarlet said.

We walked down the stairs, past administration, past the gymnasium, where the dance was being held, and past the ticket area. We were almost out the front doors of the school when I heard someone call my name. It was Dr. Lau, one of the chaperones that night. I turned to go speak to her, silently praying that Leo would know enough not to follow me.

"Good news, Anya! I've been looking for you everywhere. I wanted to tell you in person that I have just received word that your application to Teen Crime Scene Enrichment Summer has been accepted."

"Oh, wow, that's great," I replied. "I . . . I'm feeling a little light-headed. Would you mind if we talked about this more later?"

"Is something the matter, Anya?" Dr. Lau asked.

"Everything's fine," I replied. "I need a little fresh air. I'll be back in five minutes." I pushed open the heavy double doors of the school and pulled Leo through them. We walked down the sidewalk. Three boys in tuxedoes were tossing a football around. Girls in long dresses were sitting on the front steps of the school. Chai Pinter was among this group, but she didn't see me. No paparazzi or reporters in sight, not that it would have mattered if there had been. Leo's ride was leaving now. There was no time to delay.

As it was a special occasion, several kids had rented cars for the evening. At the end of a row of black limousines, I spotted Leo's: a black Town Car with a green four-leaf-clover air freshener attached to the rearview mirror.

We walked the rest of the way at an even pace. No one seemed to see us. Once we were standing by the passenger-side door, I gave Leo a quick peck on the cheek. "Have a good trip!" I said. I thought it best if we avoided any sort of lengthy good-byes. "Oh, hey, would you mind giving me back Daddy's gun?"

"Why?" Leo asked.

"You won't be needing it where you're going."

Leo removed the gun from the waistband of his pants, and I put it in my handbag.

"I love you, Annie. Tell Natty I love her, too. I'm sorry for the trouble I caused you."

"Don't be sorry, Leo. You're my brother. I'd do anything for you."

Leo got into the car. "Can I come home for Christmas?"

"No, Leo, I don't think so. But let's see what happens, okay? Maybe I'll be able to come visit you someday."

"And Natty?"

"Sure, Natty, too," I lied.

I watched Leo's car drive away, then I went back into the dance. Dr. Lau wasn't in the lobby anymore, which was just as well. I wanted to go inside and dance with my boyfriend and relax for a bit. Now that I'd finally seen Leo off, the knot that I'd been holding in my stomach for these last couple weeks had finally begun to untie itself. (It wouldn't be completely untied until I heard from Yuji Ono.)

I found Win. He was talking to some of the boys he played music with. "Where were you for so long?"

"I ran into Dr. Lau on the way back from the bathroom," I said. "I got into that summer program I applied to. She was talking my ear off about it."

"Congratulations!" he said. "I'm so proud of you. How long is it again?"

"Six weeks," I admitted.

"Well, that isn't so bad. I sure will miss you though," he said as he pulled me closer.

And then Win and I danced for several more songs. I had thought I didn't like dancing, but maybe I hadn't had the right partner up until then.

"Last song," the bandleader called out. "Everyone on the dance floor."

Across the dance floor, I could see Scarlet and Gable. I decided to go mend the fence with Scarlet officially. In front of Gable, I mean. "You're my best friend," I said to Scarlet once I'd gotten up to them, "but I don't control your life. And if you want to go to a dance with this imbecile, that's your business, I suppose."

Scarlet smiled at me. "Sure, Anya. Thanks. That means a lot to me."

"Hey!" Gable said to Scarlet. "Aren't you going to say I'm not an imbecile?"

Scarlet shook her head. "Well sometimes you kind of are one, Gable."

I walked back to Win. "Let's go," I said to him.

We left the dance arm in arm. We didn't have a car waiting for us, but were planning to take the bus as usual.

"Nice night," Win said. "You can tell summer's right around the corner."

That's when I heard the gunshot.

I reached my hand into my purse for Daddy's gun.

Another shot.

Win collapsed to the ground.

"Oh, God, Win!"

I took the gun out of my purse. I cocked it, aimed it, and then I shot.

The gunman was about fifteen feet away and it was dark, but I was a good shot. Daddy had made sure of that. I shot to disable, not to kill. I landed one bullet in the person's shoulder and a second in the kneecap.

I ran over to the gunman to kick his gun out of reach, then I went back to Win. Our classmates were gathering around him. "Someone call 911. Win Delacroix's been shot." My voice was calm even though I was not.

I kneeled down by Win's side. He was passed out from the pain. Or perhaps he'd hit his head when he fell. The only wound I could see was on his thigh. It was bleeding a lot, so I took off my wrap and tied it around his leg like a tourniquet.

I ran back across the courtyard to the gunman, who was also lying on the pavement. He was wearing a ski mask. I ripped

it off his face: it was Jacks. "Please don't shoot me. I wasn't trying to kill Leo, Annie. Honestly, I swear. I was only trying to
hurt him so I could bring him back to Yuri and Mickey."

"So they could kill my brother and you'd be the big hero,
huh? Well, you moron, that wasn't even Leo. Leo's not here.
That was my boyfriend, Win."

"Annie, I'm sorry. It was an honest mistake," Jacks said.

"Nothing you do is honest, Jacks." I wondered how Jacks
had found out that Leo was at the school. Had he guessed? Or
had Leo somehow been communicating with him? Or had a different person entirely been the informant? The only people that
knew our plan were Yuji Ono and Scarlet and I highly doubted
either one of them had told Jacks. I couldn't think about this right
now. And I couldn't ask Jacks either, because if I asked him, it
would be as good as admitting that we had managed to smug-
gle Leo out of the country tonight. "You do know who my boyfriend's father is, don't you?" I asked Jacks.

"The assistant DA," Jacks said as it slowly dawned on him
just whose son he had mistakenly shot.

"Good luck with that, cousin. All of our lives are about to
become a living hell," I said.

A police car showed up. "What happened here?" a cop
demanded.

"This man, Jakov 'Jacks' Pirozhki, shot my boyfriend," I
said. The cops put Jacks in handcuffs. I saw him wince as they
pulled his arm.

"So, who shot him?" The cop was pointing to Jacks.

"I did," I said, at which point I, too, was put in handcuffs.

And then an ambulance showed up to transport Win to the

328

hospital. I was desperate to go with him, but I was restrained by the handcuffs, of course. I screamed to Scarlet that she should ride with him instead, and she did.

And then another ambulance came to take Jacks away.

Finally, a second police car came, and this one was just for me.

XIX. i enact a fair trade

I WAS QUESTIONED FOR FOUR HOURS at the police station, but I told them nothing about Leo. All they knew was that a low-level mobster had shot my boyfriend and that I had shot back in self-defense. The only charges they could pin on me were relatively minor: possession of a concealed weapon and possession of a weapon with an expired permit. Not to mention, I had saved Charles Delacroix's son's life—so what if it had been me who had put the young man in jeopardy to begin with? From the police's point of view, I was a hero. Or, at least, an antihero.

And so I was sent home under house arrest while the powers that be tried to figure out what to do with me. They did not send me to Liberty as they were wary of sending me back there after the public relations fiasco of my last stay.

What else can I tell you? Oh yes, Leo. I had just begun my period of house arrest when word came from Yuji Ono that my brother had made it to Japan and was safely among the monks of

Koya. At least it hadn't all been for nothing, I suppose. On the phone, Yuji asked me if I needed anything further. I told him I didn't. He had helped me enough.

And you'll want to know about Win, of course. Charles Delacroix barred me from Win's hospital room. Mr. Delacroix also made sure that neither calls nor things I tried to send reached his son. Win's father was nothing if not thorough, and I suppose this was something to admire about the man.

I read in the news that the bullet had gone through Win's hip socket and that his leg was being held together with a series of metal rods and pins. He would recover, but Scarlet, who had visited him, reported that he was in a lot of discomfort. She also told me that his father had him monitored by around-the-clock security guards. "In theory," Scarlet said one day when she was over at the apartment, "it's to make sure no one tries to get at Win, but the reality is Charles Delacroix wants to make sure Win doesn't try to contact you."

As usual, I could understand Charles Delacroix's point of view. In less than a year, I had landed two boyfriends in the hospital. How could I be considered anything but a plague? If I had a son I loved, I would keep me away from him, too.

"But," Scarlet said, "guess what?"

"What?"

"I have a note. He didn't have much time to write it."

Scarlet handed it to me. It was scribbled on a clean piece of gauze.

Dear Anya,
Don't listen to my father.

Please come if you can.
I still love you. Of course I do.
Win

"Can I write one for you to give to him?" I asked.

Scarlet considered this. "Hmm. It'll be harder for me to bring one back from you. The guards don't let you take anything into his room. And if they saw I had a note from you, they might not let me come back. Why don't I say something to him for you?"

"Tell him . . ." What was there to say? I was beyond sorry. "Tell him thanks for the note."

"*Thanks for the note!*" Scarlet repeated in an overly bright way. "Will do!"

Two weeks after the shooting, I was granted leave from my house arrest to face the school's administrative board. Simon Green accompanied me. The ad board's task was to decide whether or not I would be allowed to attend senior year at Holy Trinity.

I won't bother you with the details, but they voted eleven to one to expel me from Holy Trinity. (The only dissenting vote had come from good old Dr. Lau.) Despite my numerous other offenses (fighting, insubordination, excessive absenteeism), it pretty much came down to the weapon that I had used to shoot Jacks. Apparently, they didn't want someone who was packing on the Holy Trinity campus. I would be allowed to finish my junior year classwork at home, but after that, I needed to find myself another school. I added this to my list of things to do.

The school's decision? I cannot honestly say I disagreed with it.

On the way back from Holy Trinity, I asked Simon Green if we could stop at the hospital.

"Do you think that's a good idea?" Simon Green asked me. "Charles Delacroix has made his feelings toward you perfectly clear."

"Please," I begged. (Daddy always said the only thing worth begging for was your life, but maybe he was wrong. Maybe sometimes your love is a little bit worth begging for, too.) "Please." Tears were running down my face and snot was coming from my nose. I was behaving like an infant. I was loathsome and wretched and Simon Green, who was softhearted and as green as his surname, took pity on me.

"All right, Anya. We can try," Simon Green said.

We rode the elevator to the juvenile ward. How absurd that tall, grown-up Win was still considered a juvenile. By chance, it was lunch hour, so there were no guards posted outside Win's room. We knocked on the door, which was orange with a cutout of a beach umbrella pasted to it. I suppose the cutout was meant to indicate that summer was nearly here even if it didn't feel that way when you were stuck in a hospital bed.

"Come in," a female voice called. I pushed the door open. The bed was empty. Win's mother was seated in a chair by the window. When she saw me, I thought she was going to yell at me to get out, but she didn't. "Win's having an X-ray. Please come in, Anya," she said.

Simon Green and I did not have to be asked twice. I knew

that this was a gift Win's mother was giving me, so I did my best to make small talk. "How are your oranges?" I asked.

"Very well, thanks." Mrs. Delacroix laughed. "I want you to know I think that Charlie's behaving like an absolute barbarian," Mrs. Delacroix continued. "What happened isn't your fault. If anything, your quick thinking saved Win's life."

"It's not as if I didn't have something to do with putting him in that situation in the first place," I felt compelled to add.

"Well, yes . . . Nobody's perfect, I suppose. Sit down a moment. Win will be back soon and I know he wants to see you. This, by the way, is a severe understatement."

There were no other chairs so Simon Green and I sat on the bed.

Simon Green and Mrs. Delacroix did most of the talking, as I found I was too anxious to speak.

Finally, an orderly wheeled Win back into the room. He was wearing a T-shirt and a pair of sweatpants that had one leg cut off to allow room for all the black pins and other hardware holding the hip and leg in place.

My beautiful Win. I wanted to kiss him on every last broken place, but his mother and my lawyer were there. So, instead I started to cry.

I had done this to Win.

Or if not done this, I had certainly been the reason this had happened to him.

Win's injuries were not nearly as bad as what had happened to Gable, but I felt Win's so much more. I suppose the difference was that I loved Win.

"Let's give the kids a moment alone," Mrs. Delacroix said.

"The guards will be back after lunch." Simon Green and Mrs. Delacroix went out into the hallway.

At first, I could barely look at him. He looked fragile. No wonder his father had wanted to lock him away from everyone.

"Say something," Win said gently. "You can't just stand there not speaking and not looking at me. I'll think you don't like me anymore."

"I was so scared," I said finally. "And worried for you. And then they wouldn't let me see you. Or call you or anything. And now I'm here and you're all broken and hurt. Are you in much pain?"

"Only when I try to stand or sit or turn over or breathe," he joked. "Here, help me back into bed, lass." He leaned on me to stand, then he pushed himself into bed. He winced.

"Oh," I said. "Did I hurt you?"

He shook his head. "No, of course not, silly girl. You make things better." I bent down, and I kissed his leg on one of the places where the pins went in. Then I crawled into his bed and lay down next to him for a bit.

We must have fallen asleep because the next thing I knew, guards were running into the room and pulling me out of Win's bed. I fell hard on the floor and landed on my knee. It would leave a terrible bruise, but in that moment, I barely felt it.

"Leave her alone," Win said. "She's fine! She's not doing anything."

"Your father's orders," the guard replied with an apology in his voice.

"He didn't say you should throw a sixteen-year-old girl on the floor," Win yelled.

"Come on," Simon Green said. "We should go before this gets worse."

"I love you, Anya," Win called out.

I wanted to reply but they'd already shut Win's door. As Simon Green was dragging me to the elevator, he muttered, "Mr. Kipling's going to kill me for taking you here."

Simon Green dropped me back at the apartment. After my return was noted by the policeman meant to monitor my actions and protect me from the rest of my family, I went straight to my room. On my way down the hall, I was accosted by Imogen.

"What happened to your knee?" she cried. The day had been warm enough that I was wearing my school skirt and no tights.

"Nothing," I said. In point of fact, my kneecap was starting to throb. I felt silly complaining when I compared it with Win's injuries.

"It doesn't look like nothing, Annie." She escorted me into my bedroom. "Lie down," she ordered, which was the only thing I'd wanted to do anyway. I was cried out—the well never ran very deep with me—and what I wanted to do was hibernate like a bear. The good thing about house arrest, about being isolated from most everything and everyone, was that I could sleep in the middle of the day and no one cared.

Imogen returned with the ubiquitous bag of frozen peas. "Here."

"It's fine, Imogen. I just want to sleep."

"You'll thank me later," she said.

I flipped onto my back. She felt around my kneecap. Ugly bruise, but nothing was broken and she assured me that I'd live. Then she set the peas in their place.

"Why is it always peas?" I asked, thinking about the numerous times I'd rested a bag of peas on Leo's head or the night we went to Little Egypt when I gave the bag to Win. Had this been the very same bag? I could not say for sure. "Don't we ever have frozen carrots or corn?"

Imogen shook her head. "The corn gets eaten the quickest. And none of you like carrots so they're never bought."

"That seems logical," I said. Then I told her that I wanted to sleep and so she left me alone.

Late that night (Natty had already gone to bed), I awoke to a knock at my bedroom door. It was Imogen. "You have a visitor," she said. "It's your boyfriend's father. Would you rather see him in here or in the living room?"

"Living room," I said. My knee had tightened up something awful, but I did not want to encounter Charles Delacroix in a horizontal (i.e., weak) position. I pulled myself out of bed. I smoothed down my school skirt and shirt, ran my fingers through my hair, and limped out to the living room.

"I'm sorry about that," Mr. Delacroix said, indicating my knee, which ten hours later had become black, blue, puffy, and all-around spectacular. He was seated in the crimson velvet chair, and I couldn't help but think of the times I'd seen his son seated in the same place.

"I'm also sorry about the late hour. Work has forced me to keep exceptionally long hours and also, well, I did not want to make my visit to you cause for a photo opportunity."

I nodded. "Maybe you also didn't want to see me with my lawyer present," I suggested.

"Yes, Anya, you're right. I wanted to have a discussion that was only between you and me. The situation we find ourselves in is personal but it is also business. That's what makes this matter unusually complex for me."

"Business is always personal if it's *your* business," I said.

Charles Delacroix laughed. "Yes, of course. I like you very much!"

I gave him a look.

"Oh, don't be so surprised. You're terribly likable, just not for my son."

At least he was honest.

"All right, so I'm here to give you the lay of the land, if you don't mind. We tested the bullets that you used to shoot your cousin. They came from the same gun that your brother used to shoot Yuri Balanchine. So, what are we to infer from this, Anya?"

I would not help him. "Why don't you tell me?"

"Smart girl," Mr. Delacroix said. "That you saw your brother and somehow got him to a safe location at which point he gave you the gun."

I took a deep breath. I would never tell where Leo was.

"Honestly, Anya, I don't care what happened to your brother. He shot a mobster who no one much liked, even his own men. So, if you got Leo, Junior, out of the country without getting him killed, good for you. You take care of your own, I understand that. And so you'll also understand why I have to do the same. The only thing I care about is the fact that you got my son shot."

I lowered my head. "I wish I could change things. I put him in danger's way and I'll never forgive myself."

"Oh, Anya, don't be so overdramatic. I sometimes forget you're only a sixteen-year-old girl until you go and say something silly like that. Win will recover and the experience will be character-building for him. Life has been too easy on Win. At this point, the main reason I care about Win getting shot is because it puts his name in the news and it links my name with your name. You see my problem?"

I nodded.

"If I don't punish you in some way for the possession charges, I'll be seen to be showing favoritism to the girlfriend of my son. Even worse, this person is tied to the *bratva* in some way. My enemies will argue that I am weak on organized crime. I can't afford that. I announce my candidacy for DA the first week of June."

"I see."

"So, I've told you my predicament. Would you like to know what yours is?" Charles Delacroix asked.

"Go for it."

"Actually, you have several problems, poor girl. The first is your brother. I don't care where he is but others in your family do, and if I release the bullet tests, they'll know what you did. They'll track Leo down, and they'll kill him. Possibly you, too. The second is your precious baby sister, who is, for the moment, without a legal guardian. I know you're the real guardian in the situation, but people are foolish and I doubt you want, say, Child Protective Services getting in your business. The third is the possession charges. We've gone over those. And the fourth is my son. He loves you. You love him. But ugh, his father! Why is he trying to keep you apart?"

Yes, that about covered it. "Looks pretty bleak."

"I can help you," he said. "I've been thinking of the first time we met on the ferry back from Liberty. I've been thinking of something you told me your father used to say to you. Do you remember what it was?"

"Daddy used to say a lot," I replied.

"You said that your father always told you that you shouldn't make an agreement unless you knew exactly what you were going to get out of it."

"Yes, that was Daddy," I said.

"Well, Anya, I once asked you not to pursue a relationship with my son, but I didn't have a counteroffer. Today, I do. This offer only lasts for a very short time, though. I need you to decide tonight."

And so, he laid it out for me. Mr. Delacroix would make certain that the information about the bullet tests would never be released to the public, thus securing Leo's safety. In exchange, I would be sent to the Liberty Children's Facility for the summer on the possession charges so that Mr. Delacroix could show his constituents that he was not weak on crime. While I was at Liberty, Natty would be at genius camp. (I asked him how he knew about that: "I know everything, Anya—it's my job.") This arrangement would help ensure that Child Protective Services would have no need to get involved with us as Natty would never go without a guardian. Over the summer, Charles Delacroix would help to push through the paperwork that made me an emancipated minor and also Natty's official legal guardian. In exchange, I would end things with Win. I would be allowed to see him one last time before going into Liberty, but that would only be for the purposes of breaking it off.

"I'm sorry about that last part," he said. "As I said, I like you very much. But as long as you're with him, it's an ongoing problem for me. And yes, perhaps I understated my concern for Win's welfare before. Though this first bullet was character-building for the boy, I'd rather him not get shot again. I'd like my son to live to see twenty."

I considered Charles Delacroix's offer: Liberty for three months and no more Win forever in exchange for my brother's safety and my sister's safety. Two for two. Yes, this seemed fair. It wouldn't be hard to end it with Win because, in a way, this was what I wanted to do anyway. I loved him, but he wasn't safe around me. "How do I know you'll keep your word?"

"Because I have as much to gain and to lose as you do," Charles Delacroix replied.

The third Sunday in May (two weeks until Liberty), Natty and I went to church for the first time in ages. I did not confess because the line was too long, as was my list of sins. I did receive the host. The liturgy was, appropriately enough, about sacrifice: how there was redemption in it, even if it wasn't always immediately apparent. And, this was nearly enough to steel me to do what I had to do next.

After church, Natty and I went to see Win at his apartment. Charles Delacroix had eased up on the guards. Win had also been told that his father had eased up on me. (Win had not yet been informed about my forthcoming stay at Liberty, however.)

Natty had missed Win terribly, maybe as much as I had. She drew flowers on the cast that had replaced the metal pins, and she also returned his hat, which had been in her possession since prom night. "Win and I need to talk alone for a bit," I told Natty.

"Ooh, are you guys going to kiss?" Natty teased us.

"Let's go outside," Win suggested. "I'm able to get around a little now. Besides, I'm in danger of turning into a total vampire if I don't see daylight every now and again."

We went out to his mother's rooftop garden. We sat down at a picnic table as Win still needed to rest often. It was incredibly sunny and I wished for sunglasses. Win put his hand over my eyes to shield them from the sun. What a nice boy he was.

I had practiced what I would say, which made my words sound rehearsed.

"Win," I began, "during our time apart, I've been thinking and I realized something. I don't think we're suited for each other."

Win laughed at me. I would need to up my game if he was to believe me.

"I'm serious, Win. We can't be together. We can't be." I made sure to look him in the eye when I said this. Eye contact made people think you were being truthful even when you weren't.

"Did my father put you up to this?"

"No. This is me. But I do think your father's right about you," I said. "I mean, look at you. You *are* weak. There's no point. I could never be with someone like you in the long term."

He said he still didn't believe me.

"There's someone else," I said.

"Who?" he barked.

"Yuji Ono."

"I don't believe you."

"Believe what you want," I said. "But I've been seeing him since my cousin's wedding. We have the same background and interests. He understands me, Win, in a way that you never could." And then I was crying. I hoped this would make me look guilty. My sister's and brother's lives depended on it.

"You're making this up!" Win said.

"I wish I was." I cried even more. "I'm sorry, Win."

"If this is true, you're not the person I thought you were," Win said.

"That's the thing, Win, you never knew me." I stood up from the bench. "I won't be seeing you again. I'm going to Teen Crime Scene Summer"—why I told this lie, I do not know; I suppose I didn't want him to think of me locked up all summer—"and then I won't be coming back to Holy Trinity in the fall. I don't know if you've heard that I've been expelled. You . . . I really did love you."

"You just don't anymore," he said flatly.

I nodded and then I left. Had I spoken, I feared giving myself away.

I went down to Win's room to get Natty. "We have to go," I said, grabbing her hand.

"Where's Win?" she asked.

"He . . ." And here, another lie. This one so that Natty didn't ask me a lot of questions. "He ended it with me."

"I don't believe you!" Natty said, pulling her hand from mine.

No one believed me. "I'm telling you, it's true," I said. "He told me that he'd met someone. A nurse in the hospital."

"Well, I hate him, then," Natty decided. "I'll hate Win Delacroix for the rest of my life."

She took my hand, and then we walked back to our apartment. "It's just as well," she said. "You'll meet someone new in Washington. I'm sure of it."

I hadn't had the heart to tell Natty that I was going to Liberty either. Miss Bellevoir had described Natty's camp as being "isolated from the rest of the world," which meant Natty wouldn't figure out where I'd been until she got back and saw I wasn't there. (In the four-week gap between her return and my release, Imogen would watch her.) My justification for this lie was that Natty had had a hard-enough year already: Nana's death, Leo's disappearance, and everything else. Let her think I was living it up at Teen Crime Scene Summer. I wanted her to feel free to enjoy herself and be the kid genius she was meant to be without worrying about her big sister in the reformatory. I wanted her to have the summer I might have had, if only things had been different.

X X. i set my house in order; am returned to liberty

THE FIRST MONDAY IN JUNE, Natty left for genius camp with Miss Bellevoir.

Following the terms of our agreement, Charles Delacroix announced my sentence to the media on Tuesday. It came toward the tail end of a press conference that had largely been about matters relating to his recently announced candidacy. "As Miss Balanchine is only a minor," he said, "she is being given the relatively light sentence of ninety days at Liberty Children's Facility. Let us not forget that she used the gun in self-defense and that she also saved a life that night. A life very near to my heart."

"Mr. Delacroix," a reporter called out. "Is Miss Balanchine still involved with your son?"

Mr. Delacroix replied, "Sadly, no! My sources tell me she has found a new boyfriend. The course of true teenage love never did run smooth." There was mirth in his voice when he said this, and I hated him for it.

Another reporter: "Is it true that while in detainment for shooting your son Jakov Pirozhki confessed to orchestrating the Balanchine chocolate contamination?"

"Expect an announcement about that in the next several days," Mr. Delacroix replied. "But yes."

So, Jacks had done it. Though Jacks had sworn that he hadn't and had told my brother it was Mickey, this news didn't exactly come as a surprise. Jacks would have done whatever he could to improve his position in the Family. I suspect that included the particularly repellent act of convincing Leo to shoot Yuri Balanchine, who was Jacks's own father, after all. Though Yuri's heart was badly damaged, he had, more or less, recovered. In the wake of Jacks's confession and to facilitate Natty's and my safety, I felt it was time to mend fences.

Wednesday, I called a summit with Yuri, Mickey, and all the other Balanchines.

Mr. Kipling accompanied me. Before we went in, he asked me, "Are you sure you want to do this?"

I assured him that I did.

Security at the Pool had been particularly tight in the months since the shooting, and Mr. Kipling and I were both thoroughly frisked before we were allowed in the building.

The space that had been chosen for the meeting was a round conference table that was at the bottom of a lap pool. A lift had been installed along the side of the pool for Yuri's wheelchair. The rest of us had to climb down using ladders. Everyone else had already arrived. My seat was at the opposite end of the table from Yuri's, in the deep end.

I was the only female at the meeting, and I had chosen my

wardrobe carefully. Nana used to say that it alienated the men if they thought you were trying to dress like them, so a men's suit was out of the question. I had tried wearing one of Nana's old dresses, but it seemed too formal and like I was playing dress-up. What I finally settled on was my good old school uniform. It was nonthreatening, I thought, but also somehow official.

I sat down in my chair, and Mr. Kipling stood behind me, as was the custom.

"So, young lady." Yuri's voice echoed across the pool. "You called this meeting. What do you have to say for yourself?"

I cleared my throat. Daddy always said that it was a lie that you should only speak from your heart—you ought to let your brain play a part, too. I cleared my throat again. "Many of you know that tomorrow I begin a three-month sentence at Liberty Children's Facility. It's not Rikers Island but it won't exactly be a trip to Hawaii either."

The men laughed at this.

"I wanted to speak to you today because this bloodshed has to stop. In the last ten years, I have lost my mother, my grandmother, and my father. My brother may or may not be dead, but he is lost to me. The only one I have left is my sister and"—here, I paused to look at each of the faces of my ragtag band of relatives—"all of you."

There were murmurs of approval.

"I think about what Cousin Jacks did, and what I feel is incredibly sad. He truly felt his only option was poisoning the supply and my brother's mind. You might wonder if I bear ill will toward Jacks, and I am here to tell you that I do not. My deepest hope is that there will be no more retaliations in the wake of Jacks's confession and that my sister and I can live our lives in peace. I am just a girl, and even I can see that we will destroy ourselves if we don't stop fighting each other. We must treat each other as family again." I paused. "That's all I have to say."

It was not the most eloquent speech, but I had said my piece.

Yuri peered up at me. "Little Anya, who is now a grown woman, I see. Anya, you have my personal assurances that no one will seek out your brother, if he should still be alive. And that, if in some time, after emotions have cooled, he should choose to return to you, young Leo will not be harmed. It was my mistake to employ him at the Pool against the wishes of my dear departed half brother Leonyd, and I have certainly learned my lesson. You have my additional assurance that you and your sister can go about in peace. No one holds you responsible for shooting my son Jacks or for his imprisonment. It pains me to say this but he is the product of a tainted union and perhaps the bastard deserves what he got."

Uncle Yuri rolled his wheelchair toward me. The chair descended easily, as the pool floor was sloped and I was seated in the deep end.

When he got to me, the old man kissed me on both of my cheeks. "So like your father," Uncle Yuri said, and then he whispered in my ear, "You could run this place better than either of my sons."

The next day, I returned to Liberty. I was greeted by Mrs. Cobrawick. She was wary of me, but couldn't resist saying, "I had a feeling we'd be seeing each other again," before leading me to the Children's Orientation area for the long-term special (minus the tattoo, as I already had one). I found Liberty no better or worse than the last time I was there. Perhaps it was easier because I knew how long I would be there. Also, I had learned to avoid conflict. Keep your head low. Don't make eye contact.

By coincidence or design, I had the same bunkmate, Mouse. *Welcome back*, she wrote.

"What do the papers say about me this time around?" I asked.

"Mob Daughter Saves Boyfriend."

Mouse was quiet, but good company. And truthfully, I did not mind the quiet. It gave me time to think about all the things I would need to do once I got out. I had to find a school for myself. Maybe a new school for Natty, too. If she was as bright as they said, maybe a place like Holy Trinity wasn't enough for her. Maybe I'd even take time off before finishing high school. I didn't know.

Sometimes I thought about Win, but I tried not to.

In any event, I was not without visitors.

Scarlet came to see me as often as she could. Once, she even brought Gable. I suppose they were in love, as much as that disgusted me. She claimed he had atoned for his sins, but part of me would never see him as anything but that boy in my bedroom who—I can admit this now—had so terrified me. Part of me doubted that a person could ever really and truly change. I suppose I was just as prejudiced as everyone else in this stupid world.

One day, my cousin Mickey showed up. I was surprised to see him, and I didn't hesitate to tell him so.

"Dad's dying," Mickey said. "I doubt he'll make it to the end of the year. He wanted me to come and see you, though."

"Thanks."

"I was glad to. I mean, I wanted to see you. I love Dad, but he never should have been the one running this family. Dad was just a chocolate salesman. He wasn't good about being on the opposite side of the law. He let things get disorganized. He wanted to do right by people, but he didn't know how. It should have been your grandmother, but there was resistance to the idea because she was a woman."

That's not the story I had heard, but whatever. "These foolish men."

"I agree. That's why I think this family shouldn't repeat the same mistake again. You and I should run things together," Mickey said. "Chocolate wasn't always illegal, and, maybe, someday soon, it won't be again. Maybe if we're smart, we can win the fight with lawyers instead of guns. Charles Delacroix will win the election and he is a pragmatic man. I believe he will listen."

I said nothing.

"Yuji Ono thinks very highly of you," Mickey continued. "My father thinks very highly of you. My wife, Sophia, thinks very highly of you. I think very highly of you. Next year is your last year of high school. You'll have a choice to make. Whether you want to be a bystander or a participant. It's up to you.

"Listen, Anya," he continued. "I know what lengths you went to, to protect that little family of yours. Those acts did not go unnoticed. Have you ever wondered if it would be easier to protect them if you were the one calling the shots?"

"Calling the shots with you?"

"Yes, with me. You're very young. And you are, as you said, just a girl. We could be a team. I've been watching you for some time. I believe, with the right moves, our business can become completely legitimate again. And if chocolate were legal . . ."

He did not have to finish that thought. We both knew exactly what that would mean. If chocolate were legal, Natty would be safe. We wouldn't need to carry guns or involve ourselves with black market operations. And maybe I could be with a nice boy like Win again.

Or even Win himself, if he would have me.

"You and I were born into this," Mickey continued. "It was not our choice. But we can choose what happens next. Our birthright was to be Balanchines, but our birthright does not have to be violence and death. You said as much in your speech at the Pool. Violence should not always beget more violence."

I nodded. A bell indicated that visiting hours were over. "Thank you for coming," I said. "You've given me a lot to think about."

Mickey grabbed my hand. "Come see me when you're out of here. September fifteenth, right? We can talk more then." He ran his fingers through his white-blond hair. "I've been thinking about making a trip to Kyoto," he said as he was leaving. "Perhaps you'd like to come with me?"

I wasn't sure what Mickey meant by that. Was it a threat against my brother? He seemed to be on very familiar terms with Yuji Ono, so perhaps it was about seeing Yuji and nothing more.

My seventeenth birthday was August 12, and this, like every other day of that summer, was passed at Liberty. Scarlet had wanted to throw me a party in the visiting room, a proposition I seriously discouraged.

351

"But, Anya," she protested, "I hate the thought of you alone on your birthday."

"I'm not alone," I assured her. "I sleep in a room with five hundred girls."

"Can't I at least come to visit?" Scarlet insisted.

"No. I want no reason to remember my seventeenth birthday at all."

The morning of my birthday, a guard came into the cafeteria to tell me that there was a visitor for me.

Oh, Scarlet, I thought, you never listen.

I went into the visiting room. It was early, barely 7:30, so no one was there except my visitor.

His hair was cropped short and he was wearing one of his school dress shirts and lightweight pants. I had never known him in summertime, so I had never seen those pants before. I, of course, was looking especially stylish in my navy jumpsuit. I ran my fingers through my knotted hair. I knew I wasn't supposed to care what Win thought of me anymore, but I did. Had I known he was coming, I might have had time to steel myself against him. I might have refused him altogether. But my feet kept walking me ineluctably toward the table where he sat, and then into a chair that was what they considered a respectable distance away.

Had I known he was coming, I certainly would have managed to bathe. I could not remember the last time I'd seen myself in a mirror. But it was just as well, I supposed. I would treat this as a visit from an old friend.

"Good to see you, Win. I'd shake your hand," I said, "but . . ." I pointed to the NO CONTACT sign that hung on the door.

"I don't want to shake your hand," he said, looking at me with cold blue eyes. Their hue seemed to have changed from sky blue to midnight since the last time I'd seen him.

"Where's your hat?" I asked lightly.

"I've given up on hats," he replied. "I was always leaving them places, and it had only gotten worse, now I've got this cane to manage." He nodded toward a walking stick which was resting on the table.

"I'm sorry about that. Are you still in very much pain?"

"I don't want your pity," he said in a rough voice. "You're a liar, Anya."

"You don't know that."

"I do," he said. "You told me you were going to that crime scene camp, and look where I find you."

"Well, this isn't terribly far off, is it?" I joked.

He ignored me. "So when I finally heard you were here—and it was a while because of the pains I took to avoid any mention of you—I couldn't help but wonder what else you had lied about."

"Nothing," I said, willing my eyes not to tear. "Everything else was the truth."

"But we've already established that you're a liar so how can I believe anything you say?" Win asked.

"You can't," I said.

"You told me you were in love with someone else," Win said. "Was this a lie?"

I did not reply.

"Was it a lie?"

"The truth is . . . The truth is, it doesn't matter if it's a lie. If it's a lie, it's one I need to be the truth. Win, please don't hate me."

"I wish I did hate you," he said. "I very much wish I wasn't here."

"Me, too," I said. "You shouldn't have come."

And then I leaned across the table and I grabbed his hair, what was left of it, and I kissed him hard on the mouth.

For that moment, I was a person without a last name and so was he. We did not have fathers, mothers, sisters, brothers, grandparents, uncles, or cousins to remind of us of what we owed or were owed. *Obligation, consequence, tomorrow*—the words did not exist, or perhaps I had temporarily forgotten their meanings.

All I could think of was Win, and how much I wanted him.

"No kissing!" yelled a guard who had just come on duty.

I pulled away, and Anya Balanchine was restored to me. "I shouldn't have done that," I said.

That was when I kissed him again.

May God forgive me for this and all these things I've done.

GOFISH

GABRIELLE ZEVIN

What did you want to be when you grew up?

It changed every day, based on who I was talking to at the time. I never said *writer*, though, because everyone was always telling me I should be one. I don't like doing what I'm told, at least not right away.

When did you realize you wanted to be a writer?

I was always writing stories and letters and plays, so at a certain point, it became completely obvious.

What's your most embarrassing childhood memory?

Oh, that's funny. . . . I seem to have blocked it out. Actually, when I was six years old, my friend challenged me to a tree-climbing contest—you know, who could climb higher. It was toward the end of recess, and we both kept going up and up and up. I got to the highest part; I won. I was feeling really superior about my victory when the teacher blew the whistle, which meant recess was over. My friend jumped down from the tree to go inside. I was about to follow her, when I looked down and saw how high I really was. I was too afraid to go back down. All the kids went back into class, and everyone forgot all about me. I was stuck in the tree. And eventually, I had to go to the bathroom. And I did. Right there in the tree. At a certain point, I realized that I had a choice to make—I could either be stuck in a tree with wet pants for the rest of my life, or figure out a way back down. As I'm not *still* in that tree, you can figure out which I chose.

What's your favorite childhood memory?
Every year, my dad used to take me to a diner before school on my birthday. My dad also used to take me to vote with him, and I liked getting the I VOTED sticker, even though those stickers probably cost about a penny each.

As a young person, who did you look up to most?
My parents. They were so much taller than me.

What was your worst subject in school?
Geometry. I considered it a waste of time to prove things that had already been proven a million times before. The worst grade I ever received was in a course on German cinema during college, but I loved the class anyway. Incidentally, I think it's important to make the distinction between the grade you receive and your overall enjoyment of a subject. This is hard to do when you're in school because everyone is so focused on the mark.

What was your best subject in school?
English. Except in 9th grade—the teacher made us keep diaries, which he would then read and grade. I felt this was a violation of my privacy, and every time I'd sit down to write in mine, I'd find I just couldn't bring myself to do it. Sometimes, you don't do well in a class because the teacher's style

doesn't match up with yours, but that doesn't necessarily mean that you aren't good at the subject. On the other side of that, I loved Mrs. Murley for European History, because she taught history like she was gossiping about people she knew.

What was your first job?
I was a babysitter for exactly one day. When I was growing up, there was this really popular series called The Baby-Sitters Club, and I got obsessed with being a babysitter like the characters in the books. So when someone finally asked me to babysit, I was so excited. I had all these activities planned. I really thought it was going to be the greatest thing ever. But it actually turned out to be the most boring thing ever. Mainly, all the kids wanted to do was sleep, so all I really did was the dishes and watch some TV. The mother even asked me to babysit for her again, but I turned her down. That night was the beginning and end of my brilliant babysitting career.

My first job that lasted longer than one day was writing music reviews for a newspaper. When I was fourteen, I wrote an angry letter to a local paper disagreeing about a concert review they had run, and they offered me the best job ever. Here's a bad pun/moral of the story: It *pays* to express yourself.

My first soul-killing, 9-to-5 type job was selling lingerie at a department store. At a certain point, I thought I might go mad if I saw another bra.

How did you celebrate publishing your first book?
I cut off all my hair. I have long, dark hair, and Samson-like, I hadn't cut it the whole time I was working on the book.

Where do you write your books?
In my head.

What was your inspiration for *All These Things I've Done*?
Organized crime movies, fancy private schools, Prohibition stories, the global economic crisis, and the difficulties of being a woman in power. Not necessarily in that order.

How would you manage without coffee and chocolate?
Strangely enough, I'm not a huge chocolate person. I've grown an appreciation for it from the research I did for the book, but I don't crave it and I could definitely manage without it. I'd be a lot more upset about a society that banned bread! I once read an interview with Ralph Fiennes, who plays Voldemort in the movies, in which they asked him if he was a big Harry Potter fan. He replied that he wasn't, but that the man who played Voldemort probably shouldn't be. It's pretty much like that for me and chocolate. I'd miss the coffee, however. I'd probably have to quit writing if coffee became illegal.

What made you decide to write a series?
Here's the long answer. Just before I began writing *All These Things I've Done*, I was going through a Charles Dickens phase. People forget this, but he was one of the first series writers. All his books were serialized in newspapers and a novel like *Bleak House* is something like one thousand pages in all and might be published in three books or more these days. What I found when I reread Dickens was the possibilities for series writing. I had never been particularly interested in writing a series. Many contemporary series I've read sort of mark time, which is to say, the plot doesn't turn much

past the first book. What we often end up with is a promising first book that doesn't really go anywhere narratively in subsequent installments. (If readers are attached enough to the characters, they tend not to notice these things.) With Dickens, the plot is turning the whole length of the series. It had to be to keep readers coming back to those newspapers, and the characters are growing and developing the whole time, too. And that's the kind of series I wanted to write. A series that, if you put all the books together at the end, you would have a planned narrative that made sense from page one to page twelve hundred. In addition, of course, to four books that held up on their own.

The short answer is that it seemed like a good idea at the time.

Anya's story takes place in the future, but her tale is timeless. What attracted you to a future setting?
The future is sometimes depicted as if it is some far-flung and impossibly strange destination that we'll never reach. I didn't want the world of the book to feel remote because that lets a reader off the hook. The ideal reaction a young reader could have is to finish the book and say, "Hey, what in my own society is like *All These Things I've Done*? Why are things the way they are, and what can I do to change them?" Young readers are more powerful than they know, and the future is sooner than we think.

When you finish a book, who reads it first?
I do. I don't believe in punishing my friends and loved ones with early drafts—it's not fair to me, them, or the work. But assuming that I'm pretty far along, I'll show it to my partner, Hans, or my editor, Janine.

Are you a morning person or a night owl?
I usually do most of my work after midnight and before noon.
So in a strange way, I'm both.

What's your idea of the best meal ever?
Anything my mom has made especially for me. I fully believe
that food prepared with love tastes better.

Which do you like better: cats or dogs?
Dogs, but when I was young, I loved cats. I even went so far
as to subscribe to a magazine for cat lovers, but then around
twelve or so, I became allergic to them.

What do you value most in your friends?
Humor and forgiveness.

Where do you go for peace and quiet?
I take long walks with my dog, but as we live in New York
City, I don't know if most people would call them either
peaceful or quiet. I suppose I mean a kind of inner peace
and quiet.

What makes you laugh out loud?
My dog, politicians, newscasters, and good sketch comedy.

What's your favorite song?
At the moment, my favorites are "First Day of My Life" by Bright
Eyes, or maybe "Hallelujah" by Jeff Buckley—but ask me on a
different day and you'd probably get a different answer.

Who is your favorite fictional character?
Off the top of my head, Gilbert Blythe (he'd make a nice boyfriend); Holden Caulfield (he wouldn't); Humbert Humbert

(even though he's a pervert); Charlotte the Spider (good with words).

As for books I've read recently? Edward from *Twilight*—I told the author, Stephanie Meyer, that he was like Mr. Rochester *and* Gilbert Blythe.

What are you most afraid of?
Nuclear Holocaust. People who don't value their existences as much as I value mine.

What time of the year do you like best?
Fall. I like the smell of leaves and new pencils.

What is your favorite TV show?
I'm fickle and at times, tasteless. Seriously though, I am not someone who feels that television is bad and evil, and I really get annoyed with people who complain that "there's nothing worth watching on TV."

If you were stranded on a desert island, who would you want for company?
My dog and my boyfriend. Both would hate to be stranded on a desert island, by the way—my dog loves regular meals and comfy pillows way too much, and my boyfriend loves watching movies.

What would you do if you ever stopped writing?
Probably read more.

What do you like best about yourself?
My brain and sense of humor. I'm very good company for myself. Physically? I have incredibly well-arched eyebrows that require minimal grooming.

What is your worst habit?
Caring what other people think.

What is your best habit?
Sending thank-you notes.

What do you consider to be your greatest accomplishment?
I'd like to think it hasn't happened yet.

Where in the world do you feel most at home?
Where the people I love, who love me, are.

What do you wish you could do better?
I wish that I could run a seven-minute mile and that I had a quicker response time for phone calls and e-mails—those aren't really wishes, as I could probably do both if I were determined enough. So, real wishes? I wish I could sing well and figure skate. I wish I could write three-hundred-page books in a day, and without actually having to be present for the process.

Anya Balanchine is determined to follow the straight and narrow after her release from Liberty Reformatory. But when old friends return demanding that certain debts be paid, Anya is thrown right back into the criminal world.

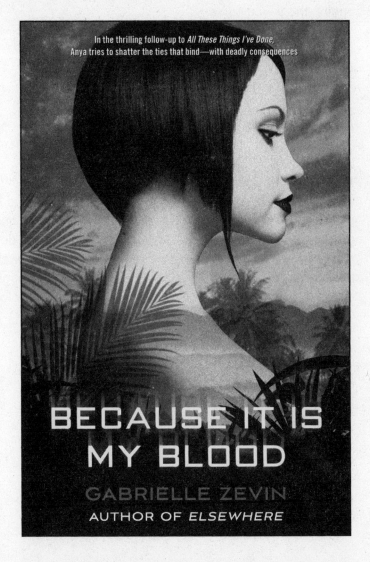

In the thrilling follow-up to *All These Things I've Done,* Anya tries to shatter the ties that bind—with deadly consequences

BECAUSE IT IS MY BLOOD

GABRIELLE ZEVIN

AUTHOR OF *ELSEWHERE*

It's a journey that will take her across the ocean and straight to the heart of the birthplace of chocolate.

I. i am released into society

COME IN, ANYA, HAVE A SEAT. We find ourselves in the midst of a situation," Evelyn Cobrawick greeted me, parting her painted red lips to reveal a cheerful sliver of yellow tooth. Was this meant to be a grin? I certainly hoped not. My fellow inmates at Liberty Children's Facility were of the universal opinion that Mrs. Cobrawick was at her most dangerous when smiling.

It was the night before my release, and I had been summoned to the headmistress's chambers. Through careful adherence to rules—all but one, all but once—I had managed to avoid the woman for the entire summer. "A situ—" I began.

Mrs. Cobrawick interrupted me. "Do you know what I like best about my job? It's the girls. Watching them grow up and make better lives for themselves. Knowing that *I* had some small part in these rehabilitations. I truly feel as if I have thousands of daughters. It almost makes up for the fact that the former Mr. Cobrawick and I were not blessed with any children of our own."

I was not sure how to respond to this information. "You said there was a situation?"

"Be patient, Anya. I'm getting there. I . . . You see, I feel very bad about the way we met. I think you may have gotten the wrong impression about me. The measures I took last fall may have seemed harsh to you at the time, but they were only to help you adjust to life at Liberty. And I think you'll agree that my conduct was exactly right, because look what a splendid summer you've had here! You've been submissive, compliant, a model resident in every sense. One would hardly guess that you came from such a criminal background."

I knew she meant this as a compliment. "Thank you," I replied. I snuck a glance out Mrs. Cobrawick's window. The night was clear, and I could just make out the tip of Manhattan. Only eighteen hours before I would be home.

"You are most welcome. I feel optimistic that your time here will serve you well in your future endeavors. Which brings us, of course, to our situation."

I turned to look at Mrs. Cobrawick. I very much wished that she would stop referring to it as "our situation."

"In August, you had a visitor," she began. "A young man."

I lied, telling her that I wasn't sure whom she meant.

"The Delacroix boy," she said.

"Yes. He was my boyfriend last year, but that's done now."

"The guard on duty that day claimed that you kissed him." She paused to look me in the eyes. "Twice."

"I shouldn't have done that. He had been injured, as you probably read in my file, and I suppose I was overcome to see him well again. I apologize, Mrs. Cobrawick."

"Yes, you did break the rules," Mrs. Cobrawick replied. "But your infraction is understandable, I think, and human really, and can be overlooked. It probably surprises you to hear an old gorgon like me say that, but I am not without feelings, Anya.

"Before you came to Liberty in June, acting District Attorney Charles Delacroix gave me very specific instructions regarding your treatment here. Would you like me to tell you what they were?"

I wasn't sure, but I nodded anyway.

"There were only three. The first was that I was to avoid any unnecessary personal interaction with Anya Balanchine. I don't think you can disagree that I followed that one to the letter."

That explained why my stay had passed in such relative peace. If I ever saw Charles Delacroix again (and I hoped I'd have no reason to), I'd be certain to thank him.

"The second was that Anya Balanchine was not to be sent to the Cellar under any circumstance."

"And the third?" I asked.

"The third was that I was to contact him immediately if his son came to visit you. Such an event, he said, could possibly necessitate a revision to both the quality and length of Anya Balanchine's stay at Liberty."

I felt myself shudder at the word *length*. I was well aware of the promise I had made Charles Delacroix regarding his son.

"So, when the guard came to me with the news that the Delacroix boy had been to see Anya Balanchine, do you know what I decided to do?"

She—horrors!—smiled at me.

"I decided to do nothing. 'Evie,' I said to myself, 'at the end of the year, you're leaving Liberty and you don't have to do everything they say anymore—'"

I interrupted the conversation she was having with herself to ask, "You're leaving?"

"Yes, it seems I've been forced into early retirement, Anya. They're making a huge mistake. Not anyone can run this kingdom of mine." She waved her hand by way of changing the subject. "But as I was telling you before . . . 'Evie,' I said, 'you don't owe that awful Charles Delacroix a thing. Anya Balanchine is a good girl, albeit one from a very bad family, and she can't help who does or doesn't visit her.'"

I offered cautious thanks.

"You're very welcome," she replied. "Perhaps someday you'll be able to return the favor."

I shivered. "What is it you want, Mrs. Cobrawick?"

She laughed, then took my hand in hers and squeezed it so hard one of my knuckles cracked. "Only . . . I suppose I'd like to be able to call you my friend."

Daddy always said that there was no commodity more precious or potentially volatile than friendship. I looked into her dark, red-rimmed eyes. "Mrs. Cobrawick, I can honestly say that I won't ever forget this act of friendship."

She released my hand. "Incidentally, Charles Delacroix is an incredible fool. If my experiences working with troubled girls have taught me anything, it's that no good ever comes from keeping young lovers apart. The more he pulls, the more the two of you will pull back. It's a Chinese finger trap, and the finger trap always triumphs."

Here, Mrs. Cobrawick was wrong. Win had visited me that one time. I had kissed him, then told him that he should never come again. To my great annoyance, he'd actually obeyed me. A little over a month had passed since that encounter, and I hadn't heard from or seen Win since.

"As you're leaving us tomorrow, this will also serve as our exit interview," Mrs. Cobrawick said. She opened up my file on her slate. "Let's see, you were brought here on . . ." She scanned the file. "Weapons-possession charges?"

I nodded.

Mrs. Cobrawick put on the reading glasses she wore on a brass chain around her neck. "Really? That's it? I seem to remember you shooting someone."

"In self-defense, yes."

"Well, no matter. I am an educator, not a judge. Are you sorry for your crimes?"

The answer to that was complicated. I did not regret the crime I had been charged with—having my father's gun. I did not regret my actual crime either—shooting Jacks after he shot Win. And I did not regret the deal I had made with Charles Delacroix that had insured both my siblings' safety. I regretted nothing. Of course, I could sense that saying this would have been frowned upon. "Yes," I replied, "I'm very sorry."

"Good. Then, as of tomorrow"—Mrs. Cobrawick consulted her calendar—"the seventeenth day of September in the year 2083, the city of New York considers Anya Balanchine to be successfully rehabilitated. Best of luck to you, Anya. May the temptations of the world not lead you to recidivism."

* * *

It was lights-out by the time I got back to the dormitory. As I reached the bunk bed I had shared with Mouse these past eighty-nine days, she lit a match and gestured that I should come sit by her in the bottom bunk. She held out her notepad. *I need to ask you something before you go*, she had written on one of her precious pages. (She was only allotted twenty-five per day.)

"Sure, Mouse."

They're letting me out early.

I told her that was great news, but she shook her head. She handed me another note.

After Thanksgiving or even sooner. Good behavior, or maybe I use too much paper. Point is, I'd rather be here. My crime makes it so I can't ever go home. When I get out, I'll need a job.

"I wish I could help, but—"

She put her hand over my mouth and handed me yet another prewritten note. Apparently, my responses were just that predictable.

DON'T SAY NO! You can. You're very powerful. I've thought a lot about this, Anya. I want to be a chocolate dealer.

I laughed because I couldn't imagine that she was in earnest. The girl was five feet tall in socks and completely mute! I turned to look at her, and her expression told me that she hadn't been kidding. At that moment, the match burned out, and she lit another one.

"Mouse," I whispered. "I'm not involved in Balanchine Chocolate that way, and even if I was, I don't know why you'd want that kind of a job."

I'm seventeen. Mute. Criminal. I have no people, no $, no real education.

I could see her point. I nodded, and she passed me one last note.

You are the only friend I've made here. I know I'm small, weak, & mousy, but I am not a coward and I can do hard things. If you let me work with you, I will be loyal to you for life. I would die for you, Anya.

I told her that I didn't want anyone to die for me, and I blew out the match.

I climbed out of Mouse's bunk and went up to my own, where I quickly fell asleep.

In the morning when she wrote and I said goodbye, she didn't mention that she had asked me to help her become a drug dealer. The last thing she wrote before the guards came for me was *See you around, A. My real name is Kate, by the way.*

"Kate," I said. "It's nice to meet you."

At eleven a.m., I was taken to change out of the Liberty jumpsuit and back into my street clothes. Despite the fact that I had been booted from the school, I had worn my Trinity uniform the day I had surrendered myself. I was so used to wearing the thing. Even three months later, as I was pulling the skirt over my hips, I could feel my body wanting to go back to school, and specifically to Trinity, where classes had started without me the previous week.

After I'd changed, I was brought to the discharge room. A lifetime ago, I had met Charles Delacroix in this same room, but today, Simon Green and Mr. Kipling, my lawyers, waited for me instead.

"Do I look like a person who has done hard time?" I asked them.

Mr. Kipling considered me before he answered. "No," he said finally. "Though you do look very fit."

I stepped out into the muggy mid-September air and tried not to feel the loss of that summer too much. There would be other summers. There would be other boys, too.

I breathed in, trying to get all that good exterior air into my lungs. I could smell hay, and in the distance, something rotten, sulphurous, maybe even burning. "Freedom smells different than I remember," I commented to my lawyers.

"No, Anya, that's just the Hudson River. It's on fire again," Mr. Kipling said with a yawn.

"What is it this time?" I asked.

"The usual," Mr. Kipling replied. "Something to do with low water levels and chemical contamination."

"Fear not, Anya," Simon Green added. "The city's nearly as run-down as you left it."